# STONE OF CHAOS

## DEMON'S FIRE BOOK 2

## CHRISTOPHER PATTERSON

*Stone of Chaos*

Rabbit Hole Publishing

Tucson, Arizona 85710 USA

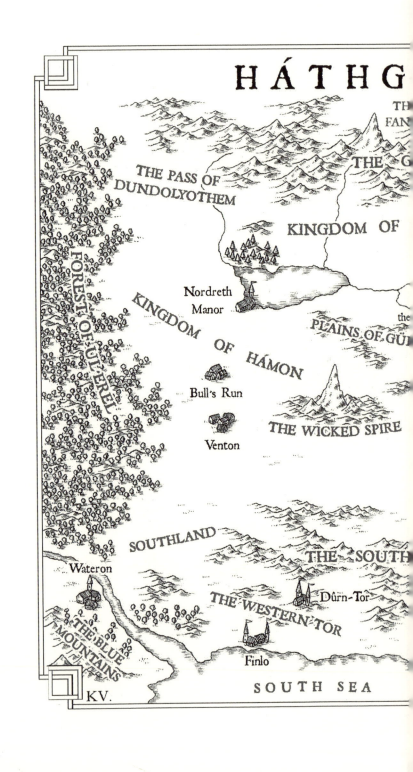

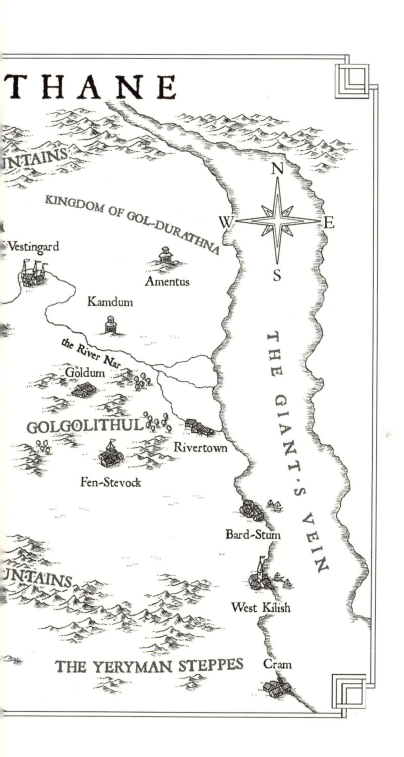

THANE

UNTAINS

KINGDOM OF GOL-DURATHNA

Vestingard

Amentus

Kamdum

the River Nar

Goldum

GOLGOLITHUL

Rivertown

Fen-Stevock

THE GIANT'S VEIN

Bard-Stum

UNTAINS

West Kilish

THE YERYMAN STEPPES

Cram

# 1

---

$\mathcal{E}$rik Eleodum watched the setting sun reflecting off the frost-covered ground. It never snowed heavily in Northwest Háthgolthane, but as the winter waxed and the temperatures dropped, the frost that covered the grass and the branches of the bare trees each morning would remain all day. A flash of purple distracted him. He leaned to his left and raised his sword, blocking the oncoming strike.

Erik grinned at his cousin, Bryon Eleodum, who was breathing heavily, sweat glistening on his face despite the cold. The purple light of Bryon's elvish sword seemed to meld with the greenish hue of Erik's dwarvish one—Dragon Tooth—and, for a moment, his cousin's snarl was illuminated, making him look angry. Erik knew he wasn't, that was the look Bryon had when they trained. Obviously annoyed Erik had blocked his surprise attack, he kicked out, pushing Erik away with his boot. Bryon was better than most, perhaps one of the best with the sword, but Erik was better. It just happened that way.

There usually wasn't much to do on a farm in the winter except to raise a few hardy crops and tend their livestock. They would service their tools and make sure they had stocked enough seed for the coming spring, but that season had also been a time of rebuilding. Erik's father's barn had burnt down at the end of autumn, and Erik had expected to spend most of the winter helping his father rebuild it.

However, within a week of the fire, a hundred dwarves from the Gray Mountains arrived at the Eleodum farmstead, and the barn had been rebuilt within several weeks. The dwarves' arrival was testimony to their generosity and recognition that Erik and his family were now, as far as they were concerned, dwarves after he had been baptized into Clan Dragon Fire.

Erik had also wanted to spend time with his wife, Simone, but her pregnancy had recently left her in bed most days, and he had no idea how to comfort her. His mother and sister, Beth, did most of what was needed, often shooing him out of his own bedroom so Simone could rest. That left little more to do than train, and so that's what Erik and Bryon did, along with their dwarvish companions, Turk, Nafer, and Bofim, and even Andu, an Easterner, who had once served the king of Hámon, a man named Bu Al'Banan, and now served the Eleodums as a head farmhand.

"Are you going to train or what?" Bryon asked, feigning a swing with his sword only to kick out again.

Bryon was tall and, even though he looked lean, was stronger than most. Their instruction had originally come from a man who once served in the Eastern Guard, the most prestigious military force in Golgolithul, a nation most these days referred to as the Eastern Empire. Wrothgard Bel'Therum was a good man and an even better teacher. Perhaps his most valuable lessons weren't about using a blade or weapon, they were the mental ones, about calming the mind, envisioning success in battle before it even happened. He taught them to understand their weaknesses and strengths and using the latter to their fullest advantage.

"What does it look like I'm doing?" Erik retorted, swatting Bryon's foot away with the broad side of Dragon Tooth's blade.

"Daydreaming," Bryon replied. "That's all you do these days ...

daydream. Do you miss the adventure that much? The fighting? The danger?"

Erik looked north, at the Gray Mountains. Low clouds covered the two tall peaks known as the Fangs. Snow covered the entirety of the mountains, even the foothills. He wondered how the people of Mayisha Maythia —once known as Fealmynster—were doing. Was Shu'ja'a as good a leader as he thought he would be? Erik shook his head, wanting to dismiss such thoughts.

"No, I don't," Erik replied. "I don't miss it at all."

Erik looked over his shoulder, back at his house, where Simone lay in bed. She would be all right, as would their baby. Erik's mother had experienced the same fatigue when she was pregnant with all four of her children—Erik, his now-deceased brother, and his two sisters—but Simone spending most of her time in bed put more stress and worry on Erik.

"You're lying," Bryon said.

"I don't lie," Erik replied.

"You just proved yourself a liar," Bryon said with a smile.

"Do you miss it?" Erik asked.

"It's all I think about," Bryon replied without hesitation.

"Truly?" Erik asked. "What about your farm? Your parents? Your sisters?"

"I am grateful for my farm," Bryon said, "and Father has been teaching me the business aspects more but, as much as I feel blessed for a renewed relationship with my family and the opportunity to run a successful farm, I find no true purpose in it."

They both looked to the Gray Mountains. Then, in unison, they looked east.

"I had purpose out there," Bryon said. "But what was it all for?"

Erik stared at his cousin, studying his face as Bryon continued to look east. The look that crossed Bryon's face could only be described as one of yearning as he remembered past days.

"What do you mean?" Erik asked.

Bryon turned to look at Erik.

"You know damn well what I mean!" Bryon replied. "What was the purpose of all of it? The dwarves? The dragon? That damned sword? Befel's life? What was it all for? So we could come back to Western Háthgolthane and live out the rest of our days as farmers? We could have done that without ever leaving. And Befel would still be alive."

There wasn't a day that Erik didn't think about his older brother, and so many things reminded him of the only man he looked up to as much as his father. From the smell of the farm to the sounds his pigs or cows made to the simple buzzing of a passing honeybee. He was a better man than all of them, loyal and strong, and he left this world the only way he would have expected to ... helping someone else.

"Maybe it was to teach us to appreciate what we have," Erik said, but he didn't sound convinced.

"Seems a harsh way to teach us that," Bryon replied. "I just feel like there is more for us. Out there."

Erik said nothing, but he agreed. In fact, he knew there was more for them. He—they—were wanted men. The Lord of the East wanted Erik's sword, once known as the Dragon Sword, and now reforged as Dragon Tooth, and therefore, wanted him dead. The north—Gol-Durathna—wanted him dead as well, for a reason Erik could only guess was to keep Dragon Tooth out of the hands of the Lord of the East. A rebel faction of dwarves, led by a politician named Fréden Fréwin, wanted him dead, thinking men were nothing but a disease. And, even though King Bu Al'Banan had stayed true to a word of truce he had given Erik, the latter still suspected the king of wishing him ill-will also. Slavers from Saman—northernmost city of Wüsten Sahil—wanted him dead. There were probably others, men he didn't even know existed, who wanted his life.

And if all these people wanted Erik dead, it meant they wanted his family dead as well. He would have to save his family, but what was it Dewin the ancient wizard had said? Something about the winds of change moving swiftly and that Erik would be called. That's when he was to leave again. But called by who and how?

*Save the world; you will save your family. Save your family; the world dies.*

Those fifteen words Dewin had spoken rattled daily in Erik's mind. The old man had put the weight of the world on Erik's shoulders, but it was all riddles. Everyone spoke to him in riddles. Andragos. Dewin. His dreams even never brought clarity. Some damned mystery he couldn't figure out. He just knew he'd become mixed up in it all and that it somehow had to do with his sword—Dragon Tooth —and a crown and a spell ... and dragons.

"Only the Creator knows," Erik finally muttered.

"What was that?" Bryon asked.

"The Creator," Erik said, speaking louder, "he knows what is in store for us. We just need to wait."

"I've been waiting," Bryon said. "We'll continue waiting and supposedly know what he had in store for us when we die and, according to you, go to meet him. I don't know that I want to keep waiting for some stupid sign."

Erik just shrugged. They continued to stare east, as the sun sat more than halfway below the horizon and remembered a different time. Erik wondered which part of all that had happened was currently uppermost in Bryon's mind. For Erik, he couldn't shut out the last time he spoke to Dewin.

The sun was almost gone when Bryon turned to Erik, extending his hand.

"Tomorrow," Bryon said.

Erik nodded with a smile and shook his cousin's hand, but Bryon didn't squeeze back. His eyes were trained on the east.

"Bryon, give it a rest," Erik said, smiling and almost laughing. "The east will be there tomorrow."

"Hush," Bryon said, letting go of Erik's hand and squinting, leaning forward. "I see something."

"It's nothing," Erik said. "Dusk always changes how things look."

"No," Bryon said. "There's someone out there."

A year ago, Erik's untrained eye would have never seen it, or he would have passed it off as an errant ray of sunlight or a distant firefly. But now, it was unmistakable. The flash of a blade.

"I see it," Erik said.

As if still instructed by Wrothgard, Erik and Bryon crouched simultaneously and began to move slowly towards the waist-high fence that surrounded Erik's home. The movement was fluid, unhurried yet deliberate. Against the gently rolling hills the farmlands backed onto, a myriad of bushes and fences marked out farm and land boundaries. Despite the different fruit and nut trees—albeit leafless in the deep winter—and farmhouses and barns that could obscure a man's vision, Erik could see shadows, and he knew Bryon saw them too. Men were moving a step at a time.

"What do we do?" Bryon whispered.

"We don't even know who they are," Erik replied. "They could be anyone."

"Who would be slinking in the shadows?" Bryon asked. "Especially in the farmsteads. Especially around your farm?"

"Children," Erik offered.

"They don't look like the shadows of children," Bryon said.

"Older boys," Erik offered, even though he didn't believe his own words.

"No. It's probably that prick Bu, going back on his truce."

"It's only a matter of weeks since that lord of his was here talking of trade agreements."

"So what? He's a tricky bastard," Bryon said. "Maybe he's decided it's time to finally take away our free lands. I think they're Hámonian."

Erik's stomach twisted, and something caught in his throat.

"If they are here to kill us," Erik said, "then they could be anyone."

## 2

"So, what do we do?" Bryon repeated.

"Sneak up on them," Erik said, "slowly."

"Get your hunting bow," Bryon said.

Erik nodded, crawled over to the gate in his fence and up onto the walkway made of polished flagstone leading to his front door. He stopped twice, his eyes trained on the shadows hidden in the night, as their unknown assailants still moved furtively. He opened the front door as quietly as possible, hoping he didn't alert his wife and the shadowy figures slinking in the darkness alike. The main living room of their home was dark, and for the first time in his short marriage, Erik was glad Simone forgot to light the candles and lantern. He reached just inside the door, where he kept his hunting bow, and grabbed that and the quiver of arrows leaning next to the weapon.

"Are they still there?" Erik asked when he returned to his cousin, still crouched next to the fence. The sun had now fully set, and it was harder to follow the shadows. The moon was low on the horizon and shed very little light.

"They've moved," Bryon said and pointed towards a copse of apple trees. They were closer now.

As his eyes became more accustomed to the darkness, Erik saw one of the figures—he surmised there were three of them—motion with an arm. Their pace seemed to pick up as they made their way across a wide road made of hard-packed dirt that passed through the Eleodum Farm. He looked down at the hunting bow and nudged Bryon.

"What?" his cousin asked.

"Here," Erik said, giving him the bow, "you're better with this than I am."

Bryon nodded, took the bow, and nocked an arrow, waiting. The figures had disappeared into a dip in the road, only to rise again. Bryon drew the bowstring back halfway.

"Shouldn't we wait to see if they're hostile?" Erik asked, looking at the half-drawn bow.

"Why don't you go over there and ask them if they mean to shove a knife up your ass or just join us for dinner?"

Erik didn't answer. He ducked down as he heard shuffling and whispering, so quiet an untrained ear might have missed it.

"They're close," he whispered.

Bryon just nodded, breathing slowly and lifting the bow.

"Are you sure about this?" Erik asked.

"Nope," Bryon whispered, shaking his head.

Erik looked down at Dragon Tooth, still sheathed. If these men were as good as he thought they were, sneaking up on them by the cover of night, Bryon would only get one shot. He would have to move quickly. He plotted his course— around his wife's rose bushes and over the fence to the right of a wagon; that would take him south of where the men were last seen. He pointed for Bryon to move in the opposite direction and then circled his finger back the other way; they would converge in the middle.

Bryon nodded his understanding and breathed out slowly and evenly. He pulled the bowstring as taut as it would go as one of the figures moved and then stopped again, low in the night. The unmistakable glimmer of the moon on the edge of a blade as the clouds shifted confirmed their expectations; they weren't friends.

"Do it," Erik said, deliberately, his voice now hard steel.

Bryon let go of the bowstring and headed right before he could even check what had happened. The arrow sounded like a quick gust of wind before Erik heard a thud and a quick cry. One of the figures stood about fifty paces away, then his body gave a quarter turn and disappeared from sight. Erik heard the unmistakable sound of a body hitting the ground.

Erik moved left around the cut-back rose bushes and leaped over the fence, head still stooped low. He ran to the left of a wagon, making sure to crouch low under its wooden sides. He inched his head around the end and waited until he heard whispers in the darkness. The language sounded familiar, and it reminded him of two soldiers from Gol-Durathna who had taken the Dragon Scroll from him, causing the dragon attack on South Gate, the poor suburb that rested against Fen-Stévock's southern wall. Another snatch of a few words confirmed to him these were Durathnans.

Their voices sounded concerned, their words quick and angry. As the moon rose higher, he saw there was one more than he had originally thought and confirmed that when he heard three distinctive voices. He presumed they were arguing over what to do next now they'd been discovered and one of their number was dead.

He ran south, hurrying past the trunks of the orange trees that ran along the eastern edge of his property; they weren't wide enough to give him coverage. He stopped again, this time behind another gray-leafed bush. The shadowy men were now quiet; they had stopped moving.

He slid under the lowest rail of the fence that separated his property from the road, slowly wiggling his back against the ground, and then turned onto his front and squinted. If these men were as trained as he expected them to be, they would see any sudden movements and have no idea if Bryon was ready to attack yet. In their haste, they failed to discuss a cue.

As if his mind was being read, Erik heard the hoot of an owl, but the feigned sound didn't fool the attackers, and in the moonlight, he could see eyes darting around in the darkness. He heard another quick gust of wind, and something thudded into the ground several paces away; another arrow from Bryon. A miss. Was it on purpose? It didn't matter, because as the three figures stood, he saw a purple glow. The shadows shouted, and the glint of steel flashed in the space between the three men and Bryon. The glow grew closer, weaving back and forth, bobbing up and down, trying to confuse. Erik unsheathed Dragon Tooth.

He didn't understand Durathnan, but when Dragon Tooth flared with its green flame, the men became excited. They knew about the sword, or perhaps it was because they were trapped between two magical blades. Whatever the case, their words were angry and hateful, regardless of the language. As he now rushed towards them, Erik saw one had turned towards him. The other two concentrated on Bryon.

The man's clothing was black, and he seemed to be wearing a dark cloth mask as well as having smothered some blackening agent on the blades of his two short swords; Erik could only see their sharp-looking edges. The man moved quickly and precisely, but as Erik closed in on him, he could the assassin blinking wildly in the green light of his sword.

Erik rolled underneath the swipes from the short swords. He came up, blocking two more overhead strikes and kicked out, the heel of his boot crashing against the man's shin. The assassin gave a short cry and attacked again. He was fast and strong and stealthy. He said something directly to Erik, but he didn't understand the words.

"I don't know what you're saying," Erik said, swatting one short sword away and then swinging down hard, knocking the other one out of the assassin's hand.

The sound of metal scraping against leather told Erik that the assassin had drawn another blade. From the corner of his eye, Erik could see flashes of purple. He felt a fist in his ribs and an elbow to the side of his head. It wasn't enough to knock him unconscious, even daze him, really, but it did push him back. This assassin knew how to fight, with both weapons and hand, but it was a style Erik was familiar with. Wrothgard had taught him, but he had also shown Erik to improvise.

He heard cloth flutter and sensed another fist, this one clutching a blade, flying towards his face again. He ducked, stomped his boot heel on the man's toe, and brought his knee up into the man's crotch. He felt balls crush under his knee and the unmistakable sound of air leaving a man's lungs. He expected the assassin to fall into him, but rather, despite his obvious pain, he rolled backward, coming up into a crouched position before lunging at Erik again. This one was rather persistent.

Erik felt the air move again as he ducked once more, a blade passing over his head. He leaped backward when another blade tried to slash at his throat and then chanced a kick, connecting with a leather greave with enough force to send his attacker to one knee. He swung downward, his blade catching in the middle of the assassin's two crossed weapons. Erik pulled his sword through and then swiped up, knocking the dagger and short sword out to the side. He saw the flick of the man's wrist and instinctively jerked to one side, a knife barely missing his cheek. It probably wouldn't have caused much damage; if these men were truly assassins, it was likely to have been poisoned.

Erik kicked up again. The assassin blocked his foot with a hand, but at the same time, he brought Dragon Tooth down, and hard. The green flame around the sword flared, and the assassin screamed as the blade cleaved through his shoulder and into his ribs, and some of his black clothing caught fire as Erik retrieved his weapon.

The Durathnan fell forward, dead, his burning clothes lighting up the scene of the fight. As much as Bryon's handling of a sword might not have been as good as Erik's, he was holding his own against the other two men, and the smell of burning flesh—together with the green of Erik's sword—told them they were now on their own.

Erik faced Bryon and gave his cousin a quick nod, just enough of a sign that he was all right, and Erik was there for him. The other Durathnans split their attention between their two opponents. The flames of burning cloth began to die, but in the dim light, Erik could see they were slight men, short and thin, wearing black clothing that hugged their bodies. Half masks covered everything but their eyes, and they wore hoods.

The Durathnan assassin facing Erik squinted, his black eyes hateful. He flicked a wrist and a small, double-bladed knife twirled at Erik, both sides undoubtedly coated with some sort of poison. He didn't know if the man meant for the attack to cause injury, or if he meant it to simply distract Erik, but it did neither. Gripping Dragon Tooth with both hands, Erik swung down hard, but the lithe attacker rolled out of the way, flicking his wrists twice more.

One of the two-sided knives caught Erik on his left hand as he brought it up to shield his face. The weapon bounced away, drawing a small trail of blood, but the wound burned. Erik hoped it wasn't a deadly poison. The assassin did a backflip, kicking up at Erik at the same time, before landing in a crouch. He wheeled his foot around, trying to trip Erik, but he jumped high over the assassin's leg. The moment he landed, Erik slashed at the man's leg, cutting flesh and causing the black pants to catch fire.

The Durathnan stood quickly as he let out an involuntary yelp and slapped his leg, trying to extinguish the fire. Erik took advantage of the distraction, and rushed in, ramming the assassin with his shoulder, grabbing his throat with his left hand, and thrusting upward with Dragon Tooth. The hateful eyes went wide, and Erik could smell the sickening combination of bile and blood, trapped between the mask covering the man's mouth and his lips.

Erik felt a knee in his side as he pressed into the dead man and saw a flash of black run past him. He looked to Bryon, pushing himself up quickly from his knees.

"Are you all right?" Erik asked.

"Never better," Bryon replied, breathing heavy. "Don't let him get away."

They both gave chase, but the assassin was fast, and the road was dark, causing Erik to stumble over a rock or a small ditch several times.

"We're going to lose him," Bryon said.

"Here," Erik said, stopping and reaching into his boot, grasping the small handle of a small knife he always kept there.

It was hardly a weapon, something meant as a tool around the farm, but it might be enough, if well aimed, to slow the assassin. Erik tossed the knife to Bryon, who caught and in one motion, threw it. Despite the darkness of the night—the moon only rising a bit more and casting its white light on the farmsteads—Bryon had an impeccable aim, and the small tool flew blade over handle, into the center of the Durathnan's back. The man yelped and stumbled forward, now tripping on the even ground until he was sliding along, face first. In moments, Bryon and Erik were on the man, kicking away his weapons, and Erik dropped on their target, holding him down.

The man struggled, but Erik drove his knee into the assassin's neck as Bryon pointed his elvish blade at the man's face, the tip sizzling as it touched his flesh. The man fell still but groaned loudly underneath his half mask.

"What do you want?" Erik asked.

The man replied in his native tongue, but with clear hatred in his voice.

"We don't speak your language, Durathnan," Bryon said, bringing the tip of his elvish blade closer to the assassin's eye.

"You," the assassin said, his accent rolling and fluid. "I want you."

"Me?" Erik asked.

"Both of you," the assassin added. "And the Dragon Sword."

"Why?" Erik asked.

He felt the man shrug under his weight.

"I do as I'm told," he said.

"It'll be to your death," Bryon said.

"Then I die fighting an enemy of the north," the man replied.

"An enemy of the ..." Erik began to say.

He grabbed the Durathnan's shoulder and pulled the man up so that he was kneeling. Erik tore away the mask, revealing a young man, clean-shaven with a strong jaw. His hair was short and either black or brown, but he couldn't tell in the moonlight.

"Gol-Durathna?" Erik asked. "I don't know why Amentus hates me. I am no enemy of the north."

"Don't banter with him, Erik," Bryon said. "He's not worth it."

Erik ignored his cousin.

"Speak," Erik said. He shook the man.

"You serve the Lord of the East," the assassin accused.

"I serve the Creator," Erik retorted, "and my family and friends. I have never *served* the Lord of the East."

The assassin shrugged again.

"The Dragon Sword is gone," Erik said, lifting up Dragon Tooth. "This is Dragon Tooth, and it is mine, no one else's."

"More will come," the assassin said. "The Atrimus never sleep. Whether you serve the Lord of the East or not, it doesn't matter. Alive, you are still a danger to my people."

"You can fight me all you wish, but leave my family alone. Take back that message, and I will let you live." Erik said.

The man looked up at Erik, the green light from Dragon Tooth reflecting across his face. He smiled.

"Never," he said.

As Erik lifted Dragon Tooth, the man threw his head back.

"Atrimus!" he shouted, and Erik brought his blade down hard.

## 3

*E*rik burst through the door of his house and ran to the bedroom. Simone was a lump under the covers and, squinting in the light that spilled into their room from the lantern in the living area, he could see her chest rise and fall, breathing gently. She was sweaty, and hair matted to her face, but she was clearly unhurt. He breathed a sigh of relief and went over to the table where they kept a pitcher and bowl of water; he wanted to clean the wound on his hand and wash his face. He was rinsing out the cleaning cloth when he heard a shuffle of feet behind him and spun around.

"Erik, what are you doing?" Simone asked sleepily as she now stood behind him. Erik let out slowly the breath he'd been holding. As her eyes focused, throwing off the normal haze of post-sleep, they opened wide.

"What happened to you?" she asked, reaching up and touching his neck.

He winced, and she showed him her finger. Blood. He hadn't noticed, but there was a small cut on his neck.

"Where is my mother?"

"Your mother?" Simone asked. "She left a long time ago, before sundown. What a silly question. Were you and Bryon training too hard again?"

Erik grabbed Simone by the shoulders. He inspected her and then stood and looked around the room, under their bed and in the small little space they used for a closet, even behind the chest of drawers her mother had given them that stood snuggly against the wall.

"Erik, what are you doing?" Simone asked, standing and stepping towards her husband. Her tone hardened. "What is going on? Speak to me."

"Why are you up on your feet?" he said, still not answering either of her questions. "Lay down. Get some rest."

"I've been resting all day long," she replied. "Now, tell me what happened to your neck?"

Erik pushed his hand behind his back and stared at his wife, her sweat smattered face, the damp neck of her gown, and her tired eyes.

"Erik ... tell me what, by the Creator, is going on."

He sighed deeply, dropping his chin to his chest, his shoulders slouching almost in defeat.

"Bryon and I were training," he said. "I guess we got a little zealous."

She stared at him, her eyes narrowing.

"And where is Bryon now?" she asked.

"Outside," Erik lied again. Bryon was looking around to make sure there was no one else about that might try and hurt them.

"Why didn't he go home?" Simone asked. "He normally goes home in a huff when you two get too serious, especially when you best him. Or did he best you today, and he wants to gloat?"

"We saw something," Erik said. "He decided to stick around a little while longer. That's all."

"Saw something?"

"Yes. It was nothing."

Simone touched his neck again.

"If this was from Bryon," she asked, "why isn't it red? Every time he accidentally cuts you, the wound gets red from the heat of his sword."

She continued to stare at him, and he found it hard to stare back, eye to eye.

"What we saw," he began.

"Yes," she said. "Go on."

"Men," Erik said.

"Men," Simone repeated. "Not so uncommon on a farmstead in the early part of the evening."

"These men ... they came for us," Erik said. "They attacked us."

"Attacked you!" Simone said, putting her hands on his chest, staring up at him with scared and worried eyes, wide and watery.

"Yes," Erik replied, pulling her close to him.

"Who was it?"

"I don't know," Erik lied.

"What did they want?" Simone asked.

Erik still didn't meet her eyes.

"I don't know," Erik said. "I think they were just some thugs ... common brigands."

"Brigands ... Here, near our farmstead?" Simone asked.

Erik could probably count on the fingers of one hand the number of times he heard of thieves or thugs harassing the farmers of Northwest Háthgolthane. It wasn't that they were an uncommon sight in the rural areas of the continent—slavers inhabiting the Blue Forest near Waterton were a testimony to that—but the farmlands near Erik's farmstead were a close community, and the people watched out for one another in an almost uncommon way. Thievery in these lands tended to be more trouble than it was worth.

"Yes," Erik said. "Is that so hard to believe? It was dark. Bryon and I were finished with our training, ready to clean up, and they came slinking down the road."

"And where are they now? These brigands?" Simone asked. She crossed her arms across her breasts.

"Gone," Erik said. "We chased them off. We scuffled. They lost. They're gone."

She glared at him.

"You're lying."

Erik lifted his head quickly, squinting angrily. He could feel his face grow hot, offended by the accusation even though it was true.

"Lying?" His pretense made him feel like a child again, about to be scolded by his mother.

"I can see it your face," she said. "I can hear it in your voice."

"How dare ..." Erik began.

"To the nine hells with you, Erik Eleodum!" she yelled. "Don't you dare turn this around on me!"

"You shouldn't be yelling in your condition," Erik said, putting his hands up defensively.

"Damn my condition!" she screamed. Simone breathed hard, her face growing redder by the moment.

"Yes," Erik said. "I'm sorry. I lied."

"Why?" Simone snapped.

"They weren't brigands," Erik said, his eyes dropping to the ground again. "They were assassins."

"They were ... what?" Simone said, her voice breathless. "As in men hired to hurt you?"

"Yes."

"Why?" Simone asked.

Erik looked up at her.

"Do you really need to ask that question?" he replied. "I am a wanted man in the eyes of many people ... of powerful people."

She still looked angry at first, ready to challenge him further, but then her expression changed to one of concern.

"And where were these men from?" she asked quietly.

"Gol-Durathna," Erik replied, his voice defeated. It was harder to fight her when she was angry. Now he felt tired, more tired than he had felt in a while.

"Now I know you're lying," she said, almost laughing as she

returned to accusing Erik. He shook his head as he reached up to wipe away blood that was still trickling down his neck. Simone took the cloth from his hand and pressed it firmly onto the wound. Erik could smell the soap in her hair despite her sweating.

"The golden city of Amentus has a dark underbelly like any other city," Erik said, his voice almost soft as he quoted his dead friend, Marcus.

"And why would the Northern Kingdom of Háthgolthane, and a nation that supposedly exemplifies goodness, want you dead?" she asked.

"Because I was seen to be working for Golgolithul," Erik replied. "I am still connected to them, I suppose, in some weird, roundabout way."

"You're ... you're not lying now ... Are you?" she said, and he shook his head. "Where are they now? These men?"

"Dead," Erik replied, and he didn't have to look at her face to know it was pale, that look of fear every person wears when they are so close to death and killing.

"Dead?" she whispered in his ear after a sharp intake of breath. Erik nodded.

"And where are their bodies?" she asked, still pressing on his neck. He could sense her eyes on his face but still couldn't look at her, ashamed of his lying.

"Out on the road," Erik replied, now chancing to lift his eyes to meet her gaze. "Bryon and I will take care of them before sunup."

Simone let go of his neck and stepped back. She now looked more horrified than angry. She knew he had killed men—she watched as he killed Bone Spear, another assassin—but she still appeared shocked at the idea.

"Are you all right?" she asked.

"I'm fine," he said, and then brought out his hand. "But this could use some attention."

Simone gasped at the sight of the cut, this one rawer looking where the poison had caused it to weep as well as bleed.

"This needs more than water," she said and went over to the cooking area and began to make a poultice from her supply of plants and herbs.

After Erik had washed his hand, he walked over to stand side by side with Simone.

"How many were there?" she asked as she mixed the different leaves with a mortar and pestle. Her voice now sounded cold and distant.

"Four."

"Oh, Erik ..." Simone said and shook her head.

"My love, I cannot remember the number of people, and creatures, I have killed. Their deaths haunt my dreams every night. I see them. Every single one of them. And not just the ones I killed, but the ones who have died because of me. Thousands of men, women, and children from South Gate ... every night ... skin blackened, eyes red, just staring at me. Wondering why. Asking. Sometimes cursing and ..."

"And your guilt makes it all right for me, does it?" she snapped as she threw the mortar and pestle into the stone sink. "As long as I know you feel bad, I don't have to worry about more people coming here?"

Erik stared at her, his mouth open. They rarely argued, although he had been gone for much of their marriage, but at that moment, she was now more angry with him than she'd ever been. Beneath her open robe, she wore her nightgown of sheer white cloth, and it did nothing to cover her nakedness. She grabbed both sides of her robe, pulling it tight across her large belly and crossing her arms over her chest. She looked at Erik for a little longer, saying nothing for a moment, and he simply looked into her face, waiting for the anger to hopefully pass. Eventually, she shook her head and returned to making the poultice.

"You ... we can't live like this, Erik," she said, keeping her focus on the grinding. Her tone had softened. "We can't live our lives always looking over our shoulders."

"What do you want me to do?" he asked as he stepped forward and put his hands on her shoulders. She shuddered when he touched her, and he quickly retracted his hands.

A lump caught in his throat because he knew she was right.

"I'll put the poultice on later," he said as he turned and walked out of the house.

The moon had finally risen in the night sky, and even though the high, wispy clouds still floated across the stars, the night had brightened. As he stood on the veranda, he saw the purple glow of Bryon's sword as his cousin walked up to his house.

"Everything all right?" Bryon asked. "I checked the road, the barn, and even the fields. I didn't see anything. The dwarves said they didn't see anything either. Turk and Nafer were already asleep, and I don't know where Bofim is."

"Okay," Erik said. "What about Andu?"

The former soldier in Bu Al'Banan's army now lived in a small, two-roomed cottage behind their barn.

"He didn't see anything either," Bryon replied.

Erik nodded. Of course not. If the dwarves didn't see or hear anything, Andu wouldn't have. His face must have given away his mood.

"What's wrong?" Bryon asked.

"Simone," Erik replied, sitting on the top step down from the veranda.

"Is she okay?" Bryon asked, sitting next to his cousin.

"She's upset," Erik said.

"Upset about what?" Bryon asked.

"The attack."

"You told her?" Bryon asked, exasperated.

"Of course," Erik said. "I can't lie to my wife."

He immediately felt another twinge of guilt in his gut. He had lied to his wife.

"Well, you probably should have," Bryon said. "At least, for the moment."

"What do we do?" Erik asked, staring up at the night sky.

"I don't know," Bryon replied, making a half-circle in the dirt with his boot, flicked from side to side on the heel. "Go to Thorakest?"

"We can't just run," Erik said, now looking out over the darkening fields of his farm.

"We need to do something with the bodies," he said.

"It's already been done," Bryon said.

"Really?"

"Aye," he replied. "Me, the dwarves, and even Andu. We moved them."

"Where?"

"Behind the barn," Bryon replied. "Turk said they would take care of them—bury them somewhere."

Erik nodded his appreciation as Bryon stood up and left without another word.

As Erik stared out but did not really see anything, he thought of Dewin, the old soothsayer in Eldmanor. He had learned that Dewin was a wizard, apprenticed by Andragos, and at one point was a powerful mage and practitioner of the dark arts. Dewin was also a dream walker, like Erik, but Erik still didn't understand why Dewin sent him the way he did to Fealmynster, telling Erik to travel a seemingly roundabout way through several life-threatening hazards.

When Erik finally returned from Fealmynster, the cursed town run by Sustenon, he stopped to speak with Dewin, and that's when the old man's words about saving the world had stuck in his head. What did it mean? How was Erik supposed to save the world, especially if he was worried about any number of people sending assassins to his home?

He looked down at his sword by his side. Dragon Tooth had once been a dagger, given to him by a gypsy and possessed by the spirit of an elf named Rako. Rako had appeared to him in a vision and told Erik how to reforge the Dragon Sword; he'd even helped him kill Sustenon the Damned. Before that, Rako, at least his voice, had been with Erik for a year, guiding him, and even being a friend. Now he was gone, but he said something to Erik before he disappeared. It was about saving him, releasing him from some magical prison called the Dragon Stone. Did that have anything to do with saving the world and, therefore, saving his family?

"Rako, I'm sorry," Erik whispered and immediately felt the gooseflesh on his arms raise. The hair on the back of his neck stood on end as something crawled up his spine.

*Erik.*

It was his own voice in his mind, but it wasn't him. He looked down at his sword again. The voice came again, faint and distant.

*Erik.*

So far away, but he recognized that voice. It was the voice of his dagger; it was Rako Rokhev, the elf warrior, the first dragon rider, imprisoned in the Dragon Stone.

"I'm here," Erik said quietly. "Rako, I'm here."

*Help me. Free me.*

"I will," Erik said, and he couldn't help feeling excited, exhilarated. The voice was back. His friend was back.

But then he was gone.

# 4

The caravan of wagons and soldiers and cavalry marched through the Plains of Mek-Ba'Dune. This wasn't Golgolithul's territory yet, but as the Lord of the East watched from the rolling tower in which he rode, he imagined it was his. Even in the coming winter, the Plains were temperate, the grass still a muddled green, and the soil rich and dark. He saw acres of farms and towns all within a day's ride, and the people appeared robust and hard working.

He would truly be an emperor, the most powerful man in not just one continent, but in two. He would extend his empire east, all the way to Tyr and the Jagged Coast. He would drain the Shadow Marshes and build port after port. Trade would flourish. His army would be vast. And all would praise his name. This was what *he* had promised him—the *Lord of Chaos*. It was his dream—his father's dream, and now, he could taste it, seeing it coming to fruition. What was the cost? Submission. Fealty. Syzbalo ground his teeth silently.

Their journey was slow, especially with the number of troops and horsemen they had brought, but one could never be too careful in the lands east of the Giant's Vein. It was, after all, barbaric and savage.

More men meant slower travel, as well as the two-story battle tower the Lord of the East insisted on, so he might stare out at all that he intended on controlling as they rode through its lands.

The Lord of the East couldn't help the small smile that touched his lips as giant, gray-skinned creatures pulled his wheeled tower. He heard that even larger versions of the creatures dwelt in Wüsten Sahil, but these smaller versions could still carry and pull a hundred times what an ox could. With their large ears and long trunks, the simple barbarians of Mek-Ba'Dune called them elephants.

"Imagine what they could do in battle," the Lord of the East said.

"The men of Wüsten Sahil use them for just such a purpose," Melanius, his Isutan advisor, said.

"Truly?" the Lord of the East asked. "Astonishing."

"Shall I command your tamers and animal handlers to train several of these creatures?" Melanius asked.

"You should," the Lord of the East replied.

Syzbalo waited a moment, doing his best to put on a facade of irritation. He turned and rolled his eyes, staring at the Isutan magician.

"Why must we come all this way to meet with Specter's daughter?" the Lord of the East said, alluding to the real reason they traveled east.

Everyone, except his inner circle—his two witches and Melanius—thought he was traveling east to sow relations with the King of Po, an attempt to form an alliance with the backward Two Towners of Mek-Ba'Dune. But his witches and magician knew he meant to meet with the Black Tigress, daughter to Bone Spear and renowned assassin in her own right ... at least, that was what he told them.

Meeting with the Black Tigress was important, of course. Erik Eleodum had to pay for his insolence and insubordination. And Syzbalo desired the Dragon Sword, which Erik now possessed. But the true reason he traveled east, the reason only privy to him, was that his new master—this mysterious Lord of Chaos—beckoned him to go east. He was to meet others who served the Chaos Lord.

"It was her father who failed me," Syzbalo continued, keeping up his pretense of annoyance. "She should come to us."

"It is not the way of my people," Melanius replied, and Syzbalo could hear the irritation in his voice. "And besides, we need her. She doesn't need us. I am sure she is not in short supply of work these days."

"I don't think I like your tone, Melanius," the Lord of the East said. He saw his advisor give him a half-hearted shrug.

"Besides, she hated her father," Melanius continued. "Although, I am sure some of her hesitation is that some farm boy killed her father, deemed immortal by most."

"This Erik Eleodum is no farm boy," the Lord of the East said.

"Be as it may, Your Majesty," Melanius said, bowing, "it came as quite a shock to most of us."

The Lord of the East thought for a moment before he nodded slightly and shrugged, returning to his seat. He swatted a fly away. For as powerful and mighty as these elephants were, they brought with them a hundred times more flies than a horse.

"Black Tigress," Syzbalo muttered with a short laugh.

"She also goes by Ankara," Melanius explained.

The Lord of the East laughed.

"You Isutans and your names," he said. "I am certain Ankara is not her real name either. What does it mean in Isutan?"

"Literally?" Melanius asked. "Her name means *Sparrow of Death.*"

Syzbalo laughed aloud.

"Where is your special and peculiar name?"

"It is the code of the Isutan guilds," Melanius replied. "They never use their real name, except for within their guild houses. For someone to know their real name outside their guild would be death and dishonor. As for me, I traded my name for power long ago."

The Lord of the East looked over his shoulder to see the old magician smiling. Syzbalo picked at one of his fingernails, taking in the vast fields of grass and listening to the low grunts and louder trumpets coming from the elephants.

"Any word on Andragos' bodyguards?"

"Terradyn and Raktas remain elusive," Melanius replied.

"Well, keep looking for them then," the Lord of the East snapped.

"My lord ..." Melanius said, and then stopped.

The Lord of the East turned in his seat and stared at his magical mentor.

"Do you believe Andragos?" Melanius asked, referring to the Black Mage, who had served Syzbalo all his life.

"Believe him?" the Lord of the East replied, but he knew what Melanius meant. He returned to his fingernails for a moment as he pondered his response.

In retaliation for the inquisitors Andragos had killed—men the Lord of the East had sent to one of Andragos' homes in search of a traitor's family—the Lord of the East required the lives of the two bodyguards. These were men who Andragos had raised from the time they were nothing but toddlers, and as well as protecting the Black Mage, they were second to none in the ways of combat.

Syzbalo supposed Andragos had every right to be upset that inquisitors showed up at his residence wishing to inspect his home. They were beneath the man. He was a great wizard ... once. And only the gods knew how old the man was. He was advisor to Mörken, Syzbalo's father, and the Aztûkians before he and his family gained control of Golgolithul.

However, Andragos had now crossed Syzbalo, this much the Lord of the East knew, and the man known to most as the Messenger of the East, or the Black Mage, or the Herald of the East, or the Harbinger of Death had, to Syzbalo's mind, grown soft. The Lord of the East had commanded that the family of a traitor to the state be executed, and Andragos had the affront to save them. The Black Mage's loyalty was now shaky at best, and to some extent, Syzbalo worried that the Messenger was actually becoming an enemy ... a powerful enemy that might need to be dealt with and soon.

The Lord of the East needed some way to test that loyalty. He had confined the Black Mage to one of his cottages and sent a hundred Eastern Guardsmen to the dwelling, ready to take his bodyguards away. But Andragos confessed they had left. He had told them of their fate, assuming they would accept it as loyal subjects, but they fled. According to the captain of the guard, Andragos cursed his bodyguards for fleeing.

"No, I don't believe him," Syzbalo finally replied, turning in his seat to watch the plains before him.

If that wasn't enough to prove Andragos had become disloyal, Syzbalo wanted one more test, so he put the wizard in charge of all his affairs while he was away. He would see what the Messenger of the East did with such power when he returned.

Syzbalo felt something catch in his throat and his stomach knot, a rare hint of the sort of emotion he would never wish to display. Andragos had raised him, tutored him, taught him, and befriended him. The Black Mage was more of a father to Syzbalo than Mörken was, and more of a mother, as well, since he rarely was allowed to see her. Now, the Messenger of the East seemed to have turned against his protégé.

"And what do you intend to do about it?" Melanius asked.

"Do not worry about that," the Lord of the East said, standing and turning as he hardened again, his softer thoughts dismissed. He stared at the closed door behind him; his witches were in there, waiting. He put a hand on the door handle and looked down at Melanius. "I will take care of Andragos when we return to Fen Stévock."

Andragos had passed his time, passed his usefulness to the east, and Syzbalo's new *master* assured him he would soon wield more power than the Black Mage could ever dream to possess.

## 5

*W*ith his red beard braided and falling to his belt, a bald head replete with blue tattoos and bulging muscles, Terradyn looked to be a man few would wish to tangle with. As he breathed, his red mustache fluttered, and he fiddled with one of his earrings, tugging on the thick, gold hoop and then rubbing the sweat from his bald head, collecting there despite the cold of winter.

"Are you nervous?" Raktas asked.

Terradyn looked to the man with whom he traveled.

"No," Terradyn lied. "Of course not."

He hadn't been away from his master, Andragos, for more than a day since he was six years old. It had been so long ago he didn't even remember his life before he was taken on to become the Messenger of the East's manservant. It did make him nervous. His whole life—however long it was; he had lost track of the years—had been consumed by protecting and serving his master. Now, he was supposed to keep someone else safe. Looking at Raktas, he knew he felt the same way.

It must have been at least a century before the current Lord of the East's father took control of Golgolithul, since he and Raktas first met. As boys, they came to serve the Messenger at the same time, and they spent every day with each other and their master, but they had never really gotten to know each other beyond their duties. They talked, but always of their responsibilities and occasionally of small things like the weather or a weapon they particularly liked.

They japed, but it was always about how some soldier pleaded for his life before one of them ran him through or of some other crude thing related to war. And they drank together, but that rarely resulted in talking and commonly caused fighting or whoring. They knew nothing of each other's past, families, or heritages; although, Terradyn really knew nothing of his own family or heritage. It was a distant memory, a dream, a fading vision, and he couldn't tell if it was real or not. He didn't know what he liked and didn't like because his daily life had been orchestrated for at least a hundred years. The only two things Raktas and Terradyn did have in common was their undying loyalty to the Black Mage ... and their ability to kill.

They had passed the last homestead of Nordeth. It was a simple country with simple folk. Terradyn had never spent much time in the place and now found he rather enjoyed it.

"Nordeth was nice," Terradyn said.

"Nice?" Raktas asked, more than a hint of cynicism in his voice.

"I liked its people," Terradyn blustered.

"You liked that whore in Nordeth Manor," Raktas said.

"I did," Terradyn replied with a laugh, "but the people were pleasant."

"Are they any different than the people in Golgolithul?" Raktas asked. "The people of Nordeth?"

"I guess I don't know," Terradyn replied.

"When we reach this Erik Eleodum's farm, what exactly are we supposed to do?" Raktas asked.

"The Master said to protect him," Terradyn replied.

"What does that mean?" Raktas asked. "Do we keep him confined to his home? Are we now his personal guards?"

Terradyn just shrugged and continued to fiddle with one of his earrings.

## 6

Hugging his knees to his chest, Erik sat on the hill. As the branches of the willow tree stooped low under a cool breeze, the lowest leaves tickled his face. The man was next to him— the one he knew but couldn't ever tell from where. Neither spoke, and Erik stared out over the vast grassland that surrounded the hill, watching the black clouds, flashing with purple lightning, scudding over the distant range of black mountains. Every once in a while, the rumble of thunder caused the ground to shake. That was unnerving. Sometimes, they weren't there. That was even more unnerving.

Erik watched the dead men and women mill about the grassy meadow. Most of them just stood and ambled slowly in a zombie-like state. Most were quiet, but Sorben Phurnan—former lieutenant in Patûk Al'Banan's army of eastern dissidents—was cursing and yelling, but Erik ignored him as did most of the dead.

The new ones tested the invisible boundary that prevented them from walking onto the hill, and among them, he saw one of the Durathnan assassins that had come for him. Because they were killers, he was surprised he only saw one in the land of dreams, but perhaps it was because they had acted out of a sense of duty, or they were forced to. Either that or they were simply somewhere else at that moment.

Erik watched all of that, in the Dream World, but none of it mattered to him. He ignored it, for the most part. All he could think about was Simone and her anger over him killing again. He did not have a choice; people wanted to hurt him and his family. He had spent so much time in this place, this realm that most people who came here never realized it was real, that his thoughts, his concerns, and his troubles from his world carried into this one.

He wanted to save Rako, the elf spirit that had traveled with him for a year, helped him, befriended him, even saved his life. He wanted to free him from a prison that sounded terrible, but he couldn't leave his wife and his family. People wanted to hurt them, as well.

"I'm sorry, Rako," Erik said to the air. "I can't leave."

He felt a tear at the corner of his eye.

"We all have to make hard decisions in life," the man under the tree said.

"But, to help one person, I have to hurt another," Erik said.

"Perhaps," the man said with a shrug. He wore wide-legged, wool pants, a cotton shirt, its sleeves rolled up to the elbow, and a wide-brimmed hat made of straw that reminded Erik of his father's hat. "When we make hard decisions, we are not necessarily hurting other people ...we are simply not helping them."

"The lesser of two evils then?" Erik asked.

"No," the man said with a slow shake of his head. "Neither is evil. Just as most of these poor souls wandering about the Dream World weren't necessarily evil. They simply made a choice, and all choices have consequences that, to one person might seem righteous, while it might seem wicked to another. Things are not so black and white, Erik."

"Then why are these poor souls here and not on a golden carriage?" Erik asked.

"It is not for me to say," the man said with another shrug. "Perhaps their choices were evil, at some point. Maybe their choices severely hurt someone, or their lack of faith dictated their choices. I am merely the keeper of this place."

"Why do my choices have to be so difficult?" Erik asked.

"If there is a right and wrong choice," the man replied, "the right one is seldom easy. And if you are a righteous man, your decisions will often be difficult. The Shadow loves to confuse. Remember that. His ally—and his enemy—is chaos."

As the light seemed to dim, Erik returned to watching the grassy plain; Sorben Phurnan stopped yelling curses and looked to the sky. It was as if the sun had disappeared behind thick clouds ... but there were no clouds. Erik knew what was coming. A new figure, seemingly a man, appeared in the middle of the dead, and they all stopped and looked. He wore a black, hooded cloak that fell to the ground and, as the dead began to converge on him—as they did with all new souls in this place—a hand emerged from the cloak. With long, bony fingers, he waved outwardly in a wide arc, and as one, all the dead began to scream and wail before their bodies slowly dissolved into black dust, blown away on a sudden gust of wind. Only Sorben was left behind.

"*What the ...?*" the former lieutenant yelled, his widened mouth revealing rotting teeth and black gums. "Who are you?"

The cloaked figure turned to face Sorben Phurnan, lifting both of its bony hands to its hood and pulling it back, revealing someone with a scalp of brown skin and wispy, thin, gray hair. Their back was to Erik, so he couldn't see what they looked like, but Sorben gasped, stepping several paces backward.

"You," Sorben hissed, and Erik heard a malicious cackle coming from the cloaked figure.

Erik didn't know if he had ever seen fear in one of the dead in this place, but the look that crossed Sorben's decomposing face was one of pure, unadulterated terror. He turned and ran, slowly disappearing into the horizon, and the cloaked man laughed even louder.

Erik stood, hand going to the handle of Dragon Tooth. He stepped forward.

"I'm getting rather tired of this new dweller of the Dream World," Erik said.

"Careful, Erik," the man under the tree said.

"Who is he?" Erik asked, taking a few more steps forward—down the slope of the hill.

"Danger," the man said. And then he added, "Chaos."

The cloaked man pulled his hood back over his head and turned to face Erik. The hood shadowed his face so that Erik could only see the outline of a bony chin. Erik walked to the bottom of the hill just before the protective barrier that kept the dead from walking onto it.

"Be careful, Erik," the man under the tree cautioned him again.

"Erik," the cloaked figure repeated, his voice a hiss. Erik thought he recognized the voice. "Fancy seeing you here again."

Erik stepped out into the grassy plain, Dragon Tooth's hilt grasped in his hand. The cloaked man laughed.

"That blade won't help you here," he said. He pointed to the ground, the earth. "This is my realm now."

"Oh, no," Erik said. "You're wrong. This is the Dream World, the realm of the Creator, and you're just another rotten dead man who hasn't come to grips with his fate yet."

The cloaked man chuckled, this time louder.

"Fool," he hissed, and the stench of rot and decay struck Erik's nose like a fist to the face. The man pointed. "Do you see? This is a place of chaos. It is becoming my realm."

He clenched the fist of his extended hand, and Erik looked over his shoulder; the man under the tree was gone. When Erik turned back around, the cloaked man was right in front of him. He couldn't help the fact that his heart quickened.

"There is great conflict in your heart, Erik Eleodum," the cloaked man hissed, his stench so strong, Erik wanted to retch.

"Back up before I send you into the oblivion," Erik said.

"Oh, such false threats," the man sneered. "You could never do such a thing to me. I am not some simple dead man wandering this place like an addled fool."

"Who are you, then?" Erik asked. "What are you?"

The cloaked man laughed again.

"I am power!" he hissed. "I am strength! Evil! Might!"

Erik cocked an eyebrow and chanced a quick laugh.

"Can you really laugh at such a time?" said the man, "a time when you are desperate to save your family? That will never happen."

Erik's stomach knotted.

"It doesn't matter what you do," he continued. "Stay, and they will die. Leave, and they will die."

Erik stepped away, but his back hit something hard. He looked over his shoulder, and it was the hill ... the barrier surrounding the hill. It wouldn't let him pass.

"The world will die," the man hissed. "It will burn and then ... chaos will reign. It will return the world to the way it was meant to be."

"The Shadow," Erik hissed, gripping Dragon Tooth with both hands and still trying to back up onto the hill, even though the barrier wouldn't let him.

The cloaked man just laughed as the sky darkened even more. The mountain range in the distance was gone, as before, the grass around them wilted as the air grew hot, and the willow tree on the hill burst into flames. And the cloaked man laughed even louder.

## 7

"*E*rik."

Simone's voice startled Erik, pulled him away from his dream ... from his nightmare. He was surprised to see the morning sun casting its dawn hues across the frosty fields of his farm. He had fallen asleep, despite the cold and the winter and the notion of assassins around the corner, on his front porch. The sunlight glimmered against the icy dew on the grass. It made the ground look like a bed of diamonds.

*This land is worth more than diamonds.*

"Erik," his wife said again.

He turned his head slightly, looking over his shoulder. He yawned and tried blinking his sleep away.

"Yes, my love," Erik replied.

"Have you been sitting out here all night?" she asked.

He nodded with as much of a smile as he could muster.

"Are you upset?" Simone asked.

"No, my love," Erik replied. "Just worried."

"I'm worried too," Simone said.

Erik stood, stretching his back before he turned to face his wife.

She pulled her robe tight across her body and shivered. He stepped to her and wrapped his arms around her. She nestled her face close to Erik's chest, and he could feel her breathing deeply. He loved these moments when he could just hold his wife. Even after just lying in bed all day, she smelled like mint and lavender.

"What are we going to do?" Simone asked.

Despite holding his wife and reveling in the comfort of her closeness, his stomach knotted. He knew what he had to do. He knew it the moment the elf Rako spoke to him. The Dragon Stone. The Ruling Stone. The Stone of Chaos.

"I don't know," Erik lied. He remembered his nightmare—the cloaked figure, the way his presence had changed the Dream World, the absence of the man under the tree, and the fire. Was that what his world would look like? He remembered a dream he had before leaving for the Gray Mountains—a dream of his farm on fire, of a vast shadow spreading black wings across the land. Did freeing Rako have anything to do with that?

Erik had learned in his travels and adventures that, often, things were connected, more connected than anyone ever guessed or expected. If he stayed and forgot about the elf, would this cloaked figure burn the world? If he left, would this cloaked figure burn his family? Did it matter?

Simone pushed away from him.

"Tell me the truth," she demanded.

"I may have to leave again," Erik said with a shrug.

"No," she said, her brows furrowed and her lips pursed.

"Simone ..." Erik said, but she backed up, farther away from him. He felt as if he was losing her, a pit growing in his stomach.

"How could you even say that?" she asked. "Your child will soon be here. You were gone for over two years, and I took you back because I love you. You left, and I let you go because I knew what you had to do was important, because I love you. Do you not love me?"

"How can you ..." Erik began to say but stopped as he felt himself on the verge of crying. He sought to gather himself, swallowing hard. "How can you say that?"

"You say you love me," she said, holding her swollen belly, "but then you leave so freely. Is it to another woman?"

"Of course not," Erik said with a vigorous shake of his head.

"Then how?" she asked again. "How can you just up and leave with no thought of me or your child?"

"Do you not think I don't think of you?" Erik asked. "It is all I think about."

Simone's face hardened, her eyes squinted.

"Clearly not."

"What if I have to do something that would save you and the baby?" Erik asked. "What if I had to do something that would save the world?"

*"To the nine hells with the world!"* Simone yelled, and then she started to cry. "You are my world, Erik. You and this baby. Am I not your world?"

Erik didn't know what to say. They had never argued like this. His wife was angry and sad, and he knew that nothing he said could make her feel better. In fact, anything he said beyond that he would stay would make things worse.

"I ... I don't ..."

"If you leave," Simone said, interrupting Erik and pointing an accusatory finger at him, "then I'm going with you."

"Absolutely not," Erik replied, quicker than he should have.

"You think you are the only one that suffers when you leave," Simone accused. "You think you're the only one that is in danger or hurts, or feels lonely."

"I know it's hard on you when I leave," Erik said, trying to reach out to her, but she stepped back.

*"You don't know!"* she shouted, and her voice echoed over their farm fields. "How could you? I am here, all by myself, worrying about you, worrying about our baby, wondering if I am going to have to raise him on my own."

"But you have my family," Erik said, "and yours."

*"They're not you!"* Simone screamed, throwing her hands down by her sides with clenched fists. "They can't hold me close at night, or speak to your son so he learns your voice. All I can do is feel helpless and ashamed when they come around offering to help on the farm, wondering if I am doing okay, and doing things for me I am supposed to do myself."

Simone's crying intensified, deep sobs that caused her shoulders to heave.

"Being here, without you," Simone said through her hot tears, "is like living in the nine hells. Every day is a lifetime of fear and frustration."

"Please, Simone," Erik said, trying to reach for his wife, but she shied away, opening the front door of their home.

"No," she said. "You can't just hold me and kiss me and make this go away."

She entered their house and slammed the door.

**8**

---

*E*rik opened his eyes to a gray sky and sat up. He was in the dream world, but it felt different. Gooseflesh rose along his skin as a chill struck him, but the air was stuffy as if it was a hot, humid day. The smell of rot hit his nose, but as he looked around, he saw no dead. The grass of the great, wide meadow was flat as if trampled by the feet of a thousand giants.

He couldn't see the hill with the great willow and the man under the tree, nor the black mountain range with the purple lightning—the realm of the Shadow. As he stood, his stomach twisted, nauseous, and churning. And then he saw him ... the cloaked man again. His back was to Erik, and someone was in front of him. They were speaking, and the other person—a man with broad shoulders and long, red hair —looked scared, eyes wide, mouth open, sweat beading into his red goatee. The cloaked man held out his hand, and the image of a large, egg-shaped, green stone floated above his palm.

"Fool," the cloaked man hissed, closing his hand into a fist and causing the image to disappear. He waved his hand, and the man in front of him dissolved into dust and floated away. Erik could see the cloaked man shaking his head, his hood wavering side to side.

"You're the fool," Erik said. Dragon Tooth was at his side, as it always was. He grabbed the sword's handle and tilted it forward, ready to be drawn. "Thinking you, thinking the Shadow, has any power or dominion in this place."

The cloaked man slowly turned, his shoulders slightly hunched, chuckling.

"The Shadow," he croaked.

"What did you do with your mountains?" Erik asked. "That's where you draw your power from, isn't it?"

"The Shadow," the cloaked man repeated. He stepped forward.

"I told you before," Erik said, "get too close, and I will strike you down. You will become nothing but specs of dust."

The hooded man tilted his head.

"We are all just dust, Erik Eleodum," the man said, lifting a fist. When he opened his hand, an image of Bryon hung there, hovering above his palm.

From underneath the hood, Erik heard the man breathe deeply, and then he blew, scattering the image of Bryon, the dust floating away until it finally hit the ground. An image of Turk appeared, and the same thing happened. And then Nafer and Bofim.

"Dust," the man repeated. "You see, my power is different. It doesn't come from the Shadow. It comes from chaos."

Erik swallowed. There was something familiar about this man ... his voice.

"I don't care for your games," Erik said.

The man cackled.

"So bold," he hissed. "No games. Only power. You should know. You have spoken with power. You have held power in your hands."

The man paused a moment, and Erik believed, if there were eyes under that hood, they stared at his sword.

"You held power," he repeated.

"The scroll," Erik muttered. "The sword."

The cloaked man laughed.

"What do you want with the Dragon Stone?" Erik asked.

The cloaked man said nothing.

"That was what you had, floating above your hand," Erik said. "That was what you were showing that man, wasn't it?"

"What do you know of the stone?" the cloaked man hissed. He stepped closer.

"It's a prison," Erik said.

"It is," the man said, a hint of maniacal delight in his voice.

"For a friend of mine," Erik added.

The man laughed.

"Do you seek the stone?" the man asked.

"Yes," Erik replied.

"Find it for me," the cloaked man said. "Bring it to me."

"Why would I do that?"

"Power," the cloaked man hissed.

"I don't want power," Erik replied.

"Lies," the cloaked man hissed, stepping closer. "We all want power."

*Chaos,* Erik thought. *He gets his power from chaos.*

"You don't call it the Dragon Stone, do you?" Erik asked. "You call it the Stone of Chaos."

Erik didn't know what that meant. He simply knew Dewin had referred to the stone by several names. The cloaked man growled.

"You will suffer," he said. "You have no idea what you are dealing with."

"You can't hurt me in this place," Erik said.

"Fool," the man said. He waved his hand, and the image of Simone, sleeping in bed appeared in front of Erik. The cloaked man clenched his hand into a fist, and Simone began breathing quickly, worry strewn across her face even though her eyes were closed. She began to sweat. Her legs kicked. And when the cloaked man released his clenched fist, she sat up.

"Erik!" she cried out.

"I'm here!" Erik yelled, but she couldn't hear him.

The man waved his hand, and the image was gone. He snapped

his fingers, and the image of Tia—Erik's youngest sister—appeared. As the cloaked man squeezed his hand into a fist again, the young girl curled up into a ball, shook, and then opened her eyes and cried. She was gone, just as Simone had disappeared, and there was Bryon. The same thing happened, and when he woke with a start, he was screaming and yelling and cursing, grabbing his elvish blade, looking as scared as Erik had ever seen him.

"Do you see?" the man said. "I can hurt you here."

"Dreams," Erik said. "Nightmares. The memory of those dreams will pass. It is nothing."

"Surely, you know dreams have power," the man said. "Dreams are real."

"Then I will fight you in my dreams," Erik said. "In their dreams. You can't hurt me. You can't hurt them."

The cloaked man laughed and then reached out towards Erik, closing his fist again. Erik felt as if someone had closed their hand around his throat, and he began to choke. He dropped Dragon Tooth and reached up to his neck, but there was nothing there. He still couldn't breathe. He felt vomit and blood rise into his mouth, and he felt his eyes bulge as he rose on the tips of his toes.

"I can hurt you here," the cloaked man hissed. "And I can hurt them. But I believe you will continue to harass me in this place, as I seek to serve my master. So I will block you from entering the Dream World. You will get your much-awaited wish ... to dream no more."

"You ... can't ... do ..." Erik began, but his vision blurred, and everything around him turned black.

Erik opened his eyes, coughing. His dream ... something was wrong. He sat up and saw his wife was there, sleeping. He breathed a sigh of relief. Whoever that was in his dream ... he was evil and powerful. And he wanted the same thing that imprisoned Rako.

As his stomach knotted, he rubbed his throat, where he had felt the pressure of someone strangling him in his dream. His neck hurt as if it had really happened. He swung his legs over the side of his bed and stood, walking to the polished silver looking glass, sitting above the washbasin in their room. In the light of the candle, he could see his neck was red, already beginning to bruise.

He turned and watched his wife sleeping, silhouetted in the bright moonlight flooding through their open window. The nighttime air of the oncoming winter was cold, but Simone was constantly hot, and she welcomed the chill. Her body moved slowly as she breathed. He wanted to lay next to her, hold her, feel her breathe, but he couldn't. She was angry, and he felt ashamed. He didn't blame her for being that way, but watching his beloved and not being able to touch her was as if the cloaked man was gripping his heart.

Erik strapped his belt around his waist and rested the palm of his left hand on the pommel of Dragon Tooth as he stepped to the bedroom window. Watching the stars in the night sky twinkle, he smiled as a single tear touched his cheek, remembering a simpler time. He had to leave. This thing in his dream wanted the Dragon Stone, and that was bad ... worse than bad. Apocalyptic. There was no other option. Simone had waited for him the first time, and she had waited for him the second time. He wasn't sure she would wait for him again, but he had to go. Without fully understanding why he knew it was the only way to save his family. But to go where? Then the answer came to him. He must visit Dewin, the old soothsayer of the village and former apprentice of Andragos, the Black Mage.

It had to have been close to midnight as Erik watched his farm and the stars and the moon. He heard a howl from a distant wolf and the answering low moan of one of his woolly cows. His animals were sturdy creatures, not so easily spooked, but then again, they were only animals. The mooing was followed by another low, reverberating growl.

Erik walked through his house and then outside the front door, Dragon Tooth drawn and ready, but the animals had seemed to have calmed down again, and he didn't hear any more growling. Perhaps it was distant and had been carried on a gust of wind.

Looking out on his farm, all he wanted to do, watching the reflection of the pale moonlight on the icy grass and frozen fallow fields, was stay and live … and that meant he must go. He would leave in the morning. But he would leave alone.

All he would have to do is ask. Ask his cousin, ask the dwarves, even ask Andu—former sergeant beholden to Patûk, then Bu Al'Banan—and they would go with him. But he wouldn't ask. It wasn't because he didn't want them to go. He wanted nothing more. Besides his wife, he coveted their company the most. But he also knew more assassins would come. Whether they were from Gol-Durathna, Golgolithul, Hámon, El'Beth-Tordûn, or anywhere else in the world, he was a wanted man, and his enemies wanted him, and his family, dead. Without Bryon or the dwarves, his family, his farmstead would be defenseless. He had thought about reaching out to the northern dwarves, and he was sure they would help, but he didn't know them … he didn't trust them like he trusted his cousin, or Turk and Nafer, or Bofim, or even Andu. Dwarvish warriors were, without question, honorable and loyal, but his true companions would willingly give their lives for him, as he would them. He was sure they would also give their lives for his wife and unborn child.

So, he would go alone. As hard as that was to stomach, he knew this mission was his calling, not Bryon's or Turk's, not Nafer's or Bofim's. Dewin said that he, not they, had to save the world to save his family. Dewin would know more.

## 9

*B*ryon pushed Erik in the chest, almost making him lose his balance. Simone had since gone in the house, having cried all her tears, her voice hoarse from screaming.

"*You flaming idiot!*" Bryon yelled.

"*Stop!*" Turk ordered, grabbing Bryon by the arm. He looked at Erik with those hard, gray, dwarvish eyes. "What are you doing, Erik?"

"There is something I have to do," Erik replied.

"And you meant to leave without telling us?" Turk asked. "You meant to leave without giving us the option to go with you?"

"Simone," Erik grumbled.

"Don't you dare blame her," Bryon said, pushing Erik again and then pointing a finger at him.

Erik knew that Simone had told the dwarves and his cousin he meant to go. He was going to try and leave without telling them. He knew they would want to go with him—they would try to go with him no matter how much he protested—but he needed them here, to stay with his wife and family. He needed to do this thing, whatever it was, alone. He didn't know why. His last dream had been two nights past, and whomever the cloaked man was in his dream had stayed true to his word ... Erik slept two nights, dreamless. The Dream World answered his questions, revealed things to him, and helped him, but now it wasn't there. When he slept, he closed his eyes to darkness, and then he opened them to morning.

"We are brothers," Nafer said in Dwarvish. "Brothers don't leave without saying anything to one another."

"Does our bond mean nothing to you?" Turk asked.

Erik felt helpless, listening to his friends chastise him.

"Beldar died for you," Bofim added, and that made Erik want to cry, "and Demik. For what? We are brothers, Erik."

"He doesn't know the meaning of brother," Bryon said as he spat at Erik's boots. "He stood by and watched his own brother die."

Turk gasped, and Erik saw red. All sound seemed too far away to truly hear anything. His vision narrowed, and in his head, he felt the steady thump of his heart quickening as his anger rose. He had let Bryon push him, and even slap him once. He knew his cousin was mad and had a right to be. But he had gone too far.

Erik lunged at Bryon, but Turk stepped in front, holding him away from his cousin while Nafer and Bofim held back Bryon.

"*What was I to do!*" Erik screamed, and he felt hot tears fill his eyes. "*You're the one who dragged him away from the farm! You son of a bitch! It was you!*"

"Bryon," Turk said, speaking to the man over his shoulder, "you've gone too far."

Bryon spat again and waved a hand at Erik. He muttered under his breath and began to turn, but stopped halfway, looking at Erik over his shoulder. He had tears in his eyes also.

"You think you're the only one in this world who hurts, Erik. You think you are the only one who is troubled by his dreams and sees the ones he has lost there. You think you are the only one who doesn't have a clue what is happening around him, who is conflicted and torn, who feels like his heart is being crushed with the weight of a thousand rocks as each day passes. You're not. And here, you have everything. I wish you good luck, cousin. Don't worry. I will watch over your family while you are gone. I will watch Simone cry everyday ... and Aunt Karita and Beth and Tia."

Bryon turned and walked away. Erik rubbed the back of his sleeve across his face, clearing away his tears.

"Prick," he muttered.

"No," Turk said, pointing a finger at him.

The dwarf had never given him that look before. It was a look of anger mixed with disappointment.

"You are the one to blame here, Erik," Turk said. "We have pledged ourselves to you. We have made a pact to fight with you, protect you and what is yours, but it is *our* pact. You have taken it upon yourself to remove any choice we might have had of going with you."

"But I need ..." Erik said.

Turk put up a hand, silencing Erik.

"It doesn't matter," Turk said. "If you had asked me to stay with your family, as much as my heart would break from not being able to go with you—my brother—I would have stayed because that is what brothers ... that is what warriors who are bonded to one another do. But you didn't ask Erik, and that hurt me deeply."

"Aye," Bofim said.

"I pray An protects you on your voyage, Erik," Turk said. "I pray that he touches your selfish heart and softens it, that you would make wiser choices as you take this journey you so desperately feel you need to take."

"I'm ..." Erik started to say, but Turk kept his hand up, shaking his head.

The dwarf turned and walked away, Bofim following him. Only Nafer stayed, watching Erik as he stood there, his heart feeling like it was stuck in a vice.

"They will be all right," Nafer said in Dwarvish.

"Are you the only one not mad at me?" Erik asked.

"Oh, I'm mad," Nafer replied with the slightest of wry chuckles, "but I also understand why you are going, what you are doing."

He stepped forward, opening his arms, and Erik leaned down and hugged his smaller friend.

"You need to trust more, Erik," Nafer said. "You are an extraordinary man ... and what is so extraordinary about you is that people follow you. You are a hero to them; you stand up for them without the need or hope for fame that causes some minstrel to sing your praises. Remember that. Remember that naïve farm boy who didn't really believe in magic or mountain trolls ... or even dwarves."

Nafer chuckled again and smiled.

"Do not think you can take on this world alone, Erik," Nafer said. "You cannot. And if you try, it will swallow you up like it has so many other righteous men with good intentions. And fear not ... your family will be safe."

With that, Nafer turned and followed the other dwarves.

Erik readied Warrior, the large warhorse that once belonged to Patûk Al'Banan, the eastern defector and leader of the largest group of men who opposed the Lord of the East. The fine animal, one certainly with a mind of his own, had then been claimed by the now Bu Al'Banan, King of Hámon.

However, Erik had learned early on that this horse really belonged to no one. He was cantankerous and mean and bit Erik once on the shoulder. He had tried to bite him several other times, but they had grown to respect one another. And Erik figured that was truly what controlled the horse ... respect.

Warrior looked back at Erik as he threw the heavy saddle onto the horse's back. The horse looked upset and snorted deeply.

"Relax," Erik said. He spoke to the animal in Westernese, although Turk, his dwarvish friend had been teaching him Shengu, so he spoke to the horse in his native language as well. The mean, old horse would have to learn to understand Erik in Westernese.

Erik patted the horse's flank, looking up at the sky as the darkness of night began to fade away, black giving way to the dark blue of early morning. He breathed deeply, securing saddlebags and rations to Warrior. He looked north, towards the Gray Mountains, and then he looked west. He knew the forests of Ul'Erel were there, vast woodlands that were supposedly the dwelling places of the elves, but he had never seen them. Even as he traveled to Finlo from Waterton, even the gypsies stayed away from the southern reaches of the mystical forests. Rako, before he disappeared for good in Fealmynster, had mentioned an elvish maiden, one that could help free him and unlock the mystery of this prison—the Dragon Stone. If he were supposed to find some elvish maiden, he would need to travel into those cursed woods eventually.

As Erik tightened the belt on his saddle, he sensed the presence of someone else and turned to see Simone standing behind him, arms crossed over her chest. Immediately he found it hard to breathe; his throat was dry, and his stomach knotted.

"You're leaving," she said. Her hair was matted against her face with sweat, her pregnant belly poking out and through her robe. Her eyes were red.

Erik stepped to her, but her eyes told him to keep his distance.

"I have to," he said. "To save you. To save our baby. To save our farm, I have to go."

"So, where are Bryon and the dwarves?" she asked.

"I'm going alone," Erik replied.

Only a moment ago, she had looked angry, her face growing red and her lips pursed. Now her eyes widened, and her mouth lay open.

"Why?" she asked, and before Erik could answer, she added, "You can't. Whatever you need to do is dangerous enough with them. Without them ... without them, you'll die."

Erik spread his hands.

"Bryon and the dwarves can protect you," Erik explained. "Andu too. They can protect the farm."

"You are such a fool, Erik Eleodum," Simone said.

"I trust Bryon and Turk, Nafer and Bofim. Andu even."

"And I trusted you," Simone said, stepping forward to fix the fire in her eyes on him, her anger blocking her tears. "I trusted you, Erik. You are my husband, the father of my child, and I trusted you. Only you."

Then, she stopped and seemed to gather herself before she began to walk away.

"I hope you find whatever you need out there," she said, without turning to face him. "I hope it is worth it."

## 10
———

*G*eneral Lord Marshall Darius, commander of Gol-Duranthna's armies, didn't bother to sit behind his desk. He sat, rather, in a wooden chair that was too small for him, passed down to him from his father, and as he rubbed the rough wood of the armrest, he would pass it down to his son. He held a cup made of stone. It was heavy, but it kept its contents cool longer than wood or pewter or iron. He swirled the liquor about, watching the fermented corn mash splash the sides of the cup before draining all of it in one gulp.

Amado stood behind him. He was a young man, too young to be a commander, but that he was—the commander of the Atrimus, the Shadow Men. It wasn't just the assassins and spies of Gol-Durathna that Amado commanded. He was in charge of units of messengers, men and women who trained doves and ravens and hawks to send vital information. He trained agents that would infiltrate the ranks of Golgolithul and educated ambassadors on how to act and what to say when visiting Nordeth, Hámon, Gol-Nornor, or even Hargoleth and Gongoreth. But his main function was steeped in the shadows.

"News?" Darius said. His voice was hard, not mean or cruel, just worn and old. He rubbed his face, feeling a week's worth of stubble. He remembered when it grew dark and brilliant. Now it was gray, barely speckled with a few black whiskers here and there.

"None, Lord Marshall," Amado replied. Darius could hear the anxiety in the man's voice. "I'm sorry."

"Peace, Amado," Darius said, looking over his shoulder and giving the Lord of Shadows a sidelong glance.

Darius stood and walked to the marble railing of his balcony, a second-story office and room in the Building of Military Affairs in Amentus, the Golden City, and capital of Gol-Durathna. Snow had just fallen, most of it melting on impact. But it created a brilliant sheen over the grass and leaves of the yard that surrounded the building, and when the sun caught the ice just right, it was breathtaking.

"Do you ever stop to watch the brilliance that is nature, Amado?" Darius asked.

"Lord Marshall," Amado replied.

"I remember being young, like you," Darius continued, "so busy, head in books, matters of state, and the task at hand. I wish I had taken the time to appreciate the world around me. Come, stand next to me. See what I see."

It seemed to take Amado a few moments, but without seeing him there, Darius could feel the man's presence next to him.

"Quite beautiful, isn't it?" Darius asked.

"Yes, Lord Marshall," Amado replied.

Darius closed his eyes for a moment, feeling the juxtaposing combination of winter air and noonday sun on his face. He loved the beginning of winter, with its crispness and coolness, but not weather that would chill to the bone yet. He breathed deep, letting the cold breath fill his lungs, and he slowly exhaled.

"This thing we are doing," Darius said, finally meeting Amado's eyes, "it is a terrible thing. My heart is heavy for even commanding such a thing ... assassinations."

Darius shook his head and turned away from the view from his balcony as if he couldn't think of killing and watching the purity of nature at the same time.

"I have ordered the death of a man who is nothing more than a farmer, Amado," Darius said.

"A man who holds the fate of Gol-Durathna in his hands," Amado added.

"It doesn't sit well with me," Darius said. "This is an evil thing we are doing."

"No more evil than a dragon destroying a city and killing thousands of people," Amado said. "No more evil than what the Lord of the East would do if he got his hands on such a weapon."

"Do you worship the northern gods?" Darius asked, and the look Amado gave him said he had taken the young man by surprise.

"Of course," Amado replied. "Mostly Sicario and Bella. I go to the Veiled Temple every morning and the Temple of Bella once a week."

Sicario, the god of spies, assassins, stealth, and one of the northern gods of death, was a popular one to be worshipped by those who took up such professions, and his temple, located underground, could only be entered by someone robed and masked, their identity hidden. And Bella, the goddess of war and one of three such deities in the northern pantheon, was a popular goddess worshipped by those who partook in battle, but not necessarily the brutal, frontal assault of war. She was a deity heralded for her wisdom and trickery on the battlefield.

"And then, twice a year, I pay homage to Piscalou, atoning for any wrongdoing I have committed as most do," Amado added. "Absolving myself of my sins."

Piscalou, a god who was often depicted as a giant coy fish, was a god who took a Durathnan's sins and buried them deep in the ocean ... for a price.

"And you, Lord Marshall?" Amado asked.

Darius shook his head slowly.

"I haven't worshipped the northern gods in many years," Darius said.

"Truly?"

"No," Darius replied, "not since I married my wife. We worship Unus, the God who is also worshipped by the dwarves, although they call him An."

"Ah, I see," Amado replied. "An intriguing god."

Darius gave the young man a quick nod and a smile.

"You see, Unus doesn't look kindly on assassinations," Darius said, simplifying the conundrum of trying to kill a man, who was largely blameless, because he served an enemy.

"The greater good," Amado said. "Should the Lord of the East get his hands on the Dragon Sword …"

Darius nodded.

"I understand," he said, even though his stomach still knotted. "Despite the loss of the Atrimus you sent, I assume you have spies still watching this Eleodum's village?"

"I do, Lord Marshall," Amado replied. "Perhaps more concerning, at the moment, are my spies reporting that the Lord of the East is in Po."

Darius shook his head.

"His ambition has no end," the Lord Marshall said. He had become especially ambitious in the recent months. "Continue to watch him, Amado, and report to me the moment anything changes."

Amado bowed, turned, and left Darius. The General Lord Marshall turned back to the yard, watching the noon sun melt what snow had stuck to the ground. He closed his eyes and sighed deeply. Dangerous times were on the horizon.

*V*ast grassy plains surrounded the city of Po, protected by a tall, wooden palisade. Several towers made of river rock and wood stood a hundred and then fifty paces in front of the city's main gate, manned by archers and small garrisons. The wooden walls might be a formidable defense for the barbarians of the eastern plains but would stand no chance against the siege weapons and might of a Golgolithulian army. However, most knew that the majority of the city lay within deep canyons hidden by the primitive defenses.

The people who founded Po used these canyons as natural defenses before ever thinking of building walls or structures outside the surface of the ravines. The first settlers had carved apartments and shops into the canyon walls, using an intricate system of ladders and internal stairs to move from one residence to the next. For primeval barbarians, it was an ingenious idea, but for the advanced peoples of Eastern Háthgolthane, it would be little more than a nuisance.

"It wouldn't even take a day to conquer this backward town," the Lord of the East said as he stepped out into the grassy plains of Mek-Ba'Dune, leaving the confines of his tall, rolling tower.

"Truly, Your Majesty," Melanius said, trailing behind his master. "It is a wonder it hasn't happened."

"The Aztûkians were weak, Melanius," the Lord of the East said. "If they had any balls, I would be the emperor of the known world right now. After the Battle of Bethuliam, they stopped eastern expansion. And my father ...well, I will be greater than him."

"Truly, Your Majesty," Melanius repeated.

A soldier appeared from one of the towers that stood before the city and rode up between the two sides of the long military train that had accompanied the Lord of the East from Fen-Stévock. The troops snapped to attention as they lined the road and as the soldier passed by, eventually stopping in front of the Lord of the East, who stood outside his tower. He looked down on the Emperor of the East with derisive eyes. He would pay for his disrespect.

The man wore a hardened, leather breastplate with nothing under the armor. His well-muscled arms were a golden brown, evidence of life in the constant sun of the Plains of Mek-Ba'Dune. He held a long spear tipped with a simple iron blade in his right hand, propped against his boot and carried a round, wooden shield painted with blue and yellow stripes in his left hand. His helmet, holding back some of his dark brown, messy hair that spilled past his shoulders, was a simple conical piece of armor also made of hardened leather. Other than dulled, iron greaves over his boots, the soldier wore no armor on his legs, opting for simple pants made of some sort of cloth.

"You should bow before the Lord of the East," Melanius said, shuffling in front of Syzbalo and pointing an accusatory, crooked finger at the horsed man.

The soldier didn't move, his face void of any emotion. A quick huff through his nostrils caused his long mustachios—his only facial hair—to flutter.

"Do you understand that I will peel your skin away, bit by bit, because of your insolence?" Melanius said.

The Lord of the East could see the soldier crack a small smirk under his drooping mustachios.

"Kimber, Krista," the Lord of the East said, and his two witches stepped from the rolling tower. Krista—with her almost white hair, pale skin, blue eyes, and sheer, black dress barely covering her unfettered breasts—and Kimber—with her dark skin, black hair, green eyes, and sheer, white dress fashioned in the same manner—stood next to Syzbalo, each taking an arm.

The soldier's eyes went wide, just for a moment, and the Lord of the East stepped forward.

"Have you come to take us to your Chieftain?" the Lord of the East asked. He spoke Shengu, but he knew the soldier heard him in his native language, as backward and primitive as it was.

"Why have you come to our sacred plains with a whole army?" the soldier asked in his native language, but the Lord of the East heard his words in Shengu.

"This?" the Lord of the East said, looking around. "This is hardly an army, nothing but a small retinue with whom I usually travel."

Clearly meant for speedy travel along the flat ground—as opposed to the great destriers of Háthgolthane that were weapons unto themselves— the soldier's sleek yellow-furred steed stamped a hoof as the soldier squinted slightly.

"I sent word to your Chieftain ahead of time," the Lord of the East said. "I am here for simple diplomatic purposes."

"Diplomacy requires so many horse and sword?" the soldier asked.

"Who are you to question what diplomacy does and doesn't require?" the Lord of the East asked, now clearly struggling to contain his temper. "Now, are you going to make me ask you to take me to your Chieftain again?"

The soldier looked around to the retinue of cavalry and soldiers that had accompanied the Lord of the East, getting more nervous as the moments passed by.

"Just you," the soldier said.

The Lord of the East shook his head and managed to squeeze out a smile.

"No," he replied, "but I will only bring a small contingent of my soldiers. Two dozen."

The soldier thought for a moment and then nodded.

"Why do you banter with this fool?" Melanius asked.

"He thinks he is powerful," the Lord of the East explained. "He will receive what he deserves soon enough, but for now, I will play his game."

A short while later, the Lord of the East, along with Melanius, Kimber, and Krista, rode in a large, four-wheeled chariot drawn by six horses. Two dozen horsed soldiers accompanied the chariot, twelve on each side, which followed this lone soldier. As they passed the defensive towers, the archers glared at them. The Lord of the East simply allowed himself a small chuckle.

"These are small people, Melanius," the Lord of the East said. "They will welcome my rule when the time comes."

The soldier of Po put a simple horn, cut from the head of a small deer, to his lips and blew. The tone was high pitched and long. In response, the main gate of the city-state opened, revealing a bustling metropolis, albeit primitive compared to Fen-Stévock.

The surface of the city of Po consisted mostly of defensive towers, barracks, and a few shops surrounding a small market area. It seemed larger than it looked from outside the walls but, rather than a wide path inclining to a tall tower atop a mound of earth as was common with palisaded, motte and bailey cities, a single, dirt road—large and lined with stone markers—led down into the canyon that was the true municipality of Po.

The whole interior of the city, at least its surface, stopped when the Lord of the East rode through Po's main gate in his large chariot. It was a combination of wood and gold, each side emblazoned with the symbol of the Stévockians: A black gauntlet clutching an arrow with red fletching and a red tip. Each wheel had twelve spokes and small spikes along their edges and horns of some nondescript animal extended from the front of the chariot, meant to look like dragon horns.

The driver of the chariot was a tall, well-muscled man with a bare chest; only his arms and legs were covered in leather and armor. He wore an iron war hat, wide-brimmed, and it had a simple visor that covered his face, dotted with holes for vision. Two other men accompanied the driver—a spearman and an archer—and were similarly dressed.

A short gate, made of mostly wood and some iron, extended from one gatehouse to another, across the path of the road that led into the canyons of Po, and the vast majority of the city. It sat open, but all the soldiers, men merely clothed with cloth or hardened leather, watched the entourage warily, clutching their iron and bronze weapons tightly. The path, wide and even, curved downwards, and when the canyons came into view, the Lord of the East, for a moment, didn't view those who inhabited the city as primitive.

The path leading from the upper portion of the walled city to the canyon ended in another road, one that wound through the natural curvatures of a canyon. The rock of the canyon walls looked segmented, as if some deity, eons before, had layered rock upon rock and pressed them all together. It was streaked with reds and oranges, yellows and whites, blues and purples, but that wasn't what was so magnificent, what made the Lord of the East want this place as part of his empire.

Shops and stores and other buildings lined the lower canyon walls, but as he looked up, he saw holes—apartments and living spaces—built directly into the walls, extending almost to the very top of the ravine. In some places, stairs had been built outside the wall, crisscrossing its face and carved directly from the stone. In other places, he assumed the stairs and ladders were inside the wall, as there was no other way to get from one apartment to the next. As they rode through the canyon, the people here stopping and staring much the same way they did on the surface, the Lord of the East saw that other canyons, most of them smaller, crossed this one, creating other neighborhoods.

"How many inhabit Po?" the Lord of the East asked the soldier leading them through the canyon city, but the man just looked at the Lord of the East over his shoulder, grunted, and turned back around.

"The insolence," Kimber hissed, and the Lord of the East could see the witch conjuring up a green ball in her right hand.

He put a hand on her wrist.

"Be calm, my sweet," he said with a rare smile. "As I said before, he will receive that which he deserves. All in due time."

The witch hissed again, in the direction of the soldier, but the ball of green magic disappeared.

The road ended at a wall of sheer rock, but this wasn't only layered and segmented stone. Ancient peoples had carved a wide opening, like that of a Háthgolthanian keep, into the wall. Parapets and lookout towers had been carved as well, spanning high above the entrance. Columns stood on either side of the opening, useless in function but ornately constructed out of the canyon's natural formations to look like any other freestanding castle.

"Buronn's Hold and the Hall of Munnarak, home to King Bucharan, Ruler of Po," the soldier leading the Lord of the East said, pulling on his horse's reins and turning the animal so that he faced the entourage. "Your warriors may wait out here. You may bring your personal guard."

The Lord of the East strode off the back of the chariot, his witches in tow, each on an arm. The spearman and bowman followed, and then Melanius. But the soldier put up a hand.

"They are not allowed," he said, pointing to the two witches. "Women are forbidden in the Hall of Munnarak."

The Lord of the East forced a smile.

"Surely, there can be ..."

"No," the soldier said, daring to interrupt the Lord of the East. "There are no exceptions. The Hall of Munnarak is sacred, and only men may step foot on its floors."

The Lord of the East patted each of his witches' hands, maintaining his smile as he loosened their grip on his arms.

"Do not worry," he said to them in the Shadow Tongue, "by nightfall, he will no longer be able to step foot in this sacred hall either."

They both hissed, their anger spoiling their beauty, but obeyed their master.

Even though the Lord of the East had never been inside a dwarvish stronghold, he had seen pictures, and he imagined that the inside of Buronn's Hold was what most dwarf castles looked like. Fake colonnades stood along the walls, which were barren save for the occasional bronze sconce burning with oil-filled lanterns. The light inside the hold was sparse, and most of it came from large caldrons filled with wood and grass. The fire created a smoky environment that stung the eyes and burned the throat.

Buronn's Hold was simple, although Syzbalo presumed there was more to the castle than he could see. They passed through an outer hall, which opened into another: The Hall of Munnarak. Here, the light was even dimmer and, rather than fake columns, the walls were lined with the remnants of animals' skulls—large elephants, reptiles, and one that even looked like a dragon. Most of the men in this part of the stronghold either looked like the soldier who led them—simply armed and garbed for Háthgolthanian standards but apparently, well-armed and armored by Mek-Ba'Dunian ones—or were cloaked men, wearing thick, white robes that covered them from head to toe. A bare-chested man sat upon a throne made entirely of elephant tusks, which rested at the end of the Hall of Munnarak, one elbow propped on his knee, his white, bearded chin resting against his knuckles. In the other hand, he held a long staff with an ornately carved ivory spearhead.

King Bucharan was once a stout and muscular man, but now, he was old and wrinkled and growing fat. He stood when he saw the Lord of the East, his tanned gut spilling slightly over his belt. His leggings, mostly browned leather, were almost the same color as the rest of his skin, and for a moment, the Lord of the East thought he was naked. He looked indifferent as the Lord of the East approached.

"To what do I owe the pleasure," the king said in his best attempt at Shengu, "of the Lord of the East visiting my humble city?"

"Diplomacy, of course," the Lord of the East said, although he couldn't wait to remove himself from this place that smelled of sweat and burning wood and animal fat.

"Diplomacy?" King Bucharan replied in a voice full of scorn. "You were not so diplomatic when your armies conquered lands along the eastern banks of the Giant's Vein."

"Lands that were once ours," the Lord of the East said, spreading his hands, "and ours once again."

"Stolen land," the king said.

The Lord of the East shrugged in an attempt to contain his temper.

"Not your land, though, either," he replied.

"I am no fool," the king said, to which Melanius gave a short laugh that only the Lord of the East could hear. "You could crush Po and take my city captive in less than a fortnight."

"I could," the Lord of the East replied, "but such a move would be costly. And I have no desire to spend reckless blood or gold."

He was more concerned about the gold, of course.

"Is it true?" the king asked. "Did a dragon attack your capital?"

The Lord of the East nodded as the king sat back down.

"I have grown too old for this mantle," the king said, looking at his staff. It didn't look like anything special, just a long piece of polished wood, but clearly it was their symbol of control, their version of a crown. "You have met my son."

The king presented the soldier that had led them into the city. Now that he looked at the man, he resembled Bucharan. It was too bad he had to die for his insolence.

"Is he your only son?" the Lord of the East asked, hoping for a positive answer.

"No," Bucharan replied, "I have five others ... and seven daughters. But Thrinn is the bravest, even though he is the youngest. So he will become king when I step away."

"Could we afford more light in here?" the Lord of the East said with a smile as he stepped towards the king.

The Lord of the East lifted his hands and, as he lowered them again, the caldrons filled with wood and sconces with either fresh fat or oil, casting a brightness onto the room that it had probably never seen in all its years. The white-robed men—shamans and healers and holy men—in the room, cowered and ducked. Bucharan and Thrinn just stared, unimpressed.

"If you are trying to impress me," Bucharan said, "I have been around the world, unlike these superstitious fools."

"Fair enough," the Lord of the East said, and the fires dimmed with another wave of his hands.

"I will treat with you," Bucharan said. "I can see that you are serious about an alliance with Po, having traveled so far. Do you intend to treat with Bum-Nur as well?"

"Possibly," the Lord of the East replied. He cared little for an alliance with Po and, soon, they would thank him for releasing them from their bucolic ways.

The king just nodded and motioned to his son. Thrinn jerked his head sideways, looking at the Lord of the East and leading him out of the Hall of Munnarak.

## 12

*T*here wasn't much in the city for his men, but Syzbalo sought to appear obliging and agreed to camp his military force outside the walls of Po. They had all the rations they needed, and there weren't enough alehouses or ale in the whole city to satiate his men's thirst. The city-state of Mek-Ba'Dune also had no brothels, outward prostitution being illegal, although some women did sneak away from the city at night in hopes of making some extra coin. And the soldiers of Golgolithul were more than willing to pay, viewing these women with their tanned skin and brown hair and simple ways as exotic.

A short man with a potbelly, shoulders built by years of farming, dark eyes, shaggy brown hair, and a bushy beard in need of combing walked through the canyons of Po. A tanned-skinned, bald man— only slightly taller—with a hooked nose and bony knees and elbows accompanied him. They stepped into a building—a small tavern— built against the canyon. They made their way through the main room and into a hallway cut into the canyon wall. A man wiping down benches gave them a quick glance, as did another stirring the contents of a bronze pot hanging over a large fire in the corner, but neither paid them any serious attention. They were the only other two ordinary-looking people that might frequent such an establishment.

The hallway, three evenly spaced doors to either side, led to a larger room. The door was open. The potbellied man nodded to the hook-nosed one, signaling him to guard the opening, and the farmer stepped inside.

The room appeared to be empty as the man scanned it. A bed sat against one wall, with a table and a single chair in the middle. The man squinted and saw the faint, translucent outline of someone—a woman—behind the table. A giggle came from the silhouette.

"You see me?" a voice said, none too surprised. "You are more powerful than I thought, more than Mclanius led me to believe."

"What is this?" the man asked.

"A disguise," the voice, feminine and soft with a rolling accent that made her Shengu sound quick and succinct. "Just like you."

"A disguise?" the man asked.

More laughter.

"Come now, oh exalted Lord of the East," the voice said.

Syzbalo couldn't help sensing the sarcasm in the faceless voice. He snapped a finger, and the short, pot-bellied man twisted and contorted until the Lord of the East stood there, a thin film of sweat beading along his bare chest and forehead. He heard the snapping of another finger. The space in front of him, surrounding the silhouette of a slight woman, shifted until a lithe woman with brownish skin and almond-shaped, emerald green eyes sat at the table, lounging back in the chair.

"The Black Tigress," the Lord of the East said.

"Syzbalo," the woman replied with a quick nod of her head.

"You're just like your father," the Lord of the East said. "Insolent."

"Perhaps," the woman replied, giving a small smile.

Her hair was jet black and straight, although she had it tied up into a loose knot atop her head. Her face was narrow, and her jaw soft, nothing like the hard, angular features of her father. Her thin neck betrayed what the Lord of the East knew to be strong shoulders. She wore knee-high boots made of soft calfskin, her wool pants loosely tucked into their tops. She rolled the sleeves of her white, buttoned blouse up to her elbows, showing off her thin arms. She left most of the top buttons undone, revealing the edges of small, round breasts and the tops of well-defined abdominal muscles.

"What shall I call you?" the Lord of the East asked. "The Black Tigress or Ankara?"

The woman narrowed her eyes, only for a moment, and then crossed one leg over the other, propping an elbow on the table.

"Whichever you prefer, Syzbalo," she finally replied nonchalantly.

"I will call you Ankara," the Lord of the East said. "Black Tigress seems silly to me."

"Very well," she said with a shrug and, even though she gave no hint of irritation, Syzbalo sensed annoyance at his accusation.

"Are you going to leave your man out in the hallway?" she asked

Syzbalo looked over his shoulder at his disguised chariot driver.

"He can wait," Syzbalo said.

"You seem irritated, my lord," she said, feigning reverence as she used Syzbalo's honorific title.

"Is this necessary?" he asked.

Ankara opened the palm of the hand resting on the table. The air above her hand shimmered, and something narrow, straight, and white rested there. She set it down on the wood and stared at it, her eyes taking on a glassy look as if she were about to cry.

"The last memory of my father," she said, her voice cracking and her lower lip pouting. "A single vertebrae from his spear."

"He thought he was more powerful than he was," Syzbalo said.

Ankara looked at him, a wide smile on her face. She snapped a finger, and the bone caught fire and burned away, leaving nothing but black ash.

"You don't believe I am a grieving daughter?" she asked with a hint of mockery in her voice.

"I know better," Syzbalo replied.

"Truly," Ankara said, standing. "He was a bastard. Although I would have liked to have his Bone Spear."

She shrugged and stood, moving closer to the Lord of the East, looking up at him as she was quite a bit shorter than the man.

"Nonetheless, the lands of barbarians aren't safe for me and my people," Ankara added.

"We are in the lands of barbarians," the Lord of the East said.

"Bah," she said with a dismissive wave of her hand. "Háthgolthane is the land of barbarians. Mek-Ba'Dune is a simple land—backward, perhaps in places—but simple. You are the conquerors. You are the ones spreading wickedness and brutality."

"And you profit from it," the Lord of the East said.

Ankara turned around, walking in a semicircle in the room, turning again to face Syzbalo.

"Yes," she said with another shrug of her shoulders. "Besides, I know this trip serves you more than one purpose. You needed to treat with Bucharan. You needed to show your strength in Antolika."

The Lord of the East nodded with a smirk. There was one other reason for this trip, something the Lord of Chaos bade him do, something that would garner him even greater power.

"Who is he," Ankara asked, "the mark? This man who killed my father?"

"Erik Eleodum," came the reply. "A farmer who is now being called Erik Dragon Slayer."

"A scary farmer," Ankara said, feigning a shiver and smiling.

"Do not make the same mistake your father made," the Lord of the East said, and the smile on the Black Tigress' face disappeared. "Whatever his past, he's a formidable foe and an adept swordsman. But, nonetheless, I want him dead. I want the sword he carries."

"And the bounty?" Ankara asked.

"What do you want?" the Lord of the East replied. "Are you like your father?"

Ankara scrunched up her face in a look of disgust.

"Certainly not," she said. "I prefer money and slaves."

"Name your price," the Lord of the East said, "and it is yours."

"I want three hundred slaves," Ankara replied, "and one hundred thousand eastern crowns."

"Slaves?" Syzbalo asked. "Who is the cruel, brutal one now?"

"But I won't drink the blood of their offspring like my dear departed father."

She must have noticed how he was looking at her now, and she smiled as she ran a slender finger along her neck and over to the open edge of her blouse, pushing it aside to reveal more of her breast. She bit her lip, eyeing Syzbalo up and down, and then she stepped closer. She was almost a head shorter than him, but at that moment, she made him feel small.

"I could care less how you treat them," Syzbalo said, now openly staring down at her breasts as a small, dark nipple escaped her blouse.

"You desire me, don't you," she said.

"I desire much," he replied, willing his skin, wanting to blush, to remain its typical pale tone.

"Perhaps that would be my price," she said. "A night with the Lord of the East."

"And you would extract more power than you could handle," the Lord of the East said. "I know how your magic works."

She stepped closer and smelled him.

"You have the stink of witches on you, Syzbalo," she said, stepping away and giggling. "I heard you liked witches. Conniving little bitches."

"And what are you?" Syzbalo asked. "A magic-wielding, Isutan woman?"

She laughed. She jerked her head towards the bed.

"Shall I show you how a real woman feels," she said with a toothy smile, "how Isutan women feel?"

He could feel her magic at work. That was her charm ... her sex. He had heard stories of the Black Tigress. She lay with men and then poisoned them ... with her magic. As her father drank blood for power, she drank a person's essence when she lay with them.

"And what would that cost me?" Syzbalo asked.

"Perhaps nothing," Ankara replied, and then her voice dropped to a whisper. "Perhaps everything."

Her eyes flashed and glowed, and he felt himself become immediately aroused. She grabbed him and squeezed, licking her lips and moaning, letting her head fall back and revealing her lithe neck.

He grabbed her wrist and stepped away.

"Three hundred slaves and a hundred thousand eastern crowns," he said, changing himself back into the visage of a man from Po. "But I have another job for you before you set off to kill Erik Eleodum."

Ankara looked disappointed at his lack of interest in bedding her.

"What's that?" she asked, pulling her blouse back into place.

"Are you familiar with Thrinn?" the Lord of the East asked.

"Bucharan's son?" Ankara replied. "I slipped into his room the other day and watched him bathe. His manhood was very underwhelming for such a muscular man."

"I need you to kill him," the Lord of the East said, and she laughed.

"Whatever for?"

"He insulted me," the Lord of the East replied.

"Oh," Ankara said, her continued laughter mocking him, "the great Syzbalo was shamed by some backward prince." She shrugged. "Everything has a price."

"Of course it does," Syzbalo replied. "You're Isutan."

"No," she said, her smile still present, "I am flesh and blood."

"Name the price for this one?" he asked.

"Leave me your man," she said, looking to the hallway outside her door.

"Why?" Syzbalo asked.

She laughed again and flashed her eyes.

"Will I get him back?" he asked.

"Maybe," Ankara replied with childish insincerity. "If he pleases me."

"Fine," Syzbalo replied.

"And ten thousand crowns," Ankara said as Syzbalo turned to walk away.

He nodded.

"All right. I will kill Thrinn. And then west I go, in search of this Erik Eleodum."

Syzbalo commanded his chariot driver to stay as he left the room, Ankara laughing behind him.

The Lord of the East walked into the grassy plains of Mek-Ba'Dune. Night fully encompassed the world and, without the various lights and fires of a large city, millions of stars twinkled overhead, all crowning a large moon that cast a pallid light across the tall, browning grass.

The grass bowed to a cold breeze that signified winter in an otherwise temperate part of the world. The wind opened Syzbalo's black robe, revealing his typically bare chest, although the cold didn't affect him as it might another person. He always felt comfortable, no matter what he wore, especially as of late ... especially as his power grew.

Syzbalo looked over his shoulder, staring at the dim lights that rose upwards from a city built into the ground, throughout a maze of canyons. It was quite genius, for such a backward people. The firelight from his army caused a glow that was twice as bright and for a brief moment, he wondered how long it would take for his relatively small contingent of soldiers to overrun Po ... but that wasn't really why he was there. The real reason was Ankara, the Black Tigress, the Isutan assassin that would track down Erik Eleodum and take the Dragon Sword and bring it to the Lord of the East. At least, that was what he told Melanius and the witches. And as much as he desired the Dragon Sword—and the Dragon Crown, the ability to control dragons almost intoxicating—that wasn't the true reason he was in Mek-Ba'Dune either. He was there because the Lord of Chaos commanded it. He was there because as he obeyed this shadowy lord, his power and magic grew. He was there because one day, Syzbalo—Lord of the East—would rule the world.

He stood amongst knee-high grass, peering out into the darkness of the plains with magical vision. He wasn't sure if his eyes glowed, but the land before him looked as if it was a lightly clouded day, the sun still able to shine through high, thin wisps of white. He didn't know when or where he would meet *them,* the ones the Lord of Chaos had directed him to make contact with. He was just supposed to walk into the plains at night and wait. He hated waiting and grumbled as he scanned the horizon before him.

"The Lord of the East, all by himself in the wilds of Mek-Ba'Dune," said a voice, growly and rough.

Syzbalo turned to see a goblin standing before him. He didn't know how the creature had snuck up on him. It stared at the Lord of the East with red, cat-like eyes, a small smirk on its wide, flat face, black lips barely cracking and two, small fangs poking upwards from its lower jaw and curling its upper lip. With a forehead that sloped backwards, the creature looked primitive, but Syzbalo could see intelligence in those eyes.

"I don't like being made to wait, goblin," Syzbalo said.

"And I don't serve you," the goblin replied. "We don't serve you."

The goblin language was crude and ugly, and if there was a language that could make Dwarvish sound beautiful, it was Goblin. It lifted its hand, and more than a dozen shadows emerged from the tall grass. They were short enough and slight enough—perhaps as tall as dwarves and yet thin and lithe—to hide in the grass, but that meant the Lord of the East had walked past them completely unaware. That irritated him.

"Yet," Syzbalo muttered, and the goblin growled. That made Syzbalo smile. "What is your name?"

"Akzûl," the goblin replied.

"Are you a male or female?" Syzbalo asked, and the goblin gave a snorting laugh.

"Foolish humans," Akzûl said. The goblin sneered. "Always trying to exert dominance. Male. Captain of the Black Wolves. Humble servant of the Lord of Chaos."

"The Black Wolves?" Syzbalo said, his voice dripping with sarcasm. "What do you want?"

"It is what *our* lord wants," Akzûl said. "You will escort the Black Wolves across the Giant's Vein and into Háthgolthane."

Syzbalo's face paled, and his jaw went slack.

"Out of the question," he said finally.

Akzûl stepped forward, looking up at Syzbalo with squinted eyes and a tilted head. He wore his black hair in a topknot that bobbed as he moved, and he scratched a thin, scraggly beard that hung from his thin, gray chin. Syzbalo thought it would be easy to count how many whiskers there were.

"This is the will of *our* master," Akzûl said. "Do you wish to disobey *our* lord?"

The Lord of the East waited a moment, looking about. He realized he hadn't swallowed and did so, his throat moving slowly as he envisioned the looks on his soldiers', his advisors', and his citizens' faces as he marched through Fen-Stévock with more than a dozen goblins in tow. Goblins lived in Golgolithul, and in many cases, served a valuable service as merchants and vendors, mostly in the slums and lower income parts of the eastern cities. But they were not allowed citizenship, and most, even the lowest prostitutes and beggars, spat in their direction. To have goblins accompanying the Lord of the East was unheard of.

"A few dozen goblins," Syzbalo said with a shrug. "I can manage the gossip that will cause for a few months. Who are they to speak anyway? I am the Lord of the East."

"Truly," Akzûl said with another smirk and, putting two fingers to his lips, whistled. Shadows from all around the night-shrouded plain rose from the knee-high grass, until at least a hundred goblins stood, surrounding the Lord of the East.

"How many of you are there?" Syzbalo asked.

"One hundred and twenty-one," Akzûl replied. "Eleven units of eleven. All Black Wolves."

As the goblin spoke the name of their unit, all one hundred and twenty-one of the goblins lifted their faces to the sky and howled at the moon.

"And once we're there?" Syzbalo asked.

"The master will tell us what to do next," Akzûl said.

"This can't be done," the Lord of the East muttered.

*It will be done.*

The voice was in Syzbalo's head, but it wasn't his. It was deep and growly and metallic. It was *his* voice.

*It will be done. This is my command. Or you will suffer the pain of disobedience.*

Akzûl laughed. The look on Syzbalo's face gave him away. The goblin knew *their* master was speaking to him.

"Fine," Syzbalo said, pulling his robe tight as if the cold affected him. "Gather your Black Wolves and bring them to my camp. Stay clear of my men."

"If they bother us," Akzûl said, drawing a cruel-looking, curved blade from his belt, "it has been a while since I have eaten man-flesh."

The goblin licked the blade.

"I will tell my men to stay clear of you, but you will do the same. You are there because of the master, nothing more. Do not think I couldn't turn every single one of you to ash or boil your blood in the flutter of a fly's wings. Is that all?"

Akzûl shook his head.

"The Blood Hawks are going north," Akzûl explained. "They are headed to the Gray Mountains. They must go unharassed. You will tell the king of Po and the warlord of Bum-Nur they are not to bother the Blood Hawks. Goblins are not openly welcomed by the Two Towners."

"I can't imagine why," Syzbalo muttered. "Anything else?"

"The Death Dogs are—"

Syzbalo rolled his eyes before he interrupted.

"Oh, by the gods, will you spare me the stupid names?"

"—the dogs are moving through the Shadow Marshes and will cross the Giant's Vein and into Crom," Akzûl finished. "Make sure your people leave them be."

"Very well. It's not like goblins don't live in Crom anyway. It will be done."

Akzûl smiled.

"You say you answer to the Lord of Chaos, but how do I know you will not cause trouble with my soldiers or in my city?" Syzbalo asked.

"For now," Akzûl said with a facetious smile and a low bow, "we answer to you, my lord."

Syzbalo looked down at the still bowing goblin. The others did the same, but it was all show. They hated him, and they hated the east. But for now, they served him, and he couldn't help the small smile that touched the corners of his mouth.

## 13

*A*s the sun crested the western horizon, Erik passed the last farmstead of northwest Háthgolthane. He rode north, towards Eldmanor and, by himself and riding hard, knew it would only take him two or three days to get there. The first day had been bitterly cold, and the night was freezing, but there wasn't any wind, so Erik huddled close to his fire. He tried bringing Warrior close, too, so the animal might warm itself, but he was his usual stubborn self. With each wolf's howl or coyote whoop, he only seemed to want to go find the source of the sound and stomp on some predator's head.

It wasn't the cold or the sounds of predators that stalked the nights of the northern reaches of Háthgolthane that kept Erik awake that night. Nor was it his dreams ... they weren't there anymore. He didn't know at first why he could not sleep, but for want of something to pass the time, he retrieved his flute from his haversack. From the moment he put the instrument to his lips, he understood.

All he could think of now was Simone and her swollen belly. Then the mental image changed to a little boy bouncing on his knee, learning how to fish with him, how to hunt, and how to farm. He left her. He left his unborn child. He left everyone—friends, parents, sisters. He was a selfish fool, and he truly didn't know if his wife would be there when he returned ... if he returned.

"Will I sleep at all on this trip, Warrior?" Erik asked, making his best attempt at Shengu.

He wasn't quite sure if he chose his words correctly but knew he had at least spoken the horse's name acceptably as Warrior finally turned and walked towards Erik, nuzzling his shoulder.

"You are a stubborn creature, aren't you?" Erik asked, scratching the animal's nose, retrieving an apple from his haversack, and feeding it to the horse. When he finally gave up trying to sleep, Erik doused his fire, mounted up, and continued north, toward Eldmanor.

Several days—and mostly sleepless nights—later, Erik reached the outskirts of the border town of Eldmanor as the sun began to rise. At first, he had planned on stopping at Hagmer's alehouse, but it was early, and the lack of sleep was getting to him, and he didn't think he had the patience for the noisy alehouse owner.

Seeing barely another soul braving the icy morning, Erik rode to the northern edges of the town, his eyes focusing on a small, straw hut. With no fence, sheep and goats and chickens roamed about, foraging with seemingly little fear of predators and no desire to run away. No doubt Dewin protected them.

Smoke escaped from a hole in the roof of the hut and, even from a distance, the smells of sage and thyme, marjoram and rosemary struck Erik's nose. He hadn't realized how hungry he was, and his stomach gurgled.

Because there was no fence, there was also no hitching post in front of the hut, and as Erik dismounted, he grabbed Warrior's reins and stared deeply into the animal's eyes.

"Are you going to wait for me here," Erik asked, "or should I find something to tie you to?"

The horse stomped its foot and snorted as its eyes met Erik's.

"Very well," Erik said, dropping the reins before he turned to face the entrance of the hut.

Stepping inside, the warmth washed over Erik, a musty, thick fog of heat that could not have only emanated from the small fire that burned in the middle of the one-room home. As the warm air chased away the chill of the outside winter, Erik saw a small figure huddled in a tattered, black robe, sitting next to the fire. When Erik had seen the old mage in his dreams, he was always a young man, vibrant and strong and with long, blond, wavy hair. But now, a frail, liver-spotted hand circled a long-handled wooden spoon in a dark pot that hung over the fire. As the food sizzled and popped, Dewin retrieved the spoon slurped at the steaming contents.

"It's good," Dewin said, his voice a faint croak. "Would you like some?"

"What is it?" Erik asked.

"Does it matter?" Dewin replied. "It is warm, and the world outside is cold ... and getting colder."

"I don't know how much time I have," Erik said, stepping deeper into the hut.

"I didn't expect to see you in person so soon, Dream Walker," Dewin said.

"Assassins came to murder me and my cousin," Erik said. "From Gol-Durathna."

"The Atrimus," Dewin said, putting his spoon back into the pot.

Erik had heard the name before, spoken by his gypsy friend Marcus. It was hard to believe that the nation who most heralded as righteous and upright would employ assassins.

"The assassins of the Golden City," Dewin said with a croaking laugh. "The doers of evil deeds."

"And here I had thought Gol-Durathna was a nation that stood for goodness and righteousness," Erik said.

Dewin laughed again.

"Now you know better," Dewin said, standing and shuffling over to a small, round table that sat at the other end of the hut. "You told your wife as much, didn't you?"

The old wizard grabbed two wooden bowls from the table and returned to the fire and the cooking pot. As Dewin rested the bowls on the dusty floor beside him, Erik could see only the old man's chin poking out from underneath his cowl, splotchy, wispy white hairs curling away from pale skin.

"It is ruled by men," Dewin said. "Are men good and righteous?"

"No, I suppose not," Erik replied.

"No, Dream Walker," Dewin said, ladling a spoon full of the cooking pot's contents—a stew of some sort—into the bowls. "No. Men are wicked, cruel creatures. As are dwarves and goblins and elves."

The old wizard, having filled both bowls, handed one to Erik and then shuffled back to the round table, sitting on a short stool. He presented another stool to Erik.

"You have time," Dewin said, his voice commanding, not asking for Erik to sit. "Come and eat."

Erik looked at the bowl and its contents. It was a reddish-brown with black colored beans and some chunky dark meat. He sat down, across from Dewin, and watched as the old man, picking up a much shorter wooden spoon, slurped his stew. He saw another spoon and started to eat.

The taste of rosemary overwhelmed the stew, and the beans themselves were bland. The meat—Erik suspected either goat or sheep—was tough and chewy, with bits of even chewier tendon. And there wasn't enough of the meat. But for all the unappetizing aspects of the meal, it was warm, and as it hit Erik's stomach, it gave him a sense of peace and comfort.

"Magic," he mumbled, looking at the bowl, the stew almost gone.

"I suppose, Dream Walker," Dewin said, "that food could have magical qualities. Although, I suspect you have not really eaten—or slept—in several days, and a full belly is what brings you comfort."

Erik nodded and smiled, putting the bowl to his lips and drinking the last bit of broth.

"Why has the Dragon Slayer come to me?" Dewin asked, setting his bowl down on the table.

"You know why," Erik said, setting his bowl down too.

"Do I, Dream Walker?" Dewin asked with a smile, barely visible under his low hanging cowl. "Yes. I suppose I do. You come seeking advice. You seek the Dragon Stone, the Ruling Stone, the Stone of Chaos. The same thing known by many names."

"Yes," Erik replied.

"This is a thing of great importance," Dewin said.

"Rako," Erik muttered, thinking of the elf whose spirit once spoke to him through a golden-handled dagger that now hung at his side as Dragon Tooth.

"No," Dewin replied, "and yes."

"I still don't understand," Erik said.

"I wouldn't expect you to," Dewin said. "Things will unfold, and the way will become clearer."

"This isn't about Rako, then?" Erik asked.

"No, not really," Dewin replied.

"Some evil has risen," Erik said. "Something that opposes both the Shadow and the Creator."

Dewin nodded.

"And what new evil is this?" Erik asked.

"New, yes," Dewin said, "and old. Very dangerous. You must tread carefully, Erik. This journey is about your future, the future of your people, and the future of the world."

"So I should forget about Rako," Erik said more to himself than to Dewin.

"No," Dewin replied. "Rako the Fallen is a friend and, as much, if you find the Dragon Stone, you will find a way to rescue Rako from his prison. But know this, finding the Stone of Chaos holds importance much greater than freeing the dragon rider."

"What do I do, then?" Erik asked. "Where do I go?"

"Why ask me? What do your dreams say, Friend of Dwarves?"

"They say nothing," Erik replied. "I haven't dreamt in days."

"Have you not?" Dewin asked, and Erik just shook his head.

The wizard turned away from Erik. This wasn't something even Dewin had expected, and that made Erik nervous.

"That's bad, isn't it?" Erik asked.

"It is not good, Dragon Slayer ... no, it is not good," Dewin replied.

"Someone, or something is blocking my dreams," Erik explained. "He was in my dreams. He wore a black robe and hood. At first, I thought he might have been Andragos."

Dewin pulled back the cowl of his robe, revealing his blind eyes and pale, thin skin, smattered with liver spots and scars. Before, Erik had marveled how the old man could be so precise in his movements and actions when he could not see, but now Erik just took it for granted. It was ... Dewin.

"Such power ... more powerful than Andragos ..." Dewin began, more to himself than to Erik. He turned his head, facing Erik, his pale, blank eyes staring at nothing, beyond Erik, searching for something. "An agent of chaos, that is who he is. As dangerous as chaos. As powerful as chaos."

Erik just stared at the fire, feeling the warmth it created in the small hut.

"You must go north, Wolf's Bane, to Hargoleth. Rako the Fallen has told you as much."

"Why do you call him Rako the Fallen?" Erik asked, interrupting Dewin.

"You know why, Dream Walker," Dewin replied. "You saw. What does it take, what line must be crossed for the righteous to become wicked? For the humble to become prideful? What is the difference between good and evil?"

"Good serves the Creator," Erik said, "and evil serves the Shadow."

"Yes ... and no," Dewin replied. "Are you good?"

Erik leaned back like he'd been slapped. The question caught him by surprise.

"Yes," Erik finally said. "I am good."

"To your family, you are good, Dragon Slayer," Dewin said.

But that made Erik think of Simone and the dwarves, of his parents and sisters and his cousin. Was he good to them? He found a lump in his throat as he tried to swallow.

"Ah," Dewin said, "I sense conflict, even in that assumption."

"I didn't leave my home on peaceful terms," Erik admitted.

"I see," Dewin said. "Yes, it must have been hard to leave a pregnant wife, good friends, and your family."

"Yes," Erik agreed, feeling the guilt rise like bile in his stomach.

"You see, we assume you to be good," Dewin continued. "To King Skella, you are good. To King Bu Al'Banan of Hámon, you are evil."

"But he serves the Shadow," Erik said.

"Does he, Friend of Dwarves? Or does he just serve himself?"

Erik looked away, staring at the fire and watching the smoke swirl about on its gravity-defying upwards journey. Erik wondered what it would be like to escape so easily from the pressures in his mind and heart.

"I suppose he might," Erik acknowledged begrudgingly.

Dewin just shrugged, and then Erik shook his head

"No. It must be the Shadow," Erik decided. "His actions say as much."

"To King Agempi of Gol-Durathna, you are evil," Dewin said, again shrugging. "Does he serve the Shadow? To Fréden Fréwin, you are evil ... is he also a follower of the Shadow? And to the families of Cliens and Ranus—the Durathnans—you are the most evil."

"But I was defending myself," Erik replied. "I was protecting my friends and my family."

Dewin yet again shrugged.

"You see, Dream Walker," Dewin continued, "the line between being righteous or wicked can be blurry. It was once clearly drawn in the sand, but now it is marred by wind and rain."

"I am not a good man, then?" Erik asked, more to himself than to Dewin.

The old man cackled, and Erik couldn't help feeling his face grow hot.

"How can you laugh," Erik said. "I am the worst kind of man. I left a pregnant wife at home. I betrayed the trust of my friends. I ..." He stopped and shook his head again.

"We all are wicked at some point," Dewin said. "But you are not the worst kind of man. Good and evil, in some cases, are as clear as black and white, but in other cases, they are gray. And the man serving the one who is deemed good and evil, are they the same?"

"What do you mean?" Erik asked.

"The soldier in the Lord of the East's army," Dewin said. "Is he evil? Or is he simply doing what he thinks best? Serving his country? Serving his lord?"

"I don't know," Erik said.

"Or the soldier serving the King of Thorakest?" Dewin asked. "Are all his dwarvish warriors as righteous as he? What of the dwarf that stuck a knife in the belly of your friend, Vander Bim?"

Erik remembered his friend—sailor turned mercenary. He was a simple man ... and he deserved a better death.

"But my wife?" Erik asked.

"What choice did you have?" Dewin replied.

Erik shrugged. He couldn't swallow and felt the recent food rise like the smoke. His stomach and head began to hurt.

"Can I ask you a question?" Dewin asked.

Erik nodded.

"Would you willingly lose your family to save them?" Dewin asked. "Do you love your wife so much that you would risk never seeing her again to know she would be safe and healthy?"

"Yes," Erik said without hesitation. "Of course."

"Then, there is no other way," Dewin said. "Something led you here, Dream Walker, and here is where you need to be. You must find the Dragon Stone—The Stone of Chaos."

Erik thought of the line in the sand, the division between right and wrong.

"Rako crossed that line, didn't he?" Erik said, looking at the ground as the images of the elf—from his dreams, his vision, and Fealmynster—ran through his head. "He thought his actions were righteous ... but they weren't."

"Now you begin to understand," Dewin said. "Rako the Fallen can be redeemed. In fact, to truly save the world from this new evil, he must be redeemed—he must be set free from his prison that is the Stone. You must find the Stone of Chaos and take it to the cursed forests of Ul'Erel, where the Elenderel dwell."

"The Elenderel?" Erik asked.

"Elves," Dewin said.

"El'Beth El'Kesh," Erik whispered.

"Yes, Dragon Slayer," Dewin said, getting up from his stool and walking to the fire, where he stood with his hands clasped behind his back. "She is a powerful enchantress ... and a princess of the elves. She has the power to release Rako from the Dragon Stone. She has the power to protect and hide the stone, the power to ..."

"To what?" Erik asked as Dewin's voice trailed off.

The mage shook his head and turned to face Erik.

"Nothing," he replied. "There are two sorcerers in Ul'Erel who can release Rako from the Dragon Stone. El'Beth El'Kesh is one of them ... and she might be willing to do so since she loved him ... once."

"Loved him?" Erik asked. "How old is she?"

"More than a millennia, Dream Walker," Dewin replied. "The elves live long lives. They were among the first works of the Creator ... and their magic is powerful. They hide away in their forests, unaffected by time like the rest of us. Beware the Elenderel, Erik. Beware."

"The other?" Erik asked. "Who else can release Rako?"

"Jart'El El'Kesh," Dewin replied. "Her brother. A prince of the elves."

"Your face and voice don't give me comfort as you say his name," Erik said.

Dewin shook his head.

"He hated Rako, Dream Walker," Dewin replied. "And he hates men. In fact, he hates anything that is not Sylvan."

When Erik cocked his head to the side and furrowed his eyebrows, it was again as if Dewin could see because he smiled.

"Fairy folk," Dewin explained.

"I see," said Erik, although he wasn't sure that was true.

"This will be a hard journey, Erik Dragon Fire. Especially since you have chosen to do it alone."

"Is there any other way?"

"There is always another way," Dewin replied, "but you must be at peace with your choice."

"So, where in Hargoleth do I go?" Erik asked.

"Hargoleth is a fragmented country," Dewin replied, "full of proud people—most of whom share bloodlines with you, the Eleodums—militant clans, and city-states barely holding alliances with one another. You will need to tread lightly, Dream Walker, and before you get to Hargoleth, you must travel through the Pass of Dundolyothum. Stay east of the Forests of Ul'Erel, but beware of the giants. Once you are through the Pass, you should make your way to Holtgaard, home of the Bear Clan."

"And once I am in Holtgaard?" Erik asked.

"By then, I hope your dreams have begun to speak to you again."

Erik nodded as he stood, intent on leaving, but before he did, he looked at Dewin once more and squinted his eyes in the smoke.

"Before ... Why did you send me the way you did?" Erik asked.

Dewin tilted his head and pursed his lips.

"Over the Ice Bridge and into that meadow that was clearly enchanted. Beldar said it was elvish magic."

"It was ... is," Dewin said. "The Tower of the White Rose, long since broken."

"What was it?" Erik asked.

"Perhaps a question for another time, Dream Walker," Dewin replied, "but I trust you found the white stone, hidden inside a statue of an elf."

Erik's back straightened. He put a hand to the pouch hanging from his belt in which sat one red and one white stone, both perfectly round and dull, drinking up any light that struck them.

"Yes, you did, so now you know why," Dewin said. "Your cousin found a similar stone in the Tower of the Black Thorn. You will need his stone, eventually."

"Tower of the Black ..." Erik whispered to himself, and then his eyes widened. "Fealmynster."

*Bryon never told me that. Why didn't he—*

"Yes," Dewin said, breaking into Erik's thoughts.

"Was that place once a meadow like the one beyond the Ice Bridge?" Erik asked.

"Once."

"So this is all some sort of fate, some destiny I have?" Erik asked, sensing the anger in his own voice.

Dewin balked.

"Ha! Fate. Destiny. Tools for fools and witches and soothsayers. It is a plan. That is all. Some plans are successful. Some plans fail."

Dewin lifted his nose and sniffed the air.

"I will try and seek out a way for you to walk the land of dreams, Dream Walker. Meanwhile, you must hurry to Holtgaard. The wind tells me it is time for you to go."

Erik walked out of Dewin's hut, and the wizard followed him. He walked over to Warrior and scratched the animal's nose. At first, Warrior looked apprehensive, and Erik was about to tell the mage he would bite, but as soon as a liver-spotted hand touched the white fur of the creature's snout, Warrior bowed his head.

"I've never seen him do that," Erik said.

But Dewin ignored him and, instead, leaned towards the horse's ear and whispered. Erik couldn't make out what the wizard was saying, but when he was done, he laughed quietly, and Warrior snorted, bobbed his head, and stomped a hoof.

"Continue to search for your dreams, Dream Walker," Dewin said, stepping away from the horse. "Hopefully, they will return soon. Stay the course, and as always, follow your heart."

## 14

Terradyn and Raktas crested a tall hill, still not entirely green where the frost clung to the ground despite the noonday sun. Atop the hillock, they could see a sprawling land filled with farms as far as the eye could see, and Terradyn couldn't help smiling. It was a pleasant sight, all the farms and little swirls of smoke trailing up from chimneys for the better part of a league. It looked like something out of a children's story, one of those tales that ended with, "And everyone lived happily." It was too bad most tales ended very differently.

Terradyn heeled his horse again, and they rode down the hill, finding a wide, dirt road that wound through the farmsteads. They followed the wide path and had passed two farms before they came to an old, grizzled farmer with a wide-brimmed straw hat. Despite the chill air, his brown, wool pants were rolled up to his knees, and a white shirt, sleeves turned back to his elbows as he worked on a repairing a fence that bordered the road.

"Aren't you cold?" Terradyn asked, riding up to the man and looking down at him.

The old man looked up at Terradyn, staring out from under his wide-brimmed hat with one eye squinted. He shrugged as he chewed something, and when he spat, just in front of his horse's hoof, Terradyn could tell it was rain leaf.

"Do you need help?" Terradyn asked.

Most men looked twice when they saw Andragos' two body-guards. Strangers didn't recognize the men as such, but their appear-ances could be jarring, with their large statures and muscles, their tattoos, and their pierced ears or nose. This man seemed to look at them like he would the cattle that grazed beyond the fence.

"Does it look like I need help?" the farmer asked with a gruff voice that spoke of too much pipeweed.

"Yes, it does," Terradyn replied.

"And are you offering your help?" the man asked.

Terradyn looked over his shoulder, at Raktas, and his friend just shrugged.

"Yes," Terradyn replied, "I suppose we are."

"Well," the man said coldly, still eyeing the two easterners, "I don't need no help."

"He speaks to us with such disrespect," Raktas whispered in Shengu. "We should remove his head from his wretched body."

Terradyn waved his companion off.

"Perhaps, then, you could help us," he said.

The man straightened and threw a small hand ax he had been working with into the frosty earth. As the blade thudded into the ground, he jammed his knuckles into his hips and spat once more.

"I'm busy," the farmer said, "and don't have much time to help no one."

"All we need is to find a particular farm," Terradyn replied.

"Which one?"

"It belongs to someone called Eleodum," Terradyn replied.

"Which one?"

"There are more than one?" Terradyn asked.

"Aye," the farmer said, retrieving his hand ax and going back to work on the wooden rail. "Three, in fact."

"Erik Eleodum," Terradyn said. "I am looking for Erik Eleodum."

The farmer stopped chewing and looked back up at Terradyn.

Roses lined the path that led up to the farmhouse. It was a decent-sized house, bigger than most of the other homes in the farmstead. The vast fields, albeit fallow in the winter, showed a wealthy farm, with an orchard of leafless apple and peach trees and a large barn.

As Terradyn tied his horse—a large, black stallion with muscles to match his master's—to a post of the fence that surrounded the house, a tall man burst through the front door. Terradyn thought he recognized the man, lean and muscular with blondish-brown hair and a well-groomed beard. He looked angry and, when he saw Andragos' two bodyguards, his face turned a bright shade of red. His hand went to the handle of a broad-bladed long sword hanging from his hip. When he drew the blade, Terradyn's eyes widened as the steel glowed a bright purple.

"What do you want?" the man shouted as he hurried down the path, looking as if he was about to break out into a run.

Terradyn saw Raktas' hand go to the two-handed sword hanging from his back. In response, the man walking up the path stopped and crouched into his fighting stance.

"No, Raktas," Terradyn said.

At the same time, a pregnant woman—a tall, blonde-haired woman with broad shoulders—came to the door. As soon as she saw the tall man ready to fight with his sword drawn, and he and Raktas, she put a hand to her mouth in surprise, and her eyes widened with fear.

"We mean no trouble. We are looking for Erik Eleodum," Terradyn said.

The tall man with the purple sword furrowed his brow.

"You belong to Andragos, don't you?" he asked.

The accusation stung Terradyn a bit. He didn't belong to anyone ... did he? Raktas grumbled, clearly irritated by the allegation as well.

"We are the Messenger of the East's bodyguards, yes," Terradyn said.

"Then what are you doing here?" the man asked. As he spoke, the pregnant woman walked out along the path, standing behind him. He looked at her over his shoulder. "Simone, get back inside."

"I told you we are not here to cause you problems," Terradyn said, irritated at having to repeat himself, "we are simply looking for Erik Eleodum."

"Why?" the woman named Simone asked.

"Are you his woman?" Raktas asked.

She stepped back and pulled a white shawl she was wearing across her shoulders tight as if the question caused an extra chill in the air. She looked at the two bodyguards, eyes wide for a moment, and then she pursed her lips and squinted.

"I'm his wife," she replied. "Why do you want him?"

"The Messenger of the East, Herald of Golgolithul," Terradyn said, stepping forward. The man blocking the path did not move, his sword still drawn and ready. "He has sent us here to protect Erik Eleodum and his family."

"Well," the man said, standing and dropping the tip of his sword, although he left it unsheathed and gripped with white knuckles, "you'll have to ride north, towards Hargoleth, because that's where the idiot has gone."

Simone, Erik's wife, began to shake her head and looked close to tears.

"Gone?" Terradyn asked.

"Yes," the man said, shaking his head and dropping his chin to his chest. "Left several days ago. Early morning. And without me."

"And you are?" Raktas asked.

"Bryon Eleodum," the man replied, "his cousin."

Raktas looked at Terradyn and shrugged. They heard a commotion behind them, shouting in Dwarvish, and both turned to see two dwarves running towards them from the barn. One held a battle-ax—half-moon blade glimmering in the sunlight—and the other carried a broadsword.

"Peace!" the man Bryon shouted in Dwarvish, and the two dwarves slowed, although they still looked alarmed.

"We have been tasked with both protecting Erik Eleodum *and* his family," Terradyn said.

"Why?" Simone said, now stepping in front of Bryon and walking towards the two men.

"People want to kill him," Terradyn replied, "and you."

"But why have *you* been tasked with protecting us?" she asked, pointing at the two bodyguards.

"It is the will of the Messenger of the East," Raktas replied curtly, a hint of irritation in his voice. "We do as we are commanded."

"Doesn't he serve the Lord of the East?" Bryon asked. "Has the Lord of the East changed his mind about wanting us dead? Or ... have Andragos' loyalties suddenly changed?"

Terradyn looked at Raktas and then back at Bryon.

## 15

Erik leaned over the dead wolf. It was stiff, partially because of the cold, but also because the kill was fresh. Now thickening blood had flowed from its neck, the only wound he could see on the large canine's body. Its fur was black and gray, and it was a giant of a beast, heavy with thick muscles. Although this wasn't a winter wolf, evident by the lack of red eyes, it reminded Erik of the sentient creatures he'd battled, ones with evil spirits that lived in the Southern Mountains, and served wicked warlords and wizards ... or dragons.

Erik's eyes went from the animal to the peaks of the Gray Mountains to the north, back to the animal, and then to the south. Whatever killed it was close by. None of it was eaten, and it must have been killed out of self-defense. The animal that killed this wolf would have been a fearsome thing, but he was glad for it. As cantankerous and mean as Warrior was, and as good a warrior as Erik had become —especially with Dragon Tooth by his side—this creature would have still been a formidable foe ... and wolves traveled in packs.

Erik's eyes went back to the Gray Mountains as he heard the distant moan of a wolf. He leaned forward, resting his left hand on the muscled shoulder of the dead creature—warmth still emanating from the body—and drew Dragon Tooth with his right hand. He squinted and felt his heart quicken as something white flashed up in the mountains, between two rocks. It was big and fast. He thought he saw it again, but then it was gone.

"Stay alert," Erik said as Warrior walked closer, nudging Erik with his nose.

He talked to his horse more and more each day, missing the company of men or dwarves, but as he did, the destrier seemed to warm to him. He had bitten him once since they had left the farmstead, and had only disobeyed Erik outright once. He was still as stubborn as any creature could ever be, but he seemingly understood their need for companionship and each other as much as Erik did.

Erik looked back down at the wolf. The day was waning, but the advent of a dead wolf, its pack somewhere nearby, and another creature that could kill such a powerful animal, meant he wanted to try and travel through the night. Besides, his sleep had still been restless as of late ... and his dreams had yet to return.

"Should we skin it?" Erik asked Warrior, reaching up and scratching the horse's nose as it nudged his shoulder. "Wolf meat isn't very good, but it might come in handy. And its fur is thick and mostly unspoiled."

Erik looked up at the horse over his shoulder. Warrior snorted and bobbed his head.

"I'll take that as a yes."

Erik used Dragon Tooth to make his first cuts, the heat of the steel easily cutting through the tough fur and skin of the wolf, even if it did give off the lip-curling smell of burnt hair. He used a home-made dagger to skin the rest of the animal, scraping away meat and tissue, and pieced up as much of the muscle as he could. He packed the meat in cloth and slung the fur over the back of Warrior, hope-fully allowing it to dry as they traveled by night. The cold days and nights had, thus far, not seen any rain.

Erik looked down at the wolf, half of its meat still clinging to its bones.

"Well," Erik said, "that will be a king's feast for any scavenger that chances by this way," he said as he mounted Warrior and continued north and west. Looking once more to the Gray Mountains, he thought he saw another flash of white from the corner of his eye.

Winter nights along the foothills were almost as cold as they were in the mountains, the winds coming down off the tall, snowy peaks with the ferocity of an angry predator. But as the mountain peaks began to disappear and give way to the wide-open space between the Gray Mountains and the forests of Ul'Erel, what most called the Pass of Dundolyothum, the mountains no longer shielded the northwest from the bone biting cold of the northern tundra. Things were now even worse, and Erik found himself shivering uncontrollably.

"Aren't you cold, Warrior?" Erik asked, speaking to the horse in Shengu.

The mean-spirited horse simply gave Erik an angry glance over his massive shoulders and snorted, steam spilling from his wide nostrils as he did so.

The stretch of land known as the Pass of Dundolyothum wasn't very wide, perhaps fifty leagues, but most of those who ventured there—adventure seekers, dwarves, gypsies, and ogres—stayed close to the mountain foothills, for fear of traveling too close to the cursed forests of Ul'Erel. As Erik had learned from both myth and his dwarvish friends, elves hated anything that wasn't elvish, and after what the dwarves called the Elvish Wars, they retreated into their vast forest kingdom, never to be seen again. At one time in his life, Erik would have said there were no such things as elves, but he would have also said that about dragons.

Erik's head bobbed, and he realized he had been falling asleep. Even his horse's steady canter had slowed, and he suspected Warrior was also getting tired, even though the horse would never admit it. He knew they needed to stop, but as he looked at the wolf fur strewn across Warrior's flanks, he didn't think it would be a good idea. And if they did stop, he wouldn't be able to build a fire, as that might attract predators.

He stared out at the cloudless night of the Pass of Dundolyothum. To his right, the mountains loomed like shadowy giants, and to his left, all he saw was a wide plain of snowy, rocky ground. The stars overhead were close, and the blackness of the sky stared back at him, going on forever into what his dagger—Rako—referred to as the cosmos. The moon looked extra-large, and streaks of green and purple and blues floated through the sky, just behind the glaring, pale orb, undulating back and forth like gentle waves lapping against the shore of some farm lake. Except for the mountains to the east, Erik could see for leagues.

"Okay, Warrior," Erik said, patting the gigantic horse's shoulder, "we'll stop. But only for a little while."

Darkness. No sound. No smell. And then he heard something. Faint. Distant.

"Dream Walker."

The voice sounded familiar. A friend, perhaps. It came once more, louder, washing over him like a sudden downpour of rain.

"Wake up!"

Erik's eyes shot open, and the smell of sweat, putrid body odor and stale blood struck his nose. Warrior was anxious, snorting and stamping his great hooves, but he remained next to Erik, who still lay on the ground. Erik rolled to his stomach, pushing himself up to his knees. The ground was wet, the temperature had risen, and misty rain had fallen while he slept. He smelled wet fur.

A low, reverberating growl cut through the darkness of night, the clear sky he had seen before falling asleep overcome now by thick, ominous clouds, blotting out stars and the moon. Still struggling with his night vision, he squinted and saw a shadow in front of him move, twenty paces away. It was large—massive even. The shadow shook with indignation, and when Erik finally saw it in focus, he froze.

It was a wolf ... a great gray wolf the size of a pony. The hair on its neck stood on end as it snarled, bearing yellow dagger-like teeth. Erik heard distant howling, but too far away to be part of this creature's pack. As the wolf stepped forward, he saw them ... its eyes. Red.

Two more shadows stepped up behind the winter wolf, an ancient creature made of evil and the Shadow. The figures behind the wolf weren't other animals. They were humanoid in shape, great hulking things. The smell struck Erik's nose again, and he knew they were giants ... two of them.

A break in the clouds, allowing for some brief moonlight, revealed the trio. The wolf, its red eyes glaring through the darkness, its breath rattling as it snarled, was gray with a black saddle. Its ears lay against its head, and old blood stained its teeth. The two giants behind it wore armor—mail shirts and greaves. They both had bushy beards that splayed out across their chests. One, with what Erik thought might be reddish hair, carried a giant ax—perhaps it was a halberd of some sort—in both his hands, while the other held a wide, wooden shield and a crudely fashioned spear tipped with what looked to be the broken blade from a short sword.

"Kill the man," one of the giants said, Erik able to understand their crude, dwarf-like language after coming into contact with other giants.

"Yeah," the other giant, the one with red hair, said. "Get on with it."

The winter wolf looked at the two giants over its shoulder, growling and snarling. These two lumbering idiots thought they controlled the wolf. Erik stood, placing his hand on the handle of his sword. He searched with his mind. Winter wolves were intelligent creatures, as intelligent as any man. And they spoke with their mind. He knew as much from the last time he encountered the foul beasts.

He found the wolf's mind and heard its thoughts. Images of ripping Erik's throat out and eating Warrior. But also images of leading an army of giants onto the farmlands of Háthgolthane. And then killing these two giants and then killing the rest of their tribe. This winter wolf led the giants, not the other way around.

The wolf turned hard to face Erik. It must have felt him searching its mind.

"Do you serve her?" Erik asked, referring to the dragon he had awoken in Orvencrest and drawing Dragon Tooth, the blade blazing with green fire. He remembered the leader of the last group of winter wolves he fought. "Do you serve Fang? Or do you serve this new evil?"

The creature's growling intensified. The dragon. The image of her massive wings spreading as far as Erik could see appeared in his mind's eye. He saw fire. He saw his brother and Bim, the dwarf that died with him. This wolf served the dragon ... and the Shadow. And when Erik suggested it might serve this other evil of which Dewin spoke, it seemed agitated and angry.

"What are you waiting for?" the red-headed giant said, slapping the wolf on the rump.

The beast turned hard on the giant and snapped at his hand. The giant pulled back quickly, rubbing his wrist where the winter wolf almost bit him. Erik took the moment to grab his shield from where it hung on Warrior. As the wolf turned back, its fur bristled even more, and its thoughts entered Erik's mind.

*Erik Eleodum, you will die. Your family will die. The world will die.*

*Erik Eleodum? You may call me Erik Wolf's Bane. That was my name after I killed several of your kin,* Erik replied with his mind, a smirk crossing his mouth.

The wolf threw its head back and howled before it finally attacked, the giants running after it, salivating and laughing.

Erik made himself ready to receive the full weight of the wolf as it leaped into the air, but just before its outstretched claws reached him, two powerful hooves slammed into the wolf's chest and sent it flying to the side, rolling over and over in a bundle of bristling fur.

Erik nodded to Warrior as the first giant reached him, the one wielding the great halberd. The giant swung downward, but Erik easily dodged the attack, the ax head thudding into the ground. He meant to cut through the wood of the shaft, but the other giant was on him, jabbing its spear with a speed that belied its size. Erik blocked another attack with his shield, swatted away the butt of the halberd, but found himself on his heels. Looking to his right, the winter wolf began to gather itself, shaking its head and then growling, glaring at Erik with its red eyes.

As the two giants pressed Erik, Warrior turned and kicked out with his two hind legs, its hooves slamming into the back of the spear-wielding giant. It didn't seem to hurt the giant much, other than surprise him, but it did give Erik a chance to regain his feet. He brought Dragon Tooth across the giant's leg, and he clenched his teeth and growled.

"When I kill him," the giant said, "I will take his little sword."

Warrior snorted and stomped, bobbing his head. He even nudged Erik with his great snout and shook his rear end.

"What?" Erik asked, and then realized what the horse had been bred for.

Erik had never really fought from horseback, but Warrior just waited. Before the giants could reach him, Erik leaped into the destrier's saddle, the winter wolf snapping at his heels. The horse wheeled hard, kicking out again at the wolf, and the beast leaped away. Then Warrior turned, so Erik could face the giants and, rearing up on his hind legs, lurched forward into a gallop.

Erik clung to the horse with his legs, his inner thighs burning. He could sense the winter wolf behind them, and that Warrior would know too. The horse kept his course initially, then moved to the side quickly, almost spinning around. Erik brought his sword across the spear-wielding giant's chest before he could raise his shield, and as Warrior turned around again, he kicked out with his hind legs once again, this time catching the giant in the groin. The giant fell to his knees just as the winter wolf leaped at Erik. He put up his shield, feeling the full weight of the beast against him, but Warrior barely moved.

The wolf's hind claws dug into Warrior's ribs, and in response, he kicked out again with his hind legs, his hooves connecting with the kneeling giant's face. The wolf's front claws tried to dig into Erik's shield, but simply skidded along the steep. It snapped at him from over top the shield, Erik pulling his face away and then jabbing underneath. The painful yelp the wolf gave, along with the stink of burning, let Erik know he struck flesh.

The wolf jumped off and tried to circle Erik and Warrior, a noticeable limp in one of its hind legs. The red-headed giant lay on the ground, unconscious, while the other, ignoring the circling standoff between Erik and the wolf, charged in. The winter wolf growled and ran at them as well.

"*Turn, Warrior!*" Erik yelled as he pulled on the right rein.

As the giant came close, Erik put up his shield, deflecting the massive ax head, but the blow sent jolts of pain through his shoulder. As Warrior turned, his powerful flanks pushed the giant to the side, shoving him into the wolf's path just as the beast pounced. The winter wolf's claws dug into the giant's back, and the large assailant screamed. Dropping his halberd and reaching back at the wolf, he opened himself, and Erik took the opportunity, driving Dragon Tooth into the giant's armpit.

Mounted on Warrior, Erik was almost eye-to-eye with the giant. The giant stopped and stared, mouth open with surprise. Erik withdrew his sword and jammed it into the giant's open maw, flesh and brain matter sizzling against the heat of the blade. As the giant fell backward, the winter wolf jumped away. It growled and crouched, looking as if it was ready to attack again, but instead, it turned and ran, howling as it did so.

"Follow it," Erik said and didn't need to even heel Warrior. The horse lurched into a gallop.

The large wolf was powerful and ran faster than any dog should have been able to run, but Warrior was its match. Erik had never truly felt the strength of the destrier, and he could tell Patûk Al'Banan had trained the animal well. His name was decidedly appropriate.

Erik and Warrior gained on the wolf, but the beast headed towards the mountains, and once it made it to the western foothills of the Gray Mountains, the horse wouldn't be able to give chase. Erik wasn't so concerned about the wolf getting away. It was injured and would take time to heal, and by that time, Erik and Warrior would be long gone. The problem was that he suspected there were other winter wolves up there in the mountains. Waiting. Or hunting.

They probably knew Erik was traveling north ... and by himself. But as they waited on their companion, it would give Erik a little time to move on, but probably not enough. If this one escaped, he expected it would be a day at the most before a whole pack of winter wolves, again leading giants perhaps, came after him. Before the wolf disappeared into the rocks, it turned to look at them and then howled again, seemingly surging with a renewed energy as it knew it could make its escape. Or so it thought.

Erik strapped his shield to his back and lifted himself to a crouching position on his horse, his feet on the broad saddle.

"Get as close as you can, Warrior," Erik said, and as if the horse knew entirely what it was Erik wanted, he moved in so that they were almost on the wolf's hind legs. Erik gripped his sword tight and shook his head. This was going to hurt.

Erik jumped, Dragon Tooth high in the air, just as the wolf, maw open and fangs bared, was about to howl again. He collided with the beast and felt his sword slip from his hand. They tumbled head over heel, Erik grunting, and the wolf growling and snapping. Erik held onto the creature, grabbing fistfuls of fur and, as they stopped rolling, came up to one knee, pulling his shield from his back.

Claws grazed the shield, and the winter wolf growled. The image that flashed through Erik's head was one of half a dozen red-eyed wolves descending onto his farm while this one held him by the scruff of his neck, forcing him to watch. After the slaughter of his family, in his mind's eye, the last thing he saw was an open mouth and fangs closing in on his face. He thought he could sense amusement in the wolf's snarl.

But, before the wolf could attack again, a giant hoof crashed down on its hip. It yelped as one of its hind legs went limp, dislocated from the socket. The beast turned as best it could to face Warrior, who snorted defiantly. Dragon Tooth lay only two paces away, and as Erik's horse reared up, fending off clawed attacks from the wolf, he ran to his blade, grabbed it, and charged the monster.

Erik punched the creature in the shoulder with his shield and jammed his blade into its ribs. It snarled, snapping at Erik, but another hoof crashed into the wolf's face, breaking fangs and crushing one of the creature's eye sockets. The evil wolf stumbled a bit, another hoof cracking its skull, and it went down, tongue lolling from its mouth as it lay on the ground, breathing slowly. Erik placed his sword at the base of the wolf's neck. The smell of burnt hair hit Erik's nose, and the wolf whined for the last time as he pushed the blade through its spine.

"You're good to have around," Erik said to Warrior, patting the horse's neck, but when he looked at his hand, it was covered in blood.

He inspected the warhorse. He had one mean looking claw mark on his neck and several more in between his ribs and hip. They were wounds that might have killed a normal horse, but as Erik continued to inspect Warrior, he saw the dozen or more scars the animal bore from other fights.

"No," Erik said, grabbing the horn of his saddle and pulling himself back onto Warrior, "these simple wounds can't kill the mighty Warrior."

The horse looked at Erik over its shoulder, snorted, and galloped back towards their original campsite. There, Erik found the unconscious giant coming to, kneeling and rubbing his head, gingerly inspecting a bloody indentation on his cheek. Erik dismounted and walked to the giant. The grotesque man-like creature saw him coming but didn't move.

"Are there more of you?" Erik asked, pointing his sword at the giant's eye.

"Bugger off," the giant said in its crude, dwarf-like language, his voice somewhat muffled from a broken cheek, possible broken jaw, and swollen lip.

Erik pushed the tip of his sword into the flesh of the giant's neck, and he groaned in pain.

"Yeah, there's more," the giant said. "There're always more."

"What about the wolf?" Erik asked.

"The little doggy," the giant said with a twisted malicious smile. "Never seen one like it. Me and my mate over there were going to eat it, but then it brings us a giant elk, all by itself. Figured we'd keep it until we got too hungry."

"Fool," Erik said. This giant clearly didn't know what the winter wolf was. "Are there more?"

"Of those wolves?" the giant asked, his eyes wide. "Are you daft? They're all over the mountains."

"No, you idiot! Ones with the red eyes?"

The giant looked as if he was thinking, shaking his head.

"No," he replied, and that was the last thing he ever said as Erik drove Dragon Tooth hilt deep into the giant's neck.

# 16

*K*ing Bucharan's eyes were red, his face drawn and tired.

"My sincere condolences, my lord," Syzbalo said with a half-hearted bow, closing his eyes and frowning as much as he could while laughing inwardly.

"He was so young and healthy," Bucharan said, looking at his hands as if they could reveal the mystery of his son's death. "It doesn't make sense."

"Who is to make sense of the sinister whims of the gods?" Syzbalo asked, seeking to convey pity in his voice.

"Damn the gods," Bucharan seethed, his hands balling into tight, white-knuckled fists.

"Truly," the Lord of the East said, folding his hands behind his back.

Ankara had taken an extra day to kill the king's son, insolent bastard that he was. At first, he thought she might have cheated him—Isutans were so hard to trust—when he had seen her riding west, presumably towards Erik Eleodum in pursuit of the Dragon Sword.

However, whatever she used to kill the man took two days, but die he did, and in his sleep, unassuming and away from anyone, especially the Lord of the East.

Sure there were no traces of poison or magic, Syzbalo even offered up his physicians to inspect the body. The man looked peaceful in a way, even happy in death. That was when the Lord of the East remembered how Ankara's magic worked: sex, lust, desire—those were her tools.

"If there is anything I can do ..." Syzbalo began to say, his words trailing off, hanging midsentence to perpetuate his ruse of concern.

Bucharan looked up at the Lord of the East, his face drawn and his mouth half-open, his eyes distant and weary, and his hair frazzled.

"You have taken to keeping the company of goblins, I see," Bucharan said. He licked his lips and closed his mouth. Syzbalo could see the muscles of his jaw working as he ground his teeth.

He was afraid the Two Towners of Po would notice the goblin presence. Goblins weren't terribly big creatures, but there were one hundred and eleven of them, and they stunk, and they were loud, taking to drinking too much, fighting, and chasing after women. Akzûl actually kept his brood calmer than most, but they were still goblins. Even if he kept them as hidden as possible within his camps outside the walls of Po, they would have eventually been sighted.

"My dealings with the goblins are none of your concern," Syzbalo said, his voice cold and hard.

"Do you know how many of my people have died at the hands of goblins?" Bucharan asked. "Those little pricks wait in the grass, raping and killing when unsuspecting Two Towners walk by. They raid homesteads and harass our farmers and ranchers."

"And how many of their kind have you killed?" Syzbalo retorted. He could have cared less, but it seemed an appropriate rebuttal as the King of Po questioned his alliances and his reasons for being in Mek-Ba'Dune. "Just you, King Bucharan ... how many goblins have you killed? Hundreds? Thousands?"

Syzbalo nodded toward one of the many white-robed priests in the hall, bearing a staff topped with the skull of a goblin, notable by its sloping forehead and tiny fangs.

"Do you fret the squashing of a bug under your foot?" Bucharan growled.

"I do not," Syzbalo said, sweeping his right hand out from behind his back and gently touching his chest, "but I am sure the bug does. You see, Your Majesty, your distaste for goblins is none of my concern —hate them all you like. But as I look to the future of my people ... and yours," he swept his arm outwards as if encompassing all of Po, "I see the need for peace—a truce perhaps."

"A truce? With animals?"

"Yes," Syzbalo replied, tired of arguing with the man. "The goblins have agreed to stop raiding your lands, and harming your people if you do the same."

"How can I be certain?" Bucharan asked. "They are tribal and fragmented. Each Chieftain decides a course of action for his brood."

"I will leave a small contingency of soldiers here," Syzbalo said, "for both your protection and as insurance our new treaty will be honored ... not by you, of course, but by the goblins."

King Bucharan studied him for a long moment. This was all a part of the Lord of the East's plan. He would leave troops in Po, thus strengthening his hold on Mek-Ba'Dune and solidifying an alliance with both the Two Towers and the goblins. Why he needed to ally himself with goblins was still a mystery to him, only that it was what the Lord of Chaos had commanded.

Bucharan slowly nodded.

"You have your alliance," the king said, "and we will leave the goblins be, as long as they do the same. I am not your vassal, though. Remember that."

Bucharan pointed a finger at the Lord of the East.

"Of course not," Syzbalo said, offering a wide, facetious smile. "You are my ally ... my friend."

"Do you plan on meeting with the Bayan?"

Syzbalo closed his eyes and sucked in a deep breath through his nose. He would meet with Bayan, the Warlord of Bum-Nur, eventually, because he would surely become jealous of the alliance Bucharan had with Golgolithul. And his jealousy would make the terms more favorable for Syzbalo, but he would make the man wait.

"No," the Lord of the East replied. "My city is in ruins, and I must return home and take care of my people."

"A dragon," Bucharan muttered, shaking his head slowly. "What has this world come to?"

Syzbalo offered a few more platitudes, and when their meeting was over, he had agreed to send monthly rations of fruit and vegetables, wheat, horses, and iron weapons. What did he get in return? A large cat indigenous to the Plains of Mek-Ba'Dune—a cat the king called a cheetah. The Lord of the East watched one of these cheetahs race across the plains toward a lithe and nimble deer. The cat ran down its prey with blinding speed, and the Lord of the East wanted them for no other reason than they fascinated him.

"Goblins?" Melanius hissed, keeping his voice low as he spoke to Syzbalo, who simply watched the horizon with his hands folded behind his back and his chest out. His two-story tower had rolled away from Po earlier that morning.

"What of them?" Syzbalo replied without turning his head, his tone flat.

"Why are you allowing them in our company?" Melanius asked, his tone unapproving and harsh.

Syzbalo wheeled around hard. He lifted his left hand, shot it up quickly, faster than he had been able to move before, and seized the Isutan magician by the throat. With barely any effort, he squeezed, and Melanius began to cough and gasp. As the Lord of the East squeezed just a little harder, the Isutan's face began to change color, turning a pale blue, and his eyes bulged, his mouth open, and his tongue licking at the air as if he could extract oxygen that way.

A smirk crossed Syzbalo's face. Life was so fragile. Just a bit more pressure and this man would die, his life snuffed out forever. Melanius was a powerful mage—not as powerful as Andragos, of course—but Syzbalo still controlled the Isutan's life, and it made him feel omnipotent.

Syzbalo released his grip, and Melanius crumpled to the ground in a heap of old skin and bones, gasping for air.

"Your job is to advise me," Syzbalo said, leaning forward, his hands once again folded behind his back, "not admonish or question me. Do you understand?"

Melanius nodded slowly.

"Remove yourself from my sight," Syzbalo commanded, and the magician did as he was told, albeit slowly thanks to his brittle joints.

The two witches looked at him, each with a hint of fear in their normally confident eyes.

"Come, my lovelies," Syzbalo said, unfolding his hands and opening his arms.

They both fell into him, wrapping their arms around him and pressing their faces to his muscular chest. He could tell they were compensating for Melanius' defiance, not wishing to feel Syzbalo's wrath themselves. He looked over and saw Akzûl watching him, the goblin's right hand resting on the hilt of a curved and serrated short sword and the thumb of his left hand tucked into a belt slightly too big for him.

"A wealthy and powerful man," Akzûl said, "one who commands mighty mages and beauties such as these."

"Your point?" Syzbalo asked. He didn't like having the goblin in his company, but he figured it necessary to help control the warriors he commanded.

"I would have killed the magician," Akzûl said as he shrugged.

"A good thing I, nor he, answers to you," Syzbalo said.

"I trust your diplomatic efforts with Po went well," Akzûl said.

Syzbalo looked down at the witches and patted each one on a curvaceous buttock to signal they should move away. They let go of him and sauntered over to their chairs, arranged at the edge of the platform on the tower so they could sit next to him and watch the horizon roll by.

"Is it any of your business?" Syzbalo asked.

He would have crushed this *creature* if he didn't serve the same master Syzbalo did.

Akzûl just stared at the Lord of the East. Syzbalo knew it wasn't any of the goblin's business, but it did affect his people.

"Yes, I am now in alliance with King Bucharan of Po," the Lord of the East said.

"And he will stop his attack on the goblin people?" Akzûl asked.

"He will," the Lord of the East replied, "as long as you stop the harassment of his people. Will you?"

"It can be arranged," Akzûl replied.

"Can I trust the word of a goblin?"

Akzûl shrugged again.

"We will see, won't we?" the goblin replied. "Why Po? They cannot give you anything you cannot take."

Syzbalo smiled and straightened his back. This goblin wanted a lesson in diplomatic tactics.

"It is not meant to bring me wealth," Syzbalo said. "Truth be told, I was there because the Lord of Chaos commanded it, among other things."

"Will you also treat with Bum-Nur?" Akzûl asked.

"Not yet," the Lord of the East said, "but eventually. For now, only with Po. It will make Bum-Nur jealous when they see the influence of Fen-Stévock on Po, the increase in wealth, prosperity, and knowledge, and they will beg me to come to them. They will beg me to control them."

"You will then be the Lord of ...?" Akzûl asked.

Syzbalo smiled.

"The Lord of Háthgolthane," he replied. "The Lord of Antolika."

"Doesn't have much of a ring to it," Akzûl said. "What about, the Lord of the World?"

Syzbalo's smile widened. He might grow to like this goblin.

## 17

*A*nkara rode hard, pushing her small, yet powerful horse. She was a loyal creature, handpicked from a herd of wild horses that roamed the southern plains of Antolika. Her reddish-brown color reminded the Isutan bounty hunter of her mother's hair. A star-shaped patch of white hair on the horse's nose had given the animal her name—that, and her speed: Nagarooshi ... Isutan for Shooting Star. She called her Naga for short.

Eventually, she stopped by a natural watering hole for them both to drink, and while Naga tore at some fresh grass, Ankara nibbled on small cakes made from the nemuri flower that grew in the dense forest of the Isutan Isles. Eaten whole, a flower might kill someone Ankara's size, but cooked down and baked into bread and cakes, it could keep someone awake for days without feeling tired.

She could have used her magic for such a task, but she needed to save her energy. She wasn't as powerful as her father—although, she hoped to be one day—and she didn't get her power from the same source; drinking someone's blood was quite abhorrent. She got her power the normal way, as most mages did, from rest. But there was another way she gained power—she smiled as she thought of it ... sex.

If this Erik Eleodum was strong enough to kill her father, then she would need to reserve as much strength as possible. Pride was her father's undoing. It wouldn't be hers.

She was hungry, though, and while the little nemuri cakes had their use, they did little to satiate her hunger, and she wondered where she might eat next. They were somewhere just west of Golgolithul and south of Nordeth. She hated Háthgolthane. For all its people's hubris, their pandering about being so advanced a society, they were still as barbaric as any other. All men, dwarves, elves, goblins, and any other creature that walked the world were savage. And the seasons in Háthgolthane were extreme—the summer too hot and the winter too cold.

Ankara stared out into the vast plain, the great field of grass glowed a brilliant green. At the edge of a small copse of woodland, she saw a lone deer, its coat heavy and thick from the winter, grazing, separated from its herd. It might have been just less than a league away, but still within her range. She removed the Bow of Sebuté from her back, a weapon as long as she was tall, and then drew a green fletched arrow from the quiver that hung from Naga's saddle. The arrowhead was the color of jade, and as she blew gently on the sharp steel, it glowed green, just like her eyes. She nocked the arrow, drew back the bowstring, took aim, and whispered, "Seek."

The arrow flew away with an almost inaudible twang of the bowstring. Ankara mounted Nagarooshi and heeled her in the direction of the deer. They came upon the animal, lying still amidst the grass, steam rising from its lifeless body. She dismounted and withdrew the arrow protruding from the deer's shoulder, placing it back in its quiver after she wiped off the blood on the animal's hide. She knelt by it and put a hand on its neck as she drew a knife. After cutting away its hide, she dug into the animal's chest cavity and removed its heart.

"I thank the old gods and this animal for its sacrifice," Ankara said, holding the heart up. She buried the heart after digging a small hole in the cold, but lush soil. It was a custom of her people, believing the heart and soul of the animal would return to the earth, only to be reborn so that it might give sustenance again.

She didn't know if she actually believed the myth that had been passed down from generation to generation. She didn't know if she believed any of the theology she had learned as a child. Some might call her, or her people, brutal and cruel, but they had a deep connection to the land. They were different from the elves. Those haughty little pricks thought they could speak with trees. Ankara laughed at such audacity. No. Her people simply realized that the world gave them everything they needed and thanked their gods, whether they were there or not, for the gifts and bounty the world gave them. And, so, she would stick with tradition ... perhaps just in case the gods were watching. Her father would have called her a fool, but she was alive, and he was dead by the hands of a farm boy. Who was the fool?

She built a fire just inside the wood and cooked and ate what she could, knowing this would fill her belly for at least several days, and then packed a little more. She mounted Nagarooshi again and headed northwest. She would kill this Erik Eleodum, kill his family too, and then take this sword to Syzbalo. She hadn't decided whether she would place it in his hands or in his heart.

# 18

---

erradyn sat at a small table in a room next to the kitchen of the Eleodum home. Simone, the wife of Erik Eleodum, set a plate of bread next to a cup of herbal tea he had been sipping. She set another plate of bread in front of Raktas, who quickly ripped off a chunk, knifed a heaping mound of soft butter from the stone dish in the middle of the table. He slathered it on the bread before biting into it with such ferocity, Terradyn might have thought the man was starving if he hadn't known better. Half a hen sat next to the butter, steam still rising from the cooked meat, but he hadn't touched it.

"You better eat your food," Raktas said in Shengu with a full mouth, pointing his knife to the small loaf sitting in front of Terradyn.

"I'm just not that hungry," Terradyn replied.

"You should be careful," a man said, standing behind Terradyn.

Terradyn remembered seeing the man he now knew as Bryon Eleodum once before, almost a year ago. He had looked younger then, with hardly a beard, narrow shoulders, and a boy's face. Now, he was a man grown, with a long, blond beard and well-worked muscles. Erik's cousin had come to the man's house to keep an eye on Simone.

At first, Raktas had joked with Terradyn that the man was surely keeping a very good eye—especially in the bedroom—on Erik's wife, but after spending several days in their company, he realized this Bryon had no intention of bedding the woman. He loved her, but like a man would love his sister, and he protected and defended her as such. However, he felt that Simone—if she weren't pregnant—would need little defending.

Terradyn didn't bother looking over his shoulder, but he saw the look Raktas gave the man. Terradyn didn't mind Bryon. The man wanted to feel like he was in charge. What did Terradyn care? But it irritated Raktas because Bryon was just like Raktas.

"Speaking Shengu in the west can get you in trouble if the wrong people hear you," Bryon added, walking into the kitchen and kissing Simone on the forehead as she handed him a cup of tea.

Bryon had just come back from patrolling the perimeter of the farm. Apparently, assassins had attacked them not long before Terradyn and Raktas showed up. From the sounds of it, they were the Atrimus, the secret society of killers Gol-Durathna and the Golden City of Amentus would like to pretend they didn't employ. So, each day, either Bryon, a man named Andu who once served Patûk Al'Banan, or one of the three dwarves that had befriended the Eleodums and lived with them, would go out and ride the outskirts of their lands.

"Duly noted, Bryon," Terradyn replied in Westernese, sipping some more tea. "That is good advice."

"Shengu is a noble and sophisticated language," Raktas whispered with the hint of a hiss, leaning forward as he spoke to Terradyn. "This Westernese is backward and bucolic."

Terradyn nodded, even though, for some reason, Westernese felt more natural to him.

"So noble and sophisticated," someone else said in Shengu, "that it is fairly new, with little in the way of linguistic evolution or the intricacies of an ancient language, like Dwarvish or the language of the north men."

One of the dwarves that had been staying with the Eleodums—Turk Skull Crusher—walked down the hallway that led to the bedrooms. Raktas grumbled.

"Truly said," Terradyn said, to which Raktas gave him another hard look.

"The people of these lands are peaceful," Turk the dwarf said, still speaking Shengu, "but they can be a superstitious people. They have seemed to warm to the presence of dwarves, but they are always suspicious of the east."

"I suppose many are suspicious of the east," Terradyn said, speaking in Westernese.

"They have a reason to be," Bryon said, sitting down at the table with a plate of bread and cheese. "Especially with an easterner sitting on the throne in Hámon."

"He is a traitor," Raktas said.

"Still," Bryon said.

"Have you seen anything of concern on your patrols?" Terradyn asked.

Bryon shook his head.

"No," the man said, and then looked at Turk. "Have you?"

The dwarf shook his head as well.

"I will admit," Bryon said, "I am a decent tracker, but not the best. Befel—my cousin and Erik's older brother—was always the best."

"We will go with you," Terradyn said, "on your next patrol. Maybe Raktas or I will see something you might miss."

Bryon simply shrugged as he tore off a piece of bread and took a large bite.

Every day, Terradyn wondered more and more why they were there. His master had tasked him with protecting Erik, but Erik was gone. Should they protect his family then? Help them in whatever way needed? They had not been able to contact Andragos. He and Raktas weren't magicians really, but serving the Black Mage for over a hundred years, they learned some magic, enough to aid them in battle and communicate over long distances ... as well as a few other tricks. It was this magic that allowed them to stay in contact with their master, but as they tried lately, he was unresponsive. It worried Terradyn.

Andragos was the closest thing he had to a father. He couldn't remember his real father, and as he watched many of the young boys growing up on the streets of Fen-Stévock, he wondered if he had what you might call a proper father, or was his mother one of the many whores who found themselves poor and pregnant with nowhere to go and no one to turn to. Her face was a distant memory, and chances were, she was long dead by now.

His childhood, as well as Raktas', was anything but typical, and Andragos was not the loving, caring father most children would want. He was a hard disciplinarian, his expectations high, and his punishment for failure brutal. Terradyn remembered at least a dozen other boys living with them, undergoing the same tutelage he and Raktas did, but they were the only two to survive. Once they did, Andragos rewarded them with power and strength and position. They were his, and he was theirs, and his life was of their utmost importance. And now he was far away, and they had no way of contacting him. Despite the dysfunction of their youth and upbringing, Terradyn missed him.

He finished his tea, eating none of the bread. When he stood, he thanked Simone and waited for his companion, who couldn't seem to eat enough, to finish before they walked outside to the front of the home. He walked over to his horse and patted the giant animal on the nose.

"How are you, Shadow?" Terradyn asked. His horse bobbed his head and stomped a hoof.

They stood in silence, apart from Raktas belching a couple of times, until Bryon Eleodum rode around from the farmstead's barn to the home's gate.

"Are you ready?" he asked.

Terradyn looked to Raktas. His compatriot nodded, grabbing the reins of his horse, a great white and gray warhorse he called Lightning.

"The dwarves?" Terradyn asked. "Andu?"

"They'll stay here," Bryon snapped. "Is that a problem?"

Terradyn shook his head.

"No, but the dwarves do have keen eyes," Terradyn said, "and if this Andu served Patûk Al'Banan, he is also probably a decent tracker."

"They'll stay here. For Simone," Bryon repeated and wheeled his horse around away from the farm buildings.

"Why is he so contentious?" Raktas asked, whispering to Terradyn.

"He is suspicious of us," Terradyn replied, "and I don't blame him. I think I would be too."

They both swung into the saddle and set off after Bryon.

The Eleodum farm was a large territory of land, one that any one of the nobles in Golgolithul would have been happy to own. Terradyn didn't see anything that marked the edge of the farmstead's boundaries, but Bryon rode north until he reached a single, large oak tree and turned his horse to the west. He looked around but continued to ride at a steady pace.

"No wonder he doesn't see anything," Terradyn muttered.

As he turned to the right and looked north, the sun was setting, and he saw a shadow. He squinted and then told the others to stop. Bryon continued for a few more paces before turning his horse.

"What is it?" Bryon asked.

Terradyn held up a hand, staring north. He closed his eyes for a moment, reciting a phrase in his head. He could feel the tattoos along his scalp glowing, the magic they gave him pulsing through his body. He opened his eyes and looked north again. He saw shadows ... men. As they had stopped, so had the shadows. He couldn't tell what lay ahead, so he nodded to the two other men.

"Keep moving."

As they did, riding west along the Eleodum farm boundaries, the shadows moved. They were certainly following them, tracking them. Terradyn's magic could only do so much, and he really couldn't make out who the men were—the Atrimus had been here and, in talking to Bryon and the dwarves, Erik had made enemies with this Bu Al'Banan and a Samanian slaver named Kehl. The men could have been any of them ... or none. They could have been from Golgolithul, or even Isuta—the Lord of the East had employed an Isutan assassin before.

"What do you see?" Raktas asked.

"Men," Terradyn replied.

"Where?" Bryon asked.

"North," Terradyn replied.

"I don't see anything," Bryon said.

"I wouldn't expect you would," Terradyn replied, "unless you had a bit of magic or a looking glass to help. They are far away and well hidden."

"But they see us?" Bryon asked.

"Aye," Terradyn replied.

"So they must have magic or a looking glass," Bryon said.

"Aye, they must," said Terradyn, realizing he should have thought of that.

"We should kill them," Raktas said, as usual seeking confrontation over strategy or diplomacy.

"No," Terradyn said as they continued to ride west, the shadows keeping pace with them from a far distance.

"Why not?" Raktas asked.

"Yeah," Bryon said, "why not?"

"I don't think they know we know they're watching us," Terradyn said. "It is possible they have been watching you, Bryon, every time you come out to patrol your cousin's lands. They are simply watching us."

"To what end?" Bryon asked, stopping his horse and turning to face Terradyn.

Terradyn noticed the shadows stopped. They congregated. They must have been talking, discussing something.

"I don't know," Terradyn replied. "We have to keep moving."

He grabbed Bryon's reins as he passed by his horse and prodded the animal on.

"We don't want to give them any indication we know they are there," Terradyn added.

"This is foolish," Raktas said.

"Maybe," Terradyn replied, "but a company of Northern assassins or Samanian warriors would be a deadly encounter, even for you and me. Would you tempt them, and bring assassins down on the lands of simple farmers?"

Raktas just shrugged.

They kept riding, and as the sun began to set, the shadows disappeared. When they had made a full circle of the farm and returned to the farmstead home, Terradyn's stomach knotted, an uneasy feeling weighing down on his shoulders.

"Have you been able to communicate with the Master?" Raktas asked as they walked to the barn where they slept.

Terradyn shook his head.

"Not for some time," he said as he opened the barn door.

"Do you think he is all right?" Raktas asked.

"I would think so," Terradyn replied.

"He seems to be at odds with the Lord of the East these days," Raktas said.

"It does seem that way," Terradyn replied.

"If he is," Raktas began, and then waited a moment, seemingly thinking about what he was going to say, "if our Master is at odds with the Lord of the East ... if he opposes him, what do we do?"

It wasn't often that Raktas asked for Terradyn's advice, and so the question caught him off guard for a moment.

"What do you mean?" Terradyn asked, squinting his eyes and scanning Raktas. He had no reason to distrust this man with whom he had served for over a hundred years, but the question gave him rise to be cautious.

"The Lord of the East," Raktas said, "he is the ruler of Golgolithul. He is calling himself the Emperor of the East. If our Master—if Andragos opposes him, whom do we serve."

Terradyn straightened his back and looked at Raktas with flat, hard eyes.

"I serve Andragos, no other," Terradyn replied, and even readied himself to draw his broad-bladed long sword. But Raktas just nodded with a wry smile.

"I as well," Raktas said.

"We will go out with Bryon on his patrols for the rest of the week," Terradyn said, relaxing again.

"Do we need to?" Raktas asked.

"We are charged with protecting Erik Eleodum and his family. Bryon didn't even realize he is being watched. What if those shadowy men decide to attack? Then what?"

"I think you are sweet on the woman," Raktas said.

"She is Erik Eleodum's," Terradyn replied.

"A woman being another man's wife hasn't stopped you before," Raktas said with a smile.

He spoke of the spoils of war. Both Terradyn and Raktas knew war all too well, and the hard truth of a battle lost was that the soldiers who died on the battlefield weren't the ones to receive the worst of the defeat. It was the civilians, the men, women, and children left behind in a village or town or city that saw the brunt of war. And any woman of childbearing age would be subject to rape. Both men had partaken in such brutality. But it wasn't for lust or pleasure ... no, such terror was as much a part of the war as the fighting. A man knowing the enemy had vandalized his woman was less likely to fight. A man knowing the enemy would slaughter all of his children was even less likely to fight. The sheer horror of such acts was sometimes enough to bring a whole army to its knees.

"We are to protect her," Terradyn said, "not stick her."

Raktas laughed.

"I see the way you look at her," he said.

"She is beautiful," Terradyn admitted, "and if I were ever able to take a wife, I would hope for one as beautiful. But I'll not touch her."

He looked at Raktas with those hard eyes again.

"And neither will you."

Raktas held up his hands and laughed.

"She's not my type anyway," Raktas said, sitting against a wooden post in the barn. "So, you wish to patrol with Bryon. To what end?"

"It is obvious that men are watching him ... watching the farm," Terradyn explained. "If they see us, perhaps they will start to rethink any harassment they have been planning. It will, at least, give us an idea of what we are dealing with."

"Very well," Raktas said with a quick nod.

The next evening, Terradyn saw the same men he had seen the night before. They followed them as they had before, this time a little longer, and they seemed to chance being a little closer. He assumed the new men with Bryon intrigued these shadowy spies. The evening after that was much the same. But as they embarked on their patrol the fourth evening, things seemed off. Nighttime fauna was typically plentiful in the evenings near the Eleodum farm—deer and rabbits and squirrels—but this night, nothing stirred, not even some distant nocturnal bird. But even more queer was that the shadowy men were not there, following them from a distance.

"Where are they?" Bryon asked.

Terradyn just shrugged.

"Maybe you scared them off," Raktas japed, "with your bald head and your large muscles."

Terradyn couldn't help laughing.

They were just about to turn south, back towards the farmhouse, when Terradyn stopped, putting up a hand.

"What is it?" Raktas asked.

But Terradyn didn't answer. He saw a wolf, a single gray wolf, larger than most any other wolf, even the great white wolves of the north. It must have been two hundred paces or more away. He concentrated, feeling his magic coursing through his body and leaned forward in his saddle. A wolf in the setting sun of the north wasn't such an oddity, even if it was by itself. But, other than its size, there was something different about this one. It watched them. Even a large, white wolf of the north would avoid a confrontation with three horsed men. It might be able to take down one, but large prey was plentiful enough, it had no need to chance life or limb unless provoked. No, this wolf watched them, tracked them, scouted them ... with red eyes.

"What is it?" Raktas asked again.

"A wolf," Terradyn replied.

"There are probably a hundred wolves out there," Raktas said. "It's dusk in the wilds of the west."

"It's tracking us," Terradyn said.

"Come now," Raktas said. "Even one of the large gray wolves of the north wouldn't be so foolish."

Terradyn ignored his companion.

"And it has red eyes," he added.

"Did you say red eyes?" Bryon asked.

"Yes," Terradyn replied. "I don't think I have ever seen such a thing."

"A winter wolf," Bryon muttered.

"What?" Raktas asked.

"A winter wolf," Bryon repeated. "Evil wolves. Intelligent wolves. We encountered them in the Southern Mountains, just after we got away from the dragon. Erik was convinced they served the dragon in some way and, according to the dwarves, a winter wolf—or a pack of them—would serve a mighty warlord or wizard if it suited their purposes. Erik even said he could hear their thoughts. Tell me a wolf could be evil and speak with its thoughts two years ago, and I would have called you insane, but I saw them with my own eyes. Saw how they worked together to attack."

Terradyn continued to watch the wolf as Bryon spoke. For a

moment, even though it was two hundred paces away, their eyes met, and the wolf was aware that Terradyn also watched it.

"Are you sure it has red eyes?" Bryon asked, and for the first time since meeting the farmer turned warrior, Terradyn thought he sensed fear in his voice.

"Yes," Terradyn said. He blinked, and when he opened his eyes, the wolf was gone.

"We need to get back to the farmhouse," Bryon said, turning his horse and heeling it hard, not bothering to wait for Terradyn and Raktas.

"Have you ever heard of such a thing?" Raktas asked as they turned their horses.

"I think," Terradyn replied, "once. Many years ago, in one of Master's lessons, one in which he spoke of monsters of the old days. If what Bryon says is true, our task has just become much harder."

They both heeled their horses and followed Bryon.

## 19

*E*rik and Warrior rode north, away from giants and evil wolves and towards a cold and dark unknown. Erik knew the people of Hargoleth were related to him. Several people, including King Skella of Thorakest, had told him as much, and that the people who inhabited the lands of Gongoreth were also related to these northerners. In fact, most of the people of Western Háthgolthane descended from these people, having come to aid Gol-Durathna and Nordeth in their battle with Golgolithul, all culminating in the Battle of Bethuliam. They were supposedly a hardy people, but fragmented and clannish. Turk had once said they resembled primitive dwarves in the nature of their governance, each clan holding allegiances, but operating as its own entity, unless some major threat came into their lands, at which time all the clans would band together.

Erik saw slow-moving figures in the distance, close enough to see there were a dozen or so, and they had arms and legs and heads, but far enough away that they were mere blue shadows on the horizon. They looked large, and his first inclination was giants, a group of them roaming and scavenging, or looking to avenge the deaths of two of their comrades. But he could see that some of the figures were smaller and, as Warrior cautiously trotted closer, he saw wagons and carts and even littler shadows trailing behind. He drew even closer and realized that this was a band of ogres.

Erik had seen an ogre in Finlo. He hadn't believed his brother, Befel, when he spoke of a large man with bulging muscles and a gentle spirit simply selling yards of cloth and metal wares, but when Erik finally saw the slow-moving giant, amazement was the best way to describe his experience. He met another ogre in Green Tree, a large outpost sitting along the road leading from Eldmanor to the tundra north of the Gray Mountains. He spoke with that ogre and, even though they moved slowly and deliberately, and they were docile to a fault, they were anything but stupid. He learned they were often dream walkers, as he was, and that there was something special, almost magical, about them.

He approached the group of ogres slowly, not wanting to appear as a threat. They clearly saw him, one of the women folk slowly moving to the rear of their train and gathering the little one to her. When they all came into view, there were two dozen, and Erik was glad they didn't care for violence. Just two of them could wreak havoc on a decent-sized town, let alone two dozen.

He stopped, but they didn't. They just kept walking, leading their trains of ox-drawn carts and carriages, the woman in the back shooing the little ones forward. Erik leaned forward in his saddle, wondering if he recognized any of them, but ogres—at least, to his eyes—looked so similar, with their plain, beardless faces and straight, gray hair. Finally, one of the men broke away from the group and turned to face Erik, allowing the carts and carriages and other ogres to go by.

Erik lifted both his hands, showing he meant no harm and held no weapons. The ogre stood still, showing no emotion, just waiting. Erik moved on again and got within ten paces of the ogre before he stopped.

"You are a long way from home, Dream Walker," the ogre said, speaking in Erik's native Westernese.

"I am," Erik said.

"Why?" the ogre asked.

"You walk the land of dreams," Erik said. "You know why."

The ogre nodded slowly.

"I have not seen you in the dream world as of late," the ogre said, slowly, his words precise and deliberate, just like every movement he made.

The ogre held a long staff, a head taller than him—which meant it was twice as long as Erik was tall. Feathers and rocks and beads hung from strings attached to the staff, and the skull of some small animals sat atop the wooden pole, staring out at Erik with blank eyes. The ogre leaned on his staff, gripping it with both hands.

Erik watched the ogre for a little while, leaning against his staff, unmoving other than the slow lifting of his chest with each breath. The last of the ogres in his group had passed by, and they were several dozen paces away.

"The dream world is ... I haven't dreamt in some time," Erik finally said.

"It is scared," the ogre said.

"What is?" Erik asked.

"Evil," the ogre replied.

"The Shadow?" Erik asked.

The ogre slowly nodded.

"The Shadow," he replied. "Other evils. Old evils. New evils."

Erik looked at the ogre with a raised eyebrow.

"Where are you going, Erik Dream Walker?" the ogre asked.

"Hargoleth," Erik replied. "Holtgaard."

"The Bear Clan," the ogre said with an affirming nod. "We are traveling no further than Örnddinas, home of the Eagle Clan, but you may journey with us until that time. It is the easternmost city and clan holding in Hargoleth."

"Why?" Erik asked.

"Why not?" the ogre replied.

"Is there payment to travel in an ogre caravan?" Erik asked.

The ogre chuckled, a low, reverberating, rumbling laugh.

"Your company is all we require," the ogre said.

Ogres seemed to travel slowly, and there were quite a few of them.

Erik shook his head.

"I appreciate the offer," Erik said, "but I think I will go it alone."

"Dream Walker," the ogre said, "we spend enough of our lives alone and afraid. If my dreams speak to me truly, where you are going, loneliness will be the least of your worries. Come with us, accompany us and tell us some stories. I like a good story. Spend a few more days around those with no desire to hurt you."

Erik thought for a moment, looking into the ogre's eyes. They were dark pools, and as he looked at them, he felt lost. He remembered a vision of the space beyond the sky of the world, and that's what he saw in the ogre's eyes. He felt his consciousness wane and, even though it had been a while since he had dreamt, he thought—for a moment—he was in the dream world.

Erik finally nodded.

"Alright," he said, and then after a pause, he added, "thank you."

The ogre simply nodded.

Erik followed the ogre as they met up again with the group with whom he traveled. They walked slowly, often stopping so the little ones, which were as big as a dwarf or a man depending on how old they were, could play and roam about. When moving on, they didn't seem to pay much attention to the little ones, but when one of the youngest ogres fell and hurt his knee, one of the women-folk rushed to him with a speed Erik didn't expect. She picked him up and carried him to one of their carts, gave him water, and soon he was out playing with the others again.

As they walked, going not even a quarter of the distance Erik could have gotten on his own, he kept looking over his shoulder, watching the slowly fading Gray Mountains as the sun began to set behind them.

"You need not worry about them following you," the ogre with the staff, presumably their leader, said, almost as tall as Erik sitting on horseback.

"Whom am I worried about?" Erik asked, straightening his back and puffing out his chest a little.

"Men," the ogre said with the slightest hint of a chuckle. "You pretend to be so brave. Is fear so cowardly? It is a normal emotion. What about sorrow? Is that weak also? These are normal feelings and, to embrace them, that is true courage."

"How?" Erik asked.

"If we recognize we are afraid," the ogre said, "then we can embrace and live out of faith, rather than that very fear we wish to throw off."

"It's just, the giants, and the winter wolf," Erik said.

"The etenweird will not bother us," the ogre said, using the dwarvish name for giants. "They are afraid of us ogres. As for the winter wolves, they are cunning and cruel and wicked, but they are also very intelligent and will not attack that which is more powerful. They too stay clear of ogres. You see, you have nothing to be worried about. Calm your mind and enjoy the journey, Dream Walker."

*What of Simone? My unborn child. Mother and Father. Tia and Beth. Bryon and the dwarves. Andu even.*

"They are alright," the ogre said.

"Who?" Erik asked.

"The ones you worry about," the ogre replied. "You love them, so you worry about them. Rest assured, they are safe."

Erik sighed.

"I have a hard time believing that," he said.

"Is faith so foreign to you?" the ogre asked.

Erik sighed deeply with irritation.

"I'm just in a hurry, and I left on bad terms with my wife," Erik said. "Is that so hard to understand? This mission I'm on ... it's important."

He didn't mean to sound harsh, angry, and irritated.

"Men are always in such a hurry," the ogre replied. "Truly, your mission will be there, waiting for you ... you will find your journey, lingering, whether it is tomorrow or next week. There is a purpose to our meeting, Erik Dream Walker."

"Fate?" Erik asked.

"No," the ogre replied, slowly shaking his head. "Purpose."

When they stopped, Erik tended to Warrior. The horse had many scars all over his body, some large and mean-looking, but none looked as severe as the two gashes a winter wolf's claws had made in the flesh of the animal's flank. Nevertheless, the destrier didn't seem to notice as Erik cleaned the wounds with fresh water and an ointment the ogres had given him. The medicine reminded Erik of his dwarvish friend, Turk, a battle-hardened warrior but, also, a healer, able to cure ailments and injuries with both the concoctions he created and his hands.

As Erik spread the healing ointment, a white, slimy balm that smelled minty and cool, Warrior watched him from over his shoulder. He shifted a few times, as Erik had to dig especially deep in the wound, but never gave a hint of discomfort. The ogre Erik presumed to be the leader of this traveling group joined him when he was done cleaning and slathering the wound with ointment and bandaged Warrior's flank with a soft cloth that could have fetched a pretty penny in any market.

"That looks like expensive fabric to be using on my horse's wound," Erik said. "It'll be ruined."

"We often forget that our animals can be as good friends as those of our own kind," the ogre replied. "And, many times, they are more loyal. Would you not use such fabric on your best friend ... or your wife or cousin?"

Erik stopped for a moment and watched the ogre work, wrapping the fabric—white and smooth—around the gash, under Warrior, around a leg, and then tying it. Warrior was a giant of a horse, and this ogre made him look small, and for the first time, the horse looked truly at peace. He didn't stomp his hooves, snort, or even shift his weight as the ogre worked.

"You seem to know mine, so what is your name?" Erik asked.

The ogre gently brushed a gigantic hand across the animal's coat as he finished with the bandage. He even scratched Warrior behind the ear and the horse snickered softly.

"There is power in a name, Dream Walker," the ogre replied. "We do not just give our names to anyone."

The ogre whispered something into Warrior's ear, and the horse walked, with a slight limp, over to one of the carts, where an ogre woman fed him from a large, wicker basket. The ogre turned back to Erik.

"Many people know your name, Erik Eleodum ... Erik Dragon Fire. You should be careful with whom you share your name."

"Why is knowing someone's name such a big deal?" Erik asked. "How is there power in it?"

He thought of Dewin, giving him the Lord of the East's name.

"A name can reveal much, Dream Walker," the ogre said. "It can reveal where someone is from, who they truly are, pulling back the veils of confusion and mystery that we create. It can be a gateway into someone's soul."

The ogre turned to watch Warrior eat.

"Take Warrior, for example," the ogre said. "Warrior is not his true name ... although he does like it. He has a warrior's spirit. And he likes you ... much more than his previous owners."

"How do you know?" Erik asked.

"I have spoken with him," the ogre replied.

"You have spoken to him?" Erik asked, almost laughing in disbelief. "My horse? You've spoken with my horse?"

"Yes," the ogre replied.

"Alright, then. What is his real name?" Erik asked, looking at the horse with raised eyebrows.

He didn't realize horses had their own names before being given one by a man.

"I will tell you since he would not be able to reveal it," the ogre said, "and I believe he would want you to know it. His name is Eroan."

"Eroan," Erik whispered to himself. "And yours?"

The ogre stared at Erik for a long moment before sighing with a smile.

"Jamalel," the ogre replied.

"No surname?" Erik asked.

"We ogres don't use them," Jamalel replied. "No two ogres are ever named the same. I am and will be, the only Jamalel this world will ever know."

With that, Jamalel turned and joined the other ogres.

---

## 20

*D*usk consumed the northern plains, west of the Gray Mountains, and made the surrounding land, with its sparse rocks, and flat, barren land, look even more dismal. For a while, the ogres simply allowed the deepening darkness to wash over them, sitting in or next to their carts, almost in silence, watching the sky as the northern lights finally began to dance across the vast sky.

It was cold, and Erik shivered uncontrollably until Jamalel eventually built a fire. Seated cross-legged on the ground, he watched the tiny pieces of ash float gently to the ground, daring to glow for a little longer when they touched the cold rock before dimming forever. The night was silent, save for the crackling and popping of the burning wood. They fluttered around the ogres too, and one of the young ones giggled.

It was then, as the sun and its fading light still clinging to the world, finally set, and the stars and moon took hold of the sky, that the ogres seemed to come back to life. Erik was now dragged from his reverie of Simone to watch the beginnings of a campfire dance. As an errant breeze teased the flames, causing the smoke to twirl and circle, like gypsies, the ogre women began swaying their hips back and forth in mesmerizing fashion.

Then they began to sing, again the women first. Their voices were low and mournful like the bells of a temple after someone's body had been consecrated in death. They sang long, fluid tones void of any recognizable language, and the music reminded Erik of the slow lapping of waves against a sandy lakeshore. Their perfect harmonies created a melodic hum that almost seemed to cause Erik's chest to vibrate, and he noticed all the little ones sitting and watching, cross-legged and mesmerized.

Now the men-folk joined in, adding melodies over the top of the women's fluid sounds, higher in pitch and timbre. Erik didn't understand the words, but each male ogre sang a different part until they created an orchestra of voices to match the sounds of the finest instruments ever crafted. Jamalel looked at Erik, his large, gray eyes meeting Erik's, and he smiled as he sang.

With almost a yearning to join in and play his part, Erik reached into his haversack and retrieved his simple, wooden flute. He studied it for a moment, closing his eyes and letting the warmth of the fire and the sound of the ogres wash over him as he discerned the notes he should play. Like a comforting blanket his mother might use to tuck in around him, he remembered a moment around a similar fire, with his brother and cousin, with the dwarves and men who were no longer living in this world, and he smiled. He put the flute to his lips and played.

As the sound of his flute melded perfectly with the ogre's voices, he looked to the darkness above and then closed his eyes. It was as if he was now seeing a place beyond the sky and the stars, beyond their world. An explosion of light appeared, and he was floating through this vast space before flying at blinding speeds out into this great openness. Things flew around him—rocks and colors and flashes of light—and then he slowed.

He floated again now, and around him were stars and suns, other worlds with their brilliant colors, Giant rocks flew through this vast space and crashed into one another, exploding with the brightest of lights, and creating new worlds and new stars and new moons. After each explosion, smoke and dust swirled around him until it dissipated, revealing even more celestial elements.

Erik was flying again, this time towards a singular orb, a planet. There were others around him, stars and rocks and worlds and suns, but this one was important for some reason. It was green and blue. It held life where the others were dead and silent. He floated above this world, and as it moved and turned in this great, dark space, it revealed a large, yellow sun. As the light of the sun lit up this world on one side, on the other, a white moon appeared. Erik, his breath caught in his chest, couldn't hold back the tears that came when he realized what he was seeing.

*Creation.*

He opened his eyes, most of the ogres still singing, but he had stopped playing his flute. He saw little white specks floating in the air, flashing in front of him and flying quickly by.

*Moon fairies.*

Erik smiled, remembering an ancient forest in the Southern Mountains and a gift of fairy dust that had saved his life several times. The ancient creatures, miniature relatives to the elves, flew all around them, and Erik also remembered his dwarvish friend, Balzarak, saying they were native to the north. They all looked the same to him as they stopped and fluttered in front of his face, seemingly unaffected by the cold. But they seemed to know who he was and congregated around him, the breeze from their wings oddly warm.

White fairy dust floated all about the camp, and the ogre children looked delighted, although not surprised. They giggled when a fairy would perch on the nose or head, and the small creatures seemed to play with them as the children gave chase. One small boy even caught a fairy—although Erik suspected she let herself be caught—cupping her in his hands. After a few moments, he let her go, and she buzzed around him. Erik heard a small cheer coming from the fairies, as they sprinkled extra dust on the boy.

"Fascinating," Erik said to himself as one fairy sat on his knee, cross-legged. Another one perched on his shoulder while he could feel, yet another, sitting on the top of his head.

Jamalel stood in front of him, a giant lumbering shadow against the campfire. Erik looked up at the ogre, as did the fairies sitting on him or buzzing around him. He handed Erik a large bowl, and he took it. The liquid inside the bowl was cool, but a vapor rose from it and mixed with the smoke from the fire as it lifted into the night sky. The fairies lifted themselves into the air, floating just above Erik, silhouetting him against the darkness of the night. It was as if they knew what was coming.

"You are a Dream Walker," Jamalel said. "We are the guides of the dream world. Drink."

Erik looked at Jamalel and then the bowl again. He put it to his lips, and the liquid was sweet and cold and, before he knew it, he had drunk the entire contents of the bowl.

"It is not pleasing to the Creator, An to the dwarves, El to the elves, that Erik Dream Walker be kept from the dream world," Jamalel said. "I will be your guide, Erik Dream Walker. Trust. Have faith. Let me lead you back into the dream world so that you might know and understand what is in store for you."

Jamalel put his massive hand on the back of Erik's head and, with slight pressure on his chest, encouraged Erik to lay back on the ground. As the ogre chanted, Erik thought he heard the moon fairies chant with him. Even though the ground was cold and hard, he felt warm with the softness beneath him of a comfortable mattress. He closed his eyes, and darkness met him. Then, a flash of light. A pinpoint in the distance. The whooshing of air in a stiff breeze. The splash of water. The splatter of rain ...

He opened his eyes, and he stood in a field of waist-high grass, a black mountain range to the east and a gentle hill to the west, a weeping willow, leaves fluttering in a soft breeze, atop it. Purple lightning flashed over the distant mountains, black and threatening. The earth beneath his feet vibrated, just the slightest of movements, when the thunder finally reached his ears. He turned and ignored it, walking towards the small, willow-topped hill. The smell hit his nose as soon as he took his first step, curling his lip. Death. Decay. Evil.

"I know you're there," Erik said.

"Who said that?" the undead asked. The voice was unmistakable ... Sorben Phurnan.

Erik faced the dead man. His body had decayed even more since Erik had last seen him.

"You look terrible," Erik said.

"You've been gone," Sorben said, a piece of his lip flapping as he spoke, barely clinging to his skull and ready to fall away with the slightest jolt. "Where have you been?"

Sorben looked ... Erik couldn't find the right word, and then it hit him. Sorben looked nervous, if a man decaying and existing between the plane of the living and the plane of the dead could feel that way. He constantly looked over his shoulder as if he were afraid.

"What is wrong with you?" Erik asked, raising an eyebrow.

"Have you seen him?" Sorben asked, stepping forward.

Erik smirked and drew Dragon Tooth. A faint green light emanated from the dwarvish steel, but when he stepped forward—toward the undead man—emerald flames consumed the blade. Sorben's eyes went wide, and he stepped back.

"Stay back," Erik said. "When I struck down your general in this place, he burst into a thousand pinpoints of light before he disappeared forever. As miserable as you must be, I am sure a prideful part of you wishes to continue your existence."

"The general," Sorben hissed. "Have you seen him?"

The undead man clasped his hands together, wringing them, dead skin flaking off as he did so.

"What are you talking about?" Erik asked. "Can the dead go mad?"

Sorben stopped and straightened. He looked at Erik, his empty, black eye sockets twisting in anger.

"You just wait, you pompous shite," Sorben hissed. "When you see him, you will know why I am so afraid. You just wait."

Sorben stepped backward. He began to fade, his body becoming translucent until he disappeared.

Erik made his way to the hill. The man was there, the one he knew, the one he recognized but could never put a finger on from where.

"It's been a while," the man said.

"Not on purpose," Erik said, sitting down next to the man.

"I know," the man said.

"The Shadow ..."

"Is afraid," the man finished.

"I didn't think the Shadow could fear," Erik said, "let alone be afraid of me."

The man slowly turned his head, his pale eyes boring into Erik.

"The Shadow is not afraid of you, Erik."

"Of course not," Erik said with a laugh. He immediately felt foolish for thinking such a thing.

"You saw what scares the Shadow," the man said.

"Was it here, in the Dream World?"

The man under the tree nodded. Now Erik remembered and understood.

"The cloaked man?" Erik asked.

The man under the tree nodded again.

"The same thing Sorben is afraid of?"

The man nodded yet again.

"Should I be afraid?"

The man waited, for just a moment, and then nodded again.

They sat together for a long time, watching the grass flutter gently in the wind, the branches of the willow tree droop and sway, and the odd beauty of purple lightning flashing from black clouds. Erik finally sensed the dream world slowly fading; it was a strange feeling, a tingling sensation like a thousand tiny insects crawling over his face. He looked at the man sitting with him, chewing on a long piece of grass. Erik wondered if the man would be there, the next time he entered the Dream World, or all would be gray again. That meant the mysterious, cloaked figure would greet him, the one evil enough to frighten the dead. The man final broke the silence.

"The Shadow. It was there, you know."

"Where?"

"In the beginning. Creation. You saw it."

Erik remembered his vision of the cosmos, of stars exploding and gigantic rocks crashing. Of suns forming and galaxies coalescing. He nodded.

"The most beautiful moment of all time," the man said, staring off as if he was reminiscing a fond memory. "Before time. Before anything."

The man shrugged, looking down at the grass on their hill and picking at some of it.

"The Shadow thought it could do better," the man said. "It coveted the Creator's power, but at the same moment, it shunned the light, goodness, even creation itself ... and became the Shadow."

"Did the Creator create the Shadow?" Erik asked.

"In a way, I suppose," the man replied. "He created the being that became the Shadow. He gave it free will. He gave it the ability to either love or hate him, to follow or oppose him. The Shadow chose poorly."

The world around Erik shimmered, and he knew he would wake soon.

"The keepers of the dream world have guided you back," the man said to Erik. "I will see you soon, Erik Eleodum. Tread carefully in the days to come."

And before Erik opened his eyes, before the Dream World faded away, Erik looked out onto the open, grassy plain and saw him ... a man cloaked in black and, even though he couldn't see the man's eyes, he knew he watched him.

Erik opened his eyes and saw morning had come around again; the sky overhead was a crystal blue with no clouds. He smiled when he saw Jamalel staring down at him

"A helpful dream?" Jamalel asked.

"Yes," Erik said.

"Good," Jamalel said in his slow, deliberate tone. "Now, it is time to move on. We will take you as far as Örnddinas. From there, you must let your dreams guide you."

## 21

*D*espite the flat, rocky terrain that was treeless and cold, Erik began to see signs of life. There seemed to be more birds now, along with some ground squirrels, and white-furred foxes. Large fallow fields surrounded small vegetable gardens, which consumed the space in front of small homes. Living must have been hard because these bore little more than leafy greens like spinach and lettuce. In some places, he did see goats, sheep, and pigs as well as several small ponds, mostly frozen over. Erik imagined he might see ducks and geese if they were passing through during the summertime. He even saw a small orchard of apple trees, but their growth seemed stunted, and most of their leaves had fallen.

"Is this Örnddinas?" Erik asked.

Jamalel shook his head.

"Not yet. These lands belong to farmers who have chosen to make their living beyond the protective boundaries of any clan or holding," the ogre explained.

"They seem poorer, but they are not unlike our farmsteads in Northwestern Háthgolthane."

"Where do you think your ancestors got the idea?" Jamalel asked with a smile.

"What does being on their own mean for these people?" Erik asked.

"For those that choose to farm and live within the borders of a clan holding," Jamalel explained, "their clan chieftain offers them protection in exchange for a portion of their crops and their swords if war were to break out."

"Like the feudal lords of Hámon," Erik added.

"In a way," Jamalel replied with a short nod. "Although these people are not forced to work the land, and the land is theirs. If they choose not to pay homage—to live outside of the clan—they receive no protection or help with seed and labor during lean seasons. Gongoreth is the same, although they have a king that rules over all their lands."

As they rode by, a tall, robust farmer walked out from his small farmhouse. When he saw the ogres passing by, he lifted a hand in salutation, but his face remained emotionless. He quickly went to work in his small vegetable garden.

If all Hargolethians were like this man, they were a large people. Erik's people were certainly bigger than many from Gol-Durathna and Golgolithul that he had met, and if he had descended from these people in the north, he now knew why he'd grown to a good size. But Erik would have been an average-sized man in Hargoleth, because this farmer was even more broad-shouldered than Erik and perhaps a hand taller. His hair was long and colored like the sun with a thick, braided beard of the same color, falling to his belly. Erik couldn't see his eyes—he was too far away—but his eyebrows were thick and shadowed his face, giving Erik the impression that the man had a permanent scowl.

As they grew closer to Örnddinas, more and more farms dotted the land until they looked much like the farmsteads of Northwestern Háthgolthane. These people were used to the ogres, and many of the women and children began following their traveling group, seemingly hoping to have first access to their wares and fabrics when they stopped to sell. None of them seemed to think it odd that a man was traveling with ogres, and one of the children was bold enough to talk to Erik.

"That's a big horse," the boy, perhaps seven summers old, said, the language of the north clearly some hybrid of dwarvish and Westernese. Erik began to understand where Westernese came from, and he understood enough of what the boy said.

"His name is ..." Erik began to say, speaking Dwarvish and watching the little boy to see if he understood, but then wondered which name his warhorse would want to go by.

"You speak Dwarvish?" the boy questioned with a tilted head and raised eyebrows.

"Aye, I do," Erik replied, equally surprised that this boy understood Dwarvish. "I lived with them for a time ... in the south."

The boy stopped and gave an open-mouthed gasp. His mother, a tall and broad-shouldered woman with two blonde braids falling to the small of her back, looked over her shoulder, clicked her tongue, and reached out, offering her hand to the boy. He hurried back to meet her and grasped her hand.

"Mother, this man lived with dwarves," the boy said, to which his mother smiled, rolled her eyes, and shook her head. She gave Erik a kind look, one that probably thanked him for entertaining her son.

"What's your horse's name?" the boy asked.

Erik looked at Warrior again and then down at the boy, his short legs moving fast to keep up with the train of ogres.

"Warrior," Erik replied.

"Is he a horse trained for battle?" the boy asked.

"He is," Erik replied with a smile as the boy tugged on his mother's arm and looked up at her with that same open-mouthed, wide-eyed look.

"Can I touch him?" the boy asked.

"I don't know," Erik replied. "I will ask him."

Erik patted his horse's massive shoulder and did just that, asking the horse if the boy could touch him in his native Shengu language. Warrior simply looked at Erik over his shoulder and neighed. Erik nodded to the boy, and he reached out and gingerly touched Warrior's gray coat at the top of a front leg. He couldn't reach any higher.

More people gathered around the ogres as they approached the walls of Örnddinas. They were a combination of wood and stone, but not as tall as the walls of Fen-Stévock. An earth embankment rose ten paces and, atop the man-made hill, stood the city defenses. Thick poles, fashioned to a point, jutted out from the raised earth, and the gate was a combination of wood and iron and was set back between two square towers. Its doors were open and its drawbridge down, although it lay on the ground as Örnddinas didn't have a moat. A band of ogres was clearly not seen as a threat, for the guards in the towers must have seen them approach from a good distance away.

Like those who relied on agriculture as their main source of income, most people had built their homes outside the city walls. Several streets crisscrossed the wide dirt path that served as the main road leading into Örnddinas, each block filled with houses and shops. Like other such towns or cities, the people of Örnddinas would have to abandon most of their possessions and flee inside the walls if aggressors arrived.

Erik followed the ogres through the front gate of Örnddinas. The city looked large enough from outside the walls, but the city defenses deceived the eye. The city's fortifications formed a large, protective circle, so all the homes and shops followed the walls. Even the roads —there were two of them—curved around in a circular fashion.

Örnddinas had some regular soldiers, most of them stationed at the front gate and the beginning and end of the rising ramp leading to the keep. They all wore hauberks of heavy cloth studded with small, iron discs and conical helms with nasal pieces protecting their nose and eyes. They held large, round, wooden shields painted in a variety of reds, greens, blues, and yellows and carried long spears, some carrying two or three in one hand. They all had either long swords, with short, rounded cross guards, or long-handled axes hanging from frogs in their belts. The city guard would not have been enough to stave off any substantial siege, but from what Jamalel had said, the rest of the able-bodied would undoubtedly help defend Örnddinas if the need arose.

Inside the defenses, a pathway led from the middle of the wide space behind the walls up to a much taller mound of earth, which rose from the back of the walled city. A tall, square tower, made all of stone, sat in the middle of this raised hill and, even though the walls of the city proper surrounded this keep, it also had its own wooden walls. The tops of each pole that made up the wall were again fashioned to a point. A single gatehouse stood at the top of the inclined path, and one would have to pass through the gatehouse to get into the courtyard of the keep.

"You've never been here before, have you?" the mother of the little boy who had wanted to touch Warrior asked as they approached the keep. She spoke to Erik in Dwarvish, which took him by surprise. She noted his reaction.

"Most of us learn the language of the dwarves. It's necessary for trade."

Erik nodded.

"Did you truly live with the dwarves," the mother asked, "or were you just entertaining my little Gwili?"

"I did," Erik said. "The southern dwarves, in Thorakest, the capitol of Drüum Balmdüukr."

The woman lifted her eyebrows a little.

"Örnddinas is one of the largest cities in Hargoleth," the woman added. "A thousand people live in or next to its walls. And another thousand, mostly farmers like my family, pay homage to the Eagle Clan."

Erik nodded as the woman spoke, her voice filled with pride as she spoke of the city's size.

"The cities of the dwarves must be massive compared to Örnddinas," the woman said.

"Thorakest was large, but nothing compares to Fen-Stévock," Erik said, looking down at the woman. She watched him expectedly. "The capitol of Golgolithul is home to over a million people."

The way in which her eyes widened, Erik wondered if she had ever considered such a large number. Her gaze went back to the city, and she pointed to the keep atop the tall mound of earth.

"This is Örnddinas Keep, home of Baltair Ornson, Chieftain of the Eagle Clan," the woman said. "He is a good ruler, and many of the other clans have suggested he be Battle Thane in times of war."

"Do I need to meet him, or one of his advisors if I plan on staying in Örnddinas for a night before passing through?" Erik asked.

The woman shook her head.

"We see travelers all the time," she replied. "If you plan on traveling farther west ..."

"I am going to Holtgaard," Erik said, cutting the woman off.

Her eyes widened.

"You will need to follow the road, then," she said. "Some of the smaller clans are more wary of travelers ... and not very welcoming of outsiders." She looked forward, her thoughts trailing off and then said, almost as much to herself as to Erik, "It's why we need one thane to unify us."

The ogres stopped at the edge of a market square and arranged their carts and carriages to sell their goods. The people who had followed them into Örnddinas were first to begin their haggling, while more people came to see what they offered. The citizens of Örnddinas looked much the same as those from the farming families, mostly with blond, red, or light brown hair. The men wore long hair like the women, and most had beards. But despite the apparent homogony of the community in their natural looks, their access to and acquaintance of travelers from all over the world was apparent.

Some people wore their clothing or hair in the style of the east or the south, and most of them ignored Erik or gave him little more than a quick glance. He looked like most of them, even if his armor—his dwarvish mail shirt with steel pauldrons, bracers, and greaves—would have been a prized possession by most northerners. Warrior, the great warhorse that he was, was just another horse in this place; the draft horses that pulled wagons and plows were just as big.

"As you continue on your journey, Dream Walker, you must remember that the people of Hargoleth are a simple people," said Jamalel as he came up beside Erik, looking Erik in the eye even though he was standing and Erik still sat astride Warrior. "Their lives are hard, and many of them are superstitious."

"Why do you tell me this?"

"It relates to that which you seek."

"The stone?" Erik asked, and the ogre nodded.

"The stone is sacred to the people of Hargoleth," Jamalel said.

"How do you know about the Dragon Stone?" Erik asked.

Jamalel didn't answer Erik as he continued, "If you fail your mission, Erik, the implications are dire."

"Why?" Erik asked. The mysteries surrounding the stone—the Dragon Stone—were still confusing to him and, perhaps, Jamalel would reveal more than Dewin had.

"The Dragon Stone, most call it," Jamalel said, "and you will hear these people call it the Ruling Stone. Some may even call it the Eastern Stone, or the Dragon Egg for its shape."

Erik remembered a dream in which a man held such a stone, glowing green and shaped like an egg.

"But its first name is the Stone of Chaos," Jamalel continued, "and it is just that. It is more than a prison for Rako. It is more than a symbol of power. It is more than a treasured relic. It is life or death."

"You know of Rako?" Erik asked, raising an eyebrow.

"I remember when he was just a boy," Jamalel replied with a smile, and Erik nodded. "But do not let your love for him cloud the true mission here, Erik. The Stone of Chaos must be recovered, and it must be delivered to El'Beth El'Kesh. You have heard her name before?"

Erik nodded.

"I was hoping to stay here, in Örnddinas, for a day, as it seems my journey will be a hard one," Erik said. "Could I stay with you?"

"I am sorry," Jamalel said, shaking his huge head. "You cannot delay. You must make your way to Wulfstaad."

"But Dewin said Holtgaard," Erik said, not expecting to have to explain to the ogre who he was talking about.

"Indeed, your journey will eventually take you to the clan holding of the Bear Clan, but first, you must stop and visit the Wolf Clan."

"I don't understand," Erik said.

"I wouldn't expect you to," Jamalel replied with a smile. "But you will find the key to the Dragon Stone in Wulfstaad."

Erik nodded.

"I will leave without delay, then," he said. "Thank you, Jamalel, for your company ... and your friendship."

"Remember, Erik," Jamalel said, "that growth in life is often painful. Do not curse your pain or your trials. I know you fear for your wife and your child ... for your family. The pain—and the guilt— you are experiencing now will only serve to make you ... and them ... stronger when the time comes."

"And when might that be?" Erik asked although he knew there would not be a straight answer.

"You'll see," Jamalel said, "eventually."

The ogre turned and placed his hand gently on the shoulder of one of his womenfolk. He whispered into the female ogre's ear, and she nodded. She handed Jamalel several yards of the same white fabric the ogre had wrapped around Warrior's flank. She then handed Jamalel another fabric—a dull purple, thin, and soft looking. He turned and handed the fabric to Erik.

"The white material will help stop the bleeding," Jamalel said, "for both you and Eroan. Use it sparingly, as a little bit goes a long way. The purple material is as warm as thick wool, much warmer than it looks. As you know, the nights here get cold. Wrap yourself in this, and you will stay comfortable, especially on evenings you deem it necessary to go without a fire."

"You don't need to ..." Erik began to say, but the ogre lifted a hand, quieting him.

"You must hurry, Dream Walker," Jamalel said. He rested a hand on Warrior's neck and whispered into the horse's ear. Warrior whinnied softly and stamped a hoof. "Go with the Creator. I will see you in your dreams."

Erik turned Warrior, nodded to Jamalel and the other ogres, and made eye contact with the mother he had been talking to. He nodded to her and then smiled and winked at her boy, Gwili. He rode back out the front gate of Örnddinas—Warrior trotting around the crowd and avoiding people without Erik's help—and made his way around the city until he found the wide, flat dirt road that continued west. It ran all the way to the horizon, twisting and turning with the natural undulations of the earth.

"Shall we, Warrior?" Erik asked.

His great warhorse stomped a hoof, bobbed his head and snorted, and then galloped west, faster than Erik had ever seen the horse move.

erradyn and Raktas continued to patrol with Bryon. They didn't see any more red-eyed wolves, but they did once find a large draft horse dead, just outside the fence that marked the boundaries of the Eleodum farm. The horses the farmers used for the plows and wagons would have been a formidable foe for even a pack of wolves or a cougar, but if they could bring one down, it would feed them for weeks. But this one was dead—a large chunk of its throat bitten away—*and* uneaten. The thing that killed this animal did so simply for the sport of it. Bryon was certain the attacker was a winter wolf.

Terradyn awoke the next day to a commotion outside the farmhouse. Stepping out onto the porch, he saw a small retinue of horsemen lined up outside the home's fence. They looked like knights, and he recognized the colors and symbols on their shields and breastplates as belonging to the Kingdom of Hámon, now ruled by a man calling himself Bu Al'Banan—as if Patûk had any legitimate children. Hámon was still a feudal country, the king relying on the goodwill and purchased loyalty of the lords of its land despite now being ruled by a Golgolithulian, a country ruled by an imperial despot.

"What is the meaning ..." Bryon, already outside, was walking towards the horsemen when he noticed a dark-haired man with a black, close-cropped beard. He was wearing gleaming plate mail that seemed to shimmer in the winter sun and a golden circlet around his head. He spurred his large destrier to the front of the line as Erik's cousin stopped.

"Oh ... It's you," said Bryon with a distinct sneer in his voice.

"That's your king you're speaking to!" one of the knights snapped, a broad-shouldered man with brown, bobbed hair and a thick beard. He drew a long, broadsword and pointed it at Bryon.

Bryon shrugged, clearly unimpressed, as several other knights and horsed men lowered lances or drew swords.

"These are free lands," Bryon replied, and Terradyn slowly walked up behind the man, Raktas just on his heels. "I have no king."

"For now," the knight replied.

"Sir Garrett," the man wearing the circlet around his head said, holding up a hand, "it is alright. Thank you."

The man looked at this Sir Garrett and nodded with a smile. The knight sheathed his sword, and the others followed suit.

"You'll have to excuse Sir Garrett," the man who this knight referred to as a king said. "He is very loyal and protective of me. Sir Garrett is well renowned in the lands of Hámon," to which the knight bowed, "and, even though he has faithfully served my most esteemed duke, Lord Alger, for many years, he is about to receive his own dukedom."

The king presented another man who seemed indifferent to being there; he looked down on Bryon over his nose, picking at a fingernail nonchalantly. The smile on the king's face seemed false, and Terradyn could see something else in the man's eyes ... hatred, anger, but whatever it was, his welcoming disposition was false.

"What do you want Bu?" Bryon asked, and Terradyn's eyes widened.

Terradyn realized this was Bu, newly self-crowned King of Hámon and a former soldier in the service of defector general Patûk Al'Banan. He frowned, and Terradyn noticed Bu's fingers tickling the hilt of his sword, one Terradyn recognized. It was Patûk's sword.

Terradyn remembered the time when Mikel Aztûk, the last Aztûkian to serve as Lord High Chancellor in Golgolithul, presented that sword to General Patûk Al'Banan. Soon after, Mörken, the Lord of the East's father, gained control back for the Stévockians. Five years after that, he was dead, and the Lord of the East was now despot of the east. Patûk defected from Golgolithul—frustrated with the rule of the Stévockians—and started his underground war. How fortuitous that this gutter rat would rise through the ranks of Patûk's army of traitors, gain the favor of a famous and successful general, gain the loyalty of his men after his death, carry his sword, and now become the king of a small, feudal kingdom. The world was indeed a strange place outside the servitude to Andragos.

"As free as you may be," Bu said, his tone and face flat, "I am still a king."

"By chance," Bryon said. "And these lands do not belong to Hámon.

Bryon was bold and not intimidated by Bu or his small entourage of soldiers. Terradyn was beginning to like this Bryon Eleodum.

"Still," Bu said. He continued to tickle the handle of his sword and, apparently, Bryon saw it.

"Very well," Bryon said with only the hint of a sigh. "What can I do for you, King Bu Al'Banan?"

"I want to speak with your cousin," Bu replied.

"You rode all this way just to have a word with Erik?" Bryon asked, the hint of disbelief in his voice.

"I did," Bu said.

"He's not here," Bryon said.

"We will wait," Bu replied.

"He's gone. Traveled north and west," Bryon said. "I don't know when he'll be back."

"Has he gone to Hargoleth?" Bu asked, and a low murmur flowed through his knights and horsemen.

"So I believe," Bryon said with a shrug.

"To what end?" Bu asked.

Bryon just shrugged again. Terradyn suspected Bryon knew why his cousin had left, but he wasn't going to tell this imposter king.

"Who knows?" Bryon said when Bu remained silent, waiting for an answer. "This is Erik we are talking about. His wife has asked me to run his farmstead while he is gone. Is there something I can do for you?"

"Has she?" Bu said with a mischievous smile.

As they spoke, Andu, Turk, Nafer, and Bofim walked up behind the horsed entourage, several other farmers with them. One of Bu's men—Sir Garrett—alerted him of their presence, and he turned his horse.

"Turk Skull Crusher," Bu said with feigned jollity, "it is good to see you again."

"Likewise," Turk replied, "I am sure."

"And Andu, I see you have finally found a place for your pathetic existence," Bu said, his voice a demeaning hiss.

Andu didn't say anything. He simply stepped back, behind Turk, not daring to look the King of Hámon in the eyes.

"I don't mean to be disrespectful," Bryon said, although the tone of his voice said he didn't care if he was perceived that way or not, "but we have a lot of work to do, with colder weather on its way."

"Very well," Bu said with a sigh. "I came to speak with Erik about opening up trade with the free farms of Northwestern Háthgolthane."

"Truly?" Bryon asked, surprise very evident in his voice.

"Yes, truly," Bu replied. "The gods have blessed you with rich soil and plentiful crops, hardworking people, and prolific hunting grounds. The lands of Hámon are not as rich as yours, and the farms are not as productive."

"That's because you have slaves farm your lands," Bryon said.

"They are not slaves," the man named Alger said, his voice hard, and his eyes narrowed. "They are free people, blessed by the generosity of the lords who own the lands they farm."

"Call them whatever you want," Bryon said as Bu held up a hand to calm the nobleman down. "Don't you wish to simply rule these lands? Why trade with us?"

"Peasants owning their own land ..." Alger began to say, but Bu cut him off.

"... is abnormal to us, even in the east," Bu concluded, and then he looked up to Terradyn and Raktas. "Even the Black Mage's lackeys could tell you that."

Terradyn heard Raktas growl.

"I am surprised to see the manservants of the Messenger of the East here at the Eleodum farm," Bu said. "Your master has removed his leash?"

Terradyn put a hand on Raktas' chest as the man moved forward.

"We go where our master bids us go," Terradyn said.

"And why did he bid you come here?" Bu asked. "Emissaries from the east ... Should you not have come to Hámon first, to ask permission to be here?"

"You have become very bold," Terradyn said, and then smiled, "for a simple gutter shite turned pretend king."

Sir Garret and the other horsemen drew their swords. They looked red-faced and angry.

"I came to talk trade," Bu said, "not fight."

"But why with Erik?" Bryon asked.

"Is the Dragon Slayer not the leader of your people?" Bu asked.

Bryon didn't say anything for a moment.

"They are free," Turk finally said. "They have no rulers. No leaders. No kings. You would have to meet with each farmer and each farm to establish trade."

Bu looked irritated, his face screwed into a pinch.

"You could speak to my uncle," Bryon said, "Rikard Eleodum. He has one of the more profitable farms. And he is well respected."

"Very well," Bu said. "Would you be willing to organize an audience with this Rikard?"

"Sure," Bryon replied. "Probably tomorrow. You can camp on one of our fallow fields in the meantime. If it's too cold, the barn is available."

Bryon turned to face Terradyn.

"You two can stay in the house for the time being," he added.

"The barn!" one of the knights exclaimed.

"That will be fine, thank you," Bu replied, but his face said he lied.

## 23

*A*nkara slowed Naga as she stared out over rolling hills that, despite the frost and wintery cold, held onto some of their green. The hillock on which she sat was tall enough that she could look down on the farmlands of Northwestern Háthgolthane for leagues, surveying the homes of people like Erik Eleodum. Each farm she could see in detail had, in addition to a small farmhouse with smoke twirling up through the chimney, a barn, a mill, and many had ponds. It was so quaint it made her sick.

Ankara hated all of Háthgolthane. She didn't much like Antolika either, but it was at least better than this cursed continent. For all of its attempts at advancing itself and expanding its lands and colonization, it was backward and brutal. Golgolithul had all but leveled all of its woodlands in the name of evolution and advancement. To the south, there were city-states, all governed differently, all terribly fragmented. One moment, their people might be free, and the next, some cruel tyrant would subjugate them to ridiculous, harsh rules. And in the north and west ... backwards farmers, forgotten by time and advancement. These people probably shuddered at the thought of life outside their farmsteads. The mention of magic made them pray, and the idea of adventure caused them to shiver.

And the women ... her gender in Háthgolthane were stifled and oppressed. Most lands didn't allow women to hold positions, and they were stuck in their homes, bearing children, cooking, and cleaning. They couldn't hunt. They couldn't fight. They had no say in council meetings and the determination and implementation of laws. And worst of all, they were called whores for loving the company of a handsome man, and yet, men could stick whomever they wanted without a blink of the eye. That alone prevented Ankara from ever living in this place. She loved men—their company, their bodies pressed against hers—and even in this place she might find some man who might be capable of pleasing her. It would not be easy, though; large and hairy, they clearly were not taught how to please a woman as the men in Isuta were.

The thing about Ankara that made men so appealing was that sex was one of the main ways she gained her magical power. It was the vice that gave her strength, deriving potency from her lovers' passions. Her father drank blood ... she lay with men. She had tried laying with women—she found beauty in everything—but they didn't give her the same joy or increase in magic that men did. Call her a whore ... she didn't care. She was more powerful than almost all men in Háthgolthane. She would seduce them, fuck them, and then drain them of all their life force, laughing at their tiny cocks just before killing them.

Háthgolthanians called Isuta a brutal country because of its slavery practices, but most of their slaves lived better than the farmers and peasants of the west—especially hers. They were almost all men, and she used them to increase her magic. How could such an existence be terrible ... used to lay with a beautiful, powerful woman? It was an excellent existence, except for those who failed her as lovers, of course.

As she gazed down at the farms, she was sure there would be some strong men who could give her a run for her money under the covers ... only to be shackled down by some plain farmwife never willing to explore their true potential. She moved in her saddle as her thoughts wandered, growing excited and aroused.

*I bet there are quite a few virgins down there.*

Her excitement grew. Virgins always gave her the most power. Another time, she thought, but she smiled and licked her lips.

Nudging Naga down the hillock, she found a dirt road that wound its way through the farmlands and pushed Naga on into a gentle trot. The fences of different farms bordered the road, and several of them, men worked replacing broken and warped beams or inspecting spots that might look suspect to any cow with true intentions of getting out of its confines.

She straightened her back as she rode, using a little bit of her magic to make her tan skin glow and her black hair sparkle in the sun, but most of the farmers didn't bother to look at her as she rode by. Some gave her a quick glance, and one scowled at her, an older fellow with one eye that squinted. She knew she looked different from everyone else in these lands, where even the women could be broad-shouldered and tall. But she didn't care. Even though most of these farmers had well-worked muscles, none of them struck her fancy. None of them even aroused her interest, let alone her loins.

As she traveled down the winding dirt road, she finally came to a small group of women. They all carried wicker baskets, either propped against their hips or strapped to their backs, filled with lettuce and tomatoes and some other produce.

"You look lost, dearie," one of them said, a chubby woman with a simple brown dress, red cheeks, and dark brown hair.

"I am, a little," Ankara replied with a smile. She was well aware of her rolling accent as she spoke Westernese, but these women seemed not to notice.

"Are you looking for someone?" the woman asked.

"I believe he goes by the name of Erik ... Erik Eleodum," Ankara replied.

"Well, you and everyone else in this cursed world are after him," another woman said, clearly not meaning Ankara to hear her. This was proven by the dirty look the chubby woman gave her.

"Can I ask why?" the woman asked.

The question caused Ankara to ponder for the best.

"That poor family has been through a lot recently," the chubby woman said when Ankara didn't immediately answer.

"Brought it on themselves, if you ask me," another one of the women added, almost under her breath.

"Hush," the chubby woman hissed.

"I have some news from the east for Erik," Ankara said, finally. "That is all. I am an Isutan messenger with important news that might contribute to his safety ... and the safety of his family."

The chubby woman looked up at Ankara, and then to the other women with her. She seemed to decide that this slip of a girl could be no threat and pointed down the dirt road.

"If you keep going along here, you'll see a large elm tree in front of another fence where this road continues north and another leads west. Take that second road," the woman said, "and it will eventually lead to Erik Eleodum's farmstead. It's the most western one in these lands."

Ankara nodded with a smile as she reached into a purse at her belt. She pulled out a gold coin and threw it to the woman who snatched it up in her fat hand.

"Thank you kindly," Ankara said, nudging Naga forward and glaring at the other woman who hadn't wanted to help her.

She soon found the elm tree and turned west. After crossing by several other roads, she came to a fence that surrounded a large farm, beyond which was only open country. She rode along the fence, passing by sheep with their thick, winter coats until she turned a corner and saw the farmhouse and a barn. A group of mounted, armored men and other people were in front of the house talking.

She reined in Naga quickly and looked across the road to another fence, the property of another farm. Bushes in need of trimming lined the fence, and she moved Naga back around the corner out of sight and tied her to the fence. She gave the horse a quick pat on the neck to keep her calm and leaped over the fence to take cover behind the bushes. She reached behind, her longbow appearing in her hand. She drew a long arrow with a broad blade from her quiver but didn't instruct the arrowhead to kill.

Among the men was a single woman who stood watching, her eyebrows curled into a look of pensiveness. She looked as if she wanted to say something, her arms crossed across her chest and her foot tapping quickly against the ground. But these men and dwarves were so consumed with their conversation ... no, it was an argument that she couldn't get a word in. Ankara now looked carefully from one man to the next. Which one was Erik Eleodum?

Syzbalo had done his best to describe the man, even attempting to transfer a vision of the farmer through his mind to the Black Tigress', but his magic—as much as he professed to be powerful—was different, almost tainted with an acrid taste. She found it odd. Magic was magic, but his was so strange. Whatever it meant, the image he conveyed was little more than a silhouette of a shadow. She knew Erik was tall and broad- shouldered with light brown or dusty blond, long hair. He had a beard and was well-muscled. He had a stern jaw. Ankara cracked a small smile. She could probably exact quite a bit of magical strength from such a man.

With a soft sigh, she released the tension in her bowstring. She didn't know which man was Erik and firing at will—killing at will— would do her no good. It wasn't what she was here for. Her father would have killed everyone, just to drain them. She could use them, but ... she smiled. She didn't have time, even if these Háthgolthanian dogs didn't last as long as Isutan men. She need only kill a few. When she knew her target, she would slip in like a shadow and then out the same way.

Her eyes glowed as she tapped into her magic. Turning herself into nothing but an outlined silhouette, barely shifting the space around her as she moved, she climbed back over the fence and tiptoed to a row of orange trees, their leaves fallen and curled brown on the ground. She crept along the line of trees, keeping her eyes on the group speaking in front of the house, and avoiding fallen leaves not to create unnecessary sound.

Her attention was so focused on the group of people arguing she didn't see the man in between two trees relieving himself. He wore a simple, cloth hauberk with a white tabard over it, covered in blue squares and a conical helm.

*What was a Hámonian doing here?*

She had nearly bumped into him as he buckled his belt and when he turned and looked in her direction, his face paled, seemingly staring at something that looked much like a ghost to him. The man's hand went to the sword at his side, and he opened his mouth, ready to cry out, when Ankara lifted her bow, her disguise disappearing, and fired an arrow through his open mouth. He lurched backward, the back of his skull exploding as the arrow passed through and thudded into the side of the farmhouse. The man fell to the ground, his eyes wide and blood pouring from his mouth.

"Damn it," Ankara hissed.

Her attention returned to the group of men, but none of them seemed to have noticed what happened. Her kill had been silent, and their conversation had covered the sound of the arrow sticking into the wooden wall of the farmhouse. She was about to breathe a sigh of relief when she noticed one of the dwarves looking her way, his bushy eyebrows lowered. She turned herself back into a silhouette with the snap of her fingers as he stared straight at her; he had seen something even though he was a hundred paces away. The dwarf grabbed the arm of one of the others of his kind and whispered into his ear. The other turned, looking in her direction as well.

*Damn dwarves.*

Ankara hated them. They were worse than elves, and their squat, hairy bodies were disgusting. The very thought of letting a dwarf stick her made her want to gag.

Both of the dwarves said something to another man, who also turned to look in her direction. As little as she knew about this Erik

Eleodum, this man could have been him. He was broad-shouldered and tall. He had a beard and sandy blond hair. He was lean and muscular. Could this be the one she would kill? She trained her ear on the men to hear what they were saying.

"What are you looking at Eleodum?" one of the Hámonian knights, sitting straight-backed on his horse, said, irritation clear in his voice.

*This was him!*

"Hush!" this man Eleodum hissed. "Turk sees something."

*Damn!*

"Edwin," the mounted knight said, speaking to another man who was heavily armored and standing next to his horse, "go see what has spooked this farmer and his dwarvish friends."

"I'll go too," said Eleodum, and the dwarf called Turk put a restraining hand on the man's arm.

"No Bryon," the dwarf said with a simple shake of his head and a concerned look in his eyes.

*It's not him! Must be a brother or cousin!*

The armored man named Edwin nodded, jerking his head sideways to another man who, with a simple cloth hauberk and conical helm, looked much like the one she had already killed. Although, certainly, they couldn't see her, they walked in her direction, and she moved behind one of the orange trees, heading back to the fence.

"It's moved," the dwarf named Turk said.

Ankara calmed herself, breathing deeply and evenly. Peering around the tree, still in the form of an almost translucent silhouette, she saw the heavily armored soldier named Edwin walking in her direction, the other soldier following him closely. She pressed her back against the tree and slinked back behind it. She closed her eyes, gripping her bow tightly, and then peered back around the tree. The men and single woman gathered in front of the house still watched in her direction, but now she couldn't see Edwin and the other soldier.

Ankara felt the wind move. She materialized from her translucent form and ducked as a broad-bladed long sword cut overhead.

She rolled and kicked out, her shin slamming against the thigh of her assailant. He was the knight, Edwin. He stumbled, but she hadn't caught him cleanly, and he lifted his sword with both hands as high as he could and brought it down. Ankara rolled out of the way, dropping her bow and producing a thin-bladed dagger seemingly out of nothing. She twirled it around so that she clutched it with an underhand grip and brought it up into the space of the knight's armor between his arm and shoulder as his sword thudded into the ground. The poison on her dagger wasn't deadly, but it was painful, and the knight screamed out as soon as her steel pierced his flesh. Leaving her blade in the man's armpit, she extended a hand again, producing a short sword, which she slashed at the back of his neck.

The knight moved just in time so that her blade glanced on the man's bevor, and he swung at her with a gauntleted fist. Ankara had never fought—she had barely seen—a Hámonian knight, but this man wasn't what she expected. She had heard of the feudal kingdoms of Háthgolthane, and that their men were haughty and flighty and prone to formal balls more than fighting. She thought they might be weak and untrained, but this man was strong. It didn't matter. For all his toughness and strength, he was no match for an Isutan assassin.

Ankara drew another thin-bladed dagger from her boot and jammed it into the knight's hip. He yelled out again, charging her angrily. She twirled past him, bringing her sword down again. This time she didn't miss. Her steel cut into his flesh, and he dropped to his knees. Ankara removed the dagger from his armpit, wrapped an arm around the knight's forehead—pulling his head back—and stabbed him in the neck. He slumped to the ground.

The other man had held back, no doubt thinking that the knight Edwin would take care of this slip of a girl, but he had been wrong. He charged Ankara, and this one was an easier kill. She simply tripped him as he rushed at her, knelt on his back as soon as he hit the ground, and sliced open his throat. She was wondering if he was some sort of vassal to this knight when another man came at her, exposed and angry. She threw a dagger at his face, the thin blade hitting his eye and driving into the socket handle deep. She was on him quickly, slicing his throat as well.

*Weaklings.*

She closed her eyes for just a moment, concentrating, and when she opened them, she saw shapes, huddled behind the barn. When she looked to the farmhouse, she saw nothing, just an aura of darkness. Her magic wasn't working on the home. She gritted her teeth and concentrated more. Still nothing. She felt a presence, someone pushing back at her with magic of their own. The presence blocked her—her vision, her hearing. She sniffed the air, trying to sense what kind of magic it was. It reminded her of the Lord of the East, only, more powerful, darker, blacker.

*Andragos!*

Now two men stepped out from the house. One was bald with glowing, blue tattoos etched into his scalp, emanating his power. His bright red beard dipped to his wide belt, and he held a massive two-handed sword; as he moved it, the muscles in his arms rippled. The other, a dark-haired man who wore two braids that extended to the small of his back, held two swords. They weren't as big as the red-haired man's blade, but just one of them would have been too much for a normal fighter to carry in two hands. He was a large, muscled man as well, and he stared at Ankara, his eyes glowing a sapphire blue. She knew who they were now.

Terradyn and Raktas—Andragos' bodyguards, manservants, personal slaves, and who knew what else. She had seen them before, many years ago, and they looked the same in their agelessness. Black magic. Andragos' black magic. Not that her magic was pure and righteous, but Andragos practiced magical arts that were even darker than that of her late father's. Some accused the man of actually being a demon.

Ankara made her short sword disappear and caused her bow to reappear. In the flutter of a fly's wings, she had an arrow nocked and let it loose. Just as quickly, Terradyn—the red-haired man—swung his sword, slicing the arrow in two just before it reached his throat. She fired two more arrows, these at Raktas. He swatted both of them away with his pair of blades. They walked toward her, slowly, methodically, the presence of their magic pushing in on her. She could feel it, cutting off her flow, restricting her, constricting her like a giant snake. It pressed down and in. They were powerful mages in their own rights for seeming like such dumb brutes.

Ankara tried to cast a spell, but her power was just out of reach, her fingertips brushing it but unable to fully grasp it. They walked towards her, tattoos and eyes glowing blue. The sight must have emboldened the others as several knights emerged from their hiding places, and the three dwarves ran to her, Bryon Eleodum following them, carrying a sword that glowed purple. She could sense the deep magic in the weapon.

Terradyn smiled. He must have known she was desperately reaching for her power. She nocked another arrow and fired, this time at one of the dwarves. He was quick, much faster than the little, bearded midget looked and raised his shield just in time. She fired another arrow at one of the advancing knights. He wasn't as lucky and went to the ground, an arrow protruding from his chest.

"Stay where you are!" the man holding the purple sword yelled.

She fired at him. His blade blazed a blinding purple, and her arrow burned into black ash when it struck the magical steel.

Ankara reached for her magic again. It was there. Just there. Just out of reach. She could feel it. Touch it. And then ...

She fired again, this time at Terradyn and Raktas. The arrow separated into fire arrows, all five of them shooting stars of flame. Terradyn batted one away while Raktas deflected another. The man wielding the magical sword ducked away from yet another, but two of them struck the farmhouse, its wood immediately catching fire. Ankara lifted a hand. Her magic was there again. They were powerful mages, these two lackeys of Andragos, but not powerful enough. Thorny vines sprouted up everywhere, digging into ankles. Men screamed, and horses panicked, creepers crawling up their legs and drawing blood.

As men and dwarves and henchmen came at her, she noticed the single woman that had been standing just inside the home's fence. She now stood halfway out of the house's front door, watching with wide, worried eyes. She was related to Erik as well—a sister or cousin ... or lover. Ankara's eyes blazed green as she scanned the woman. Her blue eyes met Ankara's. She scanned the woman's mind. It was difficult. She was strong. Ankara instantly liked her.

So, Erik wasn't there. But where had he gone? She decided north but was unsure of where exactly. In her mind, she saw a land of ice. Hargoleth, she guessed.

She looked to those trying to surround her. She could kill most of them, but it would use much of her power, and that wasn't what she was there for. Even though she knew Terradyn and Raktas would still be able to see her, and that the dwarves would still sense her, she snapped a finger and became translucent again. She ran, despite the cries of "Coward!" and "Weakling!" The accusations made her laugh. She knew the truth ... and she would be back to show them just what a coward she was.

## 24

"What are you about?" Bu said.

He had stood by and watched, along with the man named Alger and the knight named Garrett, while the rest of his men, the dwarves, Bryon, Terradyn, and Raktas, and more farmers than Terradyn cared to count, worked diligently on saving the Eleodum farmhouse from fiery destruction.

"What do you mean?" Bryon said, wiping sweat and dirt from his face.

Simone cried, sitting against one of the main poles of the fence that surrounded her little garden in the front of her home, Turk the dwarf trying to comfort her all the while.

"We arrive, and then we are attacked," the Count Alger said. "Isn't it obvious what your king is asking?"

"He's not my king ..." Bryon began to say, but Terradyn cut him off.

He stepped forward, and the count stepped back, looking at Terradyn with worried eyes.

"You think we had some assassin hidden in the bushes, just waiting for you?" Terradyn asked. He could hear the grinding of his teeth echo through his head as he clenched his jaw. "You Hámonians truly are fools."

The count's face turned a bright red, but Bu put a hand on the man's shoulder.

"I did wonder what the bodyguards of the Black Mage were doing on a farm in the far western parts of Háthgolthane," Bu said, stepping forward.

Terradyn nodded.

"I might ask the same thing of you," Terradyn said, "Bu Al'Banan. An easterner—and a gutter rat traitor at that—pretending that he is the son of a great general and somehow weaseling his way into a kingship."

The knight Garrett stepped forward, hand on the handle of his sword, but Bu just laughed.

"I am nothing but a gutter shite," Bu replied, still smiling and chuckling, "but why wouldn't I take such an opportunity? The fates and eastern gods found it pleasing to them to find favor in me ... or I was in the right place at the right time. I could give a pig fart why, but what other choice did I have than seize such an opportunity? Or die trying. You and Raktas ... you serve the second most powerful man in Háthgolthane; some may even say the most powerful man. And, if I understand correctly, you are always by his side, even when he takes a shit and beds a woman, so what business would you have with the simple free folk of Háthgolthane?"

Bu's knights watched him with inquiring eyes as he bantered with Terradyn.

"It is, perhaps, concerning that agents of the east are here in the wilds of the west," Bu continued. "When I conquered Hámon, I found a contingent of soldiers and advisors, sent by the Lord of the East. Has he done the same with you? Is he still trying to extend his reach west, just as he has in the east?"

"We serve Andragos, the Messenger of the East," Raktas said, his voice hard as steel.

"And who does he serve?" Bu asked. "You must admit that it is odd ... or perhaps peculiar would be a better word for it, that we would find you here."

Bu pointed to both of Andragos' bodyguards.

"And, it is peculiar that—what I can only assume because of your presence—we then find ourselves under attack," Bu said, "and by an assassin that looked to be Isutan."

"I'm surprised you could see her," Raktas said, "what with you hiding away like some yellow-bellied sack of dung."

"I had a good enough view," Bu said, not falling into Raktas' goading trap even though his two knights, as admitted by their faces, took great offense to the accusation.

"So, what is your business, here, at the Eleodum farm?"

"Our business is ours to know," Terradyn replied.

Bu nodded.

"Very well," he replied. "But, of course, you can understand that I am now concerned, not only about our potential trade deal with the free farmers of these lands, but about eastern incursions into these lands."

"I am certain he is concerned about our well-being," Terradyn heard Bryon mumble, but no one else heard him.

"Of course we understand," Terradyn said, looking at Bryon. Erik's cousin rolled his eyes, not at Terradyn, but at Bu's feigned concern.

"There is only one reason she would have been here," Bryon said. "She was after Erik. Not you. Not our lands."

"Who isn't chasing after Erik?" Bu muttered. It was clear he didn't mean anyone else to hear him, and he looked up quickly, glancing at Terradyn, Raktas, and Bryon, but none of them revealed they heard his muttering. "Even so, I would like to contribute to the security of these lands. To Erik's family."

"How so?" Bryon asked.

"I will leave one of my knights, Sir Willard, and his four men-at-arms with you," Bu explained.

"We'll be fine," Bryon said.

Bu put up a hand.

"No, no," he said. "It is the least I can do."

"You are too kind," Bryon said, sighing deeply and rolling his eyes again.

"When I return to Hámon," Bu continued, "I will send another score of my own personal soldiers. And you needn't house them. They will simply camp on your lands if it pleases you."

Bryon shrugged.

"What choice do I have?" he asked.

"Wonderful," Bu said, ignoring the man's sarcasm. "I feel this is the beginning of a plentiful and equally advantageous alliance."

Bu bowed, his eyes always watching Terradyn and Raktas. He spoke with Sir Willard for a little while. He was the least impressive of the knights Bu had brought with him, his hair mostly gray even though his face showed a younger man who had seen perhaps forty winters and his armor bulky-looking on his thin frame. Bu was not a tall man, but he seemed to tower over this Willard, who looked none too happy about having to stay on the Eleodum farmstead. Bu never lost his smile, even though he pulled the knight close to him and whispered something into his ear. Terradyn couldn't tell if it was a threat or a promise, but the man's eyes went wide, and his abjection turned to a sincere willingness to serve however King Bu Al'Banan needed him to serve.

Terradyn sat in the dining area of the Eleodum farmhouse. There were many people there, other farmers who came to help quickly board up the gaping hole in the side of the house. It wasn't permanent, and the whole wall would need to be replaced at some point, but it would make do for the time being. Even so, the house was cold, small drafts escaping through uneven spaces wafting through the home. Bryon and Simone sat at the dining table, along with Turk and the other two dwarves—Nafer and Bofim. Erik's father,

Rikard was there as well as several other prominent farmers in the area.

"This cannot stand," Rikard Eleodum said. "Hámonians forcing their way into our homes."

"What choice do we have, Father?" Simone said, her eyes still red-rimmed from smoke and tears.

Rikard just shook his head.

"We fight," he said finally.

"They are not invading our lands, though," one of the other farmers, a man named Ermid said. "They want to help us. Think of the trade potential, Rikard."

"Bah," Rikard replied, waving a hand in the air. "Promises laced with poison is what they are."

"You cannot fight them," Terradyn said. "Maybe before, when a feudal king still ruled the Kingdom of Hámon, but not now. They may still embrace the backward ways of feudalism, but no doubt Bu is slowly turning the western kingdom into a mirror of eastern efficiency. And he controls close to thirty thousand men aside from his Hámonian vassals."

"What do you suggest then?" Rikard asked. He was a hard man, not easily intimidated. Terradyn liked him.

"You need to wait," Terradyn replied. There was no *we*. "Watch the Hámonians with careful eyes."

"That's it?" Rikard asked, throwing both his hands in the air. "That's your wise eastern advice?"

Terradyn just shrugged.

"Nafer will go to Thrak Balduükr," Turk said. "He will petition the northern dwarves to send help as well."

"They already help too much," Rikard said.

"Not supplies, or builders," Turk said. "Soldiers. Warriors. King Stone Axe may not be able to send much, but it will at least make the Hámonians second-guess an invasion ... and perhaps stem another assassination attempt. Nafer has agreed he will leave at sunrise."

"Then do we fight?" Rikard asked.

Terradyn shook his head as Raktas gave an almost inaudible chuckle.

"When do we fight?" Rikard asked.

"Brother," another man said. This was Brant Eleodum, Rikard's brother, and Bryon's father. "What is your obsession with fighting?"

"You don't," Terradyn replied.

"What do you mean?" Rikard asked, and Terradyn couldn't help noticing the looks everyone else gave him, all asking the same question.

"To fight would be to your death," Terradyn explained. "It would be the death of all your people. It doesn't matter how many dwarves come to your aid."

"Nordeth would help us," Brant said.

"It's a nice thought," Terradyn replied, shaking his head, "and I am sure Nordeth has no love for Hámon, especially now that Bu leads from Venton's throne. But to openly oppose him would result in war. The lords of Nordeth cannot risk open war with Hámon for a group of free farmers."

"We have been free farmers for over two hundred years," Rikard said, slamming his fist against the table. Simone flinched, and Brant put a hand on his brother's shoulder.

"Yes, you have," Terradyn replied, "but you are citizens to no one. No army has an obligation to protect you or defend you. The implications of action against Hámon by any other nation are too great. You are not a nation. You are alone in this."

"So if Hámon does become hostile," Rikard asked, "and if their desire to trade is just pretense, what do we do?"

"Relent or leave," Terradyn replied matter-of-factly. "You agree to become citizens and serfs of Hámon, or you leave. Those will be your choices."

Rikard sat back in his chair, his face screwing up into an angry scowl. He didn't like that answer. None of them did. But it was the only one Terradyn could give. It was insensitive, he knew that, but Terradyn was not one for sensitivities.

"Erik," Terradyn heard Simone whisper. "Where are you?"

She looked concerned and now angry. Terradyn wasn't an expert in love or emotions for that matter, but he could tell Simone loved Erik. But she was frustrated and upset, too. He had heard her on multiple occasions curse the man for leaving. Terradyn didn't blame her. She was pregnant and, even though she had family and friends to help her, he imagined they didn't fill the void an absent Erik left.

Terradyn looked at Raktas. He knew, now, what Andragos needed him to do.

"I will go after Erik," Terradyn said.

"He has been gone for weeks," Rikard said.

"Even so," Terradyn replied. "Raktas will stay here."

"What?" Raktas said in Shengu.

"Will you bring him back?" Simone asked.

"I will make sure he is safe," Terradyn said.

"You cannot be serious," Raktas said, still speaking in Shengu.

"This is what Master wants," Terradyn said. "I know it."

"When will you leave?" Bryon asked.

Terradyn stood. He looked to men gathered in the Eleodum home. This Erik ... he was different from other men. He was starting to see what his master saw. All the people who came to him, came to his wife and family, came to serve and protect what was his. Terradyn looked to the man's wife.

"Tonight," he said and walked out of the house.

## 25

*E*rik and Warrior traveled from sunrise to sunset for six consecutive days, and Erik continued to marvel at the horse's stamina; he never seemed to tire. As the woman from Örnddinas had told him, he traveled by or through other clan holdings—those for the Fox Clan, the Elk Clan, and the Horse Clan. Several paths or more minor roads crossed the busy main one that crossed Hargoleth, and Erik presumed they led to the country's other towns and holdings. Along the way, he saw other solo travelers like himself, families with carts, and many merchants and tradespeople. Wulfstaad seemed to be a popular destination.

The end of the week brought Erik to the home of the Wolf Clan, which sat at a fork in the road. The north road led to Durnfell, a strong ally to Wulfstaad according to the gossip Erik had heard on his short travels, and the southern road to Holtgaard. Knowing he needed to give both him and Warrior time to rest, he had gone in search of somewhere to stay for the night and settled on one of several alehouses named *The Golden Fish*.

With Warrior stabled nearby and feeding happily on a bale of hay, Erik ordered drink and food and then sat at a table outside the longhouse that had been converted into a tavern and the obligatory brothel. As evening in Wulfstaad fell, so did the temperature, and most people sat inside. Erik simply pulled his cloak tighter around his shoulders, and chose to stay where he was; he wasn't in the mood for idle conversation, even if it might have stopped his thought of Simone, his guilt ever-growing as he spent each day in the saddle.

A serving woman, tall and buxom with thick brown hair, appeared by his side as the open front door of the alehouse let out light and the sound of voices, loosened and loudened by drinking. She set a wooden bowl in front of Erik, accompanied by half a loaf of bread and a large tankard of ale. He handed the woman a nondescript silver coin, one with a wreath on one side and a faded face on the other. He didn't need anyone questioning where he was from based on what coinage he used. As she tucked the money into a pocket in her apron, she smiled at him and touched his shoulder gently.

"Let me know if you need anything else," she said in her northern language as she winked at him and then bit a corner of her lower lip. Her words were close enough to Dwarvish for him to understand what she said, but her meaning would have been clear in any tongue.

"I'll be fine, thank you," Erik said and gave her a quick smile

"I'll be around," the woman said as she shrugged before turning around to head back inside.

The stew was full of potatoes, carrots and celery, and dark meat that had been cubed evenly. The broth was even darker and rich and hot. Erik shivered as the food entered his belly, giving him satisfying warmth. The bread was dense, and even when Erik sopped up the broth, it maintained its texture. He nodded as he chewed, sipping the ale—a tasty, heavy, sweet brew—to wash down the food.

As he finally pushed the empty bowl towards the middle of the table, the door to the alehouse opened again, and a thin man came tumbling out of the building. Clearly drunk and resembling a puppet whose master has loosened the strings, he tripped and fell down the stairs backward, landing hard on his back. Another man, one dressed like a soldier walked down the steps with heavy feet and stood over the drunk. Two more similarly attired men followed him out of the alehouse and circled the hapless body lying in the dirt.

"Stupid, drunken Bear Clanner," the first of the soldiers said, kicking the drunk on his thigh.

"Thieves," the man garbled, his short, blond beard matted with blood and what looked like vomit.

"Imagine that," one of the other soldiers said, standing on one of the man's hands, "a Bear Clanner calling us thieves."

"The Ruling Stone is ours!" the drunk man shouted. He pulled his hand away and tried to stand, but the lead soldier put a foot on his chest and pushed him back.

Erik was about to empty his tankard of ale, but he froze when he said *Ruling Stone.* The man had been slurring, but, even in the drunken, northern tongue, the words were unmistakable. He was speaking of the Dragon Stone ... the Stone of Chaos.

One of the soldiers whispered something to the first, both looking in Erik's direction.

"You need something?" the first soldier asked, taking several steps towards Erik.

"No, sir," Erik replied, shaking his head and putting the tankard to his mouth.

"Mind your own damn business," the soldier commanded.

Erik nodded without lifting his head; he eyes fixed on the final dregs of ale.

"Another stupid foreigner," one of the other soldiers said.

As little as he had spoken, they must have recognized Erik's accent as he attempted their northern language, similar to Dwarvish. He would have to be careful.

"What do we do with this one?" one of the soldiers asked as two of them grasped the drunk man under his arms and pulled him to his feet.

"Get your hands off me!" the man yelled. "Don't you know who I am?"

The soldiers laughed, but Erik used the distraction to peer over his now empty tankard. The drunk wore a leather jerkin over his shirt and a thick wool coat over that and his woolen pants. He had a short-cropped beard of a dirty yellow with gray interspersed here and there. His hair was long, but not as long as most of the men of Hargoleth, stopping short of his shoulders. Even though he was tall, he didn't carry the same muscle as many of the northerners. He wasn't a laborer or farmer, Erik could tell that much.

"I'm Gris Beornson! Son of Orn Beornson, Lord of Holtgaard!" the man yelled, but most of the words ran together. Erik wasn't sure if he'd heard correctly, but he stored Gris away for potential future use.

"Sure," one of the soldiers said, "and I am a prince of Thrak Baldüukr."

All the soldiers joined in the laughter.

"Take him to the jail," the first soldier said. "Disturbing the peace. Being a drunk idiot. Being a Bear Clanner. We'll see what the judge wants to do with him in the morning."

"You can't do this!" the man shouted as the soldiers dragged him away.

He tried to fight them, digging his heels in the ground and trying to pull away, but he was drunk, and these soldiers were broad-shouldered and strong. They laughed the harder he fought, punching him in the ribs and kicking him as they took him down the street. Before they turned a corner and disappeared, the first soldier looked back at Erik and stared. Whatever he did, Erik would need to be careful.

## 26

O nce they were out of sight, Erik set out to follow at a distance. They seemed to be heading away from the center of the town and towards the main gatehouse that would house the jail. The man named Gris cursed and yelled the whole way, no matter how many times his captors punched or kicked him, and the noise caused residents of the few homes dotted along the road to come and see what the commotion was. Once they saw the men dragging a drunkard away, they went back inside.

The jail sat outside the clan holding's wall and gatehouse. A waist-high perimeter fence surrounded a small courtyard, which stood in front of a mid-sized building made of roughly hewn stone. In the light of torches fixed to the building's walls, Erik could see two similarly attired and armored soldiers that stood on either side of a thick wooden door. Holding round shields and long spears and wearing conical helms, they stood to a lazy attention as the small entourage passed by, opened the door, and then slammed it shut behind them.

Unsure how quickly he would need to leave should he get to talk to the drunk, Erik hurried back to the livery stable and collected

Warrior. Back at the jail, Erik and Warrior stood under a small copse of tall pine trees across the street. The clan holding was large and brightened by torches on long poles, but this part of the street was dark, the trees situated in front of a large building—perhaps once a home—that looked abandoned.

He waited for a while, and it started to rain. The precipitation was soft at first, but then hardened, the guards in front of the jail cursing as they tried to back up closer to the building. The rain quickly turned to sleet, which caused the guards to curse even more. Erik felt a sharp shiver move up his spine as, even protected by the pine trees, the cold took its toll. He removed a purple, soft cloth from one of Warrior's saddlebags—a gift from the ogre, Jamalel—and wrapped it around his shoulders. The ogre told him it would stave off the cold and, even though skeptical, he was hopeful. Within moments, a warmth wholly uncommon in the north spread through his body.

*What kind of magic is this?*

As the sleet struck the soft, smooth fabric, it melted and pooled, rolling off in large droplets like water rolling off the back of a duck. A loud snort from Warrior not only reminded Erik that his companion was there, but caught the attention of the guards across the street. The horse's huge muscles undulated as he shivered as well.

"I'm sorry, my friend," Erik said, eyeing the guards who, for a brief moment, stepped away from the jail and into the courtyard, peering into the darkness of Erik's hiding spot. He took one end of the purple cloth—it was several yards long, and he had folded it around his shoulders—and draped it over Warrior's neck. "Is that better?"

It took only a moment, but the horse pressed himself closer to Erik, almost knocking him over, and Erik suspected, if a horse could smile, Warrior—normally cantankerous and feisty—would have.

"Did you hear that?" one of the guards asked. It sounded like he intended to whisper, but his voice carried on the breeze, and Erik was not far away.

"It sounded like a horse," the same guard said.

The other guard nodded.

"Someone out there?" the first guard said, raising his voice. "Show yourself!"

Erik remained still and quiet, gently stroking Warrior's head with the back of his hand.

"Piss on this," came the voice of the other guard. "My breeches are wet, and I'm freezing. So what if someone is out there. What are they going to do?"

The first guard looked as if he was going to retort, but the door to the jail opened, and the original captors of the drunk Gris emerged as the two jail guards were halfway towards the fence, crouched down as they peered across the road.

"What by the nine hells are you two idiots doing?" the leader of the three men asked.

Both guards were startled, and the first turned and stood at attention while the other let his shoulders drop, looking dejected as if this was not the first time he'd been in trouble.

"There's something over there," the first guard said, poking a thumb in Erik's direction. "We heard something."

The leader looked back and forth between both guards, ignoring the ever-hardening sleet, and the thunder and distant lightning that had now joined it. With his lips pursed and his brows scrunched into a scowl, he shook his head in disbelief.

"This is exactly why you will never graduate from guarding a jail," the leader said with an accusatory finger pointing back and forth between both men. "You fools. Get back to your post and make sure the man we just brought in remains secure. If you don't, you'll be spending time in one of those cells."

The guards moved back to their positions in front of the door, one hurriedly and the other slowly, while the soldiers walked through the gap in the fence and into the street. Their pace suggested a swift return to the alehouse, and without giving a look towards the pine trees, they began talking and laughing despite the weather.

"I could go for something warm to drink," the first of the jail guards said after some more time had passed, clearly shivering as he unsuccessfully avoided the now almost horizontal sleet.

Erik raised an eyebrow. He had a wineskin of his uncle's spiced wine. The man didn't drink anymore, and so he had barrels of the stuff and gave some to Erik as a parting gift. "Something to keep you warm on a cold night," Bryon's father had said. Erik had considered leaving it behind, wanting to make space for only the essentials, but it was good wine, and now he was glad he took it with him. He could use it as a bargaining tool.

"Shut up," the other guard hissed. "I just want this night to end."

"But you wouldn't say no to a drink," the first guard insisted.

"With you, I would," the second guard muttered.

Now was as good a time as ever, and Erik removed the purple cloth from his shoulders and Warrior's neck. The cold immediately bit at his flesh, and Warrior snorted angrily. The first guard looked at the other, eyes wide.

"I didn't hear anything," the second guard said.

The first guard was about to retort when Erik walked his horse into the road, approaching the fence and open gate built into its middle.

"You see," the first guard whispered, looking at the other before turning his narrow-eyed gaze towards Erik. "Stop right there."

Erik slowed, but he didn't stop, gingerly stepping to avoid slipping on the ice that had formed over the flattened and evened road. When he reached the fence that surrounded the jail, he stared at the two men but kept going, moving in front of Warrior so the horse would follow him.

"I said stop," the first guard said again. "Are you deaf?"

The other guard just watched Erik, and he couldn't tell if the guard was indifferent or planning a move.

"No," Erik said, walking towards the two men. He let go of Warrior's rein and slowly lifted his hands in a show of peace.

The first guard finally lowered his spear and began crouching into a fighting stance, but Erik suspected neither of these men were adept fighters. It was why they were stationed in front of a jail that most likely held the likes of pickpockets and drunks, those not even bad enough for a real prison.

"Steady now," Erik said. "No need for this to get ugly."

"What do you want?" the second guard finally asked.

"And where are you from?" the first guard asked. "Your accent sounds funny."

"Do you have a stable?" Erik asked. "Even a long overhang would do. Just a place to get my horse out of the weather."

"No," the first guard said. "The stables are for our horses."

"Oh, I see," Erik said. "And you have horses in there right now?"

"No," the second guard replied. "But you still can't put your horse in there."

Erik looked over his shoulder at Warrior.

"Some hospitality, eh?" he said, and the horse snorted.

"What do you want?" the first guard said, lowering his spear even more.

"As well as shelter for this poor animal, I'd like to have a word with your guest," Erik said.

"Our guest?" the first guard asked, clearly not understanding Erik's insinuation.

"Out of the question," the second guard said, partially rolling his eyes at his companion. "We are on orders to let no one disturb the prisoner."

"Oh, yeah, right," the first guard said, now getting Erik's meaning. "Where are you from?"

"Who gives a damn where he's from?" the other guard hissed.

"Tell me your names, and I'll tell you where I'm from," Erik said.

"No," the second guard said.

"Brand," the first guard replied, just as the second guard tried denying Erik his request. "And that's Adils. Now, where are you from?"

"You idiot," the second guard—Adils—muttered, rubbing a hand over his face.

The first guard was a fool, a man who couldn't make the normal militia that roamed the city outside the walls of Wulfstaad, so he was stuck with the most menial of guard duties. But the second man—Adils—there was something about him—the way he looked at Erik and his companions before they left, the way he moved, the way he took his time before speaking or acting. All that spoke of an experienced man ... an experienced soldier.

"Háthgolthane," Erik replied. "You both look cold and wet."

"What gave you that impression?" Adils asked, rolling his eyes. He looked at Brand. "Looks like we have a bright one here. Someone even more stupid than you."

Erik couldn't help chuckling.

"Did I hear someone mention a warm drink?" Erik asked. "What if I said my horse here would share some spiced wine with you if you'd let him use the stable. He looks big and grumpy, but he can be generous when treated properly.

Both men looked at him, Adils' eyes squinted, and Brand's went wide.

"You have spiced wine?" Brand asked.

"No, you idiot," Adils said, huffing and looking at his companion, "and if he did, it wouldn't be hot."

Adils gave Erik a hard look.

"What do you really want?"

"As I said, I want to talk to the man you have locked up in there," Erik said.

"Out of the question," Adils replied.

"But I do have spiced wine," Erik said. "It's in the saddlebags."

"See," Brand said in an almost mocking tone.

"You would only need to heat it up," Erik said before he added, "and I have money."

"Nope," Adils said. "Ari finds out and it'll be us behind bars in here."

Erik presumed Ari was the boss who had thrown Gris out of the alehouse and brought him to the jail. Erik stepped closer as if he had a secret to tell, and despite the freezing sleet pummeling his face, a small, seductive smile spread across his lips. While keeping his eyes level, looking from one guard to the next, he retrieved a small pouch on his belt and jiggled it. It clanked with coin, and he reached in, pulling out a Hámonian pound between his thumb and forefinger.

Erik was a wealthy man in any city, country, or continent, wealth mostly taken from the lost city of Orvencrest and its treasury room-turned-dragon lair. He had left most of his wealth at home, but he knew occasions like this might arise, so he brought enough to bribe people for information or to buy his way out of sticky situations.

"Three a piece," Erik said.

"Three," Brand gasped, but Adils shook his head.

"People will ask where we got it," he said. "I recognize Hámonian pounds, and they aren't common around here. Gold isn't much common here."

"We'll be rich," Brand said in almost a whisper.

Adils shot him a hard look.

"Hardly," he retorted, "but we'll be suspicious if we try to spend it, that's for sure."

This Adils was smart for a common jailor, furthering Erik's suspicions that he had screwed up somewhere, somehow, and this duty was his punishment.

"I have silver instead," Erik replied. "Finnish nickels, nondescript for the most part, and I'll give you ten a piece, and you can still have the Hámonian pounds as well. Use them sparingly."

Adils squinted, watching Erik for a moment. Erik wanted to say something. He wanted to sweeten the offer, either with more money or with his words, but if watching his father in the Hámonian markets taught him one thing, it was to avoid overselling. Make an offer, sweeten it a bit—not with everything you're willing to give up—and wait for a response, no matter how long it took. And that's what he'd do, no matter how hard the sleet fell, and no matter how cold and wet he was.

"What do you want with the man?" Adils finally asked.

"Just to talk," Erik replied, trying to be nonchalant.

"Why?" Adils asked.

"Who cares," Brand said, almost a whimper in his voice. Clearly, the enticement of spiced wine and money had gotten the better of him.

"Shut up," Adils hissed, looking at Brand and then turning his attention back to Erik.

Erik eyed the man for just a moment, and then smiled.

"He knows a man who has something that is mine," Erik said. "I want to know where this man is. He knows where he is."

Lying didn't come easy to Erik, and he disliked doing it, but at times, it seemed a necessity. He told himself he was simply stretching the truth.

Adils stretched out a hand.

"Coin first," he said.

"Let me stable my horse," Erik replied. "And I'll bring the wine."

"Very well," Adils said and pointed with his head towards the right side of the building.

Erik walked Warrior around the side of the jail and found a simple stable that was small, perhaps large enough for two horses, and leaky, but it would do. Warrior was clearly in a bad mood, but he seemed to calm when Erik retrieved the purple cloth again and draped it over the horse's neck and shoulders.

"That should help a little," he said, and the horse bobbed his head.

He lifted the flap of one of his saddlebags and grabbed a wineskin and an apple. The latter was gone in two bites, and Erik patted Warrior on the cheek before he returned to the two guards. His fingers were almost numb, but he sorted out the required coins and placed Hámonian pounds in the men's palms, along with the Finnish nickels.

"And the spiced wine?" Adils asked.

Erik lifted the wineskin.

"If you have a place to heat it up," he said.

Adils nodded.

"Inside," the guard said, jerking his head toward the door. "You can talk to the prisoner."

Erik smiled with a bow. With the money and the thought of the wine, Adil's mood seemed to have mellowed. As Erik moved to follow him, Brand eyed the wineskin, a small smile cracking his lips.

## 27

*T*he jail seemed bigger than it appeared from the outside. The guards' room was functional enough, with a large fireplace at one end and a table at the other. A thick wooden door stood in the middle of the rear wall, a large lock on the handle and bars covering a small opening centered and toward the top. After leaning his spear and shield against the wall, Brand sat at the table and plopped his mud-covered boots on one of the other chairs. Adils poured Erik's spiced wine into a large, black, iron pot that hung over a blazing fire that warmed the room and began to dry Erik's clothing quickly.

"Get your damned feet off my chair," Adils said, kicking Brand behind his knee and then wiping errant mud from the seat with a damp sleeve of his wool tunic before he sat down.

A few minutes later, Brand took a hearty draft of the wine and smacked his lips.

"It's good," he said.

"The best," Erik replied, his back to the guards as he warmed his hands by the fire.

"I don't know about that," Adils said, and Erik smiled to himself, knowing that he was only partially lying. The wine was good, but this man had a rich taste. He was a leader ... once.

"Now, you have your money and your wine," Erik said, turning to face them and the room. "Let me talk to the prisoner."

"Leave your sword," Brand said, waving a loose hand towards where he'd left his spear and shield.

Erik looked to Adils, who pursed his lips for a moment and then shook his head slightly.

"My sword stays with me," Erik said, looking from one to the other with what he hoped was his best look of defiance.

"You know that can't happen," Adils replied, but Erik could tell his heart wasn't really up for a fight. His Uncle Brent's wine was working its magic.

"Why not? I go in and see the prisoner, and you close the door behind me. If I kill him, the door is locked. What can I do? You call the militia and have them throw me behind bars instead. All I want is information."

"And what do we say when they ask why you were in there in the first place?" Brand said, standing and poking a finger at Erik.

"Tell them I took you by surprise," Erik replied. "Tell them I led you in here at sword point, but then you got the better of me and threw me in the cell block."

"Oh, right," Brand said, throwing his head back and rolling his eyes. "That'll be great. Just what Ari would want to hear. That we were overtaken by a single man. Then I'll never make the militia."

Erik couldn't help hearing the soft sigh Adils gave, or see his chin fall to his chest as he ever so slightly shook his head and rubbed his face.

"You're here for a reason," Erik said. "Aren't you? There's nothing more they can take away from you, is there?"

Adils gave Erik a hard look.

"Look, I don't want to kill this man," Erik explained. "I simply want to talk to him. But I won't give up my sword. I've given you the coin. I've given you the wine."

Adils stared at Erik for a few moments, barely blinking, and then he finally gave a quick nod.

"Alright," Adils said.

"What?" Brand said.

"Shut up," Adils said. He stood and retrieved a large ring of keys from his belt, walking to the door in the middle of the rear wall, one eye always on Erik.

"As soon as we are done with the wine, you're done talking to the prisoner," said Adils.

"Fair enough," Erik said.

"And if he winds up dead, or harmed ..."

"You needn't worry," Erik added, lifting his hands up defensively.

Adils unlocked the door, and as it opened, the creak spoke of rusty hinges in need of oil.

"Remember what I said," said Adils, and Erik nodded before walking through the doorway. He expected the door to close after him, but all he heard was the scrape of Adils' chair on the stone floor as he sat down again.

Three steps led down into a narrow corridor lined by three cells on either side—stone on three sides and bars facing inwards. Two torches hung on either side of the door, and two more hung on the far wall, directly opposite where Erik stood. He stepped down into the jail and peered through the bars of all cells. They were all empty except the last one on the right. It was dark inside, but he could see the silhouette of a man curled up in one corner. He looked like he was covered in straw, and Erik heard heavy breathing coming from the shadows, a drunk man's breathing.

"Wake up," Erik said loudly.

A groan met his command, and the silhouette shifted momentarily and then went still again.

"I said ..." Erik began, but the groan grew in volume.

"I bloody heard you," a voice croaked.

The shadow of a man, at first lying in a ball, moved to his hands and knees, slowly pushing himself upright, and then standing on wobbly legs. He shuffled forward. The light in the jail was dim, but the man squinted nonetheless as some of it spilled across his face. One of his eyes was almost swollen shut, and his lower lip was puffy.

"What do you want?"

"You took quite a beating," Erik said.

"I've had worse," the man—Gris—replied, his words slurred from residual alcohol and muffled from puffy, split lips.

"But have you ever been thrown in jail before?" Erik asked, remembering the man's claim to be a lordling.

The man looked as if he was thinking for a moment, swaying slightly back and forth, and then he sighed deeply.

"No."

"You've come all this way," Erik said, "to Wulfstaad ... alone."

Gris looked at him, squinting his one good eye as much as he could.

"You're a ... a ... a bloody foreigner, and you speak ..." Gris hiccupped and looked like he might vomit, "speak as if you know how ... how far Holtgaard is from here," Gris said and spat blood filled spittle mixed with bile on the floor. "No. I'm not alone. Or, at least, I wasn't."

"Bodyguards?" Erik asked.

Gris nodded slowly.

"Where are they now?"

Gris just shrugged.

"Left you to rot in a Wolf Clan jail," Erik added.

"I'm hardly rotting," Gris replied and then curled the good side of his lip, "even if I do smell like wet dog and bear scat."

Gris sighed heavily again.

"I'm tired," he said. "Unless you want to ... to continue this pleasant banter, I think I ... I think I am going to go back to my corner and fall asleep."

"You said something about the Ruling Stone," Erik said as the man turned his back to him.

Gris stopped, and his back straightened.

"What of it?" he said, his back still to Erik, his voice a little less inebriated.

"What is it to you?"

"You truly are a foreigner, aren't you?" Gris asked.

"Is it obvious?" Erik asked. He, of course, knew what the Dragon Stone was to Rako—a prison—and he knew that the stone was important, but a part of him wanted to know what importance these people placed on the artifact.

"It is ... the stone is the symbol of power in Hargoleth," Gris explained.

"And Wulfstaad stole it from your father?"

"No," Gris replied, teetering a bit. "But it's a ... a technicality. It was once ours, long ago, when the elves first gave it to my people."

"The elves?" Erik asked. He silently cursed Dewin, knowing he hadn't told him everything. Why would the elves have given the men of Hargoleth something so important?

"Why do you care?" Gris asked, rubbing his face gingerly and leaning forward to get a closer look at Erik.

"No reason," Erik said.

*They have no idea. No idea what they possess.*

"You've come in here, probably paying those idiot jailors, to talk to me—a beat-up drunk—for no reason," Gris replied with a slight chuckle. "I may be drunk ... and my father may call me a fool every day, but I'm no idiot."

Gris pointed a finger at Erik, just to make his point as he wobbled on his feet. Erik looked down for a moment. He knew he couldn't give too much away. He couldn't trust anyone here—not yet—and they couldn't trust him. He was a foreigner, after all.

"I'm concerned, that's all," Erik said.

Gris stepped forward, just one step, and then belched loudly, sharing his alcohol-fueled breath with Erik.

"Concerned about what?" he asked.

"I want to see that the stone is safe," Erik said, trying not to step away.

"Why?" Gris asked. "You're a foreigner. From where?"

The man teetered slightly again, his eyes closing halfway and his head tilting back. He was still drunk, even though his beating and a bit of sleep had sobered him a little. His eyes opened, and he lowered his head, his swollen eyes meeting Erik's.

"You're from Hámon ..." Gris slurred. "I can tell ... by your accent."

"No," Erik replied.

"Enough of their pompous *little* nobles have come through Holt-gaard," Gris said, showing a narrow gap between his thumb and fore-finger to demonstrate how small he thought the Hámonian nobles were, "for me to know a Hámonian ... when I see one."

"I'm not from Hámon," Erik replied, "but I hail from the same area."

"A Hámonian who gives two bear farts about the Ruling Stone," Gris declared, talking more to himself than Erik. Then, he shrugged. "Why?"

He looked at Erik again, his face reddening more than it already was.

"You want it, don't you?" Gris hissed, sobering even more with his realization.

"No," Erik said. "I just want to make sure it's safe. It is more than what you think it is."

"So, what is it?" Gris asked suspiciously.

"Important," Erik said. "That's all you need to know."

"I'm tired," Gris said with a sigh. He began to shuffle away. "I'm not telling you any more."

Erik pressed himself against the bars of the cell, extended his arm and hand in and grabbed a piece of the man's shirt and pulled him into the bars. Drunk and injured, Gris couldn't fight it, even though he tried. As Erik pulled him closer, he gripped the back of the man's neck and pulled his face into the cell's bars. Pressing Gris' cheek into the iron clearly sent a shock of pain through his body as he gasped.

Erik had never bullied anyone in his life before—and didn't like doing it—but felt he had no choice.

"Listen to me, you lordling prick," Erik sneered, his voice low, hoping Adils or Brand didn't hear the commotion of a man slamming into the iron bars, "you will tell me about this Ruling Stone, and I will then leave you be and spare you your miserable life. If I know only one thing about nobles, it is that they prize their lives over everything else—honor, respect, and faith included."

"Stop," Gris cried, "you're hurting me."

"Then tell me what I want to know."

Erik pressed Gris' face even harder into the bars. Several scabbed over cuts on his face began to bleed again, and he cried and drooled.

"Fine, fine, fine," Gris bleated.

"When did the elves give you this stone?"

"Years ago," Gris said. "I don't know how long ago. Centuries."

"Why?"

"I don't know," Gris said. The violence seemed to sober him a bit. "Protection. Safe-keeping some say. Although, I don't know what could be safer than something hidden within the forests of Ul'Erel?"

"Have you always known it as the Ruling Stone?"

"As far as I know," Gris replied.

"And why was it passed from Holtgaard to Wulfgaard?"

"The other clans decided it," Gris said. "Years ago. They said the Bear Clan was too powerful and was becoming too tyrannous. I am going to steal it back. Then, perhaps my father will think me worthy of replacing him as Lord of Holtgaard."

"I see," Erik said, releasing his grip on Gris, just a bit. "Where is it kept ... this Ruling Stone?"

Gris looked at Erik, tears filling his eyes, blood covering his face, and vomit dribbling off his lips. He waited a while, just watching.

"Where?" Erik said, pressing the man's face even harder against the bars.

"Supposedly in Wulfstaad's keep!" Gris yelped, and Erik eased the pressure just a little.

"Go on," said Erik.

"This guard I bribed said it's in the Lord's Chambers when he is away and then in his throne room when he is in."

"And you mean to steal it from the most well-guarded place in the clan holding?" Erik asked. "You're father's right. You are a fool."

"My men are the best thieves. When I get out of here, we will find a way. Now let me go!"

Erik released his hold on the so-called lordling, and the man staggered back into the cell, rubbing his neck where his clothes had been tightened around it.

"Doesn't seem like a well thought out plan," Erik said. "Doomed to failure, if you ask me."

"You sound like my father," Gris said, and at that moment, he seemed like a little petulant child even though he was perhaps twice Erik's age.

"Where are your thieves now?" Erik asked.

Gris didn't answer. He hurried back into the cell, vomited in a corner, and curled up into a ball, groaning. Erik knew he'd not get anything more from this pathetic drunk, but he had made some progress. Erik didn't care which clan held the stone, and certainly had no interest in the broader politics of Hargoleth or any other nation. All he knew was he needed to get it to an elf named El'Beth El'Kesh, and in her hands, the stone would save the world and release the trapped spirit of his friend Rako ... and hopefully keep his family safe.

The door to the cellblock opened, and Adils stood there, silhouetted by the flood of light from the guardroom.

"Wine is gone," the guard said, "your time is up."

Erik gave Gris one more glance before walking to the open door. He looked at the guard.

"I trust the wine was good."

"It was good," Adils said, his cheeks only a little red from the drink, "but I've had better."

"I don't doubt that," Erik said, looking the man over with a cocked eyebrow. "I would like to know your story someday."

Adils shook his head.

"None of your business," he said. "My story is mine to know. No one else."

"I figured you were the type of man to say that," Erik said as he squeezed by the guard and stepped into the guardroom.

Brand was hunched over in his chair, head resting on the table and breathing heavily. Adils kicked one of the table's legs, and his companion jolted up.

"Ari will have your ass if he sees you like this," Adils said, and then mumbled, "idiot."

Erik didn't wait for the guard to dismiss him; he just opened the door and stepped outside. Both the wind and the temperature had dropped, and the sleet had been replaced by a soft snow, falling gently and sticking to the icy ground. He walked around the corner to the stable, and when Warrior saw him, the horse snorted.

"Are you ready?" Erik asked.

The horse bobbed his head, and Erik patted its great neck affectionately.

"Tonight we need to find an inn, not a busy alehouse, but something off the beaten path. Tomorrow, we go to visit a lord."

---

## 28

*S*yzbalo stood on the platform of the black stoned keep, looking out over the city of Fen-Aztûk. This city wasn't always called Fen-Aztûk, of course, but when the Aztûkians fled Fen-Stévock for fear of death at the hands of the Lord of the East's father, they assumed this old, Mek-Ba'Dunian city for themselves and renamed it after their namesake. He growled as the words *cowards* and *traitors* passed through his mind.

The Lord of the East watched as the people below went about their daily tasks, and occasionally, some of them would chance a cautious but cold glance in his direction. Even if he was their ruler and the keep, even though it was the home of the Aztûkian ruling family, was technically his, the Aztûkians had a long history of being enemies of the Stévockians—Syzbalo's family. They didn't like him at best, despised him at worst, and most still held allegiances to the Aztûkian family, even if they pretended to bow to the seat of Golgolithulian power in Fen-Stévock.

It was a beautiful city, and even Syzbalo, who admired little beyond himself, could admit that much. The shore of the Giant's Vein was almost like a beach, where land met the ocean. And the land around this city was green and lush, whereas the development around Fen-Stévock had robbed much of the surrounding land of its vegetation; since a dragon's attack, much was barren and brown.

Fen-Aztûk offered a mix of Háthgolthanian and Antolikan architecture, with the vibrant colors and flat rooftops of the plains people of Mek-Ba'Dune and the solid, stone structures of Golgolithul. Its people were just as diverse as well, with a population roughly a quarter the size of Fen-Stévock.

The Lord of the East hadn't been to the city since he was a boy, and never since he had assumed power from his father. Indeed, he seldom traveled across the Giant's Vein. He didn't want to. He had his sights set on the west, but most of his people, his generals, and the nobles of Golgolithul still found interest in Antolika. So he used their interest as an excuse to meet with the Black Tigress, placate Po, and, most importantly, do the bidding of this Lord of Chaos, the creature that had given him much power as of late. He looked down and watched three goblins sneer at people as they walked by. He had hoped to keep them hidden, but that hope had been in vain. It wasn't all bad, however. Akzûl was proving to be a loyal and adept commander. He didn't hesitate to decapitate one of his own warriors when he found out the goblin had raped one of the serving girls in the Lord of the East's company. And under his command, the other goblins restrained themselves as best they could, although Syzbalo was very aware of the disapproving looks and hushed comments his own troops gave.

Traveling to Fen-Aztûk was also an excuse to check up on one of the only cities that still housed nobles in his empire that still openly opposed him. And as he stood there and watched the city, he realized how much it needed to be brought under his heel.

"What troubles my lord's mind?"

Most wouldn't be able to tell the voices of Kimber and Krista apart, the whispering, almost hissing, way in which they spoke, but he could. The witches had come to him five years ago after he had accepted the counsel of Melanius, the old Isutan wizard. They were still somewhat of a mystery to him and, at first, his original, boyhood advisor—Andragos—didn't see any harm in the women. They were mages in their own right, with the power of foresight and predications. In fact, Andragos appreciated their contributions to matters of the state.

Syzbalo still didn't know from where they came, exactly, and going by their appearance, it was two very different places. But they were always together. Over time, as their predictions and visions proved almost always correct, he began to trust them more and more.

Syzbalo never thought he would take a wife. He didn't know why. His father had kept him from gaining any sort of relationship with his mother, and then she had died when he was young, and he figured, with the help of both Andragos and Melanius, he would live a thousand years and, at some point, he would just find a woman to take his seed and bear him an heir. But two years ago, he held counsel with both witches, and they spoke of Golgolithul's advancement east, and then of its advancement west ... of what its future could look like. They drank wine while they spoke, a deep, sweet, strong red wine and, before Syzbalo knew what had happened, he found himself in bed with both of the women. Ever since then, he had not only enjoyed their flawless counsel but their company in his bedchamber as well.

He turned away from the city below, and the sight of the Giant's Vein's shoreline, to look at Krista, with her jet-black hair, her dark brown skin, and her deep, emerald green eyes. She stepped closer to him, her red lips pouting playfully as her body's movement caused her dress to hug her body and, especially, her unfettered breasts. He finally lifted his eyes from them but did not speak.

"I asked what troubles your mind, my lord."

"I heard you. There is nothing," Syzbalo replied.

"My lord has no reason to lie to me," Krista said, putting a hand on his bare chest and moving it up to his shoulder as she sauntered around him, her fingertips brushing his skin as she stroked his back and then moved in front of him again, leaving her hand on his shoulder.

"Where is Kimber?" Syzbalo asked, and she shrugged. "I thought you two were always together?"

"Perhaps, from time to time," Krista whispered, moving behind him and wrapping her arms around his chest, pressing her mouth close to his ear, "I would like to have you all to myself."

Syzbalo smiled.

"Now, no more lies," Krista whispered. "What troubles my lord?"

He thought for a moment, knowing that, if he let his guard down, his witch could—and would—read his mind. At times, they were able to read even Andragos' mind and, as much as Syzbalo hated to admit it, his old advisor was still more powerful than he was. That would soon change, however.

"This place troubles me," the Lord of the East replied. "Its very existence is a mockery to my rule."

"Then burn it to the ground," Krista said.

"I cannot," Syzbalo replied.

"Are you not the Emperor of the East?" she asked.

"Not yet," the Lord of the East admitted.

"You want these people to respect you," Krista said, "as their ruler."

"Yes," the Lord of the East replied.

"You must make them fear you," Krista said, running one of her hands down Syzbalo's well-defined chest, over his stomach, and into the front of his billowing, black, cloth trousers. "And you must make them love you ... all at the same time."

Syzbalo tilted his head back and closed his eyes as Krista worked a different kind of magic.

"How do I do that?" he asked.

"You must make an example of those who oppose you," Krista whispered as she played with Syzbalo's manhood. "Create a scenario in which you are justified in making them pay for their insolence."

"I should create a lie that allows me to execute the families who hate me?" Syzbalo asked, grabbing Krista's hand and removing it from his pants, turning to face her.

She smiled, biting her lower lip.

"Reveal an old inequity, something that only one of these families must pay for," she explained. "You should say that another one of these families—one that opposes you—has brought information, evidence of treason to your attention."

Syzbalo cocked an eyebrow.

"The family that brought you information will be upset at first, but you will explain to them that you will protect them, shower them with riches, make their sons generals and their daughters ladies," Krista said. "They will relent eventually and go along with the plan. Others will begin to question their own loyalty. And when you execute only the patron of this fated family, and his oldest son, sparing the rest as a sign of mercy, the people will begin to question the lies the Stévockians have told them for years."

"Should I punish the Stévockians?" the Lord of the East asked.

"No," Krista replied. "But a family of high rank. Then, lower taxes in Fen-Aztûk. Repair broken buildings and send seed and workers free of charge. The people will begin to love you ... as I love you."

Syzbalo forced a quick laugh. She didn't love *him*; she loved his power, and so did Kimber. But what did he think about her, about them? He wasn't sure he knew what love truly was. They were hungry for power, and so was he, and he didn't know if he had ever loved someone. He would like to think that he loved his mother, but his memories of her were sparse. He certainly didn't love his father. That man was unlovable, but he had respected him. The only other person in his life that he could think of, the only other person that he might have had some affection for ... perhaps even loved, was Andragos.

The thought of his former advisor made him scowl.

"What?" Krista said, seductively but she kept her hands still. "What else troubles you?"

Syzbalo was hesitant. No, he didn't love Krista, but he decided, at that moment, he trusted her ... her and Kimber, but how much? How much could he reveal to her?

"Tell me," Krista said, pressing herself close to him as her fingers ran up the inside of his thigh. He could feel her breath on his neck as she looked up at him. He could feel her magic, pulsing through her body like blood, transferring to his.

"It's Andragos," he said.

Krista growled as he spoke the Messenger's name.

"He frustrates me," Syzbalo said. "I feel like he opposes me."

"It's because he does, my lord," Krista replied.

The Lord of the East gritted his teeth and pulled her hand away.

"He has served Golgolithul for centuries," he said. "Through regime changes, government changes, wars, collapse, and rising to power ... ever since the fall of Gileliveren, he has served the east, but now he opposes me?"

"It is because he thinks he is more powerful than you," Krista said. She wrapped her arms around his waist, kissing his chest. "He has been serving the east for a thousand years, and yet, he has never been ruler. He feels slighted, and as you look to move the east into the future, he sees fragmentation. He looks to depose you, my lord. With the Lord of Chaos blessing you ... blessing us with more power, soon, you will no longer need the Black Mage. Truly, you do not need him now."

*Us.* How did the Lord of Chaos bless *them?* Syzbalo was about to question the slip, but as he looked at Krista, he began to understand. She was a part of his future. Kimber was too. Andragos was not. But how? Why? The Messenger of the East, the man who tutored him as a child, taught him everything he knew, spent more time with him than his father ... he was like his father. But as he looked down at Krista, looked into her eyes, he knew she was right. His time had passed. After a thousand years, his reign as the Herald of the East had finally seen its end.

"Come, my lord," she said, tugging on his waist, "let me take your mind off such troubling things ... at least for a little while."

Syzbalo followed Krista into the royal bedchamber of Fen-Aztûk's keep, but he didn't think anything could take his mind off his troubles.

## 29

With Kimber and Krista on either side of him, The Lord of the East sat atop a large carriage made of Yellow Wood, a tree that grew throughout the southern and central ranges of Antolika and bore a large, green fruit that was too tart for Syzbalo's tastes. The bark of the tree was a deep gray, but its wood was a bright yellow, giving it a golden quality. Artisans had filled the etchings and inlays of the carriage with gold and a train of twenty pure white horses drew it. Syzbalo knew it was ostentatious, but he couldn't resist taking it for himself after he had killed the previous owner.

They passed three wooden poles, all holding men, naked and beaten, their hands and feet nailed to the wood. The youngest of the three—a middle son of the Askari family who had spit in the face of Melanius as he came to arrest the man's father and eldest brother—was already dead, his mother curled up into a ball at the foot of his final resting place, still sobbing and ignoring the fact that her dress was torn and bloody.

The eldest Askari son was near death, his breathing slow, his arms stretched above his head, putting pressure on his diaphragm, and his eyes closed as consciousness waned. He was just over thirty winters old with a family of his own. But the last man—an older middle-aged man—glared at the Lord of the East through a bruised and puffy face as the carriage passed by. He pushed up against the nails in his feet, even though it caused excruciating pain. He refused to scream out.

The Lord of the East had chosen the Askari family as his example. They were a prominent family in Golgolithul and strong supporters of the Aztûkians, always speaking out against the actions Syzbalo took. They owned lands throughout the east, and he found it much easier than he had expected to convince the Martûkians to turn on the Askarians. They were loyal to the Aztûkians as well, but when offered the Askarian lands and a more important role in the Golgolithulian government—and presented with the reality that the Lord of the East was only going to grow more and more powerful—Samandar Martûk gladly created some accusation of treason against the Askarians, giving Syzbalo every right to exterminate the whole family. He presented himself as a merciful leader when he agreed to only crucify Gert Askari and his eldest son—although one of his middle sons made the fatal mistake of resisting—and then remove their family's title of nobility—something they had held since before the Battle of Bethuliam.

After having Gert and his two boys beaten, stripped of their clothes, and nailed to wooden poles to be displayed for anyone leaving or entering Fen-Aztûk, he promised Timrûk Aztûk III— current patriarch of the Aztûkians—slaves, workers, seed, and gold as soon as he returned safely to Fen-Stévock. Timrûk graciously accepted, and the Lord of the East couldn't help recognizing a look of defeat on the man's face. He finally realized that resistance against the current Golgolithulian regime was futile. In confidence, they spoke frankly of Patûk Al'Banan, Pavin Abashar, and some of the other generals who had defected and had opposed Syzbalo and his father. Timrûk admitted that he had financially supported some of them for a while, but hadn't sent anything to Patûk or Pavin in over four years, and the Lord of the East couldn't help thinking he may have finally defeated the Aztûkians, politically, and, perhaps, earned their loyalty ... as much as he ever would.

Gert Askari, daring death to take him, tried to spit at the Lord of the East as they passed by, but his lips were so bruised, bloody, and cracked, that the spittle simply dribbled down his chin and onto his naked chest.

"He is a bold man, isn't he?" Syzbalo suggested.

"It is pretense," Krista whispered in her hissing tone.

"Perhaps," Syzbalo replied, "but still ... I wonder if he would have been a better ally, seeming so stubborn and strong."

"Sometimes, to gain much," Kimber said, "we must make a costly sacrifice. Surely, the gods will look upon such a sacrifice with favor and continue to bless you with power."

"He should have seen this coming," Akzûl added, and the Lord of the East looked over his shoulder at the leader of the Black Wolves. The goblin had a grotesque smirk on his face and licked his lips as they passed by the dying patriarch. "You men have little knowledge in the ways of deception."

"What makes you think you can speak in the presence of the mighty Lord of the East?" Melanius said, pointing a long, thin finger at the goblin as the witches seethed.

"And who are you, feeble conjuror?" Akzûl replied.

Syzbalo put a hand up.

"Stop this," he said. "Akzûl is an advisor just as you are."

Melanius looked like he might say something else, but he relented with a quick bow.

"You have input on the matter?" Syzbalo asked of the goblin.

"You men think strength is the most important attribute," Akzûl said, "but we value cunning and guilefulness more."

"Maybe it's because you are so small in stature," Melanius mocked.

"Perhaps," Akzûl said, spreading his hands and giving the magician a feigned bow. "Coming from an Isutan, who somehow weaseled his way into the confidence of the most powerful man in Háth-golthane."

"Enough!" the Lord of the East yelled, standing.

He swiped an arm out in a wide arc, and the magic that Melanius was conjuring dissipated, but at the same time, Akzûl's eyes widened as he gasped for air.

"You and I both know why you are here, Akzûl," the Lord of the East said. "Remember that. And remember that I am the one our master has chosen to lead his followers until he returns."

The Lord of the East lifted a hand, and the goblin took in a deep breath, although he didn't show any other signs of distress. He was truly tougher—indeed, the goblins were proving tougher—than Syzbalo had thought.

"And you, Melanius," the Lord of the East added, "you are a trusted advisor, but you *will* know your place."

Melanius bowed, this time deep and sincere, and they all looked out in silence as they left the lands of Fen-Aztûk, where the people lined the street and cheered. Timrûk Aztûk had told the citizens of the city about the Lord of the East's generosity, and they were there to show their thanks. Whether Timrûk had forced them to come out to see the Lord of the East off, or they came on their own volition, Syzbalo didn't know, and he didn't care. Either way, the tides were changing ... and in his favor. The Aztûks were relenting, and the other families that opposed him would soon follow.

The royal river barge that carried the Lord of the East and his retinue—carriage and white horses included—across the Giant's Vein was a thing of opulence, large enough to handle any ocean wave the sea could produce and made of ebony and silver with sails made of Isutan silk and oars carved to look like long snakes. Timrûk's personal guard was there to see to the Lord of the East's safety, probably ensuring that Syzbalo could leave unharassed, so they would still receive what he had promised them.

The Lord of the East spent most of his time in his chambers, with

Kimber and Krista, although Akzûl interrupted him, wanting to be ensured that his goblin comrades would experience safe travels into Háthgolthane, as did Melanius wishing to discuss moving troops to their western borders and if they should send envoys to treat with the new king of Hámon, this Bu Al'Banan. Syzbalo couldn't have cared less at that moment. No man would have, in between his two beautiful witches.

"Do as you see fit," the Lord of the East said, barely giving his advisor a glance.

"As you wish, my lord," Melanius replied.

"Keep an eye on the goblin," Kimber hissed.

"Yes, a close eye," Krista added.

"Indeed," Syzbalo replied, and the Isutan bowed and left.

"It is wise that you chose Melanius as your advisor," Krista said, kissing the Lord of the East's neck.

"Yes, very wise indeed," Kimber echoed, kissing his chest.

"He will not lead you astray," Krista continued.

"No, he will not," Kimber added. "Not like Andragos."

Both witches hissed in unison at the mention of the Black Mage.

"You must deal with him," Krista said.

"And swiftly," Kimber added.

"I will," the Lord of the East said. "Believe me; I will."

## 30

*A* single candle lit the windowless room, sitting in the middle of a table. A small bit of light escaped through the bottom of the thick, wooden door, but other than that and candlelight, Darius sat in darkness. He set his helmet in front of him and sighed deeply.

"News," the General Lord Marshall said.

"King Bucharan's son, and heir to his throne in Po, is dead," Amado replied.

"King Agempi has sent his condolences," Darius said. "This is not so much astounding news, Amado."

"It is odd that it happened in conjunction with a visit from the Lord of the East," Amado added.

"Why would the Lord of the East execute Bucharan's son?" Darius asked. "Besides, the King heard it was natural causes."

Amado replied with a shrug.

"Who knows why he does what he does, Lord Marshall," Amado replied, "but our spies say many in Bucharan's court expect foul play ... magical poisoning. Bucharan's son was young and vibrant. What natural causes take a man's life when he is barely older than twenty winters?"

"True enough," Darius said. "Keep your ears open. Anything else?"

"The Lord of the East executed the patriarch of a prominent family in Fen-Aztûk," Amado replied. "Gert Askari."

Darius nodded. He knew of the Askarians, a high-ranking, aristocratic family in Golgolithul. He didn't quite understand the familial connections and what they had to do with politics in the eastern country, but they were important, nonetheless. And the Lord of the East executing one of their patriarchs and diminishing their family status was even more important.

"The Aztûkians and Martûkians are now fully supporting the Lord of the East," Amado added.

"Publicly?" Darius asked, and the Master of Spies nodded. "What about privately?"

"I am sure the Aztûkians will always work against the Stévockians in a way," Amado replied without much certainty in his voice, "but my spies say they are fully supporting the Lord of the East."

"This is not good," Darius muttered.

"The Lord of the East was dangerous before," Marcel, Commander of the Dragon Teeth, said. The stout and well-muscled man was the only other person in the room and, even though his troops were far less secretive than the Atrimus, he still operated under a certain amount of impunity and caution. "A unified Golgolithul is even more dangerous."

"Agreed," Darius replied.

"That is not all," Amado said.

"Go ahead," Darius said.

"My spies say the Lord of the East has *changed*," Amado replied.

"Changed?" Marcel asked.

"Yes. He has always dabbled in the dark arts of magic," Amado explained, "especially under the tutelage of the Messenger of the East, but my sources tell me he no longer derives advice from the Black Mage."

Darius leaned forward.

"Who gives him counsel, then?"

"An Isutan magician," Amado replied, to which Marcel growled. "And two women—witches."

"What is Syzbalo up to?" Darius said to himself.

"And, while in Antolika, he has taken on a goblin death squad," Amado added.

"Goblins," Marcel said, his voice as hard as a hammer breaking stone.

"Goblins have always lived freely in his country, but never served his military," Darius commented introspectively.

"Our spies say his power has grown?" Amado said.

"Power has grown?" Marcel asked.

"Yes," Amado added. "His magical abilities. He is getting stronger, despite not taking counsel from the Black Mage anymore. He is aggressively expanding east, and he still continues to strengthen his garrisons along Golgolithul's northern border."

"Lord Marshall," Marcel said, "war is on the horizon."

Darius closed his eyes. He said a silent prayer to Unus. He wished and prayed for peace more than anything, and a part of him cursed his life as a soldier. He had never known a time of amity, even if much of Háthgolthane believed that's what they were in. The En Conquillas was a lie. Truly, Darius might prefer a time when he knew exactly who his enemy was and could face them, rather than relying on spies and sending assassins to do a soldier's job.

"Marcel," Darius said, "send a unit of Dragon Teeth to Gol-Nornor. Pull your Dragon Teeth stationed in the north away and redeploy them to the south and east. Be prepared."

Darius began to stand.

"There's one more thing," Amado said.

Darius settled back into his seat.

"Speak."

"Erik Eleodum is gone," Amado said.

Darius stared at the table for a moment.

"Gone?" Darius asked.

"Yes, Lord Marshall," Amado replied.

"Where?"

"We're not quite sure," Amado replied, and Marcel groaned when the Commander of the Atrimus replied, to which Darius lifted a hand to quiet him. "He—he … we're not sure. My spies think he went north and west."

"This man kills Atrimus agents," Darius said as much to himself as to Marcel and Amado, "and now he evades the eyes of our spies. Curious."

"What are your orders?" Amado asked. "Do we try to give chase?"

Darius shook his head.

"With no idea where he is going?" Darius asked. "If he travels through the Pass of Dundolyothum, who knows where he will go. And why. The wilds of the north, and of Hargoleth, are vast. No. His companions went with him? His kin? These dwarves?"

"No," Darius replied.

That stunned Darius even more.

"Have your spies keep watch on Eleodum's farm," Darius said.

"Only watch?" Amado asked, and Darius couldn't help sensing some disagreement in the young man's voice.

"Yes," Darius replied. "Keep me informed."

Darius finally stood, and the two men followed suit.

"Be vigilant," Darius said. "Amado, keep me apprised of the information your spies send you. And tell them to be careful. To be caught spying on the Lord of the East is a fate worse than death. And if they are caught spying on the free farms of Háthgolthane, I don't know what the backlash will be."

Both Amado and Marcel bowed. Darius knocked on the thick wooden door. It opened to a brightly lit hallway. He looked at the two men leading his clandestine missions over his shoulder one more time before groaning, donning his helmet, and going about his daily duties.

## 31

*A*ndragos stood waiting, deep in thought, in front of the stairs leading up to the keep of Fen-Stévock. His Soldiers of the Eye stood with him, fifty to either side of the stairs, as did the Lord of the East's personal guard—at least those who stayed behind while he was gone to Antolika on a diplomatic mission. That's what he told everyone. Andragos was sure he was there for very different reasons.

The Lord of the East had fumed for days after he learned Bone Spear, the Isutan assassin and mage, was dead, and at the hands of the man he was meant to kill—Erik Eleodum. Syzbalo simply couldn't fathom how a farm boy could kill a seasoned and deadly man such as Specter. His pride was getting the better of him; that and those damn witches and that twisted, Isutan magician posing as some sort of advisor.

Erik was a remarkable man, and Andragos found something very refreshing about him. He reminded Andragos of himself long ago when he was young and idealistic. Not only had Erik killed Bone Spear, he had chased away the dragon that had burnt all of South Gate and would have otherwise destroyed Fen-Stévock. How could a young man who previously spent his time tilling the earth do such a thing? A magical scroll written by the elves certainly helped with the dragon, but it was Erik's willpower, his faith, and his love for his friends and family that had seen him achieve so much. Remarkable indeed.

And Syzbalo wanted him dead. What a fool. Why not use such a man? Why not recruit him, teach him, instruct him, and get the people of Golgolithul to love the Lord of the East because of him? He was sure that was why the Lord of the East wanted the man dead ... because he couldn't bend him. Was that what Andragos wanted, to bend Erik to his will? No, that wasn't the case. At first, he had hoped Erik would be a man who could be a champion for his people, restore the faith of Háthgolthane and Golgolithul. But now, he didn't know. Erik had a much deeper purpose, that much Andragos knew. And when he thought of Erik, he felt something deep in his gut, a change he hadn't felt in many years. It might have been the man's youth and naiveté, but whatever it was, Andragos found it refreshing, and again, it reminded him of a time many years before.

Syzbalo was such a fool, and now, he had once again recruited an Isutan assassin, Specter's daughter this time, to kill Erik and his family, and retrieve a sword rumored to have the power to kill a dragon. Andragos frowned deeply, though. The Lord of the East went to Mek-Ba'Dune to recruit the Black Tigress, but there was something else, something he wasn't telling anyone. He sensed it as Syzbalo left, a dark secret deep in the back of his mind—something dangerous and sinister.

Andragos always watched the Lord of the East carefully— whether Syzbalo was at home or away—and Syzbalo's powers had grown exponentially of late, too fast for natural results from study and practice. If the Black Mage weren't careful, Syzbalo would know he was watching him. Perhaps he did know, but he had met with goblins. Andragos smacked his lips as if he had eaten something sour. Why, by the eastern gods, had the Lord of the East accepted the company of goblins? It was a part of Syzbalo's secret, and Andragos knew it.

The cheers erupting from the city dragged Andragos from his reverie and told him that not only had the Lord of the East returned from his voyage, but he had purposely entered through the rebuilt South Gate. Syzbalo had made it seem like he diverted all resources to the repair of South Gate when in reality, he could have cared less for the people that lived along Fen-Stévock's southern wall. They were among the poorest, living in an area riddled with crime and trouble, and Syzbalo had told Andragos on several occasions he wished the whole of the southern part of the capital had burned away beyond repair. However, as he spent precious resources on rebuilding, he became a benevolent leader, one who loved his people so they would love him.

It took longer than it should have for the Lord of the East to reach the keep of Fen-Stévock's castle. No doubt, he was glad-handing the people who had come to see him arrive. It had been years since Andragos had seen the Lord of the East don armor, but as he walked up to the Messenger of the East, he wore a suit of black plate mail, expertly crafted to fit his body so that it wasn't the typical bulky protection of a knight. Syzbalo moved as if he was wearing simple clothing. He stopped before Andragos, a smile on his face, hands clasped behind his back.

"My lord," Andragos said with a bow. All one hundred of the Soldiers of the Eye came to attention, snapping their spears into their shoulders, the sound of their heels clicking as one echoing through the courtyard.

Andragos couldn't help noticing the look the Lord of the East gave his Soldiers of the Eye. He knew that, recently, Syzbalo had become suspicious of these men who owed their allegiance only to the Black Mage. He detested anyone who might serve someone over himself.

"I trust everything is well, despite my absence," the Lord of the East said.

"Yes, my lord," Andragos replied. "You will have seen that repairs on South Gate have gone as planned and ..."

"I would have thought more would be done by now. It is barely livable," said the Lord of the East, cutting Andragos off.

Andragos knew this would happen. He hadn't foreseen it in his bowl, nor had he dreamed it. It was simply his intuition. His favor with the Lord of the East was waning, and Syzbalo needed a reason to be upset with him.

"Our laborers are working as fast as they can," Andragos said, "and our resources at the moment are limited, due to your ... diplomatic trip. And, in reality, my lord, it was barely livable before its destruction."

"You don't approve of my trip to Po and Fen-Aztûk?" the Lord of the East said, loud enough that everyone around could hear.

"Of course I do, my lord," Andragos replied evenly, refusing to be drawn by Syzbalo's goading. "Although, I heard there was a little trouble in both cities."

"No trouble at all," the Lord of the East replied.

"A dead prince in Po and crucifixions in Fen-Aztûk. Is that not trouble, my lord?" Andragos asked, deciding to poke back a little.

"I don't think I like your tone, Andragos," the Lord of the East replied.

Andragos bowed, trying to show as much reverence as he dared without making it look false.

"My apologies, my lord," Andragos said. "I meant no disrespect. Should we continue into your hall?"

"Indeed," the Lord of the East replied, rolling his eyes at the witches before he began walking up the stairs that led to the keep's dais.

Andragos followed him, trying his best to control his temper after being treated more like a dog than the second most powerful man in Golgolithul. Peering over his shoulder, he saw the witches following them—at a distance. No doubt, without him around, those two bitches had spent plenty of time poisoning Syzbalo's mind. He didn't see Melanius, but the Black Mage was certain he was there, somewhere, listening with his cheap magic. A single goblin followed the witches, one that looked seasoned, a constant mocking snarl on his face. He saw Andragos looking at him, and he winked, which caused the Black Mage to growl and turn around.

The Lord of the East walked through his hall, void of the naked, lounging people and exotic animals usually there, and stopped in front of the steps leading up to the platform on which his throne sat. He turned and faced Andragos as he walked to him.

"Any luck in finding Terradyn and Raktas?" the Lord of the East asked.

"No, my lord. My apologies."

"Have you even looked?" the Lord of the East asked, folding his hands behind his back, and ensuring he made eye contact.

"Of course, my lord," Andragos replied, not dropping his gaze. He could out stare this fool all day.

"Of course," the Lord of the East said, mockingly. "Men who have served you faithfully for a hundred years, and you would have me believe you have searched for them, knowing I mean to put them to death?"

"Have I given you a reason to doubt me?" Andragos asked in an almost conversational tone that suggested he could have been asking about the weather. The twisting in his stomach told a different story.

"I don't know," Syzbalo said. "Have you?"

"My loyalties are to Golgolithul and its ruler," Andragos said, and when the Lord of the East raised an eyebrow and glared suspiciously, he added, "which ... is you, my lord."

"Your loyalties are to *me* and yet, you have men who serve you and only *you*," the Lord of the East said, turning and walking up the stairs to the hall's platform. "What sense does that make?"

The two witches brushed past Andragos, taking their place behind the throne.

"It is the way it has always been, my lord," Andragos said, the pit of his stomach growing into an even tighter knot; he knew this day had been coming. He thought he had more time—a week, a few weeks, a month—to fully prepare, but he knew, nonetheless. Andragos' presence now challenged Syzbalo—at least, that's what the witches and cheap, Isutan magician told the Lord of the East.

"It is time for change," the Lord of the East said.

"I see it is so," Andragos said as the goblin brushed past him and followed the witches onto the Lord of the East's dais. "Since when has the Lord of the East treated with goblins, let alone allow one upon his royal dais?"

"That is none of your business," the Lord of the East retorted.

"As your advisor," Andragos said, struggling to control his anger, "I disagree."

"As I said, it is time for change," the Lord of the East continued. "My alliance with Akzûl and his Black Wolves is imperative to the survival of Golgolithul and critical for our advancements east. It is unfortunate your xenophobia means you cannot recognize we must create alliances with all peoples, in both Háthgolthane and Antolika, in order to ensure the success of the east."

"I see," Andragos replied.

"You have enjoyed much in your service to our cause," the Lord of the East added, clearly ignoring the Black Mage's concerns for this goblin, Akzûl.

"I have sacrificed much," Andragos said.

"More than others?" Syzbalo said, lifting a questioning hand, but before Andragos could answer, he added, "No, I don't think so. I feel your time as my advisor is over. You have done much for your country. It is time to enjoy retirement."

Andragos raised his eyebrows.

"But why?" Andragos said with feigned surprise. Already, he had touched his power, blocking his mind from the witches, from Melanius—wherever he was, and from Syzbalo. He felt the Lord of the East probing, strong and forceful, slowly penetrating his thoughts. His power had grown, but it was tainted and even darker than before. It was something otherworldly, and that caused Andragos to wonder, but he would have to do that later.

The Lord of the East stepped forward.

"Your counsel and leadership in Golgolithul are no longer required."

Andragos made his lip quiver and shook his head. He mouthed the word *no* and even caused his eyes to water.

"Your laboratory here in Fen-Stévock's castle will be transferred to Melanius," the Lord of the East said.

Andragos had already removed all he needed from his laboratory —his chronicles and spells over the last millennia, his favorite potions and incantations, and his deepest held secrets like the family histories of all his henchmen and where the bastards of all the eastern nobles lived.

"What ..." he gasped, trying to make himself look totally surprised and upset. A look of triumph crossed Syzbalo's face as he lifted his chin and gave a little haughty smile. The look made Andragos want to laugh—or kick the man in the balls. The Lord of the East actually thought he could surprise the Black Mage, but he kept up the pretense. He even forced himself to think about being saddened and let his thoughts out into the open.

"You will turn over everything to Kimber and Krista," the Lord of the East continued. "They will now oversee the magical academies."

"Why ..." Andragos asked, forcing an almost pleading voice.

"It is time for change, Andragos," the Lord of the East said.

"Please, my lord," Andragos said, almost in a whisper.

"And, immediately, the Soldiers of the Eye will serve me, in my personal guard," the Lord of the East said. "Akzûl, for the time being, will be my master at arms, and he will command the Soldiers of the Eye for me."

That did take Andragos by surprise ... a little. He knew the Lord of the East hated the Soldiers of the Eye and would have eventually disbanded them. Andragos suspected he might even try to execute them, but so soon? They were a symbol of Golgolithulian might, the citizens of Fen-Stévock knew them, stepped aside, and cowered as they passed by. He assumed Syzbalo would simply kill his men, but assimilating them into his personal guard was a minor shock. An even greater shock was his intent on having a goblin grunt command them, further deepening the Black Mage's suspicions that something else, something truly dark and secretive was going on.

Andragos felt his power slip as he pondered this little surprise. He saw the witches eyeing him and fully grabbed at his magic again, steeling his mind against their probing tricks and keeping his thoughts like those of a distraught person.

"You cannot," Andragos said, returning to his pretense.

"I cannot?" the Lord of the East said. "I am the Morningstar of the East, the Rising Sun, the Breaker of Chains, the Emperor of the East! I can do as I wish!"

*Oh yes. Rage all you want. You are no sun, and you are the chain. You are not as powerful as you think.*

But he was growing more and more powerful, enough to challenge the Black Mage and command a company of goblins. Andragos hid that specific thought but let through that his mood had changed from shock and upset to one of anger. He clenched his fists at his sides and touched more of his magical power. Even though he needed to look angry and wild, almost uncontrolled in his ire, a part of him broke from his ruse, a hundred different spells running through his mind. He had no intention of harming Syzbalo—at least, not here and not now—but he could kill the Lord of the East where he stood, and those bitches too. Syzbalo had become powerful, but not that powerful.

He knew they would feel his power—the witches and the Lord of the East—and he let them. It was a part of his plan. All sound in the hall dissipated, and he only heard the beating of his heart. He saw the witches whispering, chanting their weak incantations, no doubt. The Lord of the East did the same. He saw Akzûl's hand go to the handle of a short sword at his hip, no doubt some enchanted blade cursed by black magic. He heard footsteps as guardsmen closed in on him ... and he breathed.

Andragos released his fists, shaking his hands out. He looked at the Lord of the East coldly and turned without a word, facing at least fifty soldiers who had started surrounding him. If he wanted things that way, they would last a mere moment before he boiled them in their black armor. Outwardly he furrowed his brows and frowned; inwardly he laughed.

He took a moment to look about the hall. His time here had passed. A thousand years and, finally, he would leave. He was angry but also even a little sad. But the biggest sensation was the feeling of relief that washed over him. Even the air had seemed to weigh down on him lately, and now, he felt light and free. He tried to hide the feeling with false thoughts of more sadness, but his frown lessened, and he gave a quick, short sigh.

He stepped out of the hall and walked to his Soldiers of the Eye.

*They are now mine,* the Lord of the East's voice said inside Andragos' mind.

*They will see me home, and then I will relinquish them to you,* Andragos thought back. It was lie, but he heard no response.

As they left the keep, the grizzled old Isutan advisor stepped from another of the Lord of the East's carriages, followed by several of Akzûl's *Black Wolves.*

"Andragos, my friend," the Isutan said, his voice as false as his face and his magic. "Where are you off to?"

"You have won," Andragos said. "Good luck."

"What do you mean, my friend?" Melanius asked.

He wasn't as good at pretending as Andragos was. He could barely contain his smile as he tried looking aghast. Andragos shook his head.

"You are a snake," Andragos said. He meant it as an insult, but the old fool was too vain. The magician cackled and, even though Andragos expected as much, he wanted to turn the Isutan's blood to ice.

When he and his hundred soldiers reached the home he kept just north of the Fen-Stévock's walls, he turned to them. They snapped to attention, standing just inside the head-high wall that surrounded the opulent home, waiting for his instructions. He liked this home the least, all gaudy and rich. It didn't feel like home; it offered as much sense of belonging as a prison.

It was time to find out just how loyal they were. For hundreds of years, men like these had served him, unwavering, unquestioning. But why? Fear. Lust for power. Indoctrination. He was still a powerful wizard, but he was no longer in a position of power.

"The Lord of the East no longer wishes me to serve him, and has decreed the Soldiers of the Eye be disbanded," Andragos said, and he waited a moment to see what their reaction might be. He saw one eye twitch. One uneasy shift of a man's hip. "You will report to the Lord of the East, where you will be integrated into his personal guard and commanded by a goblin named Akzûl."

There was a small mutter from the back, a groan from someone to the left, and one soldier looked down at his feet, which he shuffled slightly.

"My lord," one of the soldiers said. Others looked at the man as if he were crazy. Speaking while they were at attention, while the Black Mage spoke to them, was punishable by death.

"Speak," Andragos said.

"What if we do not wish to serve in the Lord of the East's personal guard?" the soldier asked, stepping forward to speak but staying in his position of attention. "What if we do not wish to be commanded by swamp-crawling goblin?"

"Why wouldn't you?" Andragos replied. "To serve in the Lord of the East's personal guard is a great honor. And if this Akzûl is to command you, he must be a great warrior."

The soldier paused a moment. Andragos could tell what he was thinking. He gulped, sighed, and moved his head to face the Black Mage directly. Other soldiers gasped, and one even whispered, "*Don't.*" They were not allowed to look at him unless he commanded them to do so. They were not allowed to speak to him unless he commanded them to do so. They were not allowed to speak to one another unless he commanded them to do so.

"We serve you, my lord," the soldier said, his eyes hard and gray. "No one else."

"And I serve the Lord of the East," Andragos said. "You will do this."

Andragos turned to walk to his house.

"No," the soldier said.

Andragos wheeled around hard. Defiance ... the ultimate crime in his hundred soldiers. He lifted a hand, squeezing it into a fist. He could see the muscles on either side of the soldier's neck flex as his esophagus closed. He could see the man's eyes widen, just slightly, as the Black Mage cut air off to his lungs, as blood stopped coursing through his veins, and as his face turned red. Blood began to trickle from the soldier's nose, but he stood still, even as his lips turned purple. He knew what he had done. He knew his insolence would ... should bring death.

Andragos released his hand. Any other man would have grasped his neck, fallen to his knees, and taken deep, heaving breaths. His soldier stood there, sucking in one, long breath through his nose.

"Why would you disobey me?" Andragos asked as the color returned to the soldier's face. "And wipe the blood from your nose."

The man did as he was told, wiping away the blood with the back of one hand.

"I serve you, my lord, and only you," the soldier said, chancing to look at the Black Mage once again. "When we started our training, you told us that we serve no other. That we, unlike every other soldier in the east, only answer to you. We are yours, my lord. I will not serve the Lord of the East. I will not serve some goblin." Andragos could tell this man wanted to spit at the mention of Akzûl, but he refrained. "Kill me if you must. Death is better than not serving you."

Almost as if it was planned, all one hundred soldiers slammed the butts of their spears against the ground and shouted in unison, "Death is better!"

"You all feel this way?" Andragos asked.

"Yes!" they all responded.

"None of you wish to serve the Lord of the East?" he asked. "If you do, you may leave. I will not stop you."

No one moved.

"Very well, then," the Black Mage said, trying to stop the smile that wanted to consume his face. "We must leave. Like me, you will all be wanted men."

"What of the trainees, my lord," the same soldier asked.

Andragos always had three levels of trainees. The first level, three hundred boys between eight and ten winters old, were often the children of whores and prisoners, with nothing more than a will to survive. Andragos called them his pages, as they simply did menial tasks for him and his soldiers. When they turned eleven, he dismissed one hundred of his pages—who mostly went to work for the Golgolithulian army as stable or drummer boys, since they had excellent training even though they didn't meet the Black Mage's standards. The remaining two hundred trainees became his squires. They trained in combative arts more diligently, learned how to break and deal with horses, and took on jobs such as cleaning armor and weapons. When they turned fourteen, the Black Mage dismissed yet another one hundred of them, most joining one of Golgolithul's special military units. These remaining young men were called recruits and would one day be a Soldier of the Eye. They had to be eighteen winters old to be eligible, so they had to train for at least four years, and once they turned eighteen, they would only be called up as a full-fledged soldier if someone in front of them died or became ill or infirm. Many of those doing training now had once served as soldiers.

"Bring all the recruits and squires. The pages may have a harder time understanding what is going on, but if there are any you already feel will be good enough to become recruits, bring them also. I feel we will need them more than ever; there is war on the horizon," said Andragos. What he did not add was that he wasn't sure on whose side they may end up fighting.

The soldier—Min Kwan—bowed. The Black Mage knew all their names and how long they had served him. Min, just a simple soldier

—even though there was nothing simple about being a Soldier of the Eye—in his unit. But Andragos had been impressed he was bold enough to speak out, willing to give his life to speak the collective mind of all his comrades. Next time he needed to promote someone— which could be soon—he'd reward Min's natural leadership.

"Captain Shudraka," Andragos said, and another one of his soldiers stepped forward. No one but he and the other soldiers knew of his rank, and the Black Mage did that on purpose. They all fought together. The enemy needn't know who his officers were. And the death of an officer, unlike other military units, wouldn't do anything to the other soldiers that the death of any other comrade might do. "Take Min Kwan with you as you ready my things for departure."

Shudraka bowed and jerked his head towards Min Kwan. Andragos turned to face the home. It was the last time he would see it, and for the first time in a long time, he felt relief.

## 32

*E*rik had found a small inn with only two rooms and a dirty old farmwife who just happened to walk in on him—twice—while he was changing. Once he'd got rid of her, he lay back on the bed and thought back on his conversation with Gris. He still didn't know what he could do about getting the stone, but he knew he had to gain entrance somehow to the Keep of Wulfstaad. He'd never done anything like this before without the wise counsel of Turk and the other dwarves—and even Bryon—and he was feeling somewhat lost. But that couldn't stop him, even if he had to make up a plan as he went along.

He had realized that, even though it might be rare, these northerners had dealings with Hámon. They probably had dealings with Nordethians as well, but he had planned on posing as a Hámonian noble. However, the Lord of Wulfstaad might know the noble families and realize Erik was lying if he gave them a false name. He had thought about pretending to be some noble from Kamdum or even Goldum, but the same fear twisted his stomach.

He finally decided he would almost tell the truth. He would go to the Lord of Wulfstaad, say he was a soldier of fortune from Northwestern Háthgolthane, and warn him about Gris and his plans for the theft of the stone. In return for this vital knowledge, the lord would accept Erik's request for a night's stay, and during the hours of darkness, Erik would steal the stone and escape. It sounded good when it first came to him, but the more he thought about it, the more he ended up with his first plan: making something up as he went along.

Erik felt the tickle of grass on his face. Looking up, the sky was blue, but not like he remembered it. It didn't have the same crispness to it, the same splendor as the Creator had intended. He sat up and saw the grass was brown yet still alive, gently stirred in a breeze that reminded Erik of the waves lapping against the shore in Finlo. He stared at the distant, black mountain range, with its black clouds and ... there was no purple lightning. He squinted as he looked to the sun, which seemed *off*, more red than a vibrant, blazing yellow. There was no other way to put it ... the Dream World had been tainted.

Erik shuddered at the thought of something so powerful, and his mind first went to the Shadow. However, the man under the tree—and the mysterious cloaked figure that had appeared in his dreams and presumably blocked them—had hinted this wasn't the doing of the Shadow.

*What, then? What could rival the power of the Shadow, other than the Creator?*

Erik stood and turned around, scanning the whole of the plain while he did. No dead. He didn't see them, and he couldn't even smell them. His eyes came to rest on the hill with the weeping willow tree, and he saw the shadow of a man sitting there, watching him. As he walked closer, he realized it wasn't the normal man who sat under the tree, always wearing a wide-brimmed straw hat and chewing on a piece of long-stemmed grass. It was Dewin, but bearing the image of his former self, the young wizard with long, wavy, blond hair.

"Come and sit," Dewin said, patting the spot next to him.

"Will the Dream World allow me up on the hill?" Erik asked.

"We will see," Dewin replied with a shrug.

Erik stepped onto the slope of the hill and walked up until he sat next to Dewin, letting out a slow sigh of relief.

"Your travels have been troubled," Dewin said.

Erik nodded.

"These northern people are a suspicious lot," Erik said, staring out on the vast plains of brown grass.

"They're people," Dewin said with a smile, and despite his younger look, that smile reminded Erik of the old, mysterious soothsayer in Eldmanor.

As Erik watched the Dream World, the cloaked man appeared—one moment not there and then he was—and then another man appeared in front of him. They spoke, but Erik couldn't hear what they said. The other man—lean, muscular, clean-shaven—wasn't someone Erik recognized, and when he shook his head, the cloaked figure yelled something Erik didn't understand but could only assume was a curse. The other man disappeared as if he were dust in the wind.

Dewin laughed—the cackle of an old, mad man. The cloaked man turned and, even though Erik couldn't see his eyes, he knew the mysterious figure stared at them.

"Laugh all you want, you old fool," the cloaked man croaked, his voice being carried on the breeze. "Your time will come. And soon. Then, you won't be laughing. You will be wailing, and begging for destruction to end the pain."

"The words of a desperate man, eh, Erik?" Dewin said, nudging Erik with an elbow.

Erik didn't know what to say. The cloaked man raised clenched fists, yelled something in a language Erik didn't understand, and disappeared again, leaving a patch of blackened earth where he had stood.

"Are you not afraid of him?" Erik asked.

"Oh, I am very afraid of him," Dewin replied. "More afraid than I have been in many years. But I won't show him."

"Who is he?" Erik asked.

"Rather, what is he," Dewin corrected. But as Erik just stared at him, he added, "Evil. Pure evil."

"This other evil," Erik said. "This thing that isn't the Shadow, nor the Creator. This *Chaos*."

"Yes," Dewin replied.

"Are you going to tell me who ... *what* he is?" Erik asked.

"Another time," Dewin said. "All I will say now is that you *must* retrieve the Dragon Stone, Dream Walker. It is now more important than ever, and you cannot fail; I have found my suspicions about the stone to be true. I don't know how these northerners have kept it for so long, how its secret has remained hidden for so long." Dewin spoke introspectively. "But evil is coming for it, an evil that could bring about turmoil and, eventually, destroy the world."

"Do I still take the stone to El'Beth El'Kesh?" Erik asked.

"Yes," Dewin said.

"With it, she will be able to save the world?" Erik asked.

"I don't know," Dewin replied, and for the first time, as he looked at Erik, his eyes showed worry.

"The Lord of Wulfstaad has it," Erik said, "and it's well protected."

"It isn't safe there," Dewin said. "Not anymore, Dream Walker. No matter what it takes, you must get the Dragon Stone to the elves."

The world around him began to fade and shimmer, and Erik knew he was about to wake up.

"I will see you, in your dreams, Dream Walker." Dewin's voice became distant, barely an echo. "Save the stone. Take it to El'Beth El'Kesh."

"We have breakfast," the old woman said as Erik walked from his room into the main quarters of the home of this farmwife and her husband. Erik wondered how many times the poor man had been cuckolded, but, as he sat at a crooked table rubbing a sweaty, bald head, he seemed to care more for the ale in front him than he did his wife.

"I'll be fine, thank you," Erik said, making for the door.

The woman moved with surprising speed as she stood in front of Erik, looking up at him with graying hair and a smile bearing crooked, yellowed teeth. Her breath smelled of onions.

*How could any man want to lie with her?*

"It's bacon and eggs," she said, trying to press herself against him. "It's included in the price of the room. There're many things that could be included in the price of the room."

"Good grief, woman," the husband finally said, "let the man be. He doesn't want breakfast, and he certainly doesn't want you."

"Shut your trap," she said, her pleasant, jolly demeanor quickly turning sour as she glared at him.

"Good wife," Erik said, gently grabbing her shoulders and moving her aside, "I am quite alright. Thank you for your hospitality."

"You like men? Is that it?" the woman asked, which took Erik by surprise. She looked angry, and in her anger, her silly jollity turned to vitriol. "You know, that's illegal here in the north."

"Truly?" Erik asked. It was the wrong question. The wrong thing to say, but in every other part of the world he had been, save for his farmstead, even if it was frowned upon, a man being with a man wasn't a legal issue. He cocked an eyebrow, suddenly aware that he needed to be very careful around this old housewife.

"Here is something extra for being so kind."

He pressed a Hámonian pound into the woman's palm.

"Hámon, eh?" she said. "Figures."

He didn't know what she meant, and he didn't care. Erik opened the door and stepped out into the street. He noticed it seemed rather empty; people simply standing on either side of the packed, dirt road while a contingent of half a dozen guards marched by. Surely, it was a market day like any other, with people crowding towards the keep to buy and sell goods? But they weren't.

Erik shrugged off his uncertainty with a guess that a market was not held every day and went to retrieve Warrior from a small stable crudely built on the side of the inn. As he mounted his horse and heeled him out into the street, he looked back at the inn, the old farmwife watching him from the doorway, a scowl across her face. He took a side road, one that crisscrossed the main road leading to the clan holding's guardhouse and passed the jail—Brand and Adils were gone, replaced by seven other men.

*Why would they need seven men to guard a simple jail meant for drunkards and curfew violators?*

Erik slowly rode towards the entrance to the keep of Wulfstaad. He raised an eyebrow as he got closer. The large, multi-storied double doors of the gatehouse were open, but the portcullis was down, blocking any entrance through the wall. Rather, the small, side door— the narrow, secondary opening most castles and keeps had—was open, and a long line of people waited as a single guard checked each person before allowing them passage through the wall. Erik dismounted and got in line, some twenty people back, as he heard angry shouting and a loud bell ring out.

*What, by the Creator, is going on?*

Erik finally made his way to the small entrance, a long line of people now forming behind him. He stood in front of a guard who was taller than Erik, with drooping mustachios and the scruffy beginnings of a beard on his face. He looked down at Erik, his sharp, blue eyes taking in Erik's face and demeanor.

"My name is Erik Eleodum," Erik said, and the guard jerked at hearing the different accent.

"I don't give a bear scat what your name is," the guard said angrily, grabbing Erik's shoulder. "On your way. You foreigners all think we should care who you are. You're holding up good people who wish to trade, so move along."

Erik shrugged from the man's grasp.

"Why isn't the main gate opened?" Erik asked

"None of your damned business," the guard replied and looked like he was about to grab Erik again.

"I wish to speak to Lord Wulfstan. Urgently," Erik said.

"You and a hundred other people," the guard replied, but he made no move to push Erik away.

"I'm ... I'm a noble," Erik said, instantly cursing himself for going back on his commitment to tell a different lie. "From Hámon. I wish to stay in Wulfstaad for a day and night. As a noble, I expect the courtesy a noble deserves, but I do have important news for Lord Wulfstan."

Erik had tried sounding as much as he could like a pompous ass who gave no concerns for anyone but himself and his own well-being. The guard looked at him with a squinted glare, but there was uncertainty in his eyes over what he should do.

"Where is your squire?" the guard asked, looking over Erik's shoulder as if somebody might be hiding behind him. "Where are your servants?"

Erik thought for a moment, and when the guard looked even more irritated than he already was, he spoke.

"I'm ... poor," Erik replied and cursed his stupidity.

"A poor Hámonian noble," the guard laughed.

"A noble, nonetheless," Erik replied, giving the man a haughty look over his nose, although he was sure he looked awkward doing it. "And you would do well to show a noble, a man far above your meager station in life, the respect he deserves."

*How could men talk like this all the time?*

This guard was just doing his job, and rather well. Erik had nothing but respect and admiration for such a man, and to guard the main gate to the Castle of Wulfstaad meant he was well-respected and an adept fighter.

The man tilted his head, still staring at Erik. He looked over his shoulder and nodded to another of the guards. The other man, older with grey hair curling from under his helm, came over, and the two spoke quietly.

"This is an odd time for a foreign noble to find his way to Wulfstaad," the older guard said.

"Why is that?" Erik asked.

"Because it's winter, of course!" the older guard replied. "Hámonians—and Háthgolthanians for that matter—never travel to the north in the wintertime. It's too cold for them."

Both men gave condescending laughs. It was a good point, and Erik cursed himself again for saying he was a noble.

"I'm traveling farther west," Erik finally replied, "and the cold has never bothered me."

The first guard whispered in the ear of the older man again, who nodded and went to speak to a third guard, this one with black hair and a thick, bushy beard.

"Fine. You are holding up the line. He will take you to the keep," the first guard said, nodding to the third man.

Erik eyed the soldier coldly, looking him up and down. He didn't have the usual look of the guards, with no shield or spear. Rather, his left hand rested on the pommel of his sword, and he wore a mail hauberk as opposed to one made of cloth. His boots weren't nearly as dirty, and his pants were thick wool and clean. The people behind him began to grumble and complain. Erik looked at them over his shoulder, back at the guards, and nodded.

"Very well," Erik said, leading Warrior through the small entrance, even though the broad horse barely fit.

The part of the town of Wulfstaad that was inside the walls looked much like Örnddinas, with a long, wooden walled walkway leading from the back of the enclosure up towards another raised mound of earth, topped with a five-story square keep, its first two stories made of stone while the others were wood. A gate blocked the way to the inclined path, its door closed and also guarded. There was very little in the way of trading going on inside the walls, although some carts and wagons had wares set out on them.

The only busy people were soldiers, who hurried about as their sergeants and captains shouted orders. A company of perhaps forty men stood at the portcullis, and when one man shouted up at the top of the gatehouse, it rose about halfway, heavy chains creaking and grinding as a massive wheel did the work it would take a hundred men to do. With another shout, the soldiers marched forward, and the portcullis lowered behind them.

"What is going on?" Erik asked, but the man leading him simply glared at him over his shoulder and kept walking towards the gate that led to the Keep of Wulfstaad.

They stopped at the gate of the walkway, and the two guards standing there moved aside without a word from Erik's escort. The causeway was long and slowly inclined, and another gate led into the keep's courtyard. Two more guards stood there, and again, when they saw Erik's escort, they moved aside.

A small boy ran to them, holding out a hand to Erik. He looked to his escort.

"Give the boy the reins to your horse. He will stable him while you meet with Lord Wulfstan."

Erik nodded and handed the boy the reins. He heard more shouting, now distant, from the city that surrounded the keep's walls. He looked over his shoulder, down at the homes and buildings, and he could see soldiers moving quickly through the streets, people scattering, and smoke from a few fires—and not from chimney stacks.

"Let's go," the escort said. Two more guards opened a thick door set in the middle of the keep.

The first level of the keep was mostly a kitchen and storage rooms. At the far end of the keep, a stone stairway wound upwards, and the second level of the keep was a wide, open space with a raised dais spanning the whole length of the room along one wall. A tall, wooden chair sat on the dais, two smaller chairs next to it. A large man with a huge, barreled chest sat on the large chair. His hair was a combination of dark yellow and gray, and even though he had a large, rotund gut that spilled over a wide, iron buckle set in the middle of an equally wide girdle that made him look uncomfortable as he sat in his chair, he looked like a formidable warrior with his wide shoulders, thick arms, and tree trunk legs. His beard spread out over his chest, and the head of a wolf, long dead, rested on his shoulder, mouth open and glass eyes staring out blankly, attached to a thick coat made of the same animal. He held a large goblet in one hand, a golden cup studded with jewels, and a simple circlet of iron sat atop his head. His other hand rested on a woman's arm sitting in the chair next to his.

The woman had curly red hair that spilled over her shoulders. She was a big-boned woman with broad shoulders and wide hips, and her dress was made of what looked like wolf fur. She also wore an iron circlet on her head, although it looked like her hair fought against it. Her skin was pale, freckles spreading out over the bridge of her nose and her cheeks. If she stood, she would have been tall, and one of her legs kicked out, the heel of her boot resting at the edge of the dais on which they sat.

Another woman, a younger girl with reddish hair laced with a mesmerizing mixture of darker auburns and deep browns, sat next to the large woman. She looked tall and lean and was more handsome than beautiful, with a stern jaw and a pointed nose, skin a little less pale, and just as many freckles dotting her face. She wore a green dress, cut low and daring to show some of her cleavage, which would have been large were she not such a strong and tall woman. Her dress hugged her body as well as her arms, showing off muscles most men would have coveted, but also accentuating wider hips, making her look a little awkward in the garb.

Half a dozen men bombarded the large man—Erik assumed him to be Wulfstan. Everyone was trying to talk at the same time, and they all looked frantic, angry, and upset; everyone but Wulfstan, who looked annoyed. The lord looked at Erik's escort, and the man nodded to his leader.

Wulfstan put up a hand and, even as frantic as the others trying to speak were, they quickly quieted. The escort approached the lord, stepping up to the dais, and whispered into Wulfstan's ear. Erik watched the lord's eyes as his bushy, yellow eyebrows scrunched, and his lips pursed. Whatever the confidant said, the lord turned his head to look directly at him, and the escort nodded. The lord nodded back.

"Approach," the escort commanded, and Erik did as he was told. "I present to you Lord Wulfstan Wulfson, Lord of Wulfstaad and Battle Commander of Hargoleth."

Erik bowed.

"What is it you want?" the woman sitting next to Wulfstan asked.

"My lord," Erik began, but the woman cleared her throat and sat forward in her chair.

"It was I, Lady Hilda, who asked the question," the woman said, her words hard and succinct.

"My deepest apologies, my lady," Erik replied. "I am a noble from Hámon ..."

"A poor noble," Wulfstan interrupted, "and one traveling in the coldest part of winter."

"Yes, my lord," Erik said, swallowing hard and bowing, trying not to reveal his nervous eyes. "Even so, as one noble to another, I am humbly asking for a soft bed and a warm meal, just for a night."

"So I have heard," Wulfstan said, his voice a deep rumble. "Your accent ... it is strange."

"How so, my lord?" Erik asked.

"It's more Dwarvish than Hámonian," Wulfstan replied. He lifted a large hand as if waving off the comment. "And which house do you hail from ... in Hámon, poor noble? My guards failed to get your name."

Erik searched his memory banks. He wasn't too familiar with the Hámonian noble families, and when he did come in contact with them, he rarely paid attention to their family names or crests."

"Al ... Algers, my lord," Erik said, remembering the name of a man who had and probably still did, harass his father on multiple occasions, wanting their farmlands and their superior crops for himself.

"Algers?" Wulfstan questioned, disbelief in his voice.

*This is not going well.*

"I have heard of Algers, the Count, but not the family," Wulfstan said.

"Are you a cousin of his?" the younger girl said, piping in and sounding excited for some reason. "An unattached cousin?"

"Yngrid," Lady Hilda hissed, and Wulfstan gave the girl Erik presumed to be his daughter a sidelong glance.

"Yes, my lady," Erik replied, straightening and looking straight at Yngrid. "Yes, I am his cousin."

"A cousin with no name," Wulfstan stated.

"Erik, my lord," Erik replied. "My apologies."

"And do you bear a sigil ring?" Lord Wulfstan asked. "Or a writ of passage? Something that bears the legitimacy of your nobility?"

Erik saw Yngrid roll her eyes and throw her head back.

"Must you pester him, Father?" Yngrid asked, but her father ignored her, and her mother squeezed her wrist. Rather Wulfstan just stared at Erik, a glare that might as well have been a thousand boulders.

Erik lifted his hands in defeat and smiled.

"I am sorry, my lord," Erik said. "I am clumsy and forgetful. I lost my signet ring a long time ago and never had enough money to replace it. And I've lost my writ of lineage."

"So, we are just to take your word that you are a noble from Hámon?" Wulfstan asked.

The others in the room, the men who were likely Wulfstan's advisors, began chattering softly, pointing at Erik. Several of them stood next to the lord and whispered in his ear as Wulfstan knuckled his chin. Erik saw Lady Hilda reach up and tug on Wulfstan's shirt. The lord leaned over, and his wife said something to him. His bushy eyebrows rose for a moment, then he smiled quickly and nodded ever so slightly.

"One night," Wulfstan said, raising a hand with his index finger extended.

"Thank you, my lord," Erik replied. "And in return for your hospitality, I must tell you about ..."

"Later," interrupted the lord. "I have other business today that's far more important than your prattling. My guards will show you ..." Wulfstan began, but his daughter cut him off.

"I can show him to his room, Father," Yngrid said hurriedly.

Her father eyed her warily as her mother glared.

"Very well," Wulfstan said, and Lady Hilda gave her husband a disapproving look.

Erik followed Yngrid up a flight of stairs to the third floor, which was a large sitting area surrounded by four rooms. The daughter of the Lord of Wulfstaad didn't lead Erik up there alone, of course, as two guards followed them. She led Erik to one of the rooms, opening the door and bowing.

"My lord," she said, straightening again and smiling.

The way Yngrid looked at him made Erik blush, and he couldn't help seeing her bite her lip as he passed by her.

"Let the guards know if you need anything," Yngrid said as Erik entered his room.

He turned.

"The guards?"

"Yes," Yngrid replied. "These two will stand guard at your door ... for your protection, of course."

"Of course," Erik replied with a smile.

He had planned on looking about the keep as much as he could and figured, as a noble, he would be allowed some freedom, but it seemed that would not be the case. His plan was falling apart even more.

"And if you do need anything," Yngrid said, "I'll get it for you. Just tell them to come and get me."

"You?" Erik asked with a cocked eyebrow.

Yngrid's girlish smile turned to a slight frown, and she looked like she was pouting.

"Do you not want me to tend to you?" she asked.

"Oh no," Erik said, "I would very much like that."

She smiled again and curtsied.

"I will see you, then, for supper," Yngrid said, and then added, "Lord Erik."

Most men probably wished for a day when someone might call them lord, but Erik hated the idea. The sooner he could find the Dragon Stone and leave this place, the better.

Erik's room was large, with two beds, a window facing south, a large washbasin, a cabinet with clothing, and even a small area blocked off by a shoulder-high wall made of straw with a large pot for when guests needed to relieve themselves. He sat on one of the beds, and it was soft and comfortable. Maybe he could stay here, just for one night. Wulfstan and his wife were suspicious of him, but no more than the rest of their people. Maybe tomorrow, when he spoke of Gris, he'd get an opportunity to find out where the stone was.

By early evening, the servants of the Keep of Wulfstaad had converted the second floor into a banquet hall. After a frustrating day when all he could think of was Dewin's urging, Erik was grateful for the distraction of joining Wulfstan and his wife, and his daughter, for dinner. There were only three other men and their wives, and they all sat at a single, long table on benches, the Lord of Wulfstaad, the only one blessed with a chair.

The meal was a simple one, with a soup that was bland and more of a broth than anything else followed by duck and beef, complemented by greens. The other men at the table consisted of a wealthy farmer from Wulfstaad and his wife, a member of the assembly from Durnfell and his wife, and an esteemed warrior from Wulfstan's court and his betrothed. As they all spoke with either the Lord of Wulfstaad or his wife, their conversations were of nothing consequential, but Erik couldn't help noticing Yngrid staring at him, resting her elbow on the table and leaning her cheek against her hand. She was pretty in her own way, perhaps in her late teens. She was a strong-willed girl ... Erik could tell that much, and in that sense, she reminded him of Simone.

"Daughter," Hilda hissed, "act like a lady. Get your elbow off the table and stop staring."

Yngrid rolled her eyes but did as her mother commanded. She still watched Erik, though.

"Is the Lady Yngrid your only child, my lady?" Erik asked.

"Why?" Wulfstan asked, beef stuffed into one cheek and his voice deep and hard. "Does Lord Erik of Hámon wish to marry her?"

"Father," Yngrid hissed, her cheeks turning a brilliant shade of red.

"You are unattached, are you not?" Wulfstan asked. "You wouldn't be poor and traveling west if you weren't."

"I am, my lord," Erik replied, "and the road is no place for a lady, especially one as lovely as Yngrid of Wulfstaad."

Yngrid blushed a brilliant color of red, and Wulfstan laughed.

"The honeyed tongue of Hámonian pricks," Wulfstan said, bits of food flying from his mouth as he laughed and the other Hargolethians joined in. "As if I would give my only daughter's hand to the likes of you."

Wulfstan pointed his knife at Erik.

"Truly said, my lord," Erik said, bowing slightly. "My apologies."

After a moment of silence, Erik looked up at Wulfstan.

"My lord, it is rather quiet in Wulfstaad today, is it not? Why the presence of so many soldiers."

Wulfstan squinted for a moment before answering.

"Look at Wulfstaad," Wulfstan said. "We constantly fight with barbarians from the north, raiding nomads from the west, giants from the Gray Mountains and even our own Hargolethian brothers—especially those from the south in Holtgaard. One day Gongoreth is our ally, and the next they are our enemy," Wulfstan went on. "Can we rely on the dwarves? Sometimes. Sometimes not. And there is even talk of movement in the forests of Ul'Erel. That is all I need ... elves harassing our southern borders. And this easterner asks why such a military presence in my city. Do you think we do not have the same problems as you in Háthgolthane?"

"No, my lord," Erik replied.

"Are we so backward that you wonder how it is we live in castles and have standing militaries?"

"No, my lord," Erik repeated.

Wulfstan, his face red, stood while he pushed his empty plate away.

"Come, Lord Erik, there is something I wish to show you."

Erik looked around for a moment, but while some of the others, including Hilda and Yngrid, hadn't finished eating, they stood and so Erik followed suit.

The lord led his wife and daughter and the other guests to the stairway leading down to the first floor.

"Please, Lord Erik, come," Wulfstan said, and Erik followed.

When he had entered the first floor of the keep, it was crowded and well lit, but now it was dark, only a single torch burning by the door. The smell of sweat struck Erik's nose, and as he turned, a large fist struck him in the jaw. He stumbled backward as two pairs of hands wrapped around his arms and something shoved him in the chest, hard enough to put him on his heels. He felt the hands pull him down and, before he knew it, he was on his back. Torches now lit up all around him, and a crowd of faces stared down at him, all wearing conical helms and pointing swords at his face. A large man pushed some of the soldiers out of the way, and Wulfstan came into view.

"You must think me a fool?" Wulfstan said.

"My lord," Erik said, struggling against the hands that held him down. "I don't understand."

"You lie," Wulfstan said, and one of his soldiers leaned over and punched Erik in the face.

The back of his head bounced against the stone floor, sending a wave of pain down his neck and into his shoulders. He felt his consciousness waning as hands stripped away his sword and boots.

"No more lies," Wulfstan said. "What was your plan? Distract me while your henchmen do their work?"

"What?" Erik asked.

Another punch, this time to the stomach.

"What do you want with the Ruling Stone? What does Hámon want with the Ruling Stone?"

"Hámon?" Erik asked, but someone slammed a heel onto his chest, and he began coughing uncontrollably.

"Did Orn Beornson send you? Surely, that prick isn't that bold."

"No one sent me," Erik said, Wulfstan blurring between one head and two.

Another fist to the face. A kick to his ribs. A boot to his balls. He groaned loudly, his stomach reeling, and his groin throbbing with pain.

"Who are your friends?" Wulfstan asked.

"Friends?" Erik asked, trying to turn onto his side, but the men holding him down pulled him onto his back again. "I don't know what you're talking about."

"Fellow Hámonians? Hired thugs? Bear Clan filth? More lies," Wulfstan said.

The soldiers kicked and punched Erik. He felt the skin on his face open, his lips crack, and one of his back teeth dislodge. He imagined that several of his ribs were broken, a sharp pain shot through his hip, and one of his shoulders felt out of place. When the beating finally stopped, Erik looked up through rapidly closing eyes and saw Wulfstan nod to his men. They let go of his arms.

As he squinted, Erik saw Hilda and Yngrid, along with the other supper guests, watching. They were all smiling apart from Yngrid. She clung to her mother's arm like a little girl, tears in her eyes.

*What's happened to the Dragon Stone?*

Erik's mind was a jumble. What could have happened? Was that why the city was quiet, save for soldiers? Did something happen to the Dragon Stone? Was that why they were so suspicious of him?

"Let's show this fool what we do to thieves in Wulfstaad," Wulfstan said. "Let's reacquaint him with his friends."

*What friends?*

Guards grabbed his arms and dragged him, following their lord, outside of the keep into the cold night. From the light of torches held by other soldiers, Erik saw another man, battered and bloodied, with his shirt ripped away and cuts all along his skin exposed to face the chilling cold. He was on his knees and swayed back and forth.

"Do you know this man?" Wulfstan said, stepping forward.

Erik shook his head, but the lord wasn't speaking to him. He was speaking to the other man. He nodded.

"I've never met him in my ..." Erik began to say, but a fist to his mouth shut him up.

"I'm sorry," the beaten man said amidst sobs. "I'm sorry ... my friend."

He had been coerced into a confession. Erik still didn't know what was happening, but the Lord of Wulfstaad clearly suspected him of being a part of some crime, most likely involving the Dragon Stone and this man. He had been beaten so badly that he would say anything ... agree to anything, even if it were a lie. Erik didn't blame him for being weak-willed. A year ago, he would have done the same thing.

"This man's confession saved his life, Erik of Hámon, if that is your real name," Wulfstan said.

The soldier who had escorted Erik to the keep stepped from the crowd of guards, a large, two-handed sword held low.

"I'm sorry, Erik," the other man said, tears filling his eyes and streaming down his face.

He didn't know Erik's name until that moment, but his apology wasn't false.

"It's alright," Erik said.

"Hold out your right hand," the black-haired swordsman commanded.

The prisoner did as he was told. The man lifted the sword high and, with a single swipe, removed the right hand from the confessor. He screamed and clutched his bleeding stump as soldiers dragged him away.

"Your other friends weren't so lucky," Wulfstan said.

"I don't have any friends here," Erik said.

"What do you want with our Ruling Stone?" Wulfstan asked.

Erik was about to claim he knew nothing about the stone again. He was about to claim his Hámonian nobility, but it was no use.

"Protect it," he replied. "I only wish to protect it."

"Bah," Wulfstan spat. "At least you finally admit you want it."

The beating came again. Erik rolled from side to side, groaning. He grabbed his crotch with both hands, intense pain traveling into his stomach and making him want to vomit. He did, turning his head just in time.

Erik thought the beating would never stop, and as soon as he would put a hand up to protect his face, a boot would catch him in the stomach. He protected his stomach only to have someone stomp on his leg. He curled his leg to his body, only to have someone punch him in the face again.

"Enough!" Wulfstan said.

The beating stopped, although one man spat on Erik.

"Stand up," Wulfstan said.

Erik rolled to his stomach and struggled to push himself to his knees. There must have been two dozen or more soldiers there, watching him. He looked beyond the soldiers and Wulfstan and saw Hilda still watching. Her face was now stoic and indifferent. Yngrid stood next to her, clinging to her mother's arms, eyes red, lip trembling. He stepped up with one foot and had to put a hand on his knee to steady himself. He finally stood, wobbly, instinctively holding out an arm for balance. He accidentally touched one of the soldiers standing around him, and the man swatted his hand away, almost causing him to fall.

"Where are you really from?" Wulfstan asked. "The north? Holt-gaard? Gongoreth?"

Erik slowly shook his head, taking deep, heavy breaths, his eyes half-closed and swaying back and forth.

Wulfstan was a big man and, even though he carried extra weight just above his belt, he was larger and stronger than Erik. He stepped forward and grabbed Erik's shirt, pulling him close. His breath was hot and smelled of wine and beef.

"Where?"

"Free farms," Erik replied.

"How did a farmer get such a weapon?" Wulfstan asked, extending a hand.

One of his soldiers knelt next to the Chieftain and offered him Dragon Tooth, sheathed in its finely crafted, leather scabbard. Wulfstan took the sword and pushed Erik away. He would have fallen if a soldier behind him hadn't caught him and roughly stood him up. The Lord of Wulfstaad unsheathed the sword. In his hands, the blade looked normal—just a finely-crafted weapon made from Dwarf's Iron and marked with a raven and Dwarvish runes.

"We have had peace with Durnfell for years," Wulfstan said, looking at the blade and then to his guest, who was from Durnfell, the Raven Clan. Erik saw them from the corner of his eye, and they looked suddenly frightened, stepping back. "Do they wish to break peace? Are you a spy?"

Erik's chin dipped to his chest as he shook his head. He felt like he was going to fall, his knees buckling underneath him, but several soldiers caught him under the arms and stood him up.

"Mark of the swordsmith," Erik said. "Ilken Copper Head."

"More lies," Wulfstan seethed.

A soldier's fist struck Erik's chin, and another landed squarely in his stomach. He lurched forward and vomited again, both food and blood. Pain seared through his ribs as he wretched, and he groaned loudly. He heard Yngrid whimper and saw her father look at the girl over his shoulder.

"Did you murder a Raven Clan warrior for this sword?" Wulfstan asked, showing the weapon to Erik as if he didn't know what it looked like.

"No," Erik replied, his consciousness waning.

"Are you an assassin from Holtgaard?" Wulfstan asked. "Is Orn Beornson really that stupid? He couldn't have stolen it."

"I don't ... I don't know ... know who that is," Erik replied, his voice trailing off into almost a whisper.

Wulfstan grabbed Erik by the neck, one of his hands fitting around his throat, despite the muscled thickness that it was. He pulled Erik close again.

"We will see," Wulfstan said and then let go of Erik. "Show him his friends."

He fell this time, crumpling to the ground. Soldiers dragged him down the walkway that led to the keep and the gatehouse of Wulfstaad. The men who dragged him stood him up, and Wulfstan walked in front of him. He pointed to another guard.

"Adils, is this the man who came to see the prisoner last night?"

Erik struggled to see the man, through swollen eyes, but as he walked closer, Erik recognized him. He was the guard, the one Erik thought was more than a simple guard ... once.

"Yes," Adils replied.

Another man stepped up next to Adils. It was Ari, the leader who had arrested Gris ... *Gris!* Erik's thoughts, as beaten and worn as they were, began to race.

"Why did you let him speak with the prisoner?" Ari asked. Adils was clearly worried, his nonchalant air about him gone as both his captain and the Lord of Wulfstaad questioned him.

"He carried the mark of an officer, even though he wasn't wearing his uniform," Adils said. He lied.

"What did he want with the prisoner?" Wulfstan asked.

"I don't know my lord," Adils replied.

"And where is the prisoner now?" Wulfstan asked.

"We let him go early this morning, my lord," Adils replied.

"Did a judge see him?" Wulfstan asked.

"No, my lord," Adils replied. "He was there for being a drunkard and, just before the sun rose, Ari and the militia brought in almost twenty men for brawling. We had no room, so they turned the drunk out."

"Is this true, Captain?" Wulfstan asked, and Ari bowed.

"Yes, my lord," Ari replied.

"Do you know who this man was?" Wulfstan asked. "The man this thief, this imposter, came to see."

"No, my lord," Ari replied. "He claimed to be Gris Beornson, but that is quite impossible. Why would the son of the Lord of Holtgaard be drunk in one of our alehouses?"

"Truly," Wulfstan said.

"What do you think, guard?" Wulfstan asked.

"Impossible, my lord," Adils replied, although his eyes said he believed it, and he was afraid.

Another guard approached. He had a short, squat woman with him.

"Do you know her?" Wulfstan said, pushing against Erik's swollen cheek so he might face the woman. It was the old farmwife from the inn in which he had stayed. Her eyes were red as if she had been crying. Her dress was torn. It had been dirty when he stayed in her hostel, but not torn. She wrung her hands nervously and, even though Erik's vision was blurry, he could see a welt growing on her face.

"The ... the housewife of ... of the hostel," Erik finally sputtered out.

"Tell us, good woman," Wulfstan said. "Tell us what this man did."

"He raped me," she blurted out.

Erik squinted as much as he could. He clenched his fists even though his arms were being held back.

"You bitch!" he seethed, spittle and blood dripping off cracked lips.

"Do you see?" she said, pointing at Erik. "He is a violent man, a violent foreigner. He knocked my poor husband senseless and then forced himself onto me. It was horrible."

"Liar," Erik hissed.

"Who are you to call an innocent woman a liar?" Wulfstan said, and then looked at the woman. "Thank you good wife. Rest assured, justice will be served."

Some of Wulfstaad's guards dragged Erik forward a bit more.

"Do you see your friends?" Wulfstan said, grabbing Erik's chin and jerking his head upwards, towards the top of Wulfstaad's gate-house. Five men hung there, nooses around their necks, bodies stripped of clothing, bleeding and twisted and broken.

Erik tried to shake his head, but he couldn't against the lord's grip.

"They were found sneaking around our temple, just after the Ruling Stone was discovered missing this morning," Wulfstan said.

*The Ruling Stone—the Dragon Stone is gone?*

Erik suddenly had a moment of clarity, and his mind raced. Could Gris have done this? Could he have sent these men to their deaths? He tried to stand but felt the cold, hard iron of a sword's pommel to the back of his neck, and he saw black for a moment as he went back to his knees.

"But, of course, you already knew that, didn't you?" Wulfstan said. "You think you are tough, but you *will* tell me where the Ruling Stone is. With the Creator as my witness, you *will* experience the full hospitality of the north before you take your last breath."

# 33

"Master," Terradyn said, speaking into the darkness.

He sat cross-legged on the cold ground with his eyes shut, concentrating. He could feel the blue magic pulse along the tattoos on the side of his head. Even though the air was cold—freezing—he didn't feel it. He only felt the void of the darkness, heard the nothingness of black, saw naught in the shadow. And, then, there was a flash of light. Terradyn didn't know if it was truly a pinpoint of light, but that's how he thought of it, in this dark place of magical communication.

The space around him shifted, and he heard a voice.

"Terradyn," the voice said. It was his master. It was the Messenger of the East.

"Master," Terradyn said. He tried not sounding excited, but he hadn't communicated with his master for some time and, in a way, he missed him.

"Winds are changing, Terradyn," the Black Mage said. His voice sounded distant and worried.

"I will come home, at once then," Terradyn said. He felt his body stand, even though his eyes were still closed.

"No!" the Messenger of the East said in a whispering shout. "You must stay the course. Protect Erik Eleodum."

"I don't know where he is, master," Terradyn said. "He had left his farmstead by the time we got there."

"You must go after him," the Black Mage said. "Find him."

"I am seeking to catch up with him, my lord," Terradyn said, "and Raktas has stayed behind to protect his family."

There was a long silence, even though Terradyn could still feel his master's presence.

"What is wrong, my lord?" Terradyn asked.

He heard nothing—no response.

"My lord?" Terradyn said. Still nothing. "Andragos?"

"I am no longer the Messenger of the East," Andragos finally replied, his voice even more distant. "I am no longer the Herald of Golgolithul. The Lord of the East has turned on me. It is dangerous here. Find Erik. Protect him. Contact me when you find him."

"Yes, my lord," Terradyn replied.

"And do not return until I send for you. Do you understand?"

"Yes, my lord," Terradyn repeated, even though he didn't understand anything the Black Mage said. He was the Messenger of the East. He was the Herald of Golgolithul. He had been for a thousand years. How could the Lord of the East just remove those titles?

Terradyn opened his eyes. Clouds covered the moon, but it was still lighter than the space in which he had just been. He finally felt the cold, but he ignored it. He looked to his horse—Shadow—and wondered what to do. A part of him wanted to head back to Golgolithul, ride hard east. His master, the man who had been the only father-figure in his life, was in danger, and every fiber in Terradyn's body was telling him to go ... go to his master and protect him. But that meant disobedience. He got to his feet and wandered over to the horse that had served him for more years than he could remember.

"We will ride through the night, Shadow," Terradyn said, patting the horse's neck. "Danger looms ahead, and we are needed."

Terradyn heeled Shadow, and they rode hard ... west.

Ankara knew she was being followed. She could feel it, could sense the magic of one of the men who had defended Erik Eleodum's farmstead. He was a powerful man, a servant of the Black Mage. She wasn't afraid of him, but, right now, she could ill afford any distractions, any more use of her power. She would need her magic to seek out Erik and—perhaps—kill him. He had, after all, overcome her father and taken his life when he was one of the most powerful men she had known. But then again, he was only a man.

As she nudged Naga faster, she leaned forward and stared out, searching, seeking for any glimpse or sign again. She'd already seen a group of men riding horses in the darkness of a moonless winter night, and she'd avoided them. She also saw a band of ogres and avoided them as well, those strange mystics who lied about not using magic and always spoke in riddles. They weren't dangerous, just annoying.

Now she saw a pack of wolves. Especially here in the north, such a pack might have gone out of their way to bring down a horse and its rider. Ankara, but especially Naga, would make a good meal, and fill their bellies for a week. But animals always had an innate ability to sense danger and magic, and they were the ones that avoided her, giving her a wide birth as they howled to one another, ran wide south, and then, presumably, began chasing some other prey.

That was about looking for things or people she wanted to avoid, but there was the other aspect to her searching. Erik Eleodum. She had tried avoiding the use of her magic, but now and again, she reached out with her mind, seeking a sense of her prey. She didn't know what he looked like, but after seeing his people, she had a better idea. She knew what she might look for with her magic. She could do that with her magical powers of sight. If she had an idea of what someone looked like, smelled like, sounded like, she could reach out with that special sight that most people had never tapped into and searched. Her father would do it, not from where he was now.

So, as Naga pushed on, Ankara closed her eyes once more and searched. She saw thousands of people in hundreds of dwellings and stone buildings, but none of them was the man she sought. She came upon a large building, perhaps a castle, nothing ... No, wait. She looked closer and saw a heavily fortified room with thick walls, and inside, she saw a shadow. She couldn't make the man out, hidden as he was by stone and iron, but another sense triggered her interest. Her hearing. It was a man's voice, and he was moaning in pain as he called out, desperately and quietly for someone. The name he muttered was one she had heard on the Eleodum Farm.

"Simone ..." the voice croaked. "I'm so sorry, Simone."

It was him, and he'd landed himself in some sort of trouble. She didn't care about that for his sake; if someone else killed him, she'd still claim her price from Syzbalo. Her main purpose was to recover the sword he carried. If he was in prison somewhere, hurt, dying, someone else might have it.

Ankara opened her eyes, and as she did, something caught her attention, through a quick sidelong glance. It was white, a quick flash, like a falling star but moving horizontally. She paid it no mind. She had to hurry.

"Hurry, Nagarooshi," Ankara whispered to her horse. "Fly. Fly. Fly."

The power behind the little horse seemed to increase beyond what could be considered possible looking at her, and as her hooves thudded into the hard-packed, frozen ground, the air whipped Ankara's face so hard she wondered if it might even draw blood. The thought of that spurred her on even more.

"Woe to the man who takes his sword," Ankara whispered, "for I will kill him and all his seed and leave them in a sea of blood."

## 34

*A*fter he'd been thrown into the prison cell like a sack of discarded potatoes, Erik had managed to prop himself up against the damp and cold wall. The cell was dark, with only a small amount of moonlight spilling in through a high, barred window, and the faint light of a torch from somewhere down a hallway spilling in front of his cell. Another one stood across from Erik's, but as far as he could see, no one was in it.

As he looked down through the slits that were his eyes, he saw his clothes were torn, and he felt cold. He did nothing more than shiver, but pain shot through his side, moving his broken ribs. He breathed slowly, trying not to cough, and as the ache in his chest subsided, it reared again in his groin or what felt like a hundred other places. He believed his left shoulder was broken or dislocated, and the same for the right hip. That wasn't to mention all the bruises from fists and boots.

He must have dozed for a while, but when he came back to consciousness, he needed to relieve himself. At first, he thought he'd just do it sitting there, but he couldn't. He was sure there'd be no pot in the cell, but at least he'd use a corner. How could he stand? He could only push up with one arm, his good leg, and shuffle his back along the wall. He gritted his teeth and slowly inched up the stone like a caterpillar crawling along a leaf.

When he was finally upright, he was sweating despite the icy night and shaky on his feet. Cradling his left arm against his body to avoid using his shoulder and shifting all his weight to his left leg, he tried to reach up to the window, but it sat too high in the wall. He sighed and rested his forehead against the wet wall but jerked his head away as he put pressure on one of the many bruises on his face.

He relieved himself in a corner away from where he'd sat and turned before shuffling towards the bars of his cell. Holding on to them with his right hand to stop from falling over, he looked out and saw he was in a small dungeon with five other cells, and this was no temporary home for drunks and fighters. He called out, but no one answered. Looking across to the cell facing his, he saw a shadow move, a mound of clothing on the floor. A man looked up, his face beaten and bloody, he cradled his right arm with his left. It was the confessor, the man who had lied about knowing Erik. He gasped for air, eyes widening as much as they could when they met Erik's, and he tried to mouth something. Erik thought it was 'sorry', but the effort to lift his head and speak consumed all his energy, and he collapsed into a ball of clothing again.

Wulfstan had spared this man's life, but what sort of life would he have, if he ever had one outside the walls of this prison. He would be labeled a thief, left with one hand and shunned by his own people. Better had he died with the rest of his comrades, hanging from the walls of Wulfstaad. Still, the threat of death could have been overwhelming and cause any man to seek a way to still live.

Erik returned to where he'd sat before, and by a reverse process of slowly easing his back down the wall, he sat again where he had before.

*So what now? Is this how it ends?*

He had been a guest of the dwarvish king, fought a dragon, and wielded an ancient sword, and he was now doomed to rot in a northern dungeon while his wife, his child, and his family wondered what happened to him.

"Simone," Erik muttered, and he couldn't help the tears that streamed down his face. The salty drops touched the many cuts in his flesh, and when he winced, the sudden movement hurt even more. It had been a long time since he had truly wept, but that's what he did, squeezing whatever tears he had out of his body. "I'm so sorry, Simone."

He had widowed his wife, left her to raise his child alone in a cruel world that wanted nothing more than to hurt him and his loved ones. He was so stupid. Of course, the Lord of Wulfstaad was suspicious of him. He was a foreigner and a liar. And to be outdone by a drunk nobleman?

Erik was disgusted with himself, knowing this Gris Beornson was probably well on his way back to Holtgaard, the Dragon Stone tucked into his saddlebags. He would never make it home. Erik knew others would be after the stone, just like others wanted the Dragon Sword. Who, though? The Lord of the East? Gol-Durathna? The mysterious cloaked figure from his dreams, the one Dewin was so afraid of? What did it matter? Without the stone, the world was doomed.

Eventually, his body's natural defenses forced him to sleep, and he had no idea how much time had passed when he heard a loud commotion outside his cell, the noise coming from the window that must have been at ground level outside. At first, he couldn't make out what anyone was saying, but he knew they were angry.

"Kill the thief!"

That was unmistakable.

"Back up!" a voice responded. It was Wulfstan. "This thief will feel the full weight of Wolf Clan justice!"

The others cheered loudly.

*They're talking about me.*

"And then, we will find the fool who stole our Ruling Stone!" Wulfstan shouted.

"Then what?" someone asked.

"We march on Holtgaard!" Wulfstan replied, and the crowd roared.

"Hang him!" someone shouted.

"Burn him!" another added.

Erik's stomach twisted, and he felt sick, but then he heard a different noise to the one outside, something nearer. He turned his head in the opposite direction and heard the creak of hinges echoing through the small dungeon as a door opened and then closed. His heart beat faster and began to sweat again despite the intense cold. This was it. It didn't matter how many came; he would fight them to the death.

He saw a familiar face in the faintness of the torchlight and moonlight. It was a woman, tall and broad-shouldered with long, curly hair. She had a large bundle in her arms, which looked like clothing in the darkness. Erik saw the shadow of a scabbard poking from underneath the clothing.

"Yngrid?" Erik croaked.

"Hurry," the daughter of the Lord of Wulfstaad whispered. "They're coming for you."

"Your father?"

"Yes," she replied. "The clan holding have found out the Ruling Stone is gone. They want—they need—retribution. It will start with you."

Erik could hear the commotion outside intensify. The din of people gathering rose to a deafening level.

"We don't have time," Yngrid said, producing a key from underneath the bundle of clothing and opening the door to Erik's prison cell.

"What are you doing?" Erik asked.

"Put these on," Yngrid commanded, ignoring Erik's question.

Strong and broad, Yngrid helped Erik stand and shoved the clothing into Erik's chest. As well-muscled as she was, she shouldn't have been able to knock Erik over, but she did. His hurt hip gave out from under his weight, and he crumpled to the floor.

"Oh, by the Creator," Yngrid huffed. "Are you going to make me dress you?"

She dropped the pile of clothing next to Erik and stared at him. His whole body hurt. His groin felt like his balls were stuck in an oil press, and it was as if someone stuck a hot poker inside his shoulder and wrist. The pain in his hip was unlike anything he had ever felt, and when he breathed his ribs hurt so badly he held his breath as much as he could, wheezing and gasping for air in short breaths.

"Hurry," Yngrid hissed.

His mail shirt and other pieces of armor were in the pile of clothing, along with a clean shirt and pair of pants and his heavy bearskin blanket.

"I need you to help me," Erik said, panting.

Yngrid huffed, but when she helped Erik take his shirt off, she looked shocked when she saw all the bruising. He opted to leave his armor off—he could barely stand in just his shirt, pants, and boots. She draped his bearskin blanket across his shoulders, and that was almost too heavy. The lord's daughter then put Erik's good arm across her shoulder and lifted him up. He thought his ribs had pierced his lungs, but he groaned and gritted his teeth; the woman was incredibly strong and was able to prop him up with little effort.

A loud banging echoed through the dungeon.

"Hurry," Yngrid said. "They're coming."

"Why are you doing this?" Erik asked. "Won't you be in trouble?"

She ignored him again, practically dragging Erik through the small dungeon, away from the front door.

"I barred the main door," she explained, "but it won't hold for long. There is a secret back door most of the guards won't know about."

The short hallway ended at a stone wall, two cells adjacent to the wall, and facing each other. Yngrid turned to the cell to their right and opened it.

"We never put anyone in this cell," she said as she pulled Erik to the back of the cell.

"If I'm not here," Erik said, "they'll take the other man."

"Maybe," Yngrid replied.

"I can't let him die for me," Erik said.

"He lied about you," Yngrid said. Her blazing blue eyes met his.

"How do you know he lied?" Erik asked.

"Did he?" she asked.

"Yes," Erik replied without hesitation.

"I could tell," Yngrid said. "When he saw you, outside the keep. I'm a great judge of character. I knew he was lying. His eyes said that he didn't know you."

Yngrid gave a quick, self-assuring smile.

"I knew he had lied about you," she continued, "just to get out of losing his life."

"But now he might lose it anyway," Erik said.

"He's a thief," she said, "and a liar. We need to worry about you."

"Why?"

"Will you stop asking questions!" Yngrid snapped, propping Erik against the cell wall.

Erik cradled his left arm as he shifted all of his weight to his left leg. She brushed loose straw away from the floor, revealing a small, wooden door with a round, iron ring for a handle. She gripped the handle with both hands and pulled up. The secret door opened and thudded against the floor with a loud, heavy bang.

"Come on," she said. "I can lower you down a bit, but there will still be a short drop."

Erik tried to control his breathing as he stared down into the darkness. He slid into the opening, Yngrid holding him under his arms. He clenched his teeth as more pain shot through his ribs and shoulder and did his best to land on his left foot when she let go of him, but he still felt his knees buckle and crumpled in the darkness. He heard Yngrid land next to him, even though he couldn't see her. The scratching of rock produced several sparks, and a torch anchored to the wall caught fire as one of the flashes ignited its pitch, revealing a small room attached to a dark hallway.

Erik watched as Yngrid grabbed a short ladder leaning against the wall, propped it up so she could reach into the vacant cell, closed the secret door with a loud thud, and removed the ladder once again.

"I know you want to," Yngrid said, "but we can't stay here long."

Erik heard a distant bang, undoubtedly muffled by the stone ceiling and thick, wooden door. The mob had broken into the dungeon.

"I didn't steal the Ruling Stone," Erik said as Yngrid helped him stand again.

"I know," Yngrid said, strapping Erik's belt and sheathed sword around his waist, pressing herself close to him as she did.

"How?" Erik asked.

"You couldn't," Yngrid replied, face to face with Erik and her nose and eyes too close to his for comfort. "It was Gris Beornson."

She stepped away from Erik.

"You know he was here?" Erik asked with a gasp. Her father and the captain Ari were certain only a fool would believe the lordling of Holtgaard had been in Wulfstaad.

"Of course," Yngrid replied, so sure of herself.

"Why?"

"He came to see me," Yngrid replied.

"Why?" Erik asked again.

Yngrid blushed.

"Well, he sneaks into Wulfstaad from time to time," she explained, "to come and see me."

"See you?"

"Yes," Yngrid hissed, her face a bright red. "Must I draw you a picture in the dirt. Surely, you've laid with a woman before."

"He must be twice your age," Erik said.

"Not quite," Yngrid said, stepping back a bit and looking a little hurt and offended. "Doesn't matter. Doesn't matter how much fun we had. He used me, obviously. He only ever had his eyes set on the Ruling Stone. That ass."

Yngrid clenched her fists as the muscles around her jaw flexed. Then, she looked at Erik again, her eyes squinted.

"But you wanted it too, didn't you?" she asked, stepping close.

"Not to take," Erik said, looking down and breathing heavily as adrenaline began to subside and his pain grew to levels he had never felt before. "To protect."

"To protect?" Yngrid asked.

"It's more than you think it is," Erik said, but it was even hard just to speak now. "It's ... it's more than an ancient gift from the elves."

"If you're going to start another rambling tale, that's for another time," Yngrid said, almost ducking as they heard shouting and banging, even through the stone floor and thick, wooden door. "We need to go."

## 35

As Andragos watched the black smoke rise into the air from the home he'd set on fire, its heat a contrast with the encroaching cold of winter, he knew his escape would not be so easy. The Lord of the East had spies everywhere, including several among his servants, and he had just finished choking an old serving woman, who he knew had passed information onto Syzbalo, throwing her body into the large fireplace that centered the wall of his sitting room. He rarely felt a need for servants, and the ones he had lined up in front of him were placed there by the Lord of the East. He had boiled the blood of a fat cook and made a pretty young woman stare into a looking glass as he aged her to an old hag. As soon as the spell was done, she broke the mirror and slit her own throat with one of the shards. Now they were all dead, and it was time to go.

He had already copied all of his spell books, anthologies, and volumes of histories, so he left the ones sitting on the shelves of his library to burn. The Lord of the East would not get his hands on a thousand years of work, and that Isutan magician that now served as advisor to Syzbalo would have to do his own research.

Andragos had sent his three hundred pages away first, along with twenty of his soldiers and fifty recruits. His soldiers knew where to go, to move to one of his secret homes, a former magical meadow of the elves. Then, he sent his squires, two score per group, each with two soldiers as escorts. As he finally prepared to leave himself, word came through one of his remaining loyal spies in the city that the Lord of the East had dispatched a unit, some two hundred of his elite personal guard, to seize Andragos and his precious possessions, kill his Soldiers of the Eye, and set fire to his home. They had that goblin with them, and his brood, as well.

"Goblins," Andragos spat. "What in the nine hells are you doing with goblins, Syzbalo?"

He squinted, searching his memory and thoughts, trying to figure out why Melanius, or the witches, or the Lord of the East himself would want to employ goblins. They were adept fighters, and tenacious on the battlefield, but they were unreliable and prone to infighting and thievery as much as they were to battling the enemy. And they could not be trusted, stabbing any leader in the back as soon as he turned his head for too long.

Andragos looked at the smoke again and growled. He knew Syzbalo's troops would come, so he'd done the burning for him.

They were coming sooner than he had expected, and with a unit of elite guardsmen on his tail, escape would be anything but easy. When he and the Soldiers of the Eye, along with three hundred pages, two hundred squires, and a hundred recruits were ready to depart, forty of his Soldiers of the Eye volunteered to stay behind.

"I cannot protect you," Andragos had said.

"I would be a simple street rat if it weren't for you, my lord," one of the soldiers said.

"I've lived a good life," another added.

"You have given me much, my lord," a third said. "I will willingly give my life for you."

Andragos nodded his appreciation and looked each man in the eye, something that would never have happened before.

"You will buy us much time, I know that of your skills and bravery, but once you are overrun, put your dagger to your throat. You do not want the Lord of the East capturing you. Your death will be slow and painful."

All forty of his soldiers snapped to attention and saluted him. While they were all dead men now, he knew they could probably defeat the unit of guardsmen, but Syzbalo would send many more, and these goblins—these Black Wolves—were elite fighters as well. As well trained as Andragos' soldiers were, even they couldn't fight off a thousand men and cunning goblin warriors.

As his entourage hurried into a copse of trees, one of the last true forests that existed in the vastly developed east, he looked back and saw two of his soldiers lying dead alongside the road, together with the bodies of several recruits. No doubt some of the recruits had decided they didn't want to defect from the east and rose up against their protectors. Andragos expected as much, but it also encouraged him to stay off any roads.

As he stood in front of the forest, staring at the giant oak trees along its edges, the others he had sent away earlier emerged from hiding in the darkness of the thick canopy. A quick headcount told him he had almost sixty soldiers left, some seventy recruits, a little over one hundred squires, and two hundred pages. He knew there would be losses—he had expected more—and he nodded to each of them who dared to look in his eyes. He even gave them an uneasy smile.

Ready now for his next move, Andragos picked out an especially large oak tree and began to chant. As his voice rose, he clapped loudly, and the echo met the tree, the trunk twisting, cracking and groaning as a glowing portal appeared in the thickest part of the tree. When the old wood stood split wide open, enough for the biggest of men to pass through, he nodded to Shudraka, and his captain led what was left of the Black Mage's soldiers and followers through the portal. Some of the young pages were scared to enter, but the others helped them through, either coaxing or dragging them.

Before he stepped into the portal, the last to leave, Andragos turned around to look at the country he had served for a thousand years. His stomach knotted. He would have been a fool to think his time there, his power and position would never end, but a part of him thought it wouldn't. Now it was the end of one age, and the beginning of a new one, the age of a different Andragos and era in which Syzbalo would play no part.

## 36

*Y*ngrid almost dragged Erik down a short hallway that ended in a gated door. Her key unlocked the gate and then the door, and Erik saw only darkness. The air smelled damp and musky, reminding him of the tunnels that led to the city of Thorakest, as they stepped into a rocky tunnel, cold and damp and slick with ice.

"Careful," Yngrid said once she had locked the door again behind them and lit a torch.

"What are you going to do?" Erik asked.

"Get you away from Wulfstaad."

"Won't you get in trouble?" Erik asked.

"I am a Lady of Wulfstaad," Yngrid said with a smile. "There is only so much trouble I can get in."

She looked at Erik as he hobbled along, his arm still draped over her shoulder. Her eyes were a steely blue and strong, commanding. She smiled and, as Erik looked at her, gave a quick, almost inaudible giggle. Since she'd come to his rescue, she'd seemed different to the teenage flirt at the dining table, but her youth still showed.

"And my father can be a bullish turd," she added. "He's only been Lord of Wulfstaad for five winters, just after my grandfather passed away. He was a good man, a good ruler, but he was a hard man. My father is trying to be too much like him. He had no need to behave like he did last night, and he didn't really impress anyone. Those who beat you were merely following orders."

Erik nodded his understanding, and the rest of the way through the tunnel was covered in silence save for Erik's rasping breath and grunts of pain. The tunnel curved several times before they could see moonlight and the opening to the outside world with one more gate. Yngrid unlocked that, closing it and locking it behind them, and as Erik shuffled towards some smooth, lichen covered rocks, he heard a sound that lifted his heart. He turned around, and there was Warrior. The horse stomped its hooves as he saw his master and pulled away from the northern soldier that had been holding his reins. Erik suspected he could have done that whenever he wanted but allowed the man to lead him to this place. He trotted to Erik, nuzzling him hard and almost knocking him over.

"Warrior," Erik said, resting a cheek on the horse's nose and scratching his chin, "be careful, my friend. I am hurt."

Erik looked at Yngrid.

"How?"

"The stable boy is in love with me," she said with a girlish smile. "It's cute. But he'll do anything for me. When I take horses out for midnight rides, he keeps my secrets, and all I need to do is give him a kiss on the cheek."

Erik looked at four men who stood outside the gate, waiting and watching.

"These men are loyal to me," Yngrid said, pointing to the four soldiers that met them outside the secret entrance to the keep. "They will accompany us."

Trying to be gentle but not succeeding, two of the soldiers helped Erik into his saddle, and one slid Erik's right foot into the stirrup. He wanted to scream, but Yngrid, on her horse next to him, quickly leaned over and clapped her hand over his mouth, and he yelled into her palm. Warrior turned hard on the man with a snort, biting at him.

"Easy boy," Erik said, patting the warhorse's neck. "It's not his fault. Where are we going?"

"South," Yngrid said. "After Gris and the Ruling Stone. We have to hurry. It won't be long before my father knows what has happened."

"I don't know if I can ride," Erik said, pain searing through his body, his vision blurring as he sat atop Warrior's saddle, the straddle position pushing his hip out.

"Here," Yngrid said, passing a small vial to Erik. "It will help with the pain."

"Will it dull my wits?" Erik asked through gritted teeth.

"A little," Yngrid replied. "We'll strap you into your saddle, and I'll lead your horse."

Erik shook his head.

"Don't be a fool," Yngrid said.

Erik shook his head again, and Yngrid huffed angrily.

"Men," she muttered. "Idiots."

As Erik straightened, he opened his mouth, holding back another scream with all his might. He felt hot tears at the corners of his eyes, and his hands shook. His lungs, pressing against broken ribs as they expanded, burned. His hip hurt so badly, it felt as if his leg were about to fall off, and the grip in his left hand was nonexistent. The very thought of riding Warrior made him want to weep.

"Maybe just a little," Erik said. "Half."

Yngrid nodded with a smile and handed Erik the vial. He drank half, but his pain was still there.

"How long will it take?" he asked.

"A little while," Yngrid said. "You have to be patient."

A little while might as well have been an eternity.

Yngrid had given Erik's armor to one of the men, and he stuffed the mail shirt into one of Warrior's saddlebags. His shield hung there, as well, where he had left it, as well as his hunting bow. Erik looked down at the man and the soldier up at him. He squinted and watched Erik for a long moment, his eyes questioning, cautious, and suspicious. Those were the eyes of a man who loved his master—in this case, mistress—and he feared for her.

He tied the reins around Erik's hands and used some leather laces to secure his boots into the stirrups.

"Ready?" the man asked.

Erik nodded slowly, breathing evenly as pain coursed through his body.

"Yes," Erik replied. "Thank ... thank you."

The four soldiers mounted their horses, and without a word, Yngrid clicked her tongue, and they moved off towards the south. The bounce of the trot was agony for Erik, but as the horses moved into a gallop, his chin dipped to his chest, and the potion seemed to be starting to work a little. However, it might as well have been a single bucket of water trying to put out the flames that consumed a castle. Every step Warrior took seemed to jolt every injury in his body, and he felt his consciousness wane. This was not from Yngrid's potion, but his mind seeking to shut itself down against the pain. Perhaps that would be best if he passed out.

The clan holding of Wulfstaad faded behind them quickly, especially with the speed at which they rode. It began to snow, and Erik thanked the cold as it numbed his body a little. The temperature, along with Yngrid's potion, fought like an invading army against the constant bouncing of a jerking horse, and Erik couldn't imagine what it would have been like without them. Erik gave in and asked Yngrid to stop several times, and she chided him, suggesting he ought to be a woman and try giving birth to a child.

They had ridden further, for several hours, when Erik had to call out again. They stopped, and having endured the pain for as long as he possibly could, he begged to be let down from his saddle.

"I have to rest," he said, leaning forward against Warrior and breathing heavily.

"We have to keep moving," Yngrid said. "Father will be after us soon, and Gris is certainly well on his way to Holtgaard."

"I am in too much pain," Erik said, holding his left arm. He felt tears touch the corners of his eyes. "I have suffered before, and I am not a weak man, but my injuries ... they are too much."

One of the soldiers dismounted to help Erik out of the saddle and got him seated on the trunk of tree that had been felled by the wind.

"We will give you a short while, but we must ..."

Yngrid never finished her sentence. At that moment, there was a flash like a shooting star, and one of the other soldiers flew from his saddle, landing on the ground with a thud, the long shaft of a black arrow protruding from his chest. The dead man's horse neighed loudly and then went to the ground, an arrow stuck in its chest, piercing its heart.

"Get off your horses!" yelled the soldier who had helped Erik, but he was too late for one of the remaining two. As soon as the words had left the soldier's mouth, another flash streaked through the air and an arrow struck one of the men on horseback between the eyes. He jerked backward and then toppled sideways from his saddle. Yngrid spun around on her horse, trying to see where the attack was coming from, but remained in the saddle.

Adrenaline pushed away some of Erik's pain as he pulled his shield from off Warrior's back, but his shoulder and wrist hurt so badly he could barely lift it. He heard a sound like a screeching hawk as something split the air, and with a pain-filled grunt, he lifted his shield with his right hand and promptly flew backward as an arrow struck the steel and exploded into a thousand little pieces of wood. Instinctively, Warrior stepped in front of Erik, just as the final soldier went down underneath his horse when an arrow pierced the animal's eye. The man screamed as his leg twisted oddly beneath the weight of his mount, but an arrow passing through his throat silenced his cries.

Erik's vision blurred. He couldn't move. His body had locked up, and he couldn't even breathe. He simply stared at the sky, open-mouthed, gasping like he was drowning. It was as if a thousand scorpions stung every part of his body all at once, and when their stingers stopped, and their poison had run its course, he screamed louder than he had ever screamed before, tears streaming down his cheeks. He heard laughter, far off in the distance, and tried to grab one of Warrior's stirrups, but the pain pulled him back down and rendered him helpless. He tried to lift up again, screaming as if that would help, and he heard more laughter. As Warrior stepped sideways, an arrow had grazed his chest, and blood began to seep from the wound, but he stood firm, in front of Erik. He would die protecting Erik if he didn't get them moving. Once more, Erik lifted up, this time barely gripping the stirrup with his fingers.

"Come on Warrior," he commanded. The horse looked at him, over his shoulder, and began to walk forward, dragging Erik with him by the good arm. The pain in his hip and ribs was excruciating but better than the injured shoulder.

"Over there," Erik said in Shengu and, as if Warrior knew exactly where Erik meant, he led his master to a pile of flesh, the combination of two dead horses lying next to one another and a dead soldier. It wasn't much for cover, but it would have to do.

"Hurry," Erik said, repeating the word in Shengu. Warrior began to move faster, but then snorted and neighed loudly. Erik looked up and saw the black shaft of a long arrow sticking out from Warrior's flank. The horse, true to his name, however, kept walking, keeping himself in between their hidden attacker and Erik.

When Erik made it to the pile of dead horse and man, he crawled behind the corpses. Then, he reached up to the dangling reins and pulled hard. Again, as if he knew exactly what Erik wanted from him, the horse lay on the ground as another arrow sailed high, barely missing the animal's head. Warrior lay flat and still, ignoring the arrow jutting from his flesh.

"Stay down," Erik said as he dared a peek over the mass of dead bodies that now protected him. Then he yelled. *"Yngrid! Get off your horse and come over here!"*

As she turned towards Erik, an arrow struck her in the shoulder. She screamed and, for all her strength and prowess and muscle, her cry sounded like that of a young girl, helpless and weak. She fell from her horse just as two other arrows thudded into her animal's ribs and neck. It fell on top of her, trapping her legs underneath its massive body. The last living soldier—the man who had helped Erik down from his saddle—ran to his mistress, but he never made it. As he sought to lift his shield to protect her, he jolted to the right as two arrows in quick succession thunked into his chest. Yngrid screamed, and the man let out a sorrowful cry as he hit the ground, one of the arrows snapping in half and the other one pushing all the way through his back. He reached out a hand towards Yngrid and then died, his arm still outstretched towards her.

Yngrid cried out, screaming to the sky and trying to push her dead horse off her, to no avail. As she struggled, Erik watched the horizon, peering over the dead horse in front of him as much as he dared. He saw nothing but empty space and a few sparse trees between them and their hidden attacker.

*How far away can they be?*

He looked to Yngrid and realized her screaming had stopped. She now lay still, her chest barely moving up and down, and Erik thought she was dying, but then she seemed to come to again. Panic set in once more, and she began to yell and cry again.

"Hush," Erik said, as two arrows thudded into the flesh of the horse trapping her against the ground. "You need to calm down and keep still. Whoever is out there is a marksman and could probably find your throat just by the sound of your voice."

"*Help me!*" she cried, tears filling her eyes as she tried to push the horse off her. "This thing is so heavy on my legs!"

"I will," Erik tried to reassure, "but we need to wait."

"I can't," she said. "I'm going to die."

Yngrid began to weep, and at that moment, she became Simone. Another young, strong woman, proud and independent, but sobbing as her husband left for yet another time. He pulled himself up just a little more, but an arrow thudded into the saddle of the dead horse behind which he hid.

"Yngrid," Erik said.

The woman kept crying hysterically, trying to push the horse off her and then screaming when she remembered the arrow jutting from her shoulder.

"*Yngrid!*" Erik yelled. She stopped and, tears still in her eyes, looked at Erik. "Keep your eyes on me. Don't look at the horse on top of you. Don't look at your shoulder. Just look at me."

Erik waited, looking out, and, even though she cried silently, Yngrid did as she was told, keeping her eyes on him. After a while, something appeared from within a group of half a dozen trees close to the horizon ... a shadow. It came closer, moving towards them slowly, and Erik's hand slid to the handle of Dragon Tooth.

"Be ready, Warrior," Erik said.

The shadow came closer, and Erik saw something slender and long lifted, a bow. He ducked his head and promptly heard the whooshing of air just above him.

"*Erik Eleodum! I am coming for you!*" the shadow shouted in Westernese.

The voice was heavily accented, short and robotic, and angry, and it reminded Erik of Specter. It was the same Isutan accent, but this voice was a little softer and higher pitched. It was the voice of a woman.

"*Erik Eleodum!*" the voice shouted again. "I only want you. I'm sure you know why. Come with me, and no one else dies. I'll leave your family be. I'll let this woman live."

To get to Hargoleth, this new Isutan assassin would have had to pass by his farmstead. Erik sighed heavily. If her words were true, his family was still alive, and that spurred him on to fight as best he could.

"Will you at least let me stand when you kill me?" Erik asked. Each word pressed his lungs against his ribs, shock waves of pain rolling through his body. "Let me die with a little dignity."

"Erik!" Yngrid screamed. "No!"

"Yes," the voice said. The assassin was close.

Erik looked at Yngrid and put a hand up, smiled, and shook his head. He looked to Warrior, lying patiently and waiting.

"Stay still," Erik said in Shengu. "Then take Yngrid back to her father."

Erik was sure this woman would not stick to her word. She was an assassin, a bounty hunter, a mercenary. He knew she was lying. But maybe he would give Yngrid or Warrior a chance to escape. Maybe she would think twice about going back to the farmstead and dealing with Bryon or the dwarves.

Erik rolled to his stomach and managed to get onto all fours. He knelt up, straightening his back, and looked out into the distance, seeing the small woman. He slowly stepped up with his left foot and thought he might come to his feet on his first attempt, but he wobbled and fell back to his knees. The assassin laughed again.

"Pathetic, don't you think," she said. "Especially for a man named Dragon Slayer."

*Truly.*

Erik heard her voice as if she was right beside him, but she was a good distance away.

"Magic," he grumbled.

He stepped up again, taking more time than before. As he came upright, standing mostly on his left leg, his footing was unsure, but he caught his balance and straightened his back again as much as he could. He rested his left hand on the handle of his sword. This assassin was an expert with her bow, and she was quick. He didn't know how many arrows she had left. He didn't know how fast he could draw his own sword when it was almost impossible to twist his torso the smallest amount, but he had no intention of dying without a fight.

The assassin stopped—thirty paces from Erik as he stood behind a dead horse. She was short and lithe; her hair was so dark, he could only see that it was pulled into a tight knot atop her head. Her almond-shaped eyes squinted, but he could still see they were emerald green, almost sparkling and glowing in the starlight. She watched him, intently. She knew he was false, and he knew she was false. He recognized the family resemblance.

"Another puppet letting Syzbalo pull their strings," Erik said.

The woman laughed.

"Are you trying to make me angry?" she asked. "Or just let me know you're aware of his name?"

Erik ignored her question.

"He likes Isutans, doesn't he?" Erik asked. "His mage. Those two witches."

"Those bitches are not Isutan," the woman hissed.

Erik smiled. He had struck a chord.

"Your father ..." Erik continued. "You should have seen the look on his face as he died by my sword and before he turned to dust."

"You won't stir me that easily," the woman said, regaining her composure. "Specter contributed his seed to my mother's womb, and his parenting stopped there. And let us be honest, it's not your sword."

"It is now," Erik said, not seeing the need to get into an argument with this assassin about the ownership of Dragon Tooth.

"Fine," she said. "For a few more moments."

"Does anything come from Isuta that's better than a rat turd?" Erik asked.

She chuckled.

"Show it to me," the woman said.

"What?"

"The sword," she said, "show it to me."

Erik saw her lips, a deep red as the moonlight caught them just right. They twitched, just slightly. She was excited. His right hand went to the handle of Dragon Tooth, and he slowly drew his blade. The green flame of his sword matched the brilliance of her eyes as they widened and then narrowed into a tight squint. She licked her lips.

She began to lift her bow, but not at him, at Yngrid. The girl screamed when she saw the arrow, almost fully drawn, pointed at her face.

"Keep screaming," the woman said in the northern language, "it makes the kill so much sweeter."

As if her voice had suddenly ceased working, Yngrid stopped screaming, and in surprise, Erik spun to look in her direction. Her eyes were still fixed on the assassin, but her mouth hung in surprise. Then, from the corner of his eye, Erik saw something flash, a great white mass seemingly appearing from nowhere. Erik turned his head back the other way, and as a low rumbling growl broke the tenuous silence, a great cat leaped towards the Isutan woman.

The assassin couldn't turn in enough time. As the front paws of a white, snow cat—larger than the tan plains cats that roamed the Plains of Güdal—struck the woman's shoulder, she loosed her arrow, and it sailed wide, thudding into the flesh of the horse that lay on Yngrid. Claws extended, the cat swiped at the assassin as she fell backward, but with the same speed the animal moved with, she pushed herself to her feet and jumped over her attacker.

With a sound that almost matched the cat's, the assassin snarled as she gave Erik a sidelong glance, keeping most of her attention on the snow cat. As Erik looked at the creature, he smiled through his pain; she was back. Freedom had been good to his animal friend, and she looked bigger and stronger. The cat crouched, hissing and growling as the Isutan drew a short blade with no crossguard and a gentle curve, so that it was sharp only on one side. It wasn't like the scimitars of the Samanian slavers Erik once faced near the Blue Forest—those blades thicker and capable of being wielded underhand or overhand—but it looked just as deadly.

Erik tried to step forward but felt his right leg begin to buckle under his weight. Cursing, he saw Warrior was up and next to Erik. He reached up to his saddle horn with his right hand, steadying himself, and then looked at his horse.

"Go, Warrior," he commanded as he stepped away and slapped the horse on his rump.

Warrior needed no further urging, and with a loud neigh, the horse galloped off towards the assassin. At the sound of hooves, the Isutan's eyes spun away from glaring at the snow cat that growled louder before leaping towards the woman again. The assassin attacked, slashing her blade at the cat, but the animal simply jumped to one side, one of her claws grazing the leg of the Isutan woman. She screamed, not a sound of pain, but of frustration.

She heard Warrior's thunderous hooves now right behind her as she turned, Warrior almost running her over, before she rolled to one side, dropping her bow. She retrieved another knife from her belt and threw it, not the horse, but at Erik. He swiped his sword in front of his face, Dragon Tooth flaring the same green that matched the assassin's eyes as it knocked the attacking weapon away. At the same time, the snow cat attacked, but the Isutan backflipped over the animal. As she steadied on her feet, she looked conflicted as Warrior turned and galloped towards her again, and the snow cat spun too quickly for her to get in a quick slash with her short blade.

The assassin extended her hand, and her bow flew to her before she hissed and turned, running into the darkness. She was fast, but not fast enough to disappear as quickly as she did.

"Isutan magic," Erik grumbled.

"You're a resourceful man," the woman said, her voice seemingly all around Erik. "We will meet again. Pray to your gods I do not decide to visit your family first."

Erik ground his teeth and then whistled Warrior to return. He knew the cat would come to be by his aside without any instruction.

"Help me," Yngrid whimpered. "Please."

As Warrior trotted over to stand by his side, Erik grabbed the horn of his saddle, steadying himself before he hobbled over to Yngrid with Warrior's help. As he did so, the snow cat brushed against him—almost knocking him over—and purred. Warrior snorted, but Erik patted the horse's neck.

"It's all right," Erik said. "She's a friend," he added for Yngrid's benefit.

The horse seemed to calm, although he watched the cat with wary eyes, and the girl seemed too wrapped up in her pain to bother too much about having such a huge wild animal in their midst.

Erik limped to Yngrid, blood soaking the shoulder of her heavy over cloak. He pushed on the horse laying across her legs, but it didn't move. Erik dropped to his knees and put a hand on Yngrid's head, pushing hair away from her eyes.

"Hush, girl," Erik said.

"I don't want to die," she said through soft sobs.

"You won't die," Erik said. "Our attacker is gone."

He looked at the black-shafted arrow sticking from her shoulder. It was long and thin, with wide fletching; meant for distance.

"Can you feel your legs?" Erik asked.

Yngrid nodded slowly.

"They hurt, though," she said.

"I'm sure they do," Erik replied, ruling out the more serious concern that a horse landing on her could have broken her back. He looked at the arrow shaft again. "I need to get this out, but it's going to hurt."

She nodded, started to cry, covering her face with her good arm.

"I must do this to save you," Erik said, running his hand down the shaft and then moving it slowly. It seemed to have play in it, so hopefully, the head was not buried in bone.

"I wish Turk was here," Erik muttered to himself.

His dwarvish friend—the healer. He would have been able to mend Erik, at least a little, and he would know what to do with Yngrid.

"We need to chance a fire," Erik said, "so I can close the wound when the arrow is out."

"No," Yngrid said through tears. "My father's men are following us for sure. They will see us."

"To the Shadow with your father," Erik said.

"He'll kill you," she said.

"I'll take my chances," Erik replied.

For a moment, he thought a small smile touched her lips.

"I need to get it out before it gets infected," Erik said with a stern look and a hard voice.

Yngrid just looked away again, her body shaking with silent sobs. Deciding maybe she'd be better if he freed her legs, Erik grabbed the reins of the dead horse lying atop Yngrid and tied them to Warrior's saddle as best he could with one hand.

*Is this how you felt, Befel?*

Erik looked at his own left arm, currently useless from the shoulder downwards. A slaver's knife had cut Erik's brother's left shoulder deep, leaving it almost useless. And just as he started to regain the strength in his shoulder and arm, a club injured it again. By the time Befel died, he was sure his left arm would be useless for the rest of his life.

Erik clicked his tongue and gently patted Warrior's flank, causing the horse to walk forward. The massive warhorse easily pulled the dead horse off Yngrid, the snow cat watching the whole time. When Yngrid was finally free, Erik helped her sit up. As if she knew what he needed, the snow cat plodded over to the woman and sat with her. She was apprehensive at first, but when Erik scratched the white-furred cat behind the ears, and she replied with a purr, Yngrid relaxed.

Erik built a fire, not a large one, but hot enough to heat a piece of iron. He had ignored the cold of the north, his adrenaline pushing it away while men or horse around him died, but now that a small fire dared the northern night, he realized how freezing the air actually was and shivered. Once the fire was stoked, shedding at least a little light and heat on them, Erik removed Yngrid's dagger from her belt— a fine piece of iron smithy, with a polished, bone handle, and some artist's embellishments on the blade—and stuck it in the fire.

Yngrid furrowed her brows, giving Erik a confused look. He knelt next to her as the iron heated up and tore her dress around the arrow wound. Apparently, Erik had intruded upon Yngrid's modesty, at least a little, as she blushed when he exposed more of her skin. But when Erik gently inspected the wound, which glared at him a bright red and caked with blood, before looking back at the dagger, which was now a bright reddish-white, her eyes widened, and her breathing quickened.

"You can't," Yngrid said. She tried scooting herself away as breaths and tears fought one another.

"It is the only way, Yngrid," Erik said. He caught her wrist and held her firm. "Do you trust me?"

She looked at Erik and then to the fire and back to him.

"I don't know," she said, and then began to weep, covering her face with the hand of her good arm.

"It will be quick, I promise," Erik said. He removed the dagger's leather scabbard from Yngrid's belt and then removed the dagger from the fire. He would have to work quickly, the heat of the blade already fading in the cold. "Here, bite down on this. I wish I had some sweet wine, but this will have to do."

Yngrid's breathing became even quicker, her eyes wider than they should have been able to open. The snow cat, sensing her apprehension, rested her head on Yngrid's lap. She bit down hard on the leather scabbard and closed her eyes hard.

Erik did as he promised. He jabbed the hot knife into the flesh of Yngrid's shoulder, following the line of the shaft, and she ground her teeth against the scabbard as he opened the wound and removed the arrow. He quickly discarded that and turned the blade flat, using the residual heat to cauterize the wound. The moment he moved away from her, Yngrid's mouth opened, and the scabbard fell out before she screamed and then passed out.

Erik made sure she was comfortable and then cut away a piece from the bottom of her dress, using it to bandage the wound as best he could, again with only one hand. When he decided the bleeding had just about stopped, he sat back, looked into the fire, and threw the cloth over his shoulder. He looked to the snow cat, still resting her head on Yngrid's lap, and then to Warrior.

"What do we do now?" Erik asked as if his animal friends could give him any advice.

He couldn't lift Yngrid onto Warrior and, even if he could, he couldn't walk for any distance. The snow cat got up and stretched and then moved over to Erik, now resting her head in his lap. He brushed her white fur with his hand, so soft and warm. He came to her flank and touched a rough patch of skin where the fur had not grown back over a scar.

"What happened here?" he asked.

The cat lifted her head, licked her lips, looked back at the scar, and laid her head back on his lap. He looked down at her eyes, bluish-gray and fierce.

"You've been watching me, haven't you?" Erik asked.

The cat purred.

"The wolf," Erik continued. "Creator knows what else."

He smiled and gave a short chuckle.

"I guess we wait," Erik said, turning towards the fire. He watched the small fire dare the cold. It did little for warmth, but it was enough at that moment. "Some savior you are," before his own pain and the warmth of the flames sent him too, to rest.

## 37

The temperature in the Dream World was normally comfortable, and Erik could always tell something was off when it was a little hotter or colder than usual. As he sat on the hill, the branches of the willow tree intermittently swooping down and brushing his head or cheeks in errant breezes, this world—the waist tall grass, the distant black mountains, purple lightning, and bright sun—was a fraction colder.

As Erik spent more time in this place, he began to understand it more. He could see people and places he desired to see. In this dream, he watched his wife sleep. She had awoken twice and walked to the privy, a small, wooden house just behind their farmhouse. Both times, Bryon, who slept on the floor of a small storage room, got up and made sure she was all right. It was simply the growing baby pressing on her bladder, but his cousin was concerned enough to take up sleeping at Erik's house and watching over Simone. For that, he was glad.

But there was someone else there, a large man with long, red, braided hair and a long, braided, red beard that he recognized from so long ago, and when he first saw him, Erik's heart quickened. He had stood on his hill and shouted out to his cousin as if he could hear him, but then, as he watched with a racing heart and quickened breath, the man—one of Andragos' bodyguards, named Raktas—walked through the house, slowly, and then back outside, where he sat on the front porch and simply stared out into the night.

Had Andragos sent this man to protect Erik's family? Was the Messenger of the East, an agent of Syzbalo, Lord of the East, protecting Erik? And then he wondered where the other one was? Andragos had two such bodyguards, and they always traveled together, but he only saw one.

When Erik was certain his wife and cousin were safe, he searched the Dream World for another friend, a soldier, a warrior, and a teacher. The space in front of him dimmed and swirled and shifted as if made of sand and caught by a strong gust of wind, and Erik saw the nighttime streets of Finlo. They weren't as crowded as he remembered them and armed men, all wearing short tabards bearing the emblem of a white-sailed boat, walked in twos, eyeing anyone they passed with suspicious eyes.

He found him, still, sitting in the corner of a small bar, half a dozen empty cups in front of him. Poor Wrothgard, he looked so miserable. A toothless woman sat next to him, clawing at his arm and chest, reaching between his legs, but he eventually shooed her away.

"You should have come with us," Erik said. "You would have had a purpose. And we could have used your sword."

Erik spread his hands on either side of him, staring out over a field of green grass. He saw a small group of ogres pass by, Jamalel at their front. It was the first time he had seen the ogres in his dreams, but he knew they were Dream Walkers as well. The ogre recognized him and smiled, and Erik waved in turn, but they didn't stop, even though Erik would have liked them to. They were simply passing through, watching the Dream World as the leader of this troupe of ogres said they did. It was a comforting sight, nonetheless, but then it all changed again.

Neither Dewin nor the other man sat under the tree, and soon, the cloaked figure appeared as the sky darkened, the grass turned brown, and the temperature dropped, feeling like it might even snow. Erik drew Dragon Tooth—his sword always accompanied him into the Dream World—and it felt good to hold the blade without pain racking his body.

"I'm not afraid of you," Erik said, walking down the slope of the hill and stepping to its edge.

The cowl of the figure's cloak shadowed most of his face, but Erik could see a square chin and a stern jaw from underneath the hood. He heard laughter.

"You have grown quite confident in yourself, haven't you?"

"Who are you?" Erik asked.

"Tsk, tsk," the cloaked figure said. "You know there is power in a name. Should I be so quick to give you mine?"

"What trick is the Shadow trying to play now?" Erik asked, stepping forward yet again.

The shadowy figure folded his hands within the sleeves of his cloak.

"The Shadow," he said with a hint of derision. "Dark power consumes the world, and men assume it is the Shadow. Bah. Little do they know, the Shadow's power is waning, and my master's strength is waxing. And he will soon claim that which is his."

Erik lifted an eyebrow.

"You don't know my name—then again, perhaps you do—but I know yours, Erik Eleodum. The time is coming when my master will regain his rightful foothold in this world, and chaos will reign again."

The figure unfolded his hands and lifted them over his head. Blue, green, red, and white lights danced between his open palms, rotating and pulsating as orbs. And then, in one bright flash, the color exploded, and Erik felt himself falling backward.

Erik opened his eyes and sat up quickly. He shivered and felt a tremor in his hands. The fire he had built was small, but it was long gone now, as the western horizon began to turn from black to a deep purple, and then a deep blue, signifying the coming of another day. They had slept for a whole day and night, and he could not believe they had not been found.

Yngrid was still asleep, the snow cat's head resting on her lap. She sweated profusely as she lay there, despite the cold, and when Erik felt her forehead, she was hot. It wasn't uncommon for injury and fever to accompany one another, and he wanted to let her rest even more but knew they had to move on.

*But how?*

Looking up, Warrior stood and watched. Erik knew he had to get Yngrid in his horse's saddle, and they had to get moving.

"Yngrid," Erik said, shaking the woman's uninjured shoulder. "Wake up, Yngrid."

She barely moved, small tremors wracking her body as sweat poured from her brow. Erik tried to get behind her, tried to lift her, but with his right hip and left shoulder injured, all he could do was sit her up. He looked to the snow cat, forelimbs crossed and watching intently.

"I can't leave her," Erik said. The snow cat yawned and then licked her jowls with a long, pink tongue. "If I do, though, would you stay with her? Or would you try and follow me?"

The snow cat just stared at him.

Erik heard the jingling of bells in the distance and the muffled sound of several sets of hooves. His heart sank, and as he drew Dragon Tooth, the snow cat sensed his apprehension and stood, positioning herself in front of Yngrid and Erik. Even Warrior sensed something was wrong and trotted over to Erik.

He had expected Wulfstan's men to come on quicker and stronger, to find them the previous day or during the night, but the hooves that echoed over the northern plain were trotting at best. They weren't in a hurry. He heard what sounded like wooden wheels and the oinking of pigs. He heard voices, and as the silhouettes of people and wagons began to appear along the eastern horizon—still shrouded mostly in darkness—and not the north, Erik sheathed his weapon. There was laughter, more jingling of bells, and sheep baaing.

The snow cat moved in front of Erik as he turned to face the caravan that approached them. Several horsed men or women rode in front of several carts. One of the riders put up a hand as if they were waving, but when they apparently saw the snow cat, they stopped. The voices ceased, and an errant oink was met with the din of hushing. Several other people moved up next to the two, horsed figures. Erik could see they carried bows. One of the people on horseback reached to their belt and drew what looked to be a large, curved blade.

"Come here," Erik said to the snow cat.

The animal disobeyed him, a low growl emerging from her throat. Erik slapped his leg, clicked, whistled, but nothing worked. Finally, he limped up next to the cat, grabbed the scruff of her neck as if she were a simple kitten, and pulled her back. As he tugged on the bit of loose skin all cats had around their necks, Erik realized it could have been to his death, but the large cat finally paid attention to him and moved backward, hair still bristling though and still growling.

The shadowed figures in front of them moved cautiously. Erik lifted his good hand.

"*It's all right!*" he shouted in the northern tongue.

The horsed people stopped, as did the ones carrying bows.

"*I'll come to you if you're worried. Just don't shoot,*" he added and looked down at the snow cat.

"Stay here," he said, "and don't do anything that is going to get me killed."

She didn't understand him, obviously, but when he put a hand up, she licked her jowls and sat. He looked at Warrior and, in Shengu, said, "Stay."

Dragging his bad leg, he limped towards the people in front of him, and they became less and less shadowy as the expectant sun began to light up the horizon behind him even more. He could see the horsed figure with the large sword speaking to the others around, put up a hand, and heel the horse.

*Is this the moment I die? Is he going to ride me down?*

Erik thought to place a hand on the handle of his sword but instead stopped, letting, who he could now see as a man, come to him, watching to see if he spurred his horse into a gallop and stayed at a simple trot.

The horsed man was large and broad-shouldered, that much Erik could see, as he got closer. His hair fell in tight, round ringlets past his shoulders, and a bushy beard made of the same ringlets spread out over his chest. He wore a long robe, opened and exposing a chest matted with almost black hair, and he indeed carried a large, curved sword ... a sword Erik recognized.

Erik's heart stopped.

"It can't be," he muttered to himself.

But as the horseman came closer, he began to recognize the man. He wore a much thicker beard, and his hair was longer. His muscles looked larger, his shoulders broader, his arms thicker, and he certainly wore the air of a leader about him, but he was the same man he had met almost a year before.

"Mardirru?" Erik asked as the horseman got even closer, close enough to hear him.

The horse stopped.

"Do I know you?" the man asked.

"Are you Mardirru?" Erik asked. "Are you Mardirru, leader of the Ion Gypsies and son of Marcus and Nadya?"

"Who are you and how do you know me?" Mardirru asked. Yes, it was quite clear that this man was he, son of the valiant and noble gypsy Marcus.

"It's me," Erik said, feeling several tears welling up in his eyes, "Erik. Erik Eleodum."

"Erik," Mardirru gasped, a hint of unbelief in his voice. He leaned forward in his saddle, squinting, and then his eyes widened. "By the Creator!"

Mardirru dropped the large falchion—once his father's mighty weapon—and practically leaped off his horse. He ran to Erik, and for a moment, Erik hoped his snow cat and warhorse didn't think the gypsy was attacking him.

A year ago, Mardirru was already a large man, but now he looked even bigger, and more like his father. He wrapped his arms around Erik with ease and picked him up, squeezing, and Erik screamed, a weird mixture of pain and joy coursing through his body.

"Careful," Erik said with belabored breaths. "I am hurt ... and badly."

"Oh my," Mardirru said, eyebrows lifting as high as they could as his eyes studied Erik's fist ravaged face. "Yes, you are. I was so surprised to see you, I didn't realize. you look like you've been kicked by a mule!"

He looked concerned for a moment, but then shouted, "Erik! Erik Eleodum!"

As Mardirru laughed, he heard others from the caravan shouting his name.

"Erik! It's Erik! Erik Eleodum!"

A great clamor came up from the gypsy caravan as a whole myriad of people rushed out to greet Erik.

"Careful," Mardirru commanded.

"I have a companion with me, a woman whose life I fear for," Erik said.

"Oh, by the Creator," Mardirru said, "you must let us look at you both."

"Please," Erik said.

Before Erik could lead Mardirru to Yngrid, he heard another familiar voice.

"Oh my," Bo said, "what have you done to yourself?"

"What haven't I done to myself?" Erik replied. "Please, you must look at Yngrid."

He turned and began to limp to the woman.

"Wait, Erik," Bo said. "We will bring our cart over. The way you are cradling your arm and limping, I believe you are hurt more than your face betrays."

A low growl came from the snow cat.

"Stop," Erik said, putting up a hand, and the animal obeyed, standing and staring.

"Look at this," Bo said as Mardirru commanded several of the other gypsies to bring over a cart, "Erik Eleodum has become a master of great cats. I heard he was a dragon slayer, but this ..."

"You heard about that?" Erik asked.

"The whole of Háthgolthane, Nothgolthane, Antolika, Wüsten Sahil, and beyond has heard about it, my friend," Bo replied, "and the Creator be blessed, you have come back to us, intact and well. Well, almost intact, but I think we can fix you up."

"I heard you passed through my farmstead, that you checked in on my family. I can't thank you enough for that."

Bo put up a hand.

"We have prayed for you every day," Bo said. "Dika, myself, Mardirru, all of the Ion Gypsies. We have prayed for your safety. Your brother and your cousin. Your family."

The look Erik gave Bo must have been severe as the gypsy gripped Erik's wrist with both his hands.

"What is it, my friend?"

"My cousin is well," Erik said. "He is much less stubborn, although still stubborn."

Bo laughed at that.

"And I came home to my parents and sisters ... and the love of my life," Erik explained. "We are married now, and she is expecting our first child."

"Thank the Creator," Bo said, lifting his hands in the air. "And Befel?"

Erik thought of his brother daily. And he and the dwarves and his cousin spoke of Befel almost as often, but they all knew about his death. They were all there. They all fought alongside him and broke bread with him and drank with him. Because of that, it made it easier to accept that he wasn't with them anymore. But as Erik looked into Bo's expectant eyes, the weight of Befel's loss seemed to push him to the ground, and he felt a lump in his throat.

"He is dead, Bo," Erik said. "Killed by the dragon."

Bo's smile faded. He shook his head, and Erik saw the hint of a tear at the corner of the gypsy's eye. He looked away, seemingly not wanting to make eye contact with Erik. It was hard for him, too, hearing of Befel's death.

"The cart is here," Bo said. "Let me help you."

Bo helped Erik up and to get settled. He uncorked a bottle and gave it to Erik, commanding him to drink. He recognized it as sweet wine and, even though he was typically opposed to drinking a concoction that not only dulled pain but dulled the mind as well, he hurt so badly, he gladly drained the whole of the bottle and then lay down. The snow cat leaped up into the cart, which startled the horses at first, and lay down next to Erik, resting her head on his chest.

"Yngrid," Erik muttered.

"Not to worry," Mardirru replied, resting a hand on the side of the cart, "we will tend to her. She will be fine."

"My horse," Erik said, feeling his consciousness waning. "Warrior."

"We will take care of him as well," Mardirru said.

"He is mean and stubborn," Erik said.

"Have you never met a gypsy woman?" Bo said with a booming laugh.

Even with his eyes closed, Erik smiled and then heard a loud slap.

"Ouch, woman!" Bo's voiced yelled.

"I heard you," Dika said, Bo's wife. Erik was already falling asleep, but he could smell the musty sweetness of Dika, a familiar scent that widened his smile. "Oh, my poor Erik. What have you done to yourself?"

He felt the cart move underneath him, heard the clopping of hooves, and felt the warmth of the snow cat as she rested next to him, and then unconsciousness took him again, that great healer of pain.

## 38

*A*nkara paced around Nagarooshi. Her green eyes blazed as she squeezed her hands into and out of fists, and she could feel her magic pulse all around her. An aura began to glow, red, orange, green, blue, purple, white, and then red again.

"How?" she hissed, thinking of the snow cat.

Why would such a beautiful creature fight for and protect a northern man? All these Háthgolthanians did was kill the cat's prey, take their lands, and slaughter them for their teeth and their fur. She had tried to communicate with the animal, let it know it was better off just leaving. It could eat the dead horses and the woman all it wanted. But the cat had shut itself off to her. She recalled a white flash, something fast and strong and brilliant; she had seen out of the corner of her eye as she rode north. It couldn't have been the cat. Was it?

Ankara rarely let her emotions get the best of her, but she hadn't been this indignant in a long time.

"To the fires of the nine hells with him!" she shouted, and a small, frozen bush nearby burst into flames.

Nagarooshi backed up.

"He is nothing," Ankara hissed. "A stupid, untrained man."

She realized she was frightening her horse, and rather than calm the animal, Ankara walked away into the darkness, so she might fume some more. She caused several bushes to burst into flames, and that made her feel better. She saw a little white field mouse, and she crushed its bones with a word. She felt even better. She heard an owl fly overhead, until it dropped in front of her, its body a tangled mess of feathers. Hurting things made her feel better.

"All he had was a magic sword and great snow cat as a pet," Ankara continued to say. "How, by the gods, did he kill my father?"

She knew there was only one answer. There was only one way this man, this pathetic excuse for a warrior—a man that people called Dragon Slayer, Troll Hammer, Wolf's Bane, Friend of Dwarves, and Savior—this shit of a farmer, this fool, could have killed her father ...

"Luck," she muttered.

Was it luck that he supposedly killed a winter wolf, one of those intelligent species that sold their cunningness and brutality to warlords and wizards? Was it luck that he killed mountain trolls? Was it luck that he thwarted Patûk Al'Banan? Was it luck that he found a magic scroll, defied a dragon, saved Fen-Stévock from destruction, and found an ancient, magical sword called the Dragon Sword?

"Yes," she said to the darkness. "You are a lucky bastard, Erik Eleodum. The fates have clearly smiled on you up until now. But your luck is drawing to an end. And when it does, I will be there to shoot an arrow through your heart and cut off your balls and feed them to your stupid cat."

## 39

"We buried your people, my dear," Erik overheard Dika say as she tended to Yngrid's shoulder when Erik awoke from a dreamless sleep due to the sweet wine. Looking around, he found the gypsies circled up and camped not far from where the Isutan assassin had ambushed Erik, Yngrid, and the woman's guards. At first, he was worried about Wulfstan, but then assumed they'd either lost the trail or hadn't recognized she was gone yet.

Of course, the gypsies buried her people. They were kind and generous, and the first semblance of goodly people Erik had experienced when he had left home several years before. He was gone for almost two years before meeting Marcus, once the leader of the Ion Gypsies, and all he had encountered up to that point were cruel, wicked, selfish people. At one point, he had resigned himself to going back home, thinking nothing good existed in the world outside of the Eleodum farmstead—but then he met Marcus, his Mardirru, and husband and wife, Bo and Dika.

"How are you doing?" Max, Mardirru's younger brother, asked.

When Erik last saw him, he was bald, but he had since let his hair grow, although he kept his beard close to his face save for a thick and

very heavy mustache that he curled at its ends. He was a slightly thinner, taller version of his brother, and Erik could see more of his
mother, Nadya, in him.

"Better," Erik said, and he was only half lying. His shoulder
didn't hurt as much, nor did his wrist, but his hip still screamed with
pain every time he moved. He could feel the bruising on his face
subside, but his cheeks and lips and jaw were still tender to the touch.

"Time," Max said, and then smiled, "and a little gypsy magic,
always heals wounds."

Erik chanced a laugh, even though it hurt his face.

After Bo and Dika had checked Erik's injuries, they found his
shoulder was dislocated. Dika had popped it back into place, but it
was still sore and tender and difficult to move. She gave him some
herbal treatments for the cuts and bruises but could only put new
bandages on his ribs. There was nothing that could be done for his
hip, which could well have been broken. Feeling somewhat better, he
told the gypsies what had happened, both to him and Yngrid and
their need to find Gris.

"We just came from the west," Mardirru said. "We were in the
lands of Nothgolthane, visiting the small villages and farmsteads of
northern Gongoreth, trying to help those braving the desert wilds.
We were trying to make it to Háthgolthane before it grew too cold,
but some of our old grew sick. We lost five on this journey."

Mardirru's face grew sullen as he looked down at his feet, the
reflection of a campfire—burning high despite it being midday—
dancing off the darkness of his beard.

"Why didn't you just go south, through Waterton, where the
temperature is milder?" Erik asked.

Mardirru's look grew even graver.

"I can't, Erik," Mardirru replied.

Erik gave the gypsy a questioning look.

"I don't know if I'll ever be able to go through Waterton again," Mardirru said. "It reminds me of my mother and father. Of all the friends we lost."

"I'm sorry," Erik said, putting his hand on Mardirru's shoulder.

The gypsy shook his head, rubbing his eyes with his forefinger and thumb.

"My stupidity cost five brothers and sisters their lives," Mardirru said, sitting up straight, composing himself, and taking in a deep breath.

"And what is to guarantee they would have lived, given you went south?" Erik asked. "If they were old and sickly, at least they passed from this world to the next among family and friends."

"Maybe he'll listen to you," Bo said. "I must've told this stubborn mule that very thing a hundred times, and he doesn't listen."

Mardirru looked at Bo, shaking his head with a slight smile and gave a short chortle. He looked to Erik. Those eyes, they were Marcus' eyes, and he still missed the giant of a man he knew for only a short time, but that he could trust him, and he would be a good friend.

"We will take you to Holtgaard," Mardirru said.

"I can't ask you to do that," Erik said.

"You didn't," Mardirru replied.

"Wulfstan is after me as well," Erik said.

"As you said," Mardirru replied. "It is not an issue. If they come, we will hide you. They are accustomed to gypsies, especially our clan. They would have no reason to believe we are harboring a man they think a thief."

"No," Erik said, gingerly standing. "I can't let you do that. Gris Beornson is probably already to Holtgaard, and Wulfstan Wulfson not only wants me dead, he probably thinks I kidnapped his daughter, which would put you in danger as well."

"A risk we are willing to take, Erik," Mardirru said, also getting to his feet.

In the firelight, Mardirru looked an imposing figure. In the last year, Erik had grown no taller, but wider and broader, stronger, but at that moment, he didn't think he would ever want to get on the wrong side of the son of Marcus.

"And what will you do, Erik?" Bo said, also standing. "Look what they did to you already! You are going to travel four or five days with those injuries and with an injured girl? And to what end? You may be Erik Dragon Slayer, but even heroes fall, and most times because of their hubris."

As Erik watched the dancing flames in the fire, he thought of the elf Rako, the voice that once spoke to him from a golden-hilted dagger. He remembered what the elf had told him about his hubris. It had destroyed the Dragon Sword, and it had killed many of the elf's people. It was what had imprisoned him in the Dragon Stone.

He looked at Yngrid, near a different fire, arm in a sling, talking to Dika and some of the other gypsy women. She laughed, and the light from the flames played with the deep auburns in her hair and seemed to illuminate the freckles on her cheeks. He knew she fancied him and, perhaps, in another life ...

He watched the snow cat, lounging next to Yngrid, several gypsy children scratching behind her ears, one boy even coercing the large animal to expose her belly so he might rub her tummy. The gratifying purring was so loud, Erik could well hear it. And Warrior, standing sternly next to the cart in which the gypsies had laid Erik. He was a stubborn and cranky creature, but Mardirru's sister, with her tall, lithe body and jet-black ringlets falling to the small of her back, braided his hair, and the horse let her. She even chanced to give the destrier a kiss on his great forehead, and he bobbed his head and nuzzled closer to the woman.

"I don't know how I can repay you," Erik said, sitting down again.

"Knowing that you are alive," Mardirru replied, "that the Creator has answered my nightly prayers for you, is all the payment we need."

## 40

*E*rik stood in his wide meadow, hot air stinging his face as Gris Beornson stood in front of him. The man didn't see Erik. In fact, he probably didn't realize he was dreaming. The space in front of Gris shifted, and the cloaked man appeared, the one who looked like a man of the Shadow, but he wasn't.

Gris and the cloaked figure spoke for a long while. Erik heard that same hard, raspy voice come from underneath the figure's hood.

"Give me the Ruling Stone," the figure said, "and I will give you power beyond belief."

Gris was a fool, but he was an idealistic one. He was a liar, but one with principals. He was a thief, but he was driven by a purpose. He shook his head.

"No," Gris replied with an air of haughtiness in his voice. "The stone belongs to my family, my father. And when he is gone, I will rule Hargoleth."

The cloaked figure laughed.

"Hargoleth," he hissed. "Backward barbarians. I am offering you much more. I am offering you power beyond measure. Give me the stone."

"By the Creator," Gris said as he looked around. He didn't see Erik, but he looked scared as the cloaked figure stepped closer to him.

"You call to the Creator," the cloaked man said. "Why not serve someone with balls? You have no idea what you are holding there. You have no idea how important it is."

*Neither do I,* Erik thought.

Gris tried to back up, but the cloaked figure reached out with his long, thin, skeleton-like fingers and gripped the Bear Clanner's wrist, hard.

"Let go," Gris said, trying to pull away.

He struggled for a bit as the cloaked man tried convincing him to give over the Ruling Stone. A faint outline of a stone appeared in the dream, sitting on the ground next to Gris' foot. It was egg-shaped, with the small undulations and imperfections a normal rock might have. But it was a brilliant emerald green and, even in its faintness in the dream, it glowed.

Gris stopped struggling with the cloaked figure and looked around again, giving Erik the sense the man had started to realize he was dreaming. People did that at some point, as far as he knew, especially in nightmares. They grew terrified, thinking all of their worst fears were coming to life, and then they realized it was just a dream, and woke up with an almost simultaneous sigh of relief.

"You'll never get the Ruling Stone," Gris hissed, and he faded away.

The cloaked figure didn't seem to notice Erik, sitting atop his hill and watching. He looked around, and Erik wondered if what this mysterious man saw around him was different than the wide meadow filled with knee-high grass and the hill.

The air shifted, twisted, and distorted in front of the cloaked man, and a woman appeared. She wore a loose, almost translucent, white shift dress. Her skin was tan, and she had almond-shaped eyes of a most vivid emerald green. Her arrival brought Erik to his feet; it was the Isutan assassin. Her hair fell, as straight as rain, to her lower back, and was as dark as the midnight sky. Even in the loose-fitting garment, Erik could see her muscles, belied by her lean and lithe body. She was beautiful and yet ... something about her said she would never *love* a man. The way she carried herself—flirtatious, sly—she was false.

"Ankara," the cloaked figure said.

The assassin looked to the cloaked man as if she hadn't seen him standing there, in front of her, and she squinted but didn't have the same frightened look Gris had. Instead, it was haughty as if all were beneath her.

"How do you know my name?" she asked.

"Who doesn't know the famous daughter of Bone Spear?" the cloaked figure asked.

"What do you want?" the woman asked, looking bored.

Erik couldn't tell if she realized she was in a dream. She was decidedly smarter than Gris, world-wise and, undoubtedly, a mage in some way.

"I want a stone," the man replied. "A northerner carries it."

"I don't have time for secret missions given to me in my dreams from some no-faced man," Ankara replied. "If you can speak to me in my dreams, then you know who I work for and what I seek."

"You work for a man who serves the same master as I do. You see, we are partners in the same cause," the cloaked figure said, and Erik's eyebrows shot up. The way he spoke of the Lord of the East, with such bitterness even though his words belied the sentiment, was interesting, but the Lord of the East had no master. What was this mysterious man talking about?

Ankara just shrugged.

"So what?" she replied. "He's rich and powerful and paying me for a job. If he wanted me to find some rock, he would have told me so."

"Erik Eleodum is so easy to kill, is he?" the cloaked figure said with a short laugh.

That seemed to irritate Ankara.

"I had him," she seethed, and Erik could see her clenching her fists so tightly they went almost as white as her dress.

"He is resourceful, with friends in strange places," the cloaked figure added. "Get me this stone." The cloaked figure held out his hands, and an image of the Dragon Stone appeared, floating above them, "And I will help you retrieve the Dragon Sword from Eleodum. In doing so, both of our masters will be pleased."

"I have no master," Ankara spat back.

Erik stood.

*He wants the Dragon Stone badly,* Erik thought. *But not the sword?*

"Why not just retrieve this stone yourself?" Ankara asked.

Erik nodded, agreeing with her sentiments.

"I exist in this world, for now," the cloaked man said. "And to reenter your world would take too much of my energy. At the moment. There is magic surrounding the Dragon Stone that will not let me simply take it. Someone must give it to me, here, in the Dream World."

"Dragon Stone?" Ankara asked. "Is it related to the sword?"

"It doesn't matter," the cloaked figure said. "That is but one of the names it is known by."

"It does to me if there is a connection," Ankara replied, crossing her arms like a petulant child.

"Yes, there is one, and my master, the same master the Lord of the East serves, desires it," the cloaked man said, "so in serving me, you are serving the Lord of the East."

"Your logic is infallible," the Isutan assassin said sarcastically. "If you're stuck in here, how do you plan on simply taking the Dragon Sword from Erik Eleodum?"

"I seek vengeance on this so-called Dragon Slayer," the cloaked figure hissed, almost more to himself than the Isutan woman. "What little power I have right now will not allow me to *take* the stone, but I do have enough power to kill Erik Eleodum. I will take the Dragon Sword, and I will have my revenge."

"I don't understand," Ankara said.

*Nor do I,* Erik thought.

"And you don't think I can kill this Erik?" Ankara stood, lifting her chin in defiance.

"No," the man said with a laugh. "He killed your father. How will you kill him? Let me kill him for you, and you can have the sword. That's what you really want, isn't it?"

Ankara stepped forward, towards the cloaked figure, her emerald eyes blazing like gems that had just caught the sun's reflection.

"I will get this stone for you," she said, speaking so slowly there was a moment of space between each word.

"Good," the cloaked figure said as his image began to fade.

Even when he was gone, his laughter continued to echo through the Dream World. The Isutan woman stood there for a moment, and then she turned. Her eyes met Erik's, and she was aware he was there.

"You!" she said, and Erik smiled.

Erik opened his eyes. He lay on the ground, the snow cat asleep next to him, and he looked up and watched the sky, the moon, and the stars and the northern lights. He was next to a cart and, seeking not to push pressure on his ribs, reached up and grabbed the spoke of a wheel and slowly pulled himself into a seated position. The fire in front of him blazed, and several gypsy men walked about the camp, no doubt nighttime guards. Mardirru had learned from the attack near the Blue Forest, and the Ion Gypsies would never be surprised again.

Erik was about to lie back down when he heard someone sniffle. He pulled himself to his feet—slowly and carefully using a crudely-fashioned wooden crutch Dika had given him—and limped around the cart. He saw the shadow of someone sitting on the other side, away from the fire. As he made his way across, the cold of the northern winter hit his face, and he shivered; the warmth of the gypsy fire was fading quickly.

"Yngrid?" Erik said.

The shadowy figure turned quickly, and in the dimness of the dying fire, he could see that it was the red-haired woman, her curls wild, her eyes red, and her pale face drawn and sad.

She turned back around, away from him.

"What are you doing over here?" Erik asked, walking up next to her. "You have to be cold. You're going to get sick."

"I'm used to the cold," she replied, her voice hard. "I'm a northerner."

Erik slowly lowered himself to the ground, sitting next to her, but she wouldn't look at him.

"Why aren't you sleeping?" Erik asked. "Does your shoulder still hurt?"

He gently touched her shoulder. Dika had used some of the ogre's white cloth to patch the wound as well as making the sling for the girl so she would heal quicker.

Yngrid shook her head.

"No," she replied. "I don't know what magic these gypsies practice, but my shoulder feels much better, almost like nothing happened."

"I don't know about magic," Erik said with a smile, "but the combination of sweet wine, an understanding of which wilds herbs do what, and some extra prayers might have something to do with it."

*And, perhaps, the ogres' cloth?*

"So why are you crying?" he asked. "Is it because you are away from home?"

Yngrid gave a quick, almost snorting laugh in between little sobs. She looked at Erik, and even though her eyes were red-rimmed, she gave him a mischievous smile.

"No," she replied. "I've run away from home several dozen times. Every once in a while, I just need a break from my parents. It's ...It was ..."

Erik remembered the attack. He replayed the scene in his head. The arrows. The dying. The guards with no chance. The last man that Ankara had killed and the way he reached out to Yngrid, the way she cried out when he died.

"The guard," Erik said. "The last one to fall ... he was dear to you, more than the others, wasn't he?"

Yngrid put her face in her hands and cried, nodding her head.

"Your close friend?" Erik asked. "A cousin, or even your brother?"

Yngrid shook her head, sniffing as she sat up straighter and wiping her face.

"My lover," she replied.

That surprised Erik. Was her lover aware of the flirting looks she gave him?

"Oh, I'm sorry. I don't know what to say."

She shrugged as if there was nothing that could be said. Erik tilted his head to the side and cocked an eyebrow.

"What about Gris?"

"What about him?" Yngrid asked.

"I thought ... well, I thought he was your lover," Erik said.

"Arngrim was my first love," Yngrid explained. "There were others. Sons of powerful vassals. The brothers and sons of other lords, like Gris. But they always broke my heart, and when they did, Arngrim was always there to pick up the pieces. And now he's gone."

Yngrid was probably a little younger than Erik but looked like a mature woman. She was tall and strong, and she understood politics and seemed to have watched both her grandfather and father rule. But at that moment, she looked and sounded like a little girl. No doubt, as she used the word lover and spoke of other men, she had lain with them, as a husband would lay with his wife, but she was still a girl trapped inside a woman's body.

Erik wondered if she was truly sad for the man, or that he wouldn't be there to comfort her anymore. Yngrid turned and faced him and promptly buried her head in his chest and cried. At first, he didn't quite know what to do and just stared down at her mop of red hair, but then he wrapped his arms around her and held her tight, as he might Tia or Beth if they were sad. She, in turn, wrapped her arms around his waist and squeezed. He groaned, softly, as his ribs were still tender, but he let her cry and mourn, whether it was genuine or not, her lost love. He would do the same if he had lost Simone, knowing he wanted to do that when Befel, Demik, and Beldar had died.

---

## 41

*A*nkara's green eyes glowed as she peered into the distance, watching a tall man ride towards Holtgaard. He was several leagues away, but she saw him as if the distance was a mere hundred paces. He looked nervous, and she presumed it must be because he had this stone the cloaked figure wanted so badly. She had no idea why this shadowy man who visited her dream couldn't just get the stone himself—something about not having enough power to walk in her world—but if it meant him helping her get the Dragon Sword, she didn't care. This northerner would be easy to take down.

Soon, thanks to Naga's magical speed, she was closing in on the man and, with the reins merely trapped under her thigh so they didn't get in the horse's way, she took her longbow from the sheath it hung in on her horse's saddle. She readied it in one hand and reached with the other across her body to the quiver of long arrows that hung on the other side of the saddle. She retrieved an especially long arrow, its fletching made from owl feathers. They were straight and narrow, and one of the three feathers had a little notch cut out that would cause the arrow to spin faster and, hence, be more accurate over long distances.

"Wound," Ankara said, gently.

The arrowhead, rather than the normal, triangular shape, was narrow and barely wider at the base than it was at the tip. Perfect for wounding a target rather than killing it. Ankara nocked the arrow and drew back on the bowstring. Her emerald eyes blazed as she focused on her target. He wasn't riding fast, and she had certainly executed much more difficult shots, but she didn't want to kill him; at least, not at first. She wanted to interrogate him for a while about this stone he carried. Why was it important to his people? What could this cloaked figure want with it?

She let out her breath slowly, feeling the bowstring next to her cheek. She paused a moment, gripped Naga with her thighs in a way that told the horse to move as smoothly as possible, and took aim.

The man fell from his horse, landing hard on the icy ground, and as his body bounced slightly, a sapphire-colored stone slipped from inside his tunic and rolled away. He didn't move, his chest still, his breath silent. Ankara furrowed her brows, releasing some of the tension in the bowstring. The man had looked fine in the saddle, if not a little nervous. He was barely trotting, certainly not riding hard enough that he might accidentally fall from his horse.

Ankara released all the tension in her bow and leaned forward. Something small and black stuck from the man's neck, almost invisible if it wasn't for her magical vision. She saw the silhouette of a man walking towards the fallen rider, who looked dead, his body still and his already pale skin turning whiter. He had been poisoned.

She grunted, angry and frustrated, and drew her bowstring.

"Kill," she said and now let loose her arrow.

It sailed silently towards the silhouetted man, but he turned and put up a hand. At the moment the arrow should have reached his eye, it shattered into a thousand shards of wood.

Ankara heeled Naga hard, and as the horse charged forward, she retrieved another arrow, nocked it, and fired. The same thing happened. She drew two more, with speed faster than the best archer could ever hope to achieve, and the same thing happened. Then, the silhouetted man, wearing a green, hooded cloak, flicked his wrist towards her, and even though she was still over a hundred paces away, she saw two little darts flying towards her eyes. In reality, they were tiny, black things, wooden dowels with needle-thin blades, but they glowed yellow with poison. She ducked and easily avoided them as they whizzed by her face. e

Her attacker looked just as frustrated as she had felt as he flicked his wrist twice more; Ankara knew she would have enough time. She fired two more arrows while leaning all the way to one side of her saddle, avoiding more poison-tipped darts. It had seemed a good strategy, and while the green-cloaked man put up his hand again, he was too late to destroy both arrows. One passed through whatever magic he wielded and sliced across his cheek, tearing away his hood.

Ankara pulled up as she stared at her now unmasked attacker. His eyes, shrouded by thick, dark eyebrows, were a light purple. His chin was pointed, yet strong, and his jaw firm. As he clenched his teeth in anger, a line of blood trickling down onto his collar from where the arrow had grazed him, the muscles in his neck undulated. Half of his golden-blond hair was pulled back away from his face while the lower half was allowed to fall to his shoulders. He was tall and broad-shouldered and—Ankara held her breath for a moment— quite beautiful.

But none of that was what caused her to catch her breath, not the perfect symmetry of his face; it was his ears. Tall, pointed ears.

"Elves," she hissed.

The way he squinted his purple eyes, he heard her. But, of course, he did. He was magical, and all elves were gifted with enhanced hearing and eyesight. It was the same magic that gave Ankara her enhanced sense—elf magic—but she'd never admit it.

The way the elf had stopped the rider suggested he wanted the stone as much as she did. She heeled Nagarooshi again and rode hard towards the dead man. The elf, at the same time, threw off his torn, green cloak and ran to the same target. Ankara leaped from her saddle, landing hard on her feet and immediately rolling forward, coming back to her feet, a thick curved blade in one hand and a curved kukri knife in the other. She knew the elf would see the green poison on both blades, lining their edges, but she was quick.

He stopped and drew his own blade, a long, dull gray falchion, and the wavy lines of steel told that it had been hammered and folded a thousand times before being drawn out into a sword. The blade was thinner than most falchions, and its curve was less pronounced, but it was deadly, nonetheless. The handle was long, made of some deep brown wood polished to a sheen, and as soon as the elf drew the blade, he held it with both hands.

The elf said something to Ankara. She shook her head. Elvish. They still studied it in the Isuta Isles, mostly for its magical properties. She knew the language well enough, but he spoke so quickly, she didn't understand what he had said. The elf nodded.

"You needn't die today," the elf said in Isutan with a smile, his voice soft and melodic. "I only want the stone."

Ankara laughed.

"Your charms might work on some Háthgolthanian prick," she said, "but not on me."

The elf's smile faded.

"What do you want with this man?" the elf asked.

"With him? Nothing," Ankara replied. "I want the stone."

They circled one another, watching each other closely, Ankara's eyes blazing green.

"You are a powerful mage," the elf said.

"I learned from my father," she replied.

"He must have been a powerful wizard," the elf replied.

"He was a prick," she said. "You probably heard of him, even in your hidden away cities in Ul'Erel. Bone Spear ..."

"Specter," muttered the elf, "truly useless by all accounts since I heard a farmer killed him. I suppose that makes you just as weak. I'm taking the stone, but as a souvenir of our meeting, you can have the body."

"I don't want the body," Ankara replied, taking a step forward. "I want the stone."

"But you can't have it," the elf said.

"You're wrong," Ankara said, stepping forward and the elf matching her steps.

"What could you possibly want with this stone? It's just a stone, dear to my people," the elf said, but there was something about his voice that suggested he was lying.

"I don't want it for myself," Ankara admitted. "If I deliver that stone to the man who does want it, I get my sword."

The elf furrowed his brows and pursed his lips.

"Sword?" he muttered. Then, he whispered in Elvish. *"Dragon Sword."*

He started to laugh, and then his eyes went wide.

"Was it the sword that killed your father?" the elf asked with a snicker.

He gave no warning, but simply pushed out with one of his hands and, if Ankara hadn't seen the magic coming, a gust of wind would have struck her like a fist in her chest. She dove left out of the way and, coming into a crouch, gave the elf a bit of her own magic. Dropping her kukri and lifting her hand up, she clenched a fist, and the dirt and rocks around the elf swirled about him, reddening his cheeks and scratching his skin until he shouted something in Elvish. The rubble collapsed to the ground.

It was all the time Ankara needed. She rushed towards the stone, faster than anyone should have been able to run. As she leaped towards her prize, she flicked a small belt knife at the elf. He pushed the little weapon away with his own magic and threw a dart at the Isutan, but he was too late. She rolled over to the stone and came to her feet, holding it in her left hand.

"Give it to me," the elf said. "You have no idea what that is. You have no idea what you are doing."

"I absolutely know what I am doing," Ankara said and then whistled.

Nagarooshi galloped towards her as the elf rushed her, both hands gripping his falchion. Just as he swiped his steel at her, she jumped, landing firmly in her saddle as Naga ran by. She felt the air around her move, and she leaned one way and then the other as two more darts flew by her.

"You'll have to do better than that!" she yelled, her horse racing away.

"You fool!" the elf yelled behind her. "You'll doom us all."

Ankara laughed as she rode away, but she couldn't ignore the small knot that formed in her stomach.

## 42

_A_fter more nursing and nurturing from Dika—along with Bo's sweet wine—Erik was finally able to ride Warrior. Bo had to help him into the saddle, and he couldn't do much but hold onto the reins with his left hand, but at least he felt a little more normal. Had he ridden any other horse, he would probably still be riding in Bo's wagon, but Warrior really needed no direction or prompting from Erik. The animal was even aware enough to avoid little dips in the earth or rocks, seemingly knowing those little bumps would cause his master discomfort. And Erik's snow cat plodded along beside them. The often-cantankerous horse had even grown comfortable with the cat.

Every once in a while, the cat would run off hunting, but she stayed away from the gypsies' livestock of pigs and sheep and the few cows they had. As a form of reward, Mardirru gave her the offal and fat they wouldn't eat from a hog they slaughtered the night before, and the cat seemed rather content with the offering, ending the night gnawing on a large pig femur. Nonetheless, she always returned and resumed her position next to Warrior and Erik.

Yngrid rode in Bo and Dika's wagon, mostly speaking with Dika.

Erik thought it was good for the girl. He wondered how secluded she was in the keep of Wulfstaad, and her mother did not exactly seem like the warmest person for her to talk to. As worldly as she seemed, knowing the ins and outs of the clan holding, knowing how to ride and fight, and knowing what she liked in men, she seemed immature and naïve. Of all the women in the wide world that such a sheltered girl could talk to and confide, Erik couldn't think of a better woman than Dika.

"We are one day, if that, from Holtgaard," Mardirru said, riding up next to Erik.

Erik didn't say anything. He just nodded.

"What is your plan?" Mardirru asked.

"I don't know," Erik replied. "The stone that Gris Beornson carries ... it is important."

"As you have said," Mardirru replied. "A stone that signifies who the ruling clan of Hargoleth is."

"It is more than that," Erik explained. "It is not really called the Ruling Stone, at least, not by anyone outside of Hargoleth."

"I don't understand."

"They have no idea what they have; I am certain of it. It is the Dragon Stone. Some even call it the Stone of Chaos."

"Dragon Stone?" Mardirru queried.

"I ... we retrieved a scroll for the Lord of the East, from a lost dwarvish city. Written on this scroll was an ancient spell my dwarvish friends suspected to be elvish, one that can subdue dragons, fight dragons, defeat dragons, wound dragons, control dragons, and even kill dragons."

"This is how you killed the dragon in Fen-Stévock?" Mardirru asked. "This is why you are the Dragon Slayer?"

"I didn't kill her," Erik replied. "I wounded her, but she is still alive and gaining power. You see, the spell was incomplete. It was missing several components: a Dragon Sword and a Dragon Crown. I found the Dragon Sword."

Erik drew his blade, which blazed with green fire as he held it before Mardirru. The gypsy's eyes were wide with awe. A part of Erik wanted to tell Mardirru that his sword was once the dagger he had given him, but he thought that might complicate things.

"And now you seek the Dragon Crown?" Mardirru asked as Erik sheathed his sword.

"I think, eventually, that is where the Creator will lead me," Erik replied, "but this Dragon Stone has something to do with this whole elvish puzzle, and maybe even beyond that. The Lord of the East wants the sword, and that is why he continues to send assassins after me. And he is not the only one. But someone—something else wants this Dragon Stone ... this Stone of Chaos. It is related to the scroll and the spell, but it is important for some other reason, too. I think someone named the Lord of Chaos seeks the stone. It has some importance to him."

"Who?" Mardirru asked.

Erik shrugged.

"I don't know how to explain it, but this Dragon Stone ... my dreams tell me if I retrieve it, I can save the world. If I can't, the world is doomed."

"This all sounds very complicated ... and scary."

"It is, especially for a simple farmer," Erik replied.

"Or a simple gypsy," Mardirru added with a short laugh.

"Yngrid thinks I will return the stone to her father," Erik said.

"But you cannot," Mardirru said, finishing Erik's thought.

Erik shook his head.

"I have to take it to Ul'Erel," Erik said.

"Ul'Erel?" Mardirru questioned with a gasp.

Erik nodded, slowly.

"Erik, you cannot," Mardirru said. "Anyone who enters those cursed forests never leaves. Even we gypsies stay far away."

"I have to," Erik said. "There is a she-elf I am supposed to take the stone to and, Creator willing, I will find her in Ul'Erel before whatever mysterious spirits, demons, or monsters that live there kill me."

Mardirru was about to say something else when he pulled up on his horse's reins. Like a rising tornado, a column of black ravens circled in the sky, squawking.

"Something is dead," Erik said.

"Something large for so many birds," Mardirru added. He called over his shoulder, "Move slowly and carefully."

When they arrived next to the body—seemingly that of a man—a dozen ravens hopped around it, pecking quickly and then retreating. They were nervous because of a white-feathered eagle, with talons that rivaled his snow cat's claws. It stood majestically, as tall as a dwarf, on the chest of the body and dipped down with a sharp, curved, gray beak and tore a bit of flesh from the dead person's neck.

The ravens of the north were much larger than the crows Erik was used to from the Plains of Güdal, but while they angrily squawked at the eagle, they were reluctant to compete fully for the fresh meat. The eagle pulled at a lip and this lifted the head for a moment, and Erik caught just the glimpse of the face. Albeit the skin was pale and frozen and some of the flesh was already missing from the fleshy parts of his cheek and throat, Erik knew who it was.

"Gris," Erik gasped. "That is Gris Beornson. What, by the Creator ..."

"This is the man who stole the Ruling Stone?" Mardirru asked.

Erik nodded. He looked down at his snow cat and gave a quick whistle. She was still a wild animal, by no means trained, but she seemed to have a good inclination or intuition as to what Erik wanted, and she certainly obeyed him. She looked up at him, and he looked over to the body.

"Chase them off," he said.

He heeled Warrior and the horse stepped forward, sending some of the encroaching ravens up into the air. The snow cat crouched and growled, the fur on her back standing up. She leaped and landed just at the feet of the dead Gris. The eagle stared at her, tilting its head inquisitively, a piece of Gris' lip still hanging from its gray beak. The snow cat roared, and the eagle responded with an unconcerned screech. The cat stepped forward as the eagle was about to take another bite of Gris' flesh, and the bird opened its wings—a wingspan that was as wide as Bryon was tall—ruffled its feathers, and emitted a louder and angrier screech.

In the wild, these two were formidable foes, and this eagle would be able to hold its own against almost any animal. But as it looked up and saw the encroaching men and horses, it turned and walked slowly away from the dead man as the rest of the ravens flapped into the sky. The eagle took one last defiant look at the snow cat over its shoulder before, once again, opening up its massive wings and flapping, slowly lifting itself into the air and away from Erik and the gypsies. As it flew away, the ravens gave the eagle a wide berth, perhaps hoping it didn't take a missed meal opportunity out on them.

Erik and Mardirru, along with several other gypsies and Yngrid, inspected the body. As he stared, blankly, to the sky, his chest lay open, a large gaping wound running from right shoulder to left ribs, exposing his sternum.

"That wound was made by a Hargolethian long sword," Yngrid said.

"There are any number of weapons that could have done this, my dear," Mardirru said.

"Perhaps," Yngrid replied, "but I'm sure a northerner did this. The wound is wide and deep, as our swords are heavy, and the way he was slashed from shoulder to rib ... There is no doubt that a Hargolethian warrior, or northern barbarian, did this."

"May his soul rest in peace with the Creator," Mardirru said, standing and touching his thumb to his forehead.

"He was a thief," Yngrid hissed.

"We are all sinners," Mardirru replied. "Be careful if you delight in this man's death, that you do not become like him."

Erik looked at the man's face. He was in his early middle years, but in death, he looked immature and naïve. He was a thief, but he didn't deserve this. As he searched through Gris' haversack and the saddlebags on his horse—they found the animal wandering only a hundred paces from the body—his stomach knotted, and his heart sank.

"No stone," Erik said.

"This can't be," Yngrid said.

"Whoever killed him, took the stone," Erik added. He began to wonder if a barbarian longsword really did kill him, or if Gris had been staged to look this way.

"We must go after them," Yngrid said, "whoever stole the stone."

"We can't," Erik said.

"We must," she replied, her pale face turning red, her lips pursing, and her chin quivering. "It is more important than anything."

"More important than these people, who saved our lives?" Erik asked. "They are mostly women and children, Yngrid."

"Then you and I will go," she replied.

"Truly?" he asked. "With your shoulder and all of my injuries? And with this icy ground, there are no tracks to follow. Tell me, which direction should we go?"

Yngrid looked at him in silence and then began to cry. Erik felt bad, and a part of him wanted to hold her and comfort her, but he was beginning to wonder if this was her way of getting what she wanted.

"I am only being realistic," Erik said. "I want the stone as badly as you."

"Why?" Yngrid asked. "How could you possibly want the Ruling Stone as much as me? As much as my people?"

"For your people," Erik replied, and he couldn't help noticing the look Mardirru gave him as he lied.

"I think I know who took the stone," Erik said.

"Who?" Yngrid asked.

"We will hurry to Holtgaard, as fast as we can. We will give Orn the body of his son, and I will go after the person who stole the stone," Erik said.

"He doesn't deserve the body," Yngrid said, her tears ceasing and her face turning red again. "We should leave it for the ravens."

"And if this was your child or someone else you loved?" Erik asked.

He remembered a time when such anger and hatred coursed through his veins, when dead slavers and dead soldiers littered the ground before him. And as he looked out, over the dead, all he could see were children, once innocent and uncorrupted. They, of course, weren't innocent when they died, and neither was Gris. But, nonetheless, he was simply following his father's orders, and in Erik's opinion, a parent deserved the opportunity to bury their child, an opportunity his mother and father would never have with Befel.

"We will find the stone," Erik said. "We will find it, and we will take it to where it belongs."

## 43

*H*oltgaard looked like the other clan holdings, with the majority of the city population living outside the tall, wooden walls. The keep sat on a high motte, and unlike the other fortified holdings, Holtgaard had a deeply dug ditch that surrounded both the motte and bailey. A wide permanent bridge spanned the dry moat, leading to a large gatehouse, tall, wooden statues of bears on either side of the square towers of the gate.

The soldiers of Holtgaard were clearly used to the gypsies as Mardirru led his people through the gate without a nod, word, or need for permission. Yngrid huddled up in the back of Bo and Dika's wagon, red, curly hair covered by a brown blanket, Erik's snow cat curled up at her feet, also covered by a blanket. No one knew who Erik was in Holtgaard, so he rode Warrior right next to Mardirru.

"I need to speak with Orn Beornson," Mardirru said in the northerner's language, speaking to a soldier who carried no spear or shield and wore a brown tabard with the outline of a white bear on the front, signifying him as an officer of sorts.

"You and a hundred other people," the soldier replied, huffing through wide nostrils that caused his thick, brown mustache to flutter.

He stroked his long beard, eyeing people as they walked through the gate.

"Sir, you don't understand," Mardirru began to say, but the officer wheeled on the gypsy and pointed an accusatory finger at him.

"No, you don't understand," the Bear Clanner said, "I am busy, and you need to move along."

Mardirru sighed long and deep.

"It's Lord Beornson's son," Mardirru said in a loud voice. "He's dead."

The officer stopped, as did the guards, and stared. Most of the people walking through the front gate stopped as well.

"You had better explain yourself, and quickly, before my spearmen run you through," the brown-mustached man said.

Mardirru nodded to his brother, Max, who led a cart up to the soldiers. Walking to the back of the cart, he uncovered the body of Gris Beornson. The officer gasped, and the soldiers around him lowered their spears.

"We found him," Mardirru said quickly, "on the way to Holt-gaard, alongside the road, and shooed away the carrion birds. We wrapped him up and brought him here. I would like to take him to Lord Beornson, to give my condolences, and speak with him on the matter. We have some relevant information."

The officer looked up at Mardirru, and then at Erik, and then Max, and then to the rest of the gypsies, eyes squinted.

"Men," he said to his soldiers, "grab the lordling's body. We'll see what Lord Beornson has to say about this."

One of the gate's guards blew a long note through a horn, and within moments, three dozen soldiers surrounded the gypsy caravan and led them all to the Keep of Holtgaard.

Orn Beornson stood over the body of his son, lying on a table in the main hall of Holtgaard's temple. It seemed that most of the people of Hargoleth worshipped a god similar to the Creator—called An by the dwarves—and the large circle hanging over the altar situated in the middle of the building, signifying the oneness of the Almighty and the continuum of life and death and then afterlife, would confirm that. But there was another, smaller altar against one of the walls, incense burning in small containers and the small silver statue of a woman covered in branches and leaves in its center, sitting atop a green runner made of some soft cloth. As anywhere, the people of Hargoleth and Holtgaard were diverse, which included their faiths.

The Lord of Holtgaard looked much like his son—tall and thin, yellow hair that fell to his shoulders and a short beard that looked well-groomed. Orn was so skinny, the long robe made of white bear's fur seemed to weigh him down and looked too big for him, making his movements looked forced and awkward. His face was drawn and sad, making it look even gaunter than it already was. He rubbed his forehead as he stared at his dead son.

Luta Beornson, wife of Orn and mother of Gris, stood behind her husband. She was short, with dark, bobbed hair and bangs cut too short, giving her the appearance of having a very high forehead. She was thick, with wide shoulders and wide hips, and despite being much shorter than him, she probably outweighed her husband. Her eyes were red-rimmed, and her chin quivered. She would stop crying for a moment, close her eyes and take a deep breath, open them again, tilt her head as she stared longingly at her son, and then start crying again. Orn ran a hand through his son's hair as if Gris was a little boy, and his father was messing his hair playfully.

"My son," he whispered.

Erik watched and couldn't help feeling a lump in his throat. Was this what his father would have been like, was this how he would have acted, had he been able to look upon the body of his dead son, Befel?

"We tried to clean him up as best we could," Mardirru said. "He hadn't been gone very long when we found him and the ravens and an eagle were just ... well, we did the best we could."

"And for that, I am grateful, Mardirru of the Ion Gypsies," Orn said, straightening and staring at the leader of the gypsies. "You will always be welcome in Holtgaard."

Mardirru bowed.

"One of ours says the wound on your son's chest is from a northern longsword," Mardirru said.

"How would they know?" Orn asked.

"I don't know," Mardirru replied with a shrug. "We have people who join our caravan from all over the world. They might have been a northerner, once. I didn't ask. They just said what the wound looked like."

"Undoubtedly Wulfstan," Orn seethed, clenching both his fists. "Or some agent of his."

"This wouldn't have happened if ..." Luta began to say, but Orn turned and glared at her.

*This wouldn't have happened if you hadn't sent our son to steal the Ruling Stone! That was what she was going to say?*

Erik watched Orn as he stared at his wife, fear evident on her face and in her eyes.

"What about northern barbarians?" Mardirru asked.

"This time of the year?" Orn replied. He shook his head. "No. They raid the northern reaches of Hargoleth and then retreat to the Iron Forest, having little rations to journey so far south in the extreme cold. This was the work of Wolf Clanners. And this means war."

"Husband," Lute gasped.

"No, wife," Orn snapped. "Wulfstan and Wulfstaad have thumbed their noses at us for far too long and pretended to rule Hargoleth. It is time for change."

"Why would Wulfstan kill your son?" Mardirru asked.

"I don't know," Orn replied. His response was far too quick, and the way his eyes moved said he was lying. "He's a bastard. An inadequate leader. An evil man. Take your pick. As soon as we rise up against the Wolf Clan, the others will follow."

"With war on the horizon," Mardirru said, "we will leave soon. Do we have your permission to stay in Holtgaard for a few days, perhaps a week?"

"Yes, of course," Orn Beornson replied.

Mardirru turned and nodded to Erik. They began to leave when Orn cleared his throat.

"Did you find anything else on my son?" the lord asked.

"Anything else, my lord?" Mardirru asked, pretending ignorance.

"Anything other than his belongings?" the lord added.

"Like what, my lord?" Mardirru replied.

Orn looked at Mardirru for a long while. His eyes narrowed for a moment, and then he shrugged.

"Nothing. Thank you."

With that, they left the grieving parents on their own, and once they were outside the temple, Mardirru turned to Erik.

"That should give you enough time to figure out what happened to Gris, find out where the Dragon Stone is, and let you heal, yes?" he asked in a whisper.

Erik simply nodded.

$\mathcal{A}$s Nagarooshi picked at whatever grass dared shoot up in the cold winter, Ankara sat cross-legged on the ground and inspected the stone. An elongated egg shape that fit in the palms of both her small hands, it was deep green, like the depths of a thick forest, and she thought she could see the faintest light, the hint of a spark, deep inside. It looked like it should be heavy, but it wasn't.

"Elves," she grumbled, scooting closer to her fire, but kept her back against it.

She hated the way heat felt on her face; the light from the campfire hurt her eyes, and her magic could have kept her warm. However, she had expended much of her power in fighting the elf and didn't know when she would need to tap into her abilities again. If an elf was after this stone, she knew it would be soon.

"What would an elf want with you?" Ankara asked the stone as she turned it in her hands, inspecting it.

The space in front of her shifted, and her eyes blazed. Slowly, the cloaked figure that had come to her in her dreams appeared in front of her, sitting cross legged as she was. He looked faint, almost translucent, and Ankara knew he, at least at that moment, existed in some plane in between her world and the Dream World.

"The elves want nothing good with that stone," the cloaked man said. "The elves are evil."

Haughty, arrogant, proud, conceited, reclusive, stand-offish, picky, flighty ... these were all terms Ankara had heard when people spoke of the elves, but never evil. She tilted her head, cocking one eyebrow.

"Many people mistake power for evil," the cloaked man said, "as many mistake good-will or kindness for goodness. None of which the elves have been lately, but do not be fooled, the elves are evil in their own way. They are chaotic and unpredictable, hiding away in their forest realms for a millennium, gaining power, and garnering support from the other Sylvan folk spread around the world. The stone in their hands would be terrible for the rest of the world."

Ankara didn't trust this man, who only existed in the Dream World and was, she sensed, a mage in his own right.

"And how do I know the stone in your hands wouldn't be just as terrible?" she asked.

"I ... the one I serve—the one the Lord of the East serves—only wishes to bring order to those who have none," the cloaked figure said. "And this stone would be the beginning of that."

She could care less for the other people of the world. Kicked around between destruction and order, between chaos and kindness, she had learned growing up to care only for herself. Perhaps it was the way her father, Bone Spear, left her as a child. Or the way she was shunned by many of her own people in the Isutan Isles. Nevertheless, she couldn't help wondering what type of power was truly held within this stone. But the notion that Syzbalo wanted order was almost laughable. She glared at the cloaked figure. Something—many things—were false about this man.

"If it is so powerful, why should I give it to you?" Ankara asked as she leaned forward, her emerald eyes blazing even brighter, trying to peer underneath the man's hood. "A man that only walks in the

Dream World. A man that seems more dead than alive. If you and Syzbalo serve the same master, maybe I should just give it to him. Maybe he will double my reward."

"Because, you know in your heart, it is the right thing to do," he replied. "Because twice as many slaves do not compare to what I can give you."

Ankara laughed. It was a genuine laugh. She didn't know what her heart told her. She rarely asked its opinion. As she held the stone, she felt her power and her magic grow. She felt better than when she lay with a man. She fully grasped her magic, readily available to her at a whim. It was exhilarating, intoxicating, and arousing. This was power. This was strength. To the nine hells with Syzbalo. This ...

The cloaked figure put up a hand, and Ankara's eyes turned to a much more dull, insignificant green, and she sensed her magic was gone. She could feel it, just out of reach, barely grazing it with her fingertips, but, at the moment, it was inaccessible.

She stood, quickly, and he followed suit.

"Says the man who can cut off my flow of magic," she said, seeking to retain her temper as her fingertips brushed against her short sword.

It was the cloaked man's turn to laugh.

"It will return," he said, "once I am gone."

"You know what the sword is," she said. "Why don't you want it?"

"The Dragon Sword is inconsequential to my master."

"Controlling dragons!" she exclaimed, "Being able to kill a dragon is inconsequential?"

"Yes," he replied.

"And what of the Lord of the East?" she asked.

"What of him?"

"You say dragons are inconsequential, but he wants to control them," Ankara said.

He shrugged.

"He is a puppet," the man hissed. "You are a puppet. I am a

puppet. We all have our desires, but when our master pulls our strings, we move. Deliver the sword to him. Keep it for yourself. I do not care, nor does my master. And soon enough, neither will the Lord of the East."

She looked at the stone again.

"So, Black Tigress, we have a deal," the cloaked man added, a statement more than a question.

"Yes, we have a deal," Ankara said, purposely putting the stone into a saddlebag beside her. "The stone for the sword. But you still yet have to uphold your end of the bargain, and if you know my name, should I not know yours?"

"My name is not of importance here," he replied. "Only understand that if you think to cross me, you are playing with fire. The sorrow you feel at your inability to touch your magic is nothing compared to the pain I will bestow on you for treachery."

"I like fire," she replied, and he laughed again. A strange sound, and she thought he did not do that often.

"Very well," he said. "I will retrieve the Dragon Sword. And we will have both honored our part of the bargain. But do not test me. Do not test my master. You are fooling with things that are beyond you, a power that is beyond the greatest known power in this world."

The cloaked man began to fade, and Ankara could feel her magic returning to her. He laughed again.

"When and where should we meet?" she asked.

"Travel south, towards the northern borders of Ul'Erel," the cloaked man's voice instructed as his voice faded. "I will come to you soon. Then, we will make the exchange as we have promised."

Ankara once more sat by the fire.

*We shall see, but I may find I change my mind. I am more powerful than you think, and you aren't as powerful as you want me to believe.*

## 45

Orn Beornson had given the gypsies permission to stay within the walls of Holtgaard, and they had circled their wagons and carts in the middle of the main courtyard as they would if they were out traveling in the wild. It was almost dusk, although night came on quickly in the wintery north, and Erik knew that true night-time was not far away.

"I need to get into the infirmary," Erik said to Mardirru as he was unpacking things from his carriage.

"Why?" the leader of the Ion Gypsies asked.

"I have to inspect Gris' body," Erik replied. "I have to see if there is some clue that might lead me to the Dragon Stone. I have to find it, Mardirru. Otherwise, I fear for what might come."

The large gypsy man thought for a moment and nodded.

"I will go up to the keep," he finally said. "I will ask an audience with Orn. I will say that I need to speak with him about our trade agreements with his people, especially during and after this war he wishes to wage with Wulfstaad. You will come with me, and as soon as we pass through the gate to his keep, you can steal away to the infirmary."

"I feel like I am putting you and your people in grave danger," Erik said.

"Perhaps," Mardirru said matter-of-factly, "but if you think it is important to see the body, then it is, and we will help you."

Mardirru left Max in charge as he, Bo, and a few other gypsies made their way up the inclined path that led to the keep. Erik checked in on Yngrid, who seemed content hiding herself with Dika. His snow cat also seemed to understand she needed to stay hidden, and dozed under several blankets.

"I would like an audience with Lord Beornson," Mardirru said when they reached the top of the ramp and the gatehouse that led to the keep's courtyard.

"It's late," the guard replied.

"It's important," Mardirru insisted.

The guard looked at each one of the men with Mardirru. He didn't even give Erik a second glance. As much as many of the gypsies were swarthy people with dark, curly hair, overall they were diverse. Hailing from all over the world, many different nationalities had decided to travel with this particular caravan because of the kindness and generosity shown to one and all.

"Very well," the guard said.

"Where is the infirmary?" Mardirru asked, and before the guard could question why, he added, "It is our custom to leave a gift for the dead, and I would like to do so, for the recently passed lordling, when I am done meeting with the Lord of Holtgaard."

"Along the south wall of the keep," the guard replied, and Mardirru gave the man a quick bow.

As they walked toward the keep, a two-story, wider structure than the keep of Wulfstaad, Mardirru made sure the guards had turned around and paying them no mind when he nodded quickly to Erik.

Erik found a long shadow created by the keep and rushed along the wooden wall, turning the corner and almost running into another guard. The tall soldier, holding a large, round shield and a long spear, didn't see him, and Erik backed up behind the corner.

Peering around, he saw the single, heavy, wooden door he presumed led to the infirmary, a simple wooden building built onto the keep's wall.

He waited a moment, assuming the guard might move on as he patrolled the courtyard, and so he did. As soon as the man moved away towards another building along the protective wall that surrounded the keep's courtyard, Erik pressed his back to the building, scooted along in the shadows, and crouched in the corner where the infirmary met the keep. He waited another moment before making towards the door. It was open, and he pulled on the circular handle slowly, barely making enough room for him to pass through, and stepped into a dimly lit room with a dozen beds and several shelves of medicines and surgical implements. No one was in the room, and he closed the door quietly behind him.

He wondered if he'd come to the wrong place but then saw what looked like the entrance to a stairway directly across from the door. The stairs were made of stone and curved so that he descended directly underneath the infirmary and into a morgue. Several bodies lay on slabs of stone, all wrapped in white cloth from head to toe, ready for burial. A single dwarf stood next to another body, one still being prepared for internment. Wearing a long robe, his beard and hair were equally gray, and a pair of spectacles dangled off the end of his bulbous nose. He pulled a face as he inspected the body as if something didn't look right.

The room was better lit than the infirmary above, with torches set in sconces every several paces along all four walls. There were more shelves in between the torches with different instruments and fluids —no doubt tools to help with the embalmment and preparation of dead bodies—and a wheeled cart stood next to the dwarf.

"Excuse me," Erik said in Dwarvish and stepping into the room.

The dwarf turned quickly, surprised as his eyebrows rose into high arches. Upon seeing Erik, his brows furrowed, and he grunted. He was unarmed and stepped back, grabbing a small knife from the cart.

"What are you doing here?" the dwarf asked. "You are trespassing."

Erik wanted to stop the dwarf calling out, so he lifted his hands, showing his palms.

"Wait, please," Erik said. "I mean no harm."

"You have a moment to explain yourself before I call the guards," the dwarf said in a quick, harsh tone.

"Please don't do that," Erik said.

The dwarf cocked one eyebrow, looking Erik up and down, his eyes resting on the sword sheathed at his side.

"My name is Erik Eleodum," he said.

"Is that supposed to mean something to me?" the dwarf asked.

"Some call me Erik Dragon Slayer," Erik said, slowly unbuckling the girdle from which his scabbarded sword hung from and dropping it to the ground. "Most dwarves know me as Erik Dragon Fire."

The dwarf's eyebrows shot up again, but there was disbelief in his blue-gray eyes as he watched Erik.

Erik wasn't wearing his mail shirt, and so he pulled open his shirt, revealing his left breast and the baptismal brand that sat there. The dwarf stepped forward a few paces, squinting and staring.

"Few dwarves are ever blessed with their own clan," the dwarf said, "let alone a man."

Erik couldn't tell if the dwarf approved, but he seemed a little less apprehensive.

"I know," Erik replied, "and I am grateful and blessed to have been gifted such an honor from King Stone Axe."

"You shouldn't be here, Erik Dragon Fire," the dwarf said. "If the guards find you here, it will mean trouble for you."

"I just wanted to see the body of Gris Beornson," Erik explained.

The dwarf pursed his lips.

"Why?"

"He had something," Erik replied, "something I have been searching for, and I believe he was killed for it. I thought his body might shed some light, give me some clue, as to where it is."

"The Ruling Stone?" the dwarf asked.

Erik nodded.

"Yes, only ... only it isn't the Ruling Stone," he said, to which the dwarf cocked his head to one side, his interest piqued. "It is actually the Dragon Stone."

"I don't know what that is," the dwarf said.

"The Stone of Chaos?" Erik asked.

The dwarf shook his head.

"Orn Beornson is convinced the Ruling Stone is back in the hands of Wulfstan, Lord of Wulfstaad."

"So, you know Gris stole it from Wulfstaad?" Erik asked.

The dwarf nodded.

"I don't believe Wulfstan could have stolen it back from Gris," Erik said.

"Barbarians, then?" the dwarf said.

"I don't think it was northern barbarians either," Erik said.

The dwarf sighed deeply and gave a quick huff through his nose, causing his gray mustache to flutter under his breath.

"Neither do I."

It was Erik's turn to cock an eyebrow and tilt his head.

"I shouldn't be doing this, but come here," the dwarf said.

The dwarf turned and stood next to the body he was inspecting when Erik first entered the room, and Erik moved over to join him.

Gris Beornson's body was wrapped in a white cloth from his toes to his neck, but his head lay exposed. The signs of death—pale skin, bruising, and sunken cheeks—had already set in, and he could see where the dwarf had sewn the man's mouth together where the eagle had torn away the lip.

"I have yet to paint his face," the dwarf said, looking at the dead man as if he was a dear friend, "to cover his injuries and the suture marks, to make him look like he looked in life, as much as possible at least."

"You were fond of him?" Erik asked.

"I knew him from the time he was born," the dwarf replied.

"Orn and Luta had such trouble conceiving. I had come here as their surgeon just a few years before his birth and gave both of them medicines and foods that might help. It was by the grace of An our Lady became pregnant with Gris; he was a good lad most of the time."

"I'm sorry for your loss," Erik said.

"His father had put so much pressure on him recently, and he had taken to drinking too much," the dwarf said, resting a hand on the dead man's forehead and closing his eyes for a moment. When he opened them, Erik could see the glint of tears.

"His father should never have sent him to retrieve the stone, but he was convinced his plan was foolproof. It would be a sign of loyalty and leadership, as if he wasn't already loyal to his father."

"And you don't believe the Wolf Clanners killed him either?" Erik asked.

The dwarf shook his head and pulled the cloth near the man's neck to one side. He pushed his spectacles closer to his eyes and leaned in, then pulled his head back and pointed to a spot on Gris' flesh.

"Look," he said.

Erik looked closely to where the dwarf pointed.

"Do you see it?" the dwarf asked, and at first, Erik didn't know what he was talking about. But, then, he saw it, a small puncture wound where the man's jugular would have run.

"Yes, but what is it?"

"That is what killed him," the dwarf said.

"That?" Erik said, pointing to the wound. "It's barely big enough to be an irritation."

"It's not the wound that killed him," the dwarf said. "It's what was delivered into the wound. By a small dart. You need to see this."

Erik stood and waited as the dwarf turned and grabbed a small beaker full of a yellowish liquid. He held it up so that the torchlight would illuminate it and swirled the liquid around.

"I was only able to extract a small bit," the dwarf said. "But enough poison to turn this water yellow. By the time the boy had come to me, it had already worked its way through his body."

"Do you know who would have such poison?" Erik asked.

"I believe it to be Elvish."

"Elves?"

"Aye," the dwarf replied. "Orn doesn't want to believe it, but Holtgaard is only a hard day's ride from the northern borders of Ul'Erel, and there has been evidence of elvish incursions into our land. I don't know if he even believes elves exist, but this confirms it for me."

"So, if this poison killed him, what of the other *injuries?*" asked Erik, and the dwarf shot him a glance at his emphasis on the last word.

"Done after death is my opinion," said the dwarf. "There should be more blood around his sword wound, but there is hardly any. Were he alive, his heart would have pumped so much blood, his clothes would have been saturated, but there is hardly anything."

"They looked to be done in anger to me. Perhaps Gris was killed, and then the elves discovered he did not have the Dragon Stone."

"Or someone else had taken it from Gris?" countered the dwarf, and Erik shrugged.

"Who can say right now, but I have to find it."

"If elves have taken it," the dwarf said, "and perhaps you, knowing what the stone truly is, would have a better idea as to why, then I would not chance to hope you will find it. It is in Ul'Erel by now, and that place is a tomb for anyone who is not of Sylvan blood."

*Maybe the elves should have it? If this El'Beth El'Kesh finds it, that was who I was supposed to take it to anyway.*

"You are injured," the dwarf said.

"Is it that obvious?" Erik asked with a smile.

"I can help," the dwarf said. "You have a hard road ahead of you, and pain is surely not your friend on this journey."

"Do you have healing powers?" Erik asked. "A dwarvish friend of mine has ... he has a magical touch."

"No," the dwarf said with an almost disbelieving smile. "I have no such powers. However, I do have several tinctures and mixtures that might expedite the healing process and steal away some of the pain."

He walked to one of his shelves and ran his hands over several other beakers, vials, and glasses. He collected four of them, stuffing several under his arms, and handed them to Erik.

"Take all these twice a day," the dwarf explained, "when you wake up and before you fall asleep. You have enough there for several days, and they should help a little, at least as much as you could hope without time on your side. Ideally, I would want you to rest for at least ten days, but I'm sure you wouldn't do that."

"Thank you," Erik said with a wry smile.

The dwarf closed his fist and put it to his left breast, giving Erik a quick bow.

"Go with An, Erik Dragon Fire," the dwarf said. "If you choose to enter the elvish forests, you will need him more than ever."

Mardirru brought a small wooden chest to the morgue, escorted by Bear Clan guards. Erik waited in the corner of the room when they entered and slid in amongst the gypsies that were with their leader, the guards none the wiser. He didn't know what was in the chest—perhaps some incense or herbs, knowing the gypsies—but Mardirru handed it to the dwarvish surgeon nonetheless and said a prayer over Gris' body, as well as the other two bodies that lay in the room, prepared for burial.

"I need to leave, and soon," Erik said to Mardirru as they walked down the long ramp that led up to the keep.

"You found what you needed, then?" the gypsy asked.

"Enough," Erik replied. "I fear it has made its way to Ul'Erel."

Mardirru had a perplexed look on his face.

"That is dangerous," the gypsy said. "Are you certain?"

"No," Erik replied with a quick shake of his head.

"We will go to where we found the lording's body then," Mardirru said. "Perhaps we will find some clues there, something we missed."

"We?" Erik asked.

"Yes," Mardirru replied. "If this Dragon Stone is as important as you say it is, Bo and I will go with you."

Erik looked to Bo, and the man simply smiled and nodded.

erradyn found the remnants of a battle. Graves had been dug, and the rotting carcasses of several horses littered the ground. It was too cold for flies, but other carrion eaters had been at the dead animals—wolves or foxes no doubt in this land. He found shards of iron and what looked to be the broken shafts of arrows. Black shafts.

"The Isutan," Terradyn said and then spat on the ground before he began to scan it, leading his horse by the reins.

He found the remnants of a fire. Blood. More arrow shafts. Wagon wheel tracks.

"Curious," he said to himself as he crouched down and touched the tracks.

And then he felt it.

"Magic," he said.

Terradyn concentrated, and he felt the tattoos on the side of his head flare. As he garnered the magical ability he had, he could see—through enhanced vision—traces of magic on the battlefield. It was like dozens of footsteps, splashed all over the ground. Wherever someone—the Isutan—had used magic, Terradyn saw its trace, glaring at him in mostly a green hue, but some of the residue was yellow and purple as well. He knew that the color had to do with the type of magic used, but he had yet to discover that mystery, and his master had yet to teach him.

His thoughts wandered to his master. Was he all right? Certainly, the Black Mage—he was no longer the Messenger of the East or the Herald of Golgolithul—could take care of himself. He was a thousand years old and—according to Terradyn—the most powerful man in the east. But even Andragos had his limits. Terradyn saw that, most notably, as the dragon had ravaged South Gate and the southern walls of Fen-Stévock.

Could his master stand against the Lord of the East, his other magicians, and his whole army? Terradyn shook his head. But he was resourceful and cunning. His Soldiers of the Eye were loyal, almost as loyal as he and Raktas, and he was powerful. Undoubtedly, he had stolen himself away to one of his hidden dwellings. Terradyn suspected his master was up to something and wished he could speak with him again. He would complete this mission as fast as possible, make sure Erik Eleodum was safe, and hurry back to Andragos and serve by the wizard's side. That was where he was meant to be; he and Raktas together.

## 47

"*A*re you ready to go?" Bo asked Erik.

Erik looked up at the sky, brightening as the sun crested the western horizon.

"I would like to tell Yngrid I am leaving," Erik said.

"Very well," Bo said. "Don't be too long. It'll be harder to sneak that great, white cat out of Holtgaard when everyone is awake."

Erik walked to Bo and Dika's wagon. Bo's wife was already up and preparing some bread and warm soup to break their fast.

"Yngrid," Erik said, gently shaking her uninjured shoulder.

The head cover she wore to hide her hair—a simple piece of brown cloth tied back with a thin rope—had shifted in her sleep, and when she looked up at Erik with half-closed eyes, some of her curly, red locks escaped, spreading out haphazardly. She smiled as she came to a seated position, sleep still heavy on her. She rubbed her face and yawned. Realizing her hair had escaped its cover, she untied her head cover, repositioned it, and then tightened it up again.

"Erik," she said, still smiling rather girlishly. "Why are you up so early?"

"I have to leave," Erik replied.

"Are we leaving so soon," she said, her smiling fading as she looked about as if to gather her things.

"*I* am leaving," Erik said.

"I don't understand," Yngrid replied, stopping, rubbing her eyes hard, and trying to open them a little wider.

"I'm going after the Ruling Stone."

"Then I'm coming with you," she said, the revelation seemingly waking her a little more as she scooted herself towards the rear of the wagon.

"No," Erik said. "You need to stay here with Dika. You'll be safe here. I can't keep you safe out there."

"Safe?" Yngrid gasped. "As long as I keep my hair covered and stay out of sight. Orn thinks my father killed Gris. If he finds out I am here, I am as good as dead. And perhaps these kind people too for harboring me."

"Just do as Dika tells you," Erik said, "and you'll be fine."

"What if you don't find the Ruling Stone?" Yngrid asked.

"I'll find it," he replied.

"It'll mean war," Yngrid said. "My father is probably already on his way to Holtgaard with his warriors."

"I'll find it," Erik reiterated.

"And when you do?"

Erik knew he had to be careful. If he told Yngrid he didn't mean to return it to Wulfstaad, it would cause problems. But he also didn't want to lie.

"I'll return to where it belongs," Erik said.

"You'll return it to Wulfstaad?" Yngrid asked. "To my father and my family?"

Erik paused a moment. She had no idea what had really resided within her family's clan holding for so many years. And she couldn't know. She wouldn't understand. She was too immature, too naïve, to grasp why he needed the Dragon Stone and why he couldn't return it to her family. But then he looked at her eyes, bright and filled with so much hope. They watched him longingly as she sat at the back of the wagon, her legs dangling off the edge.

"Yes," Erik lied. His eyes couldn't meet hers as she stared at him. He looked up and away but looked at her again when he felt her warmth, closer.

She had slid off the back of the wagon so that she stood directly in front of him, her breasts brushing against his chest. She smiled, and her pale cheeks blushed, a beet red in comparison to the whiteness of her skin, causing her freckles to disappear. She touched his cheek with one hand while the other grabbed the front of his belt and pulled him closer. She was surprisingly strong. Then, she kissed him.

It took Erik by surprise, and he didn't know what to do. Her lips were soft and warm, as was her body as she wrapped her arms around his waist. It had been so long since he had kissed Simone, he reciprocated at first, grabbing Yngrid's hips ...

*No! This is not Simone!*

He pulled away, reaching back to grab her wrists and unclasp her hands.

"I ... I'm sorry, Yngrid," Erik said, feeling a deep sense of guilt as his chest tightened. "I shouldn't have kissed you."

"Why?" she asked with a smile.

"I'm married," Erik replied. "I have a child on the way. My heart ... my heart is for Simone."

"But you liked it, didn't you?" she asked, and her smile was followed by the slightest, sheepish giggle.

As Erik took a small step back, he could see the childishness in her again. She hadn't a clue what love was and didn't care that Erik loved another. She wanted companionship, comfort, anything to make her feel safe and secure. Another man might fall into the trap, another man might take advantage of her naïveté and her need for intimacy. But not him.

"You are pretty and ..." Erik began to say, but Yngrid cut him off.

"Just pretty?" Yngrid said with a pouting, playful jut of her lower lip.

"I'm sorry, but I cannot reciprocate your affection. I should have pulled away as soon as you kissed me. You deserve a man who will respect you and take care of you, although, I think you are quite capable of taking care of yourself."

Yngrid's childishness began to wear away as her smile faded and her eyes looked misty and wet.

"I have to go," Erik said. "I pray the Creator blesses you with a man who will love and respect you. I will return with the Ruling Stone. That, I promise."

## 48

*I*t was still dark as Erik, Bo, and Mardirru left the city walls of Holtgaard, but Erik was still nervous over having the snow cat with them, moving in that graceful, feline way alongside Warrior. Should someone see the animal traveling with them, it might bring undue attention on the gypsies and, as a result, Yngrid.

As Erik and his companions passed the last farmstead, he was about to dig his heels into Warrior's side, when he saw a large group of ogres making their way towards the Bear Clan city. Even with the way they traveled slowly, with purpose, their long, striding gaits made them as fast as a jogging man.

"It's Jamalel," Erik said, unable to avoid smiling.

"Who?" Bo asked.

"The ogre, Jamalel," Erik replied.

"How do you know his name?" Bo asked. "And which one is he?"

"He's that one," Erik said, pointing to the large ogre he recognized as their leader, "and he told me his name."

"Truly?" Mardirru asked.

"You can tell him apart from the others?" Bo asked. "They all look the same to me."

"You know, people say that about gypsies," Erik said with another smile.

Bo laughed.

"Ogres guard their names more than their lives," Mardirru said. "I have never known an ogre to give a man his name. That is a treasured possession."

"Jamalel, my friend," Erik said as they rode up next to the ogres.

Many of them recognized and gave him a slow, methodical bow as he rode up next to them.

"Erik Eleodum," Jamalel said with a smile. He touched his thumb and forefinger to his forehead as he bowed. "It is good to see you, Dream Walker."

"I didn't think you were coming to Holtgaard," Erik said.

"We were not," Jamalel replied, "but the wind told us differently."

"The wind?" Bo asked.

"These are my friends," Erik said, presenting Mardirru and Bo to the ogres.

"The Ion Gypsies," Jamalel said, giving Mardirru the same greeting.

"Yes," Mardirru replied. "How do you know?"

"The son of Marcus is a new leader," Jamalel said with a smile, "and does not know. We ogres are Dream Walkers. The wind told me, noble gypsy, who you are."

"I didn't know ogres spoke in riddles," Bo whispered.

"Riddles to some, yes," Jamalel said, and Bo looked surprised as his cheeks blushed with embarrassment.

"And what has the wind told you recently?" Erik asked.

"The wind tells me war is at hand," Jamalel replied. "It tells me the people of Hargoleth are fragmented and that which Erik Eleodum seeks has been found and then lost again and ... may I speak of this in front of your friends?"

Erik nodded.

"The wind also tells me you cannot travel north," Jamalel continued. "The Lord of the Wolf travels south to wage war. You must go east. The woman you seek ..." The ogre paused for a moment, lifting his chin ever so slightly as if listening to something in the distance. "An assassin, and bearer of the Dragon Stone is east. Now that we have met again, Dream Walker, I will take you."

The Isutan assassin—Ankara—had taken the Dragon Stone? If so, then why the elvish poison? It all started becoming even more confusing. A possible answer crossed his mind. An elf had killed Gris for the stone—with poison—but the woman had taken it from him. That could be the reason for the body being slashed. It could have been a ruse, to misguide anyone finding the body, or it could have been in anger.

The ogre turned to his people and spoke in their language. When he had finished, one of the ogre women approached Jamalel. She had a concerned look on her face, and the ogre leader put his hands on the female's shoulders, and she leaned in, pressing her forehead to his. They stayed there for a long moment before Jamalel turned away and looked at Erik.

"It is time," Jamalel said softly.

## 49

---

With Jamalel walking alongside the horses and the cat, they traveled silently and into the night. The chill of winter seemed to deepen with each passing day, and the wind whipped their faces like knives. Even the stalwart Warrior seemed to notice as he shivered several times, and only the thick, white-furred snow cat dared the air to grow colder. Eventually, hunger stopped them, and Erik and Bo retrieved some dried meat from his saddlebag.

"Do you know her name?" Jamalel asked as clouds covered the moon and stars and northern lights, and Erik struggled to start a fire.

"The cat?" Erik asked. He looked to his white-furred companion as she lay, forelimbs crossed over each other, and waited.

"Yes," Jamalel replied, presenting a hand to Erik as he attempted to extract a spark from his stone and flint.

Erik looked at the hand and placed his flint and stone in the gigantic palm. Jamalel cupped his hands together and blew on their contents. Then, he leaned over to the pile of wood Erik had built and blew gently on the unlit campfire. He struck the stone with the flint several times, and a single, errant spark touched the piled wood, catching it aflame, and it was but a few moments before the campfire blazed, casting a much-coveted light and warmth on the campsite.

"No, I don't," Erik said eventually.

"What do you call her, then?" the ogre asked, gently sitting down cross-legged in front of the fire and warming his hands. The snow cat plodded to Jamalel and rested her head on his lap, the ogre scratching her behind the ears while she purred deeply.

Erik shrugged.

"I guess I don't call her anything," he replied.

"Really?" Jamalel said, stroking the white coat of the cat. He leaned down and nuzzled her neck with his nose, and Erik thought he heard the ogre speak to the cat in his strange language. "I am sure she doesn't like that at all."

Erik watched the pair for a while, the cat turning this way and that so the ogre could rub her belly and her back. He spoke softly to the animal, and she continued to purr.

"Her name is Thala," Jamalel said.

"Thala," Erik repeated, and the snow cat lifted her head up and looked at Erik, yawning.

"She has much to say about you, Erik Dream Walker," Jamalel said. "She is a loyal friend and will remain so. You saved her life, she says."

Erik smiled, and Thala stood and plodded over to him, rubbing her whole body along his, almost knocking him over as he sat there, before lying down and resting her head in Erik's lap.

By then, it must have been midnight. Erik hadn't been able to sleep, and Bo and Mardirru's rest looked troubled at best. Jamalel didn't sleep either, but the ogre didn't say anything. He just sat and watched the fire, so Erik did the same, Warrior standing to one side of him and Thala still lying with her head in his lap. The fire had kept them relatively warm, but in a singular moment, a strong wind crept up and caused Erik to shiver. It challenged the fire, too, as some of the flames died down.

Jamalel looked to the east as Thala woke, her ears perked upright like sentinels snapping to attention. She stood, stepped next to the ogre, and stared east as well. The cold stirred the two gypsies, and as they sat up, Warrior stomped his hooves and snorted loudly.

"Do you see them?" Jamalel asked as he slowly stood.

Erik peered into the darkness.

"Shadows," he said.

The ogre slowly nodded his head.

"The Shadow," Erik said as he searched for the smell of the dead.

Jamalel shook his head.

"No, not the Shadow," he said. "Evil, yes. But a different evil. Chaos."

Erik remembered the shadowy figure from his dreams. Evil, but not the Shadow.

A cloaked figure came into full view of the campfire—the figure from Erik's dreams. He couldn't properly see the other shadows with the figure, but it looked as if they walked on all fours, hunched over creatures who growled in an oddly familiar way.

Erik's heart quickened as he stood, and his stomach knotted as one of the shadows came into view, their fire reflecting off the smooth, gray dome of a head, void of eyes or a nose. Slime drooled from the creature's wide maw as it exposed dagger-like fangs and a long, snake-like tongue. It's gray skin stretched over lean and knotted muscle and its fingers—long and thin—ended in sharp, bony protrusions rather than nails.

"Shadow Children," Erik gasped. "Tunnel crawlers. But how?"

Jamalel didn't say anything as he got to his feet. The hair on Thala's back stood on end as she growled. Warrior snorted loudly, waking the gypsies who quickly stood. Mardirru drew his falchion while Bo drew his own sword.

A cackle escaped the hood of the cloaked figure as he stepped forward. Both bony hands reached up to grasp the edge of the cowl, and he pulled it back.

"*No!*" Erik gasped. "It can't be. You're dead. Not just dead. You were destroyed."

Patûk Al'Banan broke into laughter, his croaking cackle grating, like fingernails on slate. He looked much the same as he did in life, although he was thinner. Dark circles surrounded his eyes, and his hair was thin, revealing some of a pink scalp. His jawline was still stern and strong, but the skin on his face looked stretched as if it was about to tear. Cracks ran along his lips, and as he laughed, he revealed a mouth full of browning teeth.

"You look surprised," Patûk said.

"How?" Erik said, stepping forward.

"Warrior," Patûk said, his sunken eyes seeing the mighty destrier as he stamped his front hooves and snorted loudly. "My old friend."

Erik looked to the great warhorse, his gray coat shimmering in the contrasting darkness and light of the campfire. If a horse could, he looked confused. His eyes met Erik's, but then he snorted and stepped forward.

"Yes," Patûk hissed. "Come to me. Serve me once again."

"Warrior," Erik said. "No!"

Thala growled, and the horse snorted in response.

"I am his master, Erik Eleodum," Patûk said. "I broke him. I raised him. He belongs to me. He is my Warrior."

Erik watched as the horse took his first steps towards his old master, then he spoke one word in a quiet voice. "Eroan."

The horse stopped and looked at Erik over his shoulder as he spoke the horse's true name. Warrior looked back at Patûk, snorted indignantly, and then trotted towards Erik, pressing his snout to Erik's chest and letting the man scratch him behind the ear.

Patûk scowled and grunted something, Erik still in shock over seeing a man he had not only killed but destroyed in the Dream World.

"How are you here?" Erik asked. "You shattered into a thousand points of light."

Before the old dead general could reply, the tunnel crawlers—there must have been at least several dozen of them—growled or howled and looked as if they were going to attack. Patûk held up a hand, and they stopped.

"A man will do many things when faced with his own utter destruction."

"Like bargaining with the Shadow," Erik suggested.

"Bah!" Patûk said, swiping a hand across his face as if pushing someone aside. "The Shadow. The Shadow threw me out like rubbish, and as I watched my whole life fade away, another came to me, offered me power and life in return for service to him. I accepted, and he brought me back. Gave me a new army."

"Chaos?" Erik asked.

Patûk Al'Banan nodded with a smile.

"Yebritoch," Jamalel said.

The tunnel crawlers all hissed and howled at the name of a demon that once served the Shadow. Erik remembered the name from when Nafer explained to him what the tunnel crawlers were. A demon, strong and powerful, a general in the Shadow's armies, he had waged a deadly war on the world, and his army was what would eventually become tunnel crawlers—shadow children. But the Creator defeated him, and the Shadow punished him by casting him away. Ever since, according to legend, the demon had both opposed the Creator and the Shadow.

"Indeed," Patûk replied, a hint of awe in his voice.

"What does he want with me?" Erik asked, drawing Dragon Tooth, the dwarvish blade burning bright with its green flame as he held it by his side.

"He cares nothing for you," Patûk replied. "You are a pittance to Yebritoch the Powerful, the Lord of Chaos."

The tunnel crawlers, again, grew excited at their master's name.

Erik looked down at Dragon Tooth.

"The sword then?" he asked.

"He cares nothing for your sword, either," Patûk replied, watching the blade and licking his cracked lips with a pink tongue.

"Although, it might be a sword worthy of my hands and skills as a warrior. No, he desires the stone."

"The stone?" Erik asked, his eyes widening as his brow arched. "The Dragon Stone? I don't have it."

"Oh, I know," Patûk said, "but your sword is simply a key to get the stone. And I will exact my revenge for your treachery."

"My treachery?" Erik asked.

"You were not—are not—worthy of taking my life," Patûk said. "You have no idea what horrors I have endured to come here to repay the favor of death."

"What do you want with the Dragon Stone?" Erik asked, but then his eyes widened. It was also called the Stone of Chaos, and Yebritoch was known as the Lord of Chaos.

Patûk laughed while the gypsies looked on in horror, and Jamalel just watched intently.

"The Dragon Stone. A foolish name. The—"

"Stone of Chaos," Erik interrupted.

"Yes. Very good," Patûk said with a smile. "And it is my master's, one of four such stones. And it, they, will once again be my master's."

"You've become nothing more than a footstool."

"A very powerful footstool," Patûk yelled, reaching into his robes and drawing a long, black-bladed sword, clenching the fist of his other hand.

Patûk hissed some word of command, and the tunnel crawlers howled like a pack of evil wolves and attacked. Thala killed the first, leaping through the air, her jaws clamping around its thin neck. Warrior turned and with his back legs, kicked two more in their blank, gray faces, dropping them instantly. Jamalel's hand easily enveloped a tunnel crawler's head, and he threw the creature into the campfire, the flames arching and rising with the fresh, stinking fuel.

As Erik brought Dragon Tooth down upon a thin shoulder, the gray skin catching fire and burning the creature, Mardirru appeared next to Erik, his falchion removing the head of a tunnel crawler that would have at least scratched its claws along Erik's mail shirt, if not worse, had he not been there. Bo jumped in on the other side of Erik. He wielded two short swords, each cleaving, thin, gray skin. Meanwhile, Warrior turned again, and he reared up, bringing his massive, feathered hooves down on heads.

Patûk commanded at least fifty tunnel crawlers initially, and as the shadow children spilled from the darkness, two replaced each one that fell. Unlike those Erik had faced in the Gray Mountains, these creatures seemed to move with a purpose beyond hunger. Their attacks were coordinated as Patûk directed them. One would sacrifice itself so that two or three more could press an assault. These were the shadow children of old, the demon warriors of Yebritoch.

Dragon Tooth cleaved one in two, each half bursting into flames while another broke its long, gray claws on Erik's shield, only to be shorn in two by the mighty falchion of Mardirru. Bo supported his leader, finishing off any enemy that had been cut by the gypsy's sword, but not killed. Thala and Warrior worked in harmony, the great snow cat catching gray flesh with her claws and throwing her prey into the path of the warhorse.

And for all of Jamalel's slow and deliberate movements, in battle, he was a flash of lightning, snatching up tunnel crawlers with his large hands and crushing their skulls with a single squeeze. Or kicking two or three away into the darkness with his thick boot. They would leap at him, and he would catch them midair, his hands wrapping around their grossly thin torsos, breaking ribs and rupturing organs.

Patûk screamed and cursed and lifted a hand into the air. He chanted something in a language Erik didn't recognize, and a white flash flew from the palm of his hand to the sky. It was already dark, but Erik could see the clouds—black and angry—growing overhead. They flared with lightning as two bolts struck the ground in front of the ogre. The accompanying thunder roared with deafening fury, causing everyone and everything to stop, save for Patûk and Jamalel. The ground shifted and rumbled as small mounds of dirt began to rise and take the shape of large men, almost like the ice golems of the ice bridge in the Gray Mountains Erik had fought on his way to Fealmynster. But these were larger, at least as tall as Jamalel, their faces blank and formless and their bodies lumbering and craggy.

One earthen golem stepped forward, its leg breaking free from the earth, and a great maw opened in the middle of what would be its face. A roar erupted, dirt in place of spittle flying from its mouth, and it swung an arm at the ogre, rock replacing a hand so it might use it as a club. Pebbles rained down on the whole battlefield as the arm struck Jamalel in the chest. The ogre stepped back, only to receive the same attack from the other golem. For the first time, Erik recognized emotion on the ogre's face as Jamalel frowned, his pale skin growing red, his giant, bushy, gray brows furrowing. The ogre clenched his fists and punched one of the golems. The animated monster's head exploded into a thousand tiny rocks, and the creature crumpled to the ground, nothing more than a mound of dirt. As the second golem came on, Jamalel did the same thing, reducing it to nothing more than rubble.

As the broader battle resumed, Erik's hip was getting weaker, and his ribs hurt with every labored breath. His shoulder still hurt as he did his best to hold up his shield, knocking away tunnel crawlers as he slashed at them with his sword in his other hand. He groaned as he glared at the dead general, who was lifting his hand once more to conjure earthen golems.

Gripping Dragon Tooth tightly, he rushed in as fast as he could, his limp still very much present. He swatted away several tunnel crawlers, their skin catching fire and burning them until he reached the general. At first, Patûk seemed to take no notice of Erik, chanting the same words as before, but then he glanced at the man and chanced a small smile as he moved into his fighting stance, drawing a black-bladed sword he held with both hands.

"You surprised me once," Patûk croaked, "but you won't do it again. You weren't worthy of granting me my death, which wasn't the glorious thing it should have been. Once I slide my blade into your gut, my revenge will be complete."

"You got exactly what you deserved," Erik replied, taking his own stance. "Death at the hands of a farmer, in the middle of nowhere, so that no one will ever remember who you were. In a generation, no one will remember the name Patûk Al'Banan!"

"Pathetic lies!"

Erik gave a slight smirk as he saw the stretched, pale skin of the dead general redden, his jaws trembling.

"But the name of Erik Eleodum," Erik added, "the name of Erik Dragon Fire, Erik Dragon Slayer will live on forever."

The dead were never nimble or strong. Whatever fight they had in their bodies, it was always spurred on by Shadow magic, as their muscles and skin decayed, leaving tightly wound ligaments and bone. Patûk did not fight like the dead.

The general moved as he had in life; better in fact. He came in fast and hard, his blade poking, prodding, and then slashing. Erik blocked the downward arc of the black sword, but as the steel truck the dwarvish shield, it sent tremors through his whole body, and every injury and bruise sent pain signals to his brain. The worst was his shoulder that had taken the brunt of the blow, and it felt dislocated again.

With his hip feeling even more like it might give way, Erik had no time to recover as Patûk swung again, barely missing Erik's head, and then the old general laughed. He stood there, in front of Erik, barely breathing and not showing any signs of physical exertion. When Erik finally launched his counteroffensive, Patûk moved with a serpent's speed, easily dodging slashes and jabs. He was thin and emaciated-looking, but he felt strong and heavy when he leaned into Erik, his breath hot and a putrid wave and Erik felt himself gagging.

"Do you see?" Patûk said. "I am stronger now than I was before, and you have no chance. You are not worthy."

The general attacked again with a downward strike, which skidded off Erik's shield and struck his left thigh. Erik screamed out as the weapon dug into his flesh, burning him where it touched. He instinctively slashed out with his own sword, the flaming, green blade catching Patûk's shoulder. The cloth of his robe caught fire, and the general let out his own scream as he threw off the covering, revealing a mail shirt of black ringlets hanging loosely from narrow, boney shoulders.

The wound to his shoulder only seemed to energize the general more as he came on stronger, slashing and swiping and stabbing. When Jamalel, Mardirru, Bo, or even Thala and Warrior tried to come to Erik's aid, the tunnel crawlers would swarm, readily giving their bodies to protect Patûk. And they came on in uncountable numbers, flocking from the darkness that surrounded the camp. A bony fist crashed against Erik's chin, and he reeled backward, on his heels. The tip of a black-steeled sword grazed his neck, drawing a line of blood while a boot connected with his right knee, buckling his leg underneath him. As Erik struggled to stand, a crowd of tunnel crawlers grew, gathered around the general, panting, growling, and salivating. Patûk pointed at Erik, and the tunnel crawlers lunged forward.

Just then, Jamalel lifted his head and looked to the clouded, dark sky overhead. He flexed his arms, balled his hands into fists, and let out a thundering yell, low and reverberating. Erik felt his body shake as a wave of sound from the ogre struck him harder than the general's fist.

The sound continued, on and on, as if the ogre had no need to breathe, and as the sound struck Patûk and the tunnel crawlers, they stepped back. The shadow children howled and screamed in response, and Patûk fell to his knees. The tunnel crawlers' skin ripped and tore as blood poured from the wounds until, with a final wave of sound, every remaining tunnel crawler burst into a myriad of pieces of flesh, as if something inside of them had exploded.

Patûk wavered back and forth for a moment, clearly affected by the ogre's voice, but still very much on his feet. The effort, though was too much for Jamalel, and he crumpled to his knees, his breath ragged, and his eyes closed. He looked drained, barely holding onto consciousness as Bo and Mardirru ran to him.

Patûk groaned and stood more upright, shaking his head until he looked up and saw Erik standing there, blood trickling from his throat, wincing as he breathed. He dropped his shield, his shoulder so racked with pain again he could no longer hold it. The general smiled a toothy smile.

"Your ogre's magic is strong," Patûk chided, "but not strong enough."

Patûk stepped forward, and Erik swallowed hard. The general looked to his left, and as Erik followed his gaze, he saw the silhouette of a large man on a horse, watching a short distance away. Patûk began to laugh when he lifted a hand, causing lightning to strike in front of the distant figure. The earth rolled, and two more earth golems sprang up where the unknown man was standing.

"Come, Erik Eleodum," Patûk said, gripping his black-steeled sword in both hands, "let us finish this, so that your precious name may live on forever."

"It'll be my pleasure killing you twice," Erik said, limping forward, but his stomach knotted, and he felt his heart flutter. His strength had waned rapidly while Patûk's only seemed to grow stronger.

erradyn felt the gooseflesh rise along his arms. Magic. It was powerful, almost as powerful as that Andragos wielded. In the darkness of the night, he saw a bright, white flash in the distance. For a moment, it disrupted his enhanced vision, and he stopped his horse, blinking wildly until his eyesight came back into focus.

It was a dark, moonless night, but the sky had been clear. Black clouds billowed overhead now, and several more flashes spoke of lightning strikes. It was unnatural. More magic. Terradyn spurred his horse on, and the animal galloped at a surprising speed. He looked down at the ground and saw dead things—rabbits, squirrels, several deer, a fox, even a wolf. They were torn to pieces, bone, ligaments, and entrails strewn about. Something leaped at Terradyn from the darkness.

It was as if a shadow loomed around him, his magical vision touching just the edges of a black bubble that consumed him. And this thing had been hiding, just out of sight, waiting. He caught it by the throat. It was a creature he had never seen before, and it gnashed sharp teeth and flailed a long, pink tongue about as Terradyn squeezed.

He held a humanoid looking creature, with two arms and two legs, although both arms and legs looked to be the same length. Its skin was a pallid gray and stretched tightly over bone. As it reached out at Terradyn and scratched at his arm, he realized its fingers had no nails; they simply ended in long claws. Even though the wounds healed as soon as they were created, they burned with a black magic Terradyn had never felt before.

As Terradyn squeezed the creature's throat harder, it gurgled and struggled even more. Its head was an egg-shaped dome but with no eyes and only holes for nostrils and a mouth. He squeezed as hard as he could until he heard the breaking of bone, and the creature went limp. As he dropped it, Terradyn felt the tattoos on the side of his head flare as growling and howling surrounded him. He drew his massive sword, and as he brought it down, cut another one of the creatures in two, each half of its body flopping on the ground and jittering for a moment. He turned his horse just as another leaped from the darkness. It met a similar fate, and another and another and another. They were all around him. Dozens. Scores. Hundreds perhaps. Too many.

His magic wasn't as strong as Andragos', not even close, but being the servant of a mage, he learned how to be a magician in his own right. He concentrated for a moment, closing his eyes and thinking of the ancient words the Messenger of the East had taught him. He spoke them in his mind and clenched the fist of his other hand. He felt the tingle of electricity flow through his body, and when he opened his eyes and his hand, felt a surge of power pour outwards, into the blackness of the choking night.

A swarm of the sightless creatures was there, climbing over one another like a pack of hungry dogs, but as a wave of white electricity hit them, their gray skin caught fire, and they burned, giving light to the otherwise dark landscape. There were almost fifty, Terradyn suspected, but by the time his power had washed over the last of the creatures, they were all dead, nothing more than burnt and crooked shapes.

The extreme darkness that had consumed the space around Terradyn dissipated, and as the clouds rolled away, Terradyn heard shouting, and spurred his horse on towards to the source of magic he had felt. It wasn't far away, and soon he could make out an unnatural shadow that loomed over a campsite, a large fire burning in the middle. Those same gray creatures were there, along with a cloaked man, fighting someone Terradyn recognized. Erik Eleodum. He saw two other men, a large, white-furred snow cat, and a giant of a warhorse, and an ogre. He hadn't seen an ogre in years.

Terradyn leaned forward in his saddle; the man who fought Erik looked familiar too. Terradyn squinted his eyes, and they blazed white as his vision amplified and cleared. He sat back, his mouth open.

*It can't be.*

Patûk Al'Banan was dead, but if that was him fighting Erik, there was powerful and dark magic indeed. He looked a ghost of his former self, but that was the old General nonetheless. As he fought Erik, he pushed the farmer backward, on his heels, cutting him. Terradyn shook his head. Erik was supposed to be a great fighter, but he looked injured. He limped, and his left arm hung awkwardly. Erik was losing.

This was what Andragos had sent him away for, to protect and help Erik, and he looked like he'd failed in his task. With his sword about to swing down at Erik again, Patûk turned his head and glared at Terradyn, who was just about to jump down from his still moving horse. The general knew he was there. He lifted a hand, the same white flash as Terradyn had seen before exploding from his palm. Clouds billowed overhead. Two bolts of lightning flashed from the heavens and struck the ground in front of him.

*I'll deal with you later.*

The thought passed through Terradyn's mind, and it was Patûk's voice.

Terradyn fell backward as the ground in front of him undulated. The earth rose, almost twice his height, and then moved and twisted. Both tall mounds began to take shape, with what looked like heads sitting at their tops. There were no eyes, but both heads turned and *looked* at Terradyn. The middle of the heads opened into wide maws, and they screamed as arms erupted from their sides, and their lower halves began to split into legs. They pulled at their legs, trying to lift them, and as they ripped away from the ground, the earthen giants screamed again.

The golems had no hands or feet ...simply stumps. One of them swung at Terradyn, and he rolled underneath the attack, only to find the other one trying to step on him. He jumped out of the way as the stump crashed to the ground and slashed at its leg. His sword took a large chunk out of the golem's appendage, but the monster didn't seem to notice.

Beyond the two golems, Terradyn could see the fight between Patûk Al'Banan and Erik. It wasn't going well, and as the men and ogre and animals that looked to be allies of Erik tried to come to his aide, the general would cast some magical spell causing the earth to rise in front of them or lightning to strike the ground, pushing them back. But when Terradyn tried to rush through the two golems so that he might help Erik, the animated monsters crashed together, blocking his path.

A golem swung at him again. This time he swung his massive sword hard in a downward arc, severing the limb. It crashed to the ground and turned to dirt. He then swung at its leg, biting away rock and rubble until the golem was unsteady and began to tilt to one side. Its giant maw opened, and it screamed as it went down to what would have been its knee, but before Terradyn could slash at its blank face, the stump of the other golem thudded into his chest, sending him through the air. He landed on his back, the air hastily escaping his lungs, and he had to take a moment to regain his wits.

The mobile golem came at him. He could feel the earth under his body rolling and shaking, and he rolled out of the way just as the stump of an earthen foot crashed down. Terradyn ran to the other golem as it tried to stand, only to have its leg crumple underneath it. It opened its maw, screaming and sending sharp rocks out at Terradyn. He ignored the projectiles as they cut his face and drove his sword into the golem's mouth. He twisted and slashed sideways and then ripped the blade through, cutting the upper half of the animated monster's head off. The golem went slack and turned to nothing more than a mound of dirt and rock.

As the other golem came at him, Terradyn rolled underneath a swinging arm and cut away at both earthen legs. The golem fell, face first in front of the man. The golem pushed itself up, howling, but Terradyn brought his sword down on top of its head, splitting the rock in two, and like the other one, the golem turned to nothing more than a mound of rubble.

Terradyn turned back to the fight between Erik and Patûk Al'Banan. He whistled, and his horse came, but as he was about to mount the animal and ride to Erik's help, Patûk stabbed Erik in the shoulder.

Erik cried out, gripping the black blade and trying to stop Patûk from driving it into his flesh any further. Blood seeped through Erik's fingers, and as the general retrieved his blade, Erik looked to the sky.

"I'm sorry, Simone!" Terradyn heard him cry just as Patûk drove his sword into Erik's belly.

Everything seemed to stop. Erik's friends looked on in horror, and Terradyn watched in disbelief, one boot in his saddle's stirrup and one still on the ground. Patûk pulled his sword from Erik's belly, and the man fell to the side, dropping his sword. The green flames that had burned along the sword seemed to diminish until they finally faded away, leaving nothing more than a finely crafted weapon. Patûk laughed. He looked at Erik, then at Terradyn, and then Erik again.

"*Revenge!*" he shouted and leaned over, picking up Erik's sword.

As Terradyn rushed forward, sword drawn, a shadow swirled around Patûk Al'Banan as the space in front of the dead man shimmered. In moments, Patûk was gone. Now Terradyn turned towards Erik's body and saw both men and ogre standing over him. A great white snow cat prowled up and down the side of the campfire, and a huge horse stamped its hoof and snorted. Terradyn stopped.

"Is he dead?" Terradyn asked as one of the men put several fingers to Erik's neck.

The man, a broad-shouldered fellow with a mop of curly, dark hair, looked up at Terradyn with red-rimmed eyes and nodded.

"Who are you?" the other man asked. He looked similar to the first, and Terradyn thought they were gypsies.

"Terradyn," he replied.

"Servant of Andragos, the Black Mage," the ogre said.

"Aye," Terradyn said. "How do you know?"

"My dreams tell me many things," the ogre replied in a slow, methodical tone.

"Why are you here?" the first man said, still leaning over Erik's body.

"I was sent to protect him," Terradyn replied, and his stomach knotted at the futility of his statement. "I was sent to protect Erik Eleodum."

"Well, lot of good you did," the second gypsy added.

The ogre walked to Erik's body. He bent down and scooped the man up as if he was a baby.

"What are you doing with the body?" Terradyn asked.

"We will take him back to Holtgaard," the ogre replied.

Without another word, the ogre began walking west, the great warhorse Terradyn now recognized as Warrior following, along with the snow cat. The two gypsies followed on their horses, and after a moment, Terradyn remounted and heeled his horse after them, keeping his distance as the snow cat watched him over its shoulder.

"I'm sorry, master," Terradyn whispered. "I have failed my mission."

He couldn't return to his master now. What would the Black Mage think? His stomach knotted again, and he felt a wave of something he hadn't felt since he was a child. He couldn't put a finger on the feeling of the foreign emotion that seemed to be consuming him, but he wondered if it was sadness.

## 51

*E*rik woke. He was in a field of tall grass, lying down and staring at the sky. It wasn't the blue of a morning or the darkness of night. It was gray and dull. He sat up and looked around, noting that the grass was still and brown, and there was no breeze to flutter it back and forth. He looked over his shoulder, and the mountain range was there, black as it always was, but there were no clouds nor any lightning. His hill stood in front of him, but no man sat under the great, looming willow tree.

The whole of the Dream World seemed different. The sounds were always so clear, the colors so vibrant, as if the real world was actually some dull copy of this one, where the brilliance of everything couldn't quite be copied, But now, in this dream, it was the opposite. Everything was dull, quiet, and somber as if sadness and grief could take the form of a landscape.

Erik stood and slowly walked towards his hill, and the fact it was so hard to move his legs reminded him of his baptismal vision. It was as if he had, once again, stepped in thick mud. He sighed, the sound of his breath a distant echo when he finally reached the bottom of the hill. He rubbed his face with the palm of his hand but, no matter how hard he pressed, he felt nothing. He bit a finger. Nothing. His stomach should have knotted, but it didn't. Something was very wrong.

Erik faced his hill again. If he could just sit there, under the tree, everything would be right again. He stepped onto the hill, or at least, he tried. The moment he lifted his foot and tried to step onto the gentle slope, it was as if some invisible rope was tied to his ankle and someone was holding him back. He tried and tried, always stopping just short of getting a first foot onto the incline in front of him.

Finally, he tried to just drop onto the slope, but a powerful force stopped him, and he found himself flat on his back again, staring up at the sky. Sitting up, he saw he was in the same place as before when he had first opened his eyes. He stared at the distant hill and told himself not to give up. He ran to it, and when he reached it, he threw himself onto it again. It was no good. Again, some force held him at bay, pushed him back, and he opened his eyes to stare at a pallid gray sky.

He stood in front of it again, and this time, he felt a small breeze pick up. He closed his eyes and smiled. It was a familiar feeling. A bit of warmth hit his body, and he felt a ray of sunlight strike his face. When he opened his eyes, he saw a golden carriage in front of him. The sunlight illuminated the carriage and, when the door opened, a man clothed in black robes emerged. Erik knew this man.

"What are you doing here?" Erik asked. "There is no one to take."

"It is time, Erik," the robed man said. He extended a black-gloved hand.

"Time for what?" Erik asked.

"Your time," the robed man said. He always came for the dead, never the living that happened to walk the land of dreams, and Erik cocked an eyebrow.

"My time?" Erik asked.

"Erik," the robed man said, taking a step forward. "You are going to be alright."

"I'm fine already," Erik said. "What is going on with this place? Why is it different?"

"Because you are different, Erik," the robed man replied.

"I don't understand," Erik replied.

"Yes, you do," the robed man said. "You just don't want to believe it."

Erik looked down at his hands. They were pale, so light-skinned it was as if he had never spent time in the sun. As he touched his hands, he felt nothing. He rubbed them together hard, pinched the skin and twisted his fingers, but there was no change. He slapped his hands together and then slapped his face as hard as he could. He barely felt anything, let alone pain.

"This can't be," Erik said, but then he remembered.

He had simply assumed he had fallen asleep and awoken in this place like he did almost every night, but now his memories surged back into his mind. He remembered Patûk Al'Banan and his dark magic. He remembered pain, unbearable pain in his shoulder and hip, his ribs, and then his belly. He remembered staring into those blank, dead eyes of Patûk, as the undead general plunged his black-bladed sword into Erik's stomach. The feeling of despair and regret, hopelessness and loneliness engulfed him as his mind filled with the vision of Simone wearing the black of a widow and his child growing up without a father.

Erik wept, but there were no tears.

"It is time," the robed man said.

"*No!*" Erik shouted. "It's not supposed to end like this."

"It never is," the robed man replied, still holding out a hand to welcome Erik into his carriage.

"I still have so much left to do," Erik said.

"You always will," the robed man said. "Erik, we must leave. It is time. Join your grandfather. Join your fallen friends. Join your brother. It is time."

Erik backed away, but whatever force kept him from stepping foot on his hill now would not let him move away from the robed man. Then he remembered again. There was always the force that stopped the dead moving onto the hill.

*The dead.*

"This is wrong," Erik said. "You're wrong."

The black-robed man gave a short nod and folded his hands into the sleeves of his robe.

"Very well," the robed man said. "I will be back. Just remember, I will only come for you so many times before you will be left to wander as the other lost ones do."

He turned, stepped into the golden carriage, and it floated away.

Erik sat down, his back to the hill, and buried his face in his hands.

## 52

*A*ndragos opened his eyes. He didn't know when he last felt anxious or worried or even sad, but that feeling crept up on him like a spider stalking an insect. He looked down at a bowl of water sitting in front of him. A black ink-like substance floated along the top, like oil, but other than that, there was nothing—no vision, no picture, no image of Erik. Something was wrong. Andragos closed his eyes again and reached out, searching. He was wanting to speak with Terradyn, to see if he had caught up with Erik yet, but felt Dewin's presence.

"Dewin," Andragos said.

"Andragos," Dewin replied. The image of young Dewin began to appear in Andragos' mind. He stood in the small room in which the Black Mage sat, his long, wavy, brown hair fluttering even though there was no wind.

"I don't see Erik anymore," Andragos said.

"Nor do I," Dewin replied. "His essence in the Dream World has changed, shifted somehow."

"It can't be," Andragos said.

"I am afraid so," Dewin replied.

"He's dead," Andragos gasped. "How? Ankara?"

Dewin shook his head.

"No," the soothsayer replied. "You did not sense him?"

"Who?" Andragos asked.

"Yebritoch," Dewin said.

Andragos stopped breathing for a moment. The image of Dewin shimmered in front of the wizard as his concentration wavered. Yebritoch? The demon who once served the Shadow. The demon who once challenged the Shadow. The Lord of Chaos, the master of the Beasts of Chaos, creator of the shadow children, and scourge of any living, good thing was back, and Andragos couldn't understand how he hadn't sensed such a presence.

Yebritoch was one of the first demons to side with the Shadow in the beginning, trying to depose the Creator. Over time, many had forgotten about these truths, turning to worship the many other powerful deities and demons who had grown into power over thousands of centuries. Even though Andragos had never been a follower of the Creator—and ignored most of his teachings—he recognized his existence and hand in creation. The Shadow and Yebritoch had once waged war against each other, and the result was not only the imprisonment of Yebritoch in the deepest layer of hell but the imprisonment of the demon's four beasts, the chaos beasts. It also left the world in ruins.

"How? Why," Andragos asked.

"Yebritoch wants what he has always wanted," Dewin said, "power. And time has rusted his prison chains. He has enlisted a man named Patûk Al'Banan as his agent in the dream world."

"Patûk Al'Banan?" Andragos exclaimed. "Erik killed him!"

"Aye," Dewin replied. "As I have searched the Dream World, I have seen this Patûk broken, twisted, and black. Yebritoch offered him life for service, and the demon has given the old general power beyond anything he ever possessed in life. It is he that killed Erik, took the Dragon Sword, and will soon have the Stone of Chaos. This will mean a world in ruins once more."

"The Stone of Chaos?" Andragos asked.

"The Dragon Stone," Dewin replied.

"What does he want with the Dragon Stone?" Andragos asked.

"Truly?" Dewin replied, clearly taken aback. "You do you not know, teacher?"

"No," Andragos said, his voice short and steely.

"The Dragon Stone is one of the four prisons," Dewin replied, and when Andragos raised an eyebrow, he added, "those which hold Yebritoch's Beasts of Chaos."

Andragos' eyes went wide.

"Do the elves know?" Andragos asked.

"They are the ones who imprisoned the beasts in the first place, many millennia ago. We must rely on them again now, to stop Patûk Al'Banan. Lest, he release one of the chaos beasts onto the world."

"Who then, replaces Erik?" Andragos asked. "I thought he was the one to connect with the elves and raise the Dragon King, so there must be another. Who will take his place?"

"His cousin, perhaps?" Dewin suggested.

Andragos shook his head.

"Bryon is a good man," Andragos said, "but he is stubborn and not the leader that Erik was. I don't know, Dewin. Whoever it is, we must start an urgent search."

Dewin nodded and the image of his old pupil shimmered, and he disappeared. *Pupil? The old man knows more than me now. I am failing myself.*

Andragos stood and opened the door to his small cottage, stepping outside and breathing in the fresh air. This dwelling was far away from Golgolithul, and one the Lord of the East had no knowledge of. Andragos knew his previous master had been searching for him, to what end, he didn't know, but it could only mean trouble. Syzbalo had been absent from Golgolithulian court for some time, and he knew his former Black Mage was growing restless and concerned about the course he was taking their country. The Lord of the East had started referring to it as an empire and now the man at the heart of Andragos' plans to stop his former master was dead.

*Erik ... I'm sorry.*

Sadness was an emotion he hadn't felt in hundreds of years, but he felt it now. And worry.

## 53

*A*s they got closer to the Hargolethian clan holding known as Holtgaard, the home of the Bear Clan, a thick cloud hung in the air. The two men who looked like gypsies watched it with curiosity, but Terradyn knew very well what it was from.

"What's going on?" the smaller of the two gypsies asked.

"It's a siege," Terradyn replied, speaking the same Westernese the man spoke.

The gypsy looked at Terradyn over his shoulder with wide eyes.

"That is the smoke from the many fires of a waiting army," Terradyn added.

"How do you know?" the other gypsy asked, his voice hard and commanding. He was used to being in charge.

"I've seen it before," Terradyn replied. "It is unmistakable."

As they neared the walls of Holtgaard, Terradyn's explanation was proven true as what must have been at least a thousand warriors congregated around the city walls, some fifty paces from the archers and slingers standing atop the walls. Those warriors harassed the citizens of the Bear Clan that hadn't found their way behind the city walls, taking what food and money they had, but that was it; Terradyn had seen far worse.

These soldiers seemed to have some level of respect for the people of the Bear Clan. Typically, those poor souls too late to find protection behind a city wall and closed gate met a far worse fate. Rape and torture, all eventually ending in a much-anticipated death, were the worst of the inflictions imposed on poor, small folk of a nation that weren't privy to the comforts afforded those living closer to a city center. And the attacking force always used such acts as a threat, as if the nobles and wealthy that lived in protection gave a moment of thought to those poor people.

"Stop! What is your business here?" said a member of the sieging army as the small entourage neared the gates of Holtgaard.

He spoke in a language Terradyn had not heard in a long while, but thanks to his master, he was well versed in many different tongues.

"We mean to enter the city," the larger gypsy said.

"No one in or out," said the warrior, a tall and broad-shouldered man with long, blond, braided hair and a long beard of the same color.

"My people are in there," the large gypsy said.

"Don't care," the warrior replied. "And, I think I will be procuring your horses today. Consider it a tax to your soon to be Lord Wulfstan of Wulfstaad."

"I don't think so," the larger gypsy said as the snow cat began to growl.

The warrior clearly hadn't seen the large cat and took a step back, his eyes wide, placing a hand on the handle of his long sword. Terradyn heeled his horse, riding past the snow cat and the two gypsies and the ogre holding Erik's body. He stopped short of the Hargolethian warrior, staring down at the man. The warrior's wide eyes spoke of surprise, even though he tried to keep his composure, sliding his sword from its scabbard halfway.

"I wouldn't do that," Terradyn said slowly. He watched the man,

watched his face and eyes. He was scared, and several of his compa-
triots had taken notice of the situation and begun to walk towards
them. "We have a dead man with us, a relative of these gypsies, and
an ogre—beholden to no law and allowed to travel and trade freely
even in Golgolithul. They are no threat to you or your lord. Let them
pass so they may grieve with their kin."

"And who are you?" the warrior asked, a little bolder as two other
soldiers joined him, standing to either side of him.

"Their friend," Terradyn replied, looking at the gypsies and ogre
over his shoulder.

The soldier looked to the other two men who had joined him and
then back at Terradyn. Finally, he nodded.

"Fine," he said. "Follow me."

But then, a loud commotion arose from within the army that
surrounded the clan holding of Holtgaard. The warriors congregated
in front of the main gates parted as a large man wearing a mail
hauberk riding a large draft horse turned into a warhorse emerged. A
thick coat of wolf skin hung from his shoulders, the head of the wolf
resting on his right shoulder. Several other horsed men followed, all
riding slowly from the ranks of the army. He stopped just short of the
Holtgaard's gatehouse, five other horsemen stopping behind him.

"Orn!" the man yelled. "Show your face!"

"You tell 'em, Lord Wulfstan," one of the warriors in front of
Terradyn said, clapping one of the other men on the shoulder with a
smile on his face. "Show these bear shaggers what a real lord is
about."

"What is happening?" Terradyn asked.

"Orn Beornson not only sent his thieving son to steal the Ruling
Stone," one of the soldiers said, and then spat, "but he has also
kidnapped the lass Yngrid, Lord Wulfstan's daughter. Blood will spill
if he doesn't give both back."

Terradyn looked over his shoulder at his entourage.

"Come on," Terradyn said, jerking his head sideways and then
heeling his horse.

"Whoa!" the soldier said, stepping in front of Terradyn's horse. "Where do you think you're going?"

"Get out of my way," Terradyn said, lowering his voice and glaring at all three men who stood in front of him.

With his tattooed head, he was a formidable sight, and the soldiers gave each other worried glances and then, without a word, they all three stepped aside and let the small group pass by. When they got closer to the gates, Terradyn stopped and looked up to where a tall, thin man stood atop one of the gatehouses of Holtgaard, looking down at an assembly of at least one thousand soldiers accompanied by another hundred horsemen.

In the east, that was barely enough men to make up a single unit in the Golgolithulian army, but here in the north and west, it was a sizeable army and must have looked intimidating. However, the man atop the defenses—Orn Beornson, Terradyn presumed—gave no indication he was nervous.

"You best move your mongrel horde away from my clan holding, Wulfstan, lest your people need to find a new lord," Orn yelled from the gatehouse.

"You have my daughter, you prick!" Wulfstan yelled. "And the Ruling Stone!"

"You are a fool!" Orn yelled back.

"Liar!" Wulfstan screamed, his face growing as red as his hair.

His men began to shout and chant, feeding off his anger and intensity. He put up a hand and silenced them as Orn simply stared.

"You killed my son," Orn said. "My Gris. You murdered him in cold blood. You left his flesh to be picked on by scavengers. You are a disgrace and undeserving of the Ruling Stone."

"So you did take it?" Wulfstan asked, leaning forward in his saddle.

"I don't know where the Ruling Stone is," Orn replied, skirting the question.

"But you did send your thieving bastard son to steal it, didn't you?" Wulfstan accused.

Orn didn't answer at first. Terradyn squinted, staring at the Lord of Holtgaard. His eyes looked watery, his cheeks wet.

"You didn't have to kill him," Orn finally said, his voice softer, his words wavering. "He was the son of a Hargolethian Lord."

"A thief is a thief," Wulfstan replied, murmurs of agreement coming from the crowd of Wolf Clan soldiers gathered behind him. "But I didn't kill him. Nonetheless, you have my daughter and the Ruling Stone. Give them back, and I might forget your thieving ways."

Orn flexed his jaw.

"I told you ... I don't have your daughter, and I don't know where the Ruling Stone is," Orn yelled.

"Thief and liar!" Wulfstan shouted. "You, your family, and your people will suffer for your iniquity!"

The Wolf Clan soldiers shouted again and, as Wulfstan looked up at Orn, the Lord of the Bear Clan turned and left the top of the gatehouse. Wulfstan's face grew even redder, and he turned his horse to face his men.

"Let the siege commence!" he shouted.

Another cheer went up, and the soldiers dispersed through the dwellings sitting in front of Holtgaard's walls, setting fire to anything that would burn. They wouldn't need their own fires to keep warm that night.

Women screamed, children cried, and men shouted. Sieges like this were always worst for the small folk. In the east, every woman unwilling to take her own life would have been raped and every man would have been run through with a sword, but here, in the north, the Wolf Clan simply burned their homes and killed their livestock.

"Admirable, I suppose," Terradyn muttered to himself. He looked to the small group following him. "Let's go."

"You'll stay right there," the soldier who had originally stopped them said, putting up a hand.

"Put your hand down before you lose it," Terradyn said.

It took more persuasion than a simple threat of life and limb to get the Bear Clan guards to open the small door built into the larger gatehouse doors and let them into the clan holding, but eventually they did. People gasped at the sight of the snow cat, but when she plodded over to a small circle of gypsy wagons, they shrugged their shoulders and went about their business. Gypsies procured many oddities in their travels, including animals.

*A*nkara waited next to a tree. It was the only one for a league and looked out of place, its trunk wide and gray and its leaves a dark green despite the freezing cold. She shivered as the wind picked up and swirled through the high, gnarled branches of the tree. The rest of this northern world was so bleak and barren. No wonder the people that lived there were hard and cold and simple ... they resembled their land. She longed for the temperate weather, cool water, and vast greenness of the Isutan Isles. She could lounge on the white, sandy beaches for hours, just watching the Isutan fisherman dive for their quarry, emerging from the water, the crystalline blue wetness streaking down their tanned bodies, knotted with hard earned muscle. She shivered again, this time from a moment of excitement, her body warming and her sex wanting as she thought of the men back home.

The thought passed, and she was back in the northern lands of Háthgolthane, far too close to the Forests of Ul'Erel. Even in the waning moments of the day, she could see the distant, light blue outline of the gigantic trees of the elvish forests. The people of Háth-golthane and Nothgolthane and even Antolika didn't really believe elves still existed there—although, they kept their distance as if it was full of demons and ghosts—but she knew better, even before being recently attacked by elves. The elves in their haughtiness had spent much time in Isuta. The islands were magical, its people natural mages and wizards and conjurors. And when they Sylvan people finally retreated into their secluded forests, they left behind plenty of evidence of their existence on the Isles. They were anything but good and being even a league away from them made Ankara's skin crawl.

They thought themselves superior to everyone else, referring to themselves often as the "First Ones." Oppression and subjugation were their tools, bending others to their will through magic and might and their relationships with the more magical creatures of the world, including dragons and drakes.

When the elf had attacked her, it wasn't the first time she had seen one. Not all the Sylvan folk had retreated to Ul'Erel. Some had created similar forest kingdoms in other parts of the world, including the Isutan Isles. However, on the Isutan Isles, it was the elves that were afraid of humans. The ones brave enough to emerge from their forest hidey-holes were either killed or enslaved. An elf made the best slave, once he or she was broken. They were strong, had the endurance of an ox, and their innate magical abilities were always an added benefit.

Another shiver crawled up Ankara's spine like a small spider, but it wasn't from the cold or an errant breeze. An odd smell struck her nose, and her upper lip curled.

"I still don't know why I couldn't just steal the sword away from this Erik," Ankara said.

"You cannot simply steal away the Dragon Sword," the voice behind her said. It was the black-cloaked man from her dreams. It was already freezing in the north, but his presence brought with it an unworldly chill … and he smelled rotten. "I had to kill him to take his sword."

"I could have killed him," The Black Tigress replied. "You under-estimate my abilities."

"It is you that overestimates. Erik was not some simple man."

"Was?" the Black Tigress questioned.

"He is dead," the voice said, "and it took a true warrior ..."

The cloaked figure didn't finish. Ankara spun hard to face him, just a step away. Her short sword was out, pointed at the man's face, but when she saw him, his hood pulled back, she held her breath. His skin looked stretched over his skull, his lips cracked and his teeth— bared as he gave her a rictus snarl of a smile—were brown. He looked like he had been strong—once. What caught her by surprise even more than his appearance was the tip of a blade at her throat, pressing ever so gently against her flesh so as not to draw any blood.

"I am an adept warrior," Ankara said, chancing a swallow and feeling her throat roil against the steel against her skin.

"I am better," the cloaked figure replied.

He looked dead, but he wasn't. He breathed, and the thick blue veins in his neck and face thumped with the pulsation of blood.

"Don't be a stupid girl," the man said, his smile widening, causing the cracks in his lips to divide, and they bled. He licked his lips and seemed to delight in the taste of his own blood. "You'll have your Dragon Sword. I'll have the stone. We'll both be happy."

Ankara watched the man's eyes, sunken and blank. She lowered her short sword.

"Good girl," the man said, and as he called her a *girl*, she felt the artery in her neck thump harder and faster and could feel her hands shake.

He removed the sword from Ankara's throat and flipped it over, gripping the tip and presenting the handle of the Dragon Sword to the Black Tigress. She grasped the handle of the sword but, as she tried to take it from the mysterious man, he held it firm, and she couldn't retrieve it.

"The stone, girl," the man said, that same smile still strewn across his face.

Ankara groaned as he insisted on calling her girl. She reached into her cloak, into a pocket that seemed endlessly deep, allowing her to hold far more than her simple clothing should have been able to. She retrieved the stone and held it out. The large sapphire-blue stone seemed to drink up any light that struck it. The man in front of her stared at it as if he was inebriated.

He reached out for the stone, his grip on the sword relaxing as he did. His fingertips seemed to sparkle, almost glowing as they neared the stone. But just as he fully touched the stone, Ankara felt an errant wind blow past her face, and a white-fletched arrow thudded into the man's shoulder. He called out in both surprise and pain, and reached into his own robe, retrieving a black-bladed longsword. Ankara spun as two more arrows flew past her face, one drawing a neat line of blood along her cheek. Before her stood at least a dozen elves, and in the center, the one she bested before.

"Need your friends this time, do you?" she mocked as she reached out with her left hand, producing her bow and nocking one of her own arrows.

She took aim and released, her arrow striking an elf in his chest. He cried out and fell backward, although it was unlikely he was dead. She fired at another one, but he dodged the arrow, spinning with his own bow in hand, his blond-white hair fluttering about his face. Now crouching and firing his own arrow, she jumped behind the tree, and the arrow dug into the bark. She was about to fire back when the cloaked man extended his left hand, said something she didn't understand, and then squeezed his hand into a fist. The elf gasped, mouth open and eyes wide, and dropped his weapon as he gripped his chest. Blood poured from his nose and mouth, and his body shook until he fell to his knees and slumped over dead.

The elf she had fought before seemed to be directing the others, and Ankara fired at a she-elf, her arrow striking the warrior in the leg, and then she kicked out at another who had advanced towards her, her boot striking the elf in the chest, driving him back enough so she could fire an arrow into his chest. This time, her attack was deadly.

The cloaked man crushed another warrior's throat with his clenched fist magic, and as all the remaining elves moved closer, he slew two more with his black sword. With their attackers too close to use it, Ankara caused her bow to disappear and gripped the Dragon Sword with both hands. It was a bigger weapon than she was used to, but it felt good in her hands, and when she swung it at the nearest elf, the blade cut through a green-shaded mail shirt like it was nothing, and she almost cut the elf in half.

The elf leader began to chant a spell in a language she didn't recognize, and as he concentrated on his words, she made for him. However, she had only covered a few steps when he opened his eyes, and they had been replaced by two green flames, burning inside his sockets. It was not her he looked at, but the Dragon Sword, and it flared with a green flame, instantly burning Ankara's hands. She yelped and dropped the sword as the palms of her hands began to blister.

Now the elf clapped his hands, just as the cloaked man threw two balls of what looked like black flame at the elvish leader. The balls of black flame dissipated as soon as they reached the elf, and when he parted his hands, a wave of energy shot out, knocking Ankara backward, flying beyond the cloaked man, and onto her back.

Dazed, she heard a hateful cry, filled with pain, and she looked up to see the space around the cloaked man fluttering and twisting and shimmering. Then, in a single blink, he was gone. The elvish leader walked to where the Dragon Sword lay and picked it up. He looked it up and down, the green flames in his eyes dying and a smile spreading across his lips. Then, he walked to the stone, fallen where the cloaked man had disappeared. The Black Tigress tried to stand, but the elf waved his hand, and she flew backward again.

"You would do well not to follow us, Ankara," she heard. It was the elf. The elvish accent as he spoke her language was unmistakable. "I have spared your life this one time. You are a formidable warrior, and I respect that. I will not do so again, and your death will be slow and painful."

Ankara groaned as she moved, every muscle and bone in her

body in pain. She finally sat up, and the elves were gone, even the dead ones. The Dragon Sword and the stone were gone as well.

"Damn elves," she muttered.

"Girl," a voice said. It sounded distant, almost an echo.

She stood and waited.

"Ankara," he said.

"What do you want now? Because of you, the sword is gone, lost into Ul'Erel, as is your stone! For all I know, the Lord of the East will now send an assassin after *me*."

"You need to recover the stone," the voice said, sounding more and more distant. The use of his magic had clearly weakened him

"Get it yourself," Ankara snapped. "You're a great warrior, right?"

"I cannot," the voice replied. "The elves' magic ... it's done something to me. You must do it."

"No," she replied.

"My master will make you more powerful than you could ever imagine," the voice said.

She was about to tell this mysterious figure who dwelt in between two realms to piss off, but as he mentioned power—and after seeing the power he had been given—she stopped herself. Power. The elf had already said how good she was. With this *creature's* kind of power, it would make her the strongest mage, the strongest assassin, and the strongest fighter on Isuta. People would fear and respect her. Men like Syzbalo would cower before her and bow to her. The thought of it was almost as good as sex, and she could feel her blood racing. Killing was a show of power. Death and sex. Killing proved her power. Getting paid to do it was even better; killing without emotion. But to kill by simply squeezing her hand?

"How?" she asked.

There was a long pause, and for a moment, she thought the voice was completely gone.

"Are you still there?"

"My name is Patûk Al'Banan," the voice said. "You know who I am. I was dead. My master brought me back from death and gave me the power I now possess. He can do the same for you. Retrieve the stone. You must do that before ... before it's too late."

"Too late for what?" Ankara asked, repeating herself several times, but the voice was gone.

*What, by the eastern gods, is going on?*

She knew who Patûk Al'Banan was. She had seen him once when she was a girl. And she knew he was dead, killed in the Southern Mountains by something or someone. The news of such an important death traveled through magical channels quickly so, she knew he was dead. But he wasn't. And he was a warrior, not a powerful wizard from the outset, but the magic he wielded was mighty ... and black.

Ankara stared at the distant blue shadows, obscured by the atmosphere and space in front of her, of the Forests of Ul'Erel. She sucked in a deep breath, let it out slowly, and made wide circles with her head, reveling in each pop of her neck as she loosened it. She whistled, and her horse, Nagarooshi, appeared, previously hidden by a simple spell. She rubbed her horse's nose and nuzzled her face against the animal's cheek. She was the only thing in this world Ankara truly cared about.

"I can't take you with me," she said. "Not in there."

She rubbed the horse's nose once more.

"I will call for you when I return," Ankara said. "For now, fly. Fly away, my little shooting star, my little sparrow."

A light flashed in front of Ankara, and Nagarooshi instantly turned into a brown sparrow, fluttering away into the sky. She would call for her, and Naga would hear her magically, and it would only take her a matter of moments to reach the assassin once more. Ankara sighed as the little sparrow disappeared from view, and then she turned and stared at Ul'Erel. Finally, she took a deep breath and walked towards the elvish forest.

**55**

---

"What is your name?" the larger of the two gypsies asked.

"Terradyn," he said. "Yours?"

"Mardirru. Leader of the Ion Gypsies."

"Erik was your friend?" Terradyn asked.

Mardirru nodded.

"He will be missed," the gypsy said.

"Yes, I am sure he will," Terradyn agreed.

Terradyn saw the mistiness in the gypsy's eyes. He had cared for Erik. The mention of his death affected him.

"Patûk Al'Banan?" Mardirru asked.

"Aye," Terradyn replied, "which is surprising because last I heard, he was dead."

"He didn't look alive," Mardirru said.

"No, he didn't," Terradyn replied. "And he hated wizards and mages. But he wielded powerful magic. Dark magic."

"The Shadow," Mardirru muttered.

"No. Yebritoch," Terradyn said. "A demon. That is whom he serves. Still bad."

Mardirru nodded his understanding and looked like he was about to say something else when he was distracted by a loud commotion that rose from the nomadic people.

*"What are you doing?"* he heard a woman shout.

Terradyn watched as Bear Clan soldiers pushed gypsies aside, holding them at bay with swords and spears. The northern clans of Hargoleth were friendly with gypsies or any other nomads and traders, relying on them for information and goods they otherwise couldn't get their hands on, which meant something was wrong. Hargolethian soldiers normally wouldn't bother or harass these people.

"What is going on?" Mardirru asked, trying to push his way towards the soldiers, but a large fellow with red, braided hair that reminded Terradyn of Raktas, pushed the gypsy back.

Orn Beornson walked between his soldiers as they held the gypsies back.

"Lord Beornson," Mardirru said, but before he could add anything else, the Lord of the Bear Clan spun and faced the gypsy, his bobbed hair whipping around as he pointed a long, accusatory finger.

"Do not speak," the Lord of Holtgaard said. "I have trusted you, your father, and your people for a long time, and for you to lie to me ... in my own home."

"I don't ..." Mardirru began, but one of Orn's personal guards drew his broad-bladed longsword and pressed the tip of the blade to Mardirru's neck, causing a woman somewhere within the caravan to scream.

"If my information is correct," Orn Beornson said, "you and your people are no longer welcome here."

Mardirru shook his head, clearly confused, as Terradyn slowly placed his right hand on the handle of his sword. The Lord of the Bear Clan stopped at a wagon. The other gypsy that had traveled with the ogre and Mardirru stood in front of the wagon, along with a gypsy woman. Orn motioned for the gypsy to move, and the man shook his head, causing several soldiers to force him and the woman aside, pushing him to the ground. The woman fell over him, protectively, and cried as one of the soldiers drew his sword and pointed it at the man.

Orn pulled aside a thick blanket, revealing a broad-shouldered young woman with wild, curly, red hair hiding underneath. Some of the Bear Clan soldiers gasped, and Orn gave a quick, loud, mirthless laugh. Terradyn heard a low growl and looked down to see the great white snow cat crouching behind him. She looked ready to pounce, to protect the red-haired woman.

Terradyn put his hand out. He felt one of his tattoos on the side of his head hum and tried his hardest to keep it from glowing.

"Easy, girl," he whispered. "You'll do no good dying today."

She looked up at him and licked her lips. She seemed to calm a bit, even though she watched the soldiers closely.

"Wulfstan's daughter!" Orn shouted, grabbing the girl's arm and shaking her none too gently.

The soldiers with the lord shouted with him, cheering.

"To what end, gypsies?" Orn asked.

"They didn't know," the girl said through short sobs.

"Shut your mouth!" Orn shouted.

The girl had her right arm in a sling, but the man didn't care and continued to shake her. He pushed her to the ground, and she landed on her face with only one arm to brace herself. He pointed to Mardirru.

"Leave!" he yelled. "Never come back!"

He looked down at the girl.

"As for you, Yngrid Wulfson," Orn said, "you will pay for your father's crimes. You will pay for the murder of my son."

The woman, Yngrid, looked up at the Lord of Holtgaard defiantly, ignoring the blood slowly trickling from her nose, her eyes red but no longer crying.

"Your son was a thief," Yngrid said and spat a bloody glob onto Orn's boot, "and he got what he deserved."

The Lord of Holtgaard backhanded the woman and then turned to his soldiers.

"Open the gates and bring her," Orn said.

Most of the gypsies tended to their own, but Mardirru followed the entourage of soldiers, roughly dragging Yngrid to the clan holding's front gates. Terradyn followed close behind as well. Orn nodded to the men standing atop the gatehouses. They shouted to other men, and in moments, the gates cracked open. A line of Wolf Clan soldiers stood on the other side, a hundred paces away, and they looked like they were about to charge until Orn stepped to the front of his men, one of his guards bringing Yngrid with him.

Orn stepped just between his gatehouses and grabbed Yngrid's arm, pulling her close to him.

"Wulfstan!" Orn shouted.

The giant of a man and lord of Wulfstaad rode to the front of his troops, a hard, stoic look on his face, but when he saw his daughter, his mouth opened, and his eyes went wide. Terradyn didn't know if he had ever seen a man's face grow so red, and the Lord of the Wolf Clan's composure went from one of shock and surprise to pure fury.

"Unhand her!" he shouted, heeling his horse, but two arrows thudded just in front of him.

"Father!" Yngrid shouted, collapsing against Orn and weeping, but the Lord of Holtgaard threw a hip into her and forced her to stand.

"Orn!" Wulfstan said. "If you knew what was good for you ..."

Orn laughed.

"You are a murderer," Orn said. "Which is the more severe crime? Stealing or murder? Ask any of our judges. Ask any of our holy men. You know as well as I do that murder is more severe, especially the murder of another lord's child."

"I did not kill your son," Wulfstan seethed through clenched teeth. He shook, his face still a deep red, and tears began to pour from his eyes.

"I see the pain in your face, Wulfstan," Orn said. "It is the same pain I felt when I looked upon the decaying face of my son, Gris. The pain will deepen, Lord Wulfson, when you see your daughter hanging from my walls."

"The whole of Hargoleth would join me in tearing your clan holding down, brick by brick," Wulfstan seethed.

"Empty threats," Orn replied, "especially once they've learned her execution was justified by your murder of my son, and her sneaking into my city. To what end, Wulfstan? Were you going to have her murder my wife in her sleep?"

"I didn't know where she was," Wulfstan replied. "You know that."

"More lies," Orn said. "On the morrow, she dies. Close the gates."

Orn pulled Yngrid back. She fought against him, and Terradyn was impressed with her strength, but with only one good arm and his guards to help him, she could only fight so much.

"*Father!*" Yngrid shouted.

"*Yngrid!*" he replied.

Wulfstan shouted a command, and his men rushed the gates, but they were shut before they could reach them. Then, with a nod from Lord Beornson, archers atop the gatehouses and walls began to fire, and Terradyn could hear the cries of the Wolf Clan soldiers as the missiles found their mark.

Orn stopped in front of Mardirru.

"You will watch me execute her," Orn said, handing Yngrid off to one of his soldiers who, presumably, dragged her to the clan holding's dungeons, "and then you will remove your people from Holtgaard, lest I remove them for you."

"This is not right, Lord Beornson," the ogre that had been fighting alongside Erik and Mardirru said. "And you know it isn't."

"You and your ilk will leave as well," Orn said. "You are also no longer welcome here."

"It seems to me that it is the Creator who is no longer welcome here," the ogre said, "as you have decided you will no longer follow his laws."

Orn waved him off and walked away.

"How did they find out she was hidden within our caravan?" Mardirru asked.

"Spies," Terradyn said.

"Spies?" Mardirru asked. "They are my people."

Terradyn shrugged.

"Perhaps it is the Creator's will," the ogre said in his slow, methodical way, "for this only solidifies what I know I must do."

"What is that?" Mardirru asked, but the ogre simply smiled and plodded away towards his own people.

"Who would spy on us?" Mardirru asked. "We have been good to the people of Holtgaard for a long time."

Terradyn looked to his side and, in the distance, saw a dwarf staring at them with a worried look on his face. He wore the smock of a surgeon. When he met Terradyn's eyes, he turned and walked away.

## 56

$\mathcal{T}$erradyn wrapped his hand around the dwarf's throat, lifting the surgeon off the ground. His face turned a bright red, his eyes bulging as he struggled to breathe.

"Why did you tell Orn about the girl?" Terradyn asked.

Terradyn could feel his anger rising. He didn't know why. He cared nothing for this Yngrid, this daughter of the Lord of Wulfstaad. Perhaps it was the death of Erik that irritated him, but other than failing the instructions given to him by his master, Andragos, he shouldn't have cared about that either. In a hundred years of service, he wasn't always able to serve his master successfully. He had failed him before, and in more significant ways. But as he watched the Lord of Holtgaard pull and hit that girl, and as he heard the pain in both her and her father's voices, he felt his rage thicken.

He looked down. He hadn't realized that the dwarf had stopped moving. His face was purple, and his lips were blue. Terradyn released him, and the dwarf collapsed to the floor, didn't move or say anything for a long moment, and then violently sucked in a very long breath. It sounded as if it was painful, and the surgeon followed up the long breath by several shorter ones. He coughed and rubbed his throat, looking up at Andragos' bodyguard.

"Why?" Terradyn repeated.

"I didn't know about the girl," the dwarf replied finally, coughing up a bit of blood and then sitting up. "At least, not at first."

"Then how did Orn find out?" Terradyn asked. "You said something to him."

"I told him about Erik," the dwarf replied. He jerked his head over to one of the tables in his examining room, on which Erik's body lay.

"Why?"

"Erik Dragon Fire," the dwarf replied. "He was baptized as a dwarf, even though he is a man. He is a significant person, an honored guest. I told Lord Beornson about him. He should know that such an esteemed guest was in his clan holding. I believe he sent one of his heralds to fetch him from the gypsies, and his man saw the Lady Wulfson."

"It is because of you that she is to be executed," Terradyn said, bending down and poking a finger in the middle of the dwarf's chest.

"If I had known what was going to happen," the dwarf said, rubbing his chest where Terradyn had poked him, "I wouldn't have said anything. I harbor no ill will against the Wulfsons or the Wolf Clan."

Terradyn just glared at the dwarf; all he could think of was killing him. Then he looked at Erik, lying dead on the examining table. He couldn't go back to the Eleodum farm; he couldn't go back to his master, either. Something tugged at him, twisting his stomach and tightening his chest. He needed to finish what Erik had started. He would protect the woman, Yngrid, and he would find the Dragon Stone.

He looked at the dwarf again.

"You had better hope I can avert this," Terradyn said. "Your life depends on it."

Terradyn turned and was standing by the door, about to leave the morgue, when the ogre that had traveled with Erik entered. He had an odd smile on his face as he passed Terradyn, nodding to the man slowly and methodically. He whispered something to the dwarf, and the surgeon pointed to Erik, lying on the examining table, skin pale and ashen. The ogre touched a finger to his forehead and then bowed to the dwarf.

The ogre stood next to Erik, closed his eyes, and began to hum. He swayed back and forth and laid both of his hands on Erik's chest. Terradyn stepped forward and looked at the dwarf, but the surgeon just shrugged and shook his head. The ogre's hum rose in volume until he began to chant—at first—and then sing in a language Terradyn didn't recognize. As the volume of his singing increased, the dim candles and torches in the room brightened. Terradyn tried to touch his magic but found it cut off from him. It was like reaching up to grasp an apple from the tree, but only being able to brush the fruit with his fingertips. He tried and tried but to no avail.

The ogre stopped singing and opened his eyes. He patted Erik's chest and then looked at Terradyn.

"Your magic will not work here," the ogre said in Westernese.

"What?" Terradyn asked.

"You needn't bother trying to touch your magic here," the ogre repeated. "A deeper magic is in this place. Your abilities will return. Fret not, Terradyn."

Terradyn stepped back, closer to the door, and nodded.

"You must continue to watch him," the ogre said. "You must protect him."

"He's dead," Terradyn said. The ogre just smiled.

The ogre cupped his hands together and gently blew into them. As he did, his hands began to glow a bright yellow as if he had breathed a small sun into his palms. As he stared at his hands, his smile grew wider, and he gave a deep sigh, one like a huge sense of relief. As Terradyn became even more transfixed in the moment, an even deeper sense of calm seemed to overcome the ogre, and he looked to the ceiling and nodded. He put his cupped hands over

Erik's face, and the bright, yellow light moved from his palms into Erik's mouth.

Terradyn could see the glow as the light traveled from his mouth into the rest of his head and throat. It then moved down into his chest, and when it reached where his heart would be, the light spread from there into his belly and his limbs. Erik's skin brightened and went from a pallid, ashen color to the color of living flesh. Finally, Erik's chest lifted, his eyes shot open, and he took a deep breath.

The Dream World faded as the carriage carrying the ogre floated away up into the sky. Erik looked over his shoulder at the man sitting under the willow tree. The man smiled and nodded, and Erik returned the greeting. Everything around him went black, and when his vision came back, he found himself breathing deeply, gasping for as much air as possible. When he felt calmer, he sat up and recognized the room, the morgue of Holtgaard. He saw the dwarvish surgeon, and then Terradyn and finally, Jamalel.

Erik reached out to Jamalel, and the ogre took his hands. He stared at the ogre's great, gray eyes. Kindness, compassion, love, joy, respect, he saw all of those things and more. He had no idea how old the ogre was. They looked like ageless beings. But from what Jamalel had told him, he suspected the ogre had been in this world for a long, long time.

"How can I thank you?" Erik asked.

"Live your life. Listen to your calling," Jamalel said. "That is all the thanks I need."

Erik dropped his hands by his sides and felt a tear touch his cheek as the ogre began to fade. He didn't lay down and die. He didn't age. He simply began to fade from existence, becoming translucent, his visage shimmering. He held that smile on his face the whole time, and when he finally disappeared from this world, his clothing fell to the ground in a heap.

"How?" the dwarf gasped. He stepped back, away from Erik. He put a hand to his mouth. "What sorcery is this? What evil?"

Erik swung his legs over the side of the examining table and, ignoring the dwarf's accusations, pushed himself off and onto the stone floor. It felt cold on his feet, but his hip felt healthy, as did his shoulder. He stretched his arms and legs. It was as if nothing had happened. He touched his naked skin, and the mark of his baptism was still there. There was nothing different except for a new finger-length scar—thick and red—just above his belly button.

"The work of the Shadow," the dwarf whispered, and Erik turned to him and smiled.

"Not the Shadow," Erik said. "This did happen because of evil, though. This is a gift, the gift of life."

"Men don't just come back to life," said a strange-looking man standing close to the door to the room. He looked familiar, but Erik could not quite place him.

"No," Erik replied.

"Your injuries and wounds?" the dwarf asked, eyes still wide.

"Gone," Erik said, "save for this one," he added, pointing to his stomach. "I will wear this scar proudly, a sign that Patûk and his demon god had no sway over me."

"This is ... this is ..." the dwarf said, "this is unbelievable."

Erik just shrugged.

"Your hair," the dwarf said.

"What?" Erik asked.

"Some of it has turned white, as has your beard."

Erik ran a hand through his hair and beard. It didn't feel any different.

"Do you have a looking glass?"

The dwarf reached up to a shelf and produced a small mirror. Erik saw a line of white hair traveling just to the left of the center of his head, from the forehead towards the back of his head. White also touched the edges of his hair, just above his ears, and traveled into the top of his beard. Another streak also touched the hair to the left of his chin.

"Odd but perhaps distinguished," he suggested, and the man nodded in agreement.

Erik looked down at his nakedness. It was cold—he knew it was—but he didn't feel it. He felt warm, comfortable, and at peace.

"Do you have any clothes?" Erik asked the dwarvish surgeon.

"I have your clothes," the dwarf replied and pointed to a pile of clothing lying on a wheeled cart.

Erik sifted through the clothes. They looked new. His shirt was once riddled with holes, tears, and stained with blood, but looked as if it had just been sewn. The links of his mail shirt should have been broken where the shirt lay over his belly, but they weren't. His pauldrons and bracers and greaves were all shiny and polished.

"Your work?" he said to the dwarf.

"Yes, I was told to prepare you for an honorable burial."

Erik nodded his appreciation and dressed and donned his armor. As he buckled his belt, he looked down at an empty scabbard. Dragon Tooth. It was gone. Surely, Patûk Al'Banan had taken it. His stomach twisted. He would have to find it. The vision of a vast forest popped into his head.

*Ul'Erel.*

Erik knew it to be true. As he searched for and found the Dragon Stone, he would also find his sword, Dragon Tooth. He would find them in the forests no one else wished to enter.

Feeling ready to leave, he looked up, then he recognized the man.

"Terradyn, I believe," he said, and the man nodded his tattooed head. "Why are you here?"

"To protect you," Terradyn replied.

"Andragos' orders?"

Terradyn nodded again.

"I don't need your protection," Erik said. "Go protect my family if you must protect someone."

"Raktas is with them," Terradyn replied. He raised one of his eyebrows. "Besides, your ogre friend also told me I needed to protect you."

"Did he?" Erik asked, more to himself than anyone else.

"Then are you ready?" Erik asked.

"Sure," Terradyn said with a shrug. "Why not? A man was dead. He came back to life. Everything is normal. Yeah, I'm ready. For what, who knows? More resurrections, perhaps. You lead, I follow."

As they exited the room, the dwarvish surgeon still staring on in wonder, Erik heard Andragos' bodyguard whisper to the dwarf, "You're lucky."

## 57

*E*rik emerged from the infirmary, Terradyn on his heels, and immediately put his nose to the air and sniffed.

"War," he said. "It smells like war."

"Yeah," Terradyn replied. "How'd you know?"

Erik just shrugged.

"Wulfstan Wulfson," Terradyn explained. "He is laying siege to Holtgaard. He has accused Orn Beornson of stealing some ruling stone. Orn Beornson is accusing Wulfstan of killing his son. He found Wulfstan's daughter hidden in the city, and Lord Beornson is now going to execute her as payment for the death of his son."

"Yngrid," Erik muttered.

"That's right," Terradyn replied. "He is going to hang her from the walls of Holtgaard."

"I need to speak with Mardirru," Erik said, again more to himself.

"The gypsy?" Terradyn asked.

Erik turned to face Terradyn.

"Yes," he said, raising an eyebrow.

"They are leaving," Terradyn said. "They have been expelled from the clan holding for hiding Yngrid."

"We will see," Erik replied and made for the spot where the gypsies had circled their wagons.

As Erik and Terradyn approached the gypsy caravan, men and women were busy packing things onto their wagons and carts and carriages. Three soldiers watched the gypsies, occasionally prodding them with their spears to hurry up, but mostly they looked bored. Then a woman screamed, and they snapped to attention, spinning around to see what had caused the outburst and came face to face with the two men. A woman appeared to have fainted, but the soldiers didn't seem concerned, they just stared at Erik.

"By the Creator," a familiar voice gasped, and Erik saw Bo staring at him.

"Bo," Erik said with a smile.

"Get back to work," one of the soldiers said, pushing Bo with the butt of his spear.

"Erik!" Dika said, stepping up next to her husband and covering her mouth with her hands. "How?"

"I said ..." the soldier said again, raising his spear higher, ready to strike Dika, but stopped as Terradyn reached out and gripped the shaft of the spear with one hand.

The soldier looked at the large man, equally a well-muscled and tall fellow, and Terradyn shook his head.

"Leave these people alone," Erik said. The other two guards moved nearer to him; they looked angry and pointed their spears in his direction. "They've done nothing to you. They're packing, and they will move on. Leave them be."

The guards looked to one another, and after a moment, the anger in their faces dissipated. Terradyn released the one soldier's spear, and they all stepped back, still watching the gypsies but ceasing their harassment.

"What is the meaning of this?" Mardirru said, stepping next to Bo and Dika.

Dika uncovered her mouth and ran to Erik, wrapping her arms

around his waist and squeezing him hard. Bo followed suit, and with both of them hugging him, he found it difficult to breathe. He couldn't help smiling.

"You are ..." Mardirru began, "you were dead."

"I was," Erik replied.

"How are you here, speaking to me then?" Mardirru asked.

"A miracle," Bo said, releasing Erik and looking at him with tears in his eyes.

"A gift," Erik said with a smile. "A most precious gift. I have once again brought you trouble, and I mean to set that straight."

"What are you talking about?" Mardirru asked.

"This man, Orn Beornson," Erik said, "he is a stupid man, but he is banishing you because of Yngrid, because of me. I will fix it. But first, I must save Yngrid."

"She is too be hung as we leave," Mardirru said. "And you have no weapon. How will you save her in the clan holding of a powerful enemy?"

Erik looked down at the empty scabbard hanging from his belt.

"I had a sword," Erik muttered. When he looked up, Mardirru was holding his father's falchion. He extended his arm.

"Here," Mardirru said. "Take it. Use it as long as you need. But I still don't know how you plan on saving a condemned girl when enemy soldiers surround you."

Erik took the falchion. When he first saw the blade, a year ago, he didn't think he would have been able to wield the weapon. It was long and curved and wide, the single-edged blade glimmering in the sun. But now, it felt good in his hands. Not as good as Dragon Tooth, but good enough.

Erik turned and saw an entourage of soldiers marching through the middle of Holtgaard. Behind the train, two men escorted Yngrid, her hands in shackles, and chained together. Orn Beornson walked behind her, flanked by two more soldiers. She saw him, and, even though her eyes were already filled with tears, she began crying even more, but she didn't say anything. He sensed she thought she was protecting him.

"Are you ready?" Erik said, looking at Terradyn.

"For what?" the large man asked.

Erik smiled.

Erik rushed through the soldiers that surrounded the gypsy caravan. When they finally realized he was running towards the Lord of Holtgaard, it was too late. Erik lowered his shoulder, ramming the lord in the ribs and knocking him to the ground. Several people cried out, and the entourage of soldiers stopped. Terradyn watching his back, Erik grabbed the tall, lanky man by the front of his shirt and pulled him to his feet. He grimaced as he breathed, and Erik may have broken several ribs, but he didn't care. He shook him roughly and then put the blade of the falchion under the man's chin.

"Get back!" Erik said, holding Orn's shoulder with one hand and pressing his steel to his flesh with the other.

The soldiers that were with him, marching in front of him, and surrounding the gypsies didn't look like they wanted to listen, so Erik pressed the blade to the man's skin a little harder, and a quick gasp said he had drawn blood. The soldiers stopped.

"Terradyn, release Yngrid," Erik commanded.

Terradyn drew his sword, and as he approached the woman, the two soldiers leading her backed up, eyes wide.

"Hold out your hands," Terradyn said, and when Yngrid complied, he struck her chains away.

"Walk," Erik said, pulling Orn around to face the clan holding's gates. "Terradyn, watch my back. Yngrid, follow me."

They made their way to the gates of Holtgaard, soldiers, and a crowd of people making a tight path for them. Erik watched everyone intently, staring at the eyes of the Bear Clan warriors, knowing they would pounce given the chance. And he knew Terradyn did the same. The crowd tightened.

"Back!" Erik shouted, pressing his blade to Orn's chin even harder. "Back, or I'll kill him."

"He'll kill him anyway!" someone shouted.

"If you want to live, tell your people ..." Erik began to say but heard a loud growl and saw a flash of white leap over the heads of the crowd nearest him. Thala landed in front of Erik and turned, facing the people and growling again. She crouched, ready to pounce. Ready to kill.

The crowd backed up as if a fire had flared in front of them.

"*Open the gates!*" Erik shouted. But no one moved. He shook Orn. "Tell them."

"*Do it!*" Orn yelled. "*By the Creator and the old gods! Do it!*"

The sound of the gates opening echoed off the palisade walls of the clan holding, and when they were full agape, Erik could see a line of warriors, headed by Wulfstan Wulfson, his wide, red beard spread out over his chest, the head of a dead wolf resting on his shoulder.

"Father!" Yngrid yelled.

"Wait," Erik said even though her father heeled his horse, moving the creature several steps forward.

Erik looked up at the walls and the tops of the gatehouses. As the Lord of Wulfstaad moved forward, archers tightened their grips on their bows. He pushed Orn. They walked past the gatehouses and out to Wulfstan.

"You!" Wulfstan shouted when he saw Erik, leaning forward in his saddle. "I knew you were false."

"Father, stop," Yngrid said.

"Tell your archers to lower their weapons," Erik whispered into Orn's ear, and he complied. "Tell your men to get back, Wulfstan Wulfson!"

"The nine hells I will!" the Lord of Wulfstaad replied.

"Then you truly don't want your daughter back," Erik replied, and he saw the hard look Yngrid gave him.

Wulfstan watched Erik for a while and then nodded, turned in his saddle, and told his men to move back. Erik walked Orn and Yngrid out to Wulfstan.

"Dismount," Erik said as he lowered the falchion from Orn's chin.

The Lord of Holtgaard rubbed his neck, several streaks of blood on the palm of his hands. Wulfstan dismounted and stood in front of Orn. He was as tall but far broader, and the Bear Clan leader's eyes went wide as he stood there, face to face with the leader of the Wolf Clan. Yngrid ran to her father, wrapping her arms around the man's waist, but he didn't seem to notice as he glared at Orn.

"We are going to settle this right now," Erik said. And before either man could say anything, added, "none of this would have happened if Orn hadn't sent his son to steal the ruling stone."

Orn stammered and looked surprised but said nothing.

"And Wulfstan, your rage and anger is what led Gris to steal the stone and caused your brave daughter to come to my rescue, putting herself in harm's way for another. Both you Lords are to blame for what has happened."

The two accused looked at one another from the same side of the fence for once. It was clear no one, certainly since they were children, had ever spoken to them that way.

"Nothing can bring your son back," Erik continued, "especially the murder of another. But you should know Orn that Wulfstan did not kill Gris. Ask your own surgeon. He would have told you the truth of your son, but he is so afraid of what you might do, or of what you might accuse him. It was a poison that only elves possess that killed your son."

"Elves?" Orn gasped. "Preposterous."

"Ask your dwarvish surgeon. You know it's true."

Orn stared at Erik for a while, then his shoulders finally slumped.

"I am going after the Ruling Stone," Erik said. "It is the elves who hold it now."

"Erik, you can't, I ..." Yngrid began, but Erik held up a hand.

"But I won't be returning it to either of you," he continued. Both men looked shocked with that, but Erik kept talking. "Its true name is the Dragon Stone, and it serves a much grander purpose than deciding which clan should rule in Hargoleth. You both should look to Örnddinas, and the Eagle Clan, for leadership. A dear and trusted friend told me that clan is the best suited for leadership. You both believe in the Creator. Have humility and ask for his guidance. He will tell you what I say is true."

Both men stiffened their backs but said nothing.

"My name is Erik Eleodum. I am also known as Erik Dragon Slayer or Erik Dragon Fire."

The men's eyes went wide. They had heard of him, even in Hargoleth.

"I will remember your name," Wulfstan said, finally looking down at his daughter. "I will remember how you saved my daughter, and I apologize for how you were treated."

"I will remember your name also," Orn said, rubbing his neck, "and the *kindness* you've shown me."

"You will let the gypsies return in the future and stay as long as they need to," Erik said, ignoring the man's sarcasm.

Orn thought for a moment, perhaps wondering if he should protest, but then shrugged and gave a quick nod.

Erik turned to Yngrid. She moved to embrace him, but he put up a hand again.

"You are a good woman, Yngrid," Erik said, "and I believe you will one day be a fierce and loyal ruler to your people. And I believe you will one day find happiness with a good man worthy of your affection."

"Erik ..." she began to say, but he cut her off with a look and raised a finger. He had already told her where his heart lay.

Yngrid's bottom lip trembled, and she sought to hide her face in her father's chest. He kissed the top of his daughter's head and rubbed her hair, causing Erik to wonder how long it was since he gave her any sign of affection. He looked down at the snow cat and then to Terradyn, saying nothing more before turning back towards Holtgaard just as the gypsy caravan was exiting the clan holding, followed by the tribe of ogres Jamalel had led.

"Orn agreed to let you stay again if that is your wish ... if you'll find good business here," Erik said as Mardirru walked up to Erik, leading Warrior.

"You are beyond a good man, Erik," Mardirru said, resting a hand on Erik's shoulder.

"As are you," Erik said, returning the gypsy's smile as he presented the falchion to him.

"Keep it," Mardirru said, putting up a hand. "You have a dangerous road ahead of you."

"It was your father's sword."

"He would want you to have it in such a time of need."

Erik nodded his appreciation and turned towards the tribe of ogres when he noticed one of their women walk past the gypsy caravan and approach him. He looked up to her, her face calm and serene. She cupped his face with her hands, her palms and fingers almost engulfing his whole head. Her smile reminded him of Jamalel. Her touch, the feeling of her hands on his skin, all felt familiar, and he found himself pressing a cheek against one of her palms.

"I will see you again, my heart," the ogre said softly.

Erik's eyebrows rose.

"I don't understand," Erik said.

"Jamalel made a good choice," the ogre said. She nodded and leaned forward, resting her large forehead against Erik's. "Be worthy of his gift."

She turned around and rejoined her tribe as a child, almost as tall as Erik, walked up to her, and she ruffled his hair in her slow, methodical way. She nodded to the rest of the ogres in her group, and they moved on, walking towards the west.

Warrior trotted from behind the gypsy caravan, stopping just in front of Erik. The horse pressed his nose into Erik's chest.

"You still wish to serve me over your previous master?" Erik asked in Shengu, scratching the animal's nose.

The horse tamped a front hoof and snorted.

"I don't blame you," Erik said with a smile.

"Before you leave, Erik," Bo said, holding Erik's shield.

Erik gave his friend a quick bow, took the shield, and mounted Warrior, Terradyn mounting his own horse, and Thala stood ready behind them.

"Are you ready?" Erik asked.

"You lead, I follow."

# 58

*A*nkara crouched behind the thick root of a tall tree, its trunk so wide it might have taken ten men holding hands to surround it. The lowest branches were a hundred paces from the ground, and its deep green leaves were broad and angular. Those that had fallen carpeted the forest floor, but rather than drying and growing brittle, they remained green and soft. With cold detachment, she watched two children playing with the fallen leaves, throwing armfuls into the air, and crying out with glee as they floated back to the ground.

So thick was the canopy of trees, it should have discouraged anything to grow, but where the shed leaves were patchy, little yellow flowers glowed like tiny beacons. In the air, lighted specs hovered around like dust motes caught in the sunshine through a window, but no sun's rays broke through the canopy.

Ankara's lip curled. Maybe someone would have found these children cute, enchanting even, but in her eyes, they were ugly. She couldn't tell if the two young elflings were boys or girls. One had silver hair while the other had golden-red hair. The one with silver hair had purple eyes while the other had crystal blue eyes. Their ears looked overly large, as did most elvish children's as if their bodies had to grow into their ears. Even at a young age, the magical aura that surrounded the two children was strong. The Isutan assassin produced her bow and nocked a black arrow.

"Ye'ladem," the voice was soft and feminine, calling for the elflings, but Ankara couldn't tell if it was their father or mother. Elvish sex seemed so ambiguous.

The children looked up and dropped the leaves as an elf stepped out from behind another large tree. With pale skin and soft blue eyes, almost purple-silverish hair hid her ears, but the elf's breasts gave away her sex. Lean and tall, with an angular face, the she-elf wore a long, white robe that trailed behind her. She smiled when she saw the children waiting for her, but as she walked towards them, she stopped, her brow furrowing. She knew Ankara was there.

As the mother urged her children to hurry to her, Ankara ducked lower behind the large root, reaching into her own magic to seek to hide her presence. She knew it would have worked with a simple witch, but an elf that had never studied magic was still as powerful as most of the wizards living among the lands of men. Ankara could feel the she-elf's power; she was an adept mage but not the strongest the Isutan had ever met.

Ankara risked peeking over the top of the root and saw the elflings take their mother's hands as she turned around, leading the children away. Ankara thought she might have got away with being discovered, but then she heard a voice in her head.

*Cin baur na tir daquin neheless.*

Ankara sighed, breathing out slowly as she released the barrier she'd sought to create around her. She would have to watch herself in this place. She eased herself to her feet and was about to step around the tree when she heard several voices, all shouting angrily. She closed her eyes, whispered an incantation, and when she opened them again, she was standing on a thick branch of the tree. She was at least a hundred and twenty paces above the ground, but as she looked up, the tree extended yet another hundred paces above her.

She looked down and saw ten elves come into the clearing where the children had been playing. They had longswords and bows, and when one of them looked up, she pressed herself close to the trunk of the tree, closed her eyes, and concentrated her mind. From her saddlebags she had already chosen clothing that would help camouflage her in wooded areas—tools of her assassin's trade—and now her skin turned rough and brown, her hair green, fluttering in a breeze as if it were leaves. Now all she had to worry about was that she was too far away for them to sense her presence as the mother had done.

She waited a long while, slowing her breathing and keeping her eyes closed while she silently chanted her spell to keep it working. When she finally dared open her eyes and look down, the elves were gone, and the floating light and glowing, yellow flowers had dimmed. She looked to her right and saw a large, red squirrel sitting on her branch, watching her. It had a tail that was bushier than any she had seen before and had long ears that ended in black tufts. It just stared at her, and she finally gave it a loud hiss. It scurried away, but, as it stopped at the end of the branch, where one tree melded into another, it looked back at her, and its eyes glowed purple. She understood the message ... they would be coming again.

## 59

*E*rik and Terradyn traveled south for two days, Thala plodding alongside them until they had built a fire each night, and then the snow cat would wander off to feed. One night, when Erik and Terradyn had been discussing stocking up on their food supplies, she returned with a small deer in her mouth. Terradyn looked wide-eyed at Erik, but the latter just shrugged.

"One night, she bought me a goat," he said.

After eating, Terradyn would soon be snoring, Erik would just sit and wait for sleep to come eventually. Whereas one time, when he'd first entered the Dream World, he dreaded his eyes closing, now, he almost craved a return to that other place in which he existed.

The first night after they left Holtgaard, he saw the ogres, but they didn't come near the hill on which he sat. And then, when he finally dozed off that night, the distant black mountain range returned to as it had before Patûk had appeared, with its black clouds and purple lightning. The man he usually sat with wasn't there, so Erik just leaned against the trunk of the great willow tree and reveled in a cool breeze until he woke. He felt different in the Dream World now.

He had already grown comfortable in the place that separated the world of the living and that of the dead, but since dying himself, and then being given his life back, he felt much more a part of that alternate realm. It was an extension of him, and he could feel it, touch it, and see it even when he was awake. Perhaps that was how the ogre and other dream walkers felt. He would like to discuss that with Dewin, to ask if Jamalel was now a part of him. The way his wife looked at him when they stood outside of Holtgaard, it was as if she were staring at her husband.

"Do you see the edges of Ul'Erel?" Terradyn asked as they rode south again the next morning. The winter of the north was deepening, but somehow, the closer they got to their destination, the temperature rose.

"Interesting," Erik replied as the blue silhouettes of large trees lined the horizon. "Have you ever been?"

"No," Terradyn replied. "Although ... I think ..."

"What?" Erik asked as Terradyn's voice trailed off. He looked over his shoulder at the large man, always riding just behind him.

"This land is familiar to me," Terradyn said. "Not the north, but the west, at least."

"You are from the west?"

"I don't know from where I hailed originally," Terradyn replied. "But I think Westernese was my first language."

"How don't you know where you are from?" Erik asked.

"I have been serving Andragos since I was a little child," Terradyn replied. "It's been a long time."

"Even so," Erik said, "you are, what, forty summers old?"

"I have seen over a hundred winters come and go," Terradyn replied with a short laugh.

"Andragos' magic," Erik said.

"Undoubtedly," Terradyn agreed.

"You don't remember your family, your parents?" Erik asked.

Terradyn just shook his head.

"Raktas is the same," Terradyn said. "We came to Andragos at the same time."

"Are you from the same lands?"

"No," Terradyn replied. "I don't think so."

"That's a little sad if you think about it," Erik said.

"Sad?" Terradyn replied, and Erik could sense a little hurt mixed with anger in his voice. "I serve the second most powerful man in the world. Should I be a poor farmer, or a collector of pig shit, or some whore monger on the streets of Bull's Run?"

Erik chanced a short laugh.

"I didn't mean to offend you," Erik replied, not bothering to look over his shoulder. Any other man might fear for his life, given Terradyn's response, but the man was loyal to Andragos—to the death—and the Black Mage had commanded him to protect Erik.

"I would just think that you might wonder who your mother or father was from time to time," Erik suggested.

There was a long silence, and Erik knew he had struck a chord with Terradyn.

"I do wonder, sometimes," Terradyn said, just as Erik was about to turn in his saddle and apologize to the man.

Erik slowed Warrior so that he rode side by side with Terradyn.

"Not so much about my father," the large man continued. "In my experience, if they stay around, most fathers turn out to be pricks, so I like to think of Andragos as my sole parent sometimes. Seems like your father is different, though."

"My father is a good man," Erik replied with a genuine smile. "He could be hard when I was younger, but he is loving and kind and a little bull-headed. Bryon—my cousin—his father is a good man too. He used to drink too much, but he hasn't touched a drop of orange brandy since we've been back."

"That's good," Terradyn said. "You're lucky. I do think about my mother from time to time. No doubt, she's long dead, but I think a little part of me remembers her holding me in her arms and singing to me. There's this little tune that plays in my head when it's really quiet and been a long day. I think it's a tune she used to sing."

Erik watched the man's face. It was flat except for his eyes. They were thinking, remembering, and wondering ... almost sad. And then his face reddened, and his lips pursed as his brow twisted.

"I want to remember a loving woman, and then I wonder why she gave me up," Terradyn said, his voice hard. "I've watched hundreds of women on the streets of Fen-Stévock give up their children to thieves and pickpockets, or whorehouses, or slavers. Why would my mother be any different? I was just lucky enough that, when the gods cast my lot, I found myself with the most powerful wizard in the world, and the other bastards found themselves bedding strangers and pilfering purses."

"You've never asked Andragos?" Erik asked.

"Why would I?" Terradyn replied. "He's given me everything. He commands, and I obey."

"I think you should ask him," Erik said.

"Be careful, Erik Eleodum," Terradyn said. "He is powerful and dangerous, and while he might be on your side right now, he can be crueler than the worst tyrant ever to walk this world. You serve a purpose, so he has an interest in you and your safety. The moment your purpose passes, so does his favor."

Erik looked at Terradyn, studied the man's face.

"And I serve him," Terradyn added, "absolutely."

"Your master may yet very well surprise you," Erik said, and just before heeling Warrior forward, added, "and you may very well surprise yourself."

## 60

*E*rik would have thought it impossible, but the trees of Ul'Erel seemed even bigger as they finally reached the forest. Erik had never seen any living thing so large, even in the deepest parts of the Gray Mountains. Their branches and leaves intertwined to form a canopy that he was sure would shut out any light, and peering into the distance, even after only a few paces, the woodland looked black.

*How does anyone live in here?*

A forest, especially one so large and deep, always had odd sounds that might cause even the least superstitious of men to catch a breath or feel a quickening of a heart. For those with more generous imaginations, it would be full of spirits and ghosts and monsters; Ul'Erel seemed like a place that would be home to the worst of those.

The distant chirp of a bird, the yelp of a small fox, a dead branch falling to the ground, or even the simple rustling of branches under an especially strong gust of wind sounded like some hidden demon in this place. Erik would put himself among the less susceptible to an overactive imagination, but this place was one he'd very much want to avoid. The dark vastness of this place only served to amplify the sounds, giving it an even more mysterious quality, and he wondered if spirits really did live in this place, along with elves.

Erik could sense even Thala's apprehension, as the great snow cat stood next to Warrior. A wall of trees, which resembled giant oaks, elms, and beech along with red-barked and white-barked pines, stood like castle fortifications, seemingly arranged in almost perfect symmetry and extending north and south as far as Erik could see. As his eyes traversed from right to left, it almost seemed that this wooden barrier moved to follow his direction. Then, as he peered further into the darkness, he saw the light and shadow move.

"Are you ready?" Erik asked, looking down at Thala and then back at Terradyn.

Terradyn simply nodded.

Erik breathed in deeply and gave Warrior a tap with his heels.

A curtain of darkness enveloped them as they rode past the forest's border trees. It was like night, and the closeness of the trees was chokingly narrow. They had to move in single file, Erik in the front, Thala in the middle, and then Terradyn.

They continued like that for some time, intermittent light poking through the dense ceiling of leaves and branches. Terradyn lit a torch and passed it to Erik, and then lit another. But far too often, an extremely heavy gust—one that should not have been able to pass through tree trunks so close together—would extinguish their flame, and Terradyn would curse loudly, the blue tattoos on his head flaring almost as much as light as their torches. He would relight the torches, and they would go through the whole process again.

"To the nine hells with this place," Terradyn hissed as he set to get a spark to relight their torches once again.

As Terradyn muttered his curse, the trees seemed to respond, shaking their branches and fluttering their leaves. Erik thought it was just more wind at first, then the ground shook, and what sounded like a deep voice moaned and echoed in the distance. Thunder clapped overhead, way beyond the tops of the trees, and the canopy flashed with a brilliant blue light. Immediately afterward, Erik heard a clatter and, looking up, expected to see and feel heavy rain, but instead, it was hundreds of pine needles that pierced their skin, causing the horses to snort and neigh. Thala growled, pacing one way and then the other, seeking to avoid the painful storm as Erik and Terradyn cursed as they covered their heads with their shields.

"*What fucking witchcraft is this?*" Terradyn shouted above the din of falling needles and more thunder as flashes of the brilliant blue lightning continued above.

"Elvish witchcraft, I would assume," Erik replied, as the thunder subsided.

As the noise around reduced to only the needles, they now heard a voice. It was distant and seemed to keep repeating the same phrase. Erik couldn't make out any language he understood, but the sound now grew closer and closer.

"*Baw wengûl. Tovan gûl. A cin a coth. Baw wengûl. Tovan gûl. A cin a coth.*"

Over and over came the same phrase, getting louder and louder until Thala began to yowl, and Erik and Terradyn were forced to put their hands over their ears. Erik's heart was racing, and sweat was beading down the sides of his face.

"*What does it mean?*" yelled Erik, looking at Terradyn, who simply shook his head.

Now, it was a scream, right in front of them and just beyond the next wall of trees. It was all around them, and gooseflesh rose along Erik's skin, and Warrior stamped his hooves. Even the great warhorse was afraid.

Then, everything stopped, and all Erik could hear was the heavy breathing of men and animals until ...

"BAW WENGÛL. TOVAN GÛL. A CIN A COTH!"

The voice struck them all, accompanied by the strongest gust of wind Erik had ever felt, air tearing at his face and stinging his eyes. Thala howled, and Warrior reared up on his hind legs, almost throwing Erik to the ground. Terradyn screamed, and then all was silent again apart from Erik's heart thumping in his ears.

He looked down, and Thala had tucked her tail underneath her body. Warrior and Shadow panted. Erik could hear Terradyn's heavy breathing. He tried to calm himself, but his throat was dry and swallowing made him want to gag. Then came a different voice, softer, that spoke in a language close to Dwarvish.

"*Turn back now, turn back now, before it's too late.*"

"I say we do exactly that," Terradyn said.

"You know we can't," Erik replied as he wiped away small trickles of blood from his cheek, caused by the falling nettles before he could raise his shield. "We *must* keep going. I have no other choice and, unless you want to get on the wrong side of Andragos, neither do you. And, by the way, I would refrain from any more curses in this place."

It was with some relief that, after a while, the forest opened up a little. While the canopy of branches and leaves overhead still blocked out the sun, and the trees were still large and grew close together, they no longer had to ride in single file. This part of Ul'Erel reminded Erik of the Southern Mountains, in the ancient woodlands of the moon fairies.

"When do you want to stop?" Erik asked as the flame of his diminishing torch began to sputter.

"In truth," Terradyn replied, "never."

Erik looked down at the snow cat, and clearly over her ordeal, she yawned, causing him to do the same. He shared Terradyn's sentiment, but they would have to stop soon. He looked around and saw a spot, not really a clearing but a larger space between trees, and pointed with a hand.

"We'll rest there," Erik said, dismounting. As he did, his torch extinguished.

"Give it here," Terradyn said, extending a hand from up on his horse, but his torch blew out as well. "Damn."

"Careful," Erik said, but in the darkness, Terradyn missed his brief smile.

Terradyn tried lighting them, but they simply wouldn't catch. And they needed them.

"Do you have more?" Erik asked.

"Yes, of course, I do, but I want to save them as much as I can," Terradyn said. "Perhaps I could use a little magic the master taught me."

"No," Erik said quickly. "I don't think that's a ..."

Erik's voice trailed off. He stared out at the forest, his mouth open, his eyes wide, his heart at a standstill.

"Look," he whispered.

As Erik looked at the forest around them, he saw tufts of what looked like freshly-opened yellow flowers that glowed like tiny lanterns. They gave off little light at first, but as darkness consumed them, as if responding to it, the flowers brightened. A bush with orange leaves interspersed among the green began to glow, and red toadstools raised their heads around the base of a massive, oak-looking tree. As a grasshopper bounced from one mushroom to the next, they brightened and dimmed. Even the grass had a luminescence to it.

As Erik breathed in, the air seemed cleaner and cooler and smelled naturally sweet. It was freezing cold outside the forest, but within the confines of the trees, in this space of meadow in which they stood, the temperature was perfect—midday in the middle of spring, not too hot and not too cold. Most of the branches were high above them, far out of arm's reach, but several bright blue jays now sat on one lower hanging branch jutting from the side of a red-barked pine.

As Terradyn now stood beside him, Erik saw a red-haired squirrel scurry in front of Warrior, and the horse snorted, stomping a hoof. The squirrel, as large as a cat, stopped and chittered, before running off into some other part of the woods.

"Do you see all this?" Erik asked.

"I do, and I don't like it," Terradyn replied quietly.

"I agree. Often, the most beautiful things in this world are the most dangerous"

"That's for sure," Terradyn agreed. "The emerald viper. The red-haired spider. A beautiful woman. All stunning. All deadly."

"We must rest," Erik said, "but we must rest quickly. To stay in one place here means death."

## 61

*E*rik lay in the grass, Thala curled up next to him, but he didn't sleep. As he stared at the canopy overhead, several times, he saw a streak of light that reminded him of the moon fairies, the way they moved in the sky. Those tiny creatures had been his saviors on several occasions, but he would not trust anything that looked friendly in this place. Eventually, he heard Terradyn moving about and stood himself.

"Are you ready?" Terradyn asked, tightening his horse's belt.

Erik nodded, stirring Thala with his boot, and as he moved over to stroke Warrior's neck, the snow cat stretched with a growling yawn. Specs of dust began to fall from the forest canopy, again reminding Erik of moon fairies and their fairy dust. These specs were all different kinds of colors, though—green, red, white, yellow, and blue. A few of them fell on his cheek and nose, and he sneezed.

"I feel tired now," Erik said. "I couldn't sleep at all before, but now ... Maybe we could rest a little while longer?"

"Tired," Terradyn said, and Erik noticed the blue tattoos on Terradyn's scalp glowing softly.

"Yeah. Groggy, really, as if I've drunk too much ale. I'm just so sleepy."

"Get on your horse, Erik," Terradyn snapped, his voice urging and concerned.

He walked over to Erik, and helped him into his saddle. Erik gave Terradyn an odd look at first, but when he put a foot in one of the stirrups, he realized he wouldn't have been able to lift himself up. He probably would have just laid back down, reveling in the soft grass. In fact, that was all he wanted to do, looking at the luminescent green carpet with envy.

"It's more elvish magic," Terradyn said.

"You don't feel the same way?" Erik asked, smiling without meaning to, his eyelids heavy.

"No," Terradyn said, but as the man spoke, Erik heard voices all around him. They were soft and gentle as if singing a lullaby, something that reminded him of his mother ... of Simone as she caressed her belly and sang to their unborn baby.

"Why not?" Erik asked, and he could hear his own voice slur as he spoke.

"Got my own magic," Terradyn said, "it protects me. Hold on to your saddle horn."

Erik smiled again, childishly as he started to giggle, but he did as he was told. Terradyn wrapped a piece of thin rope around Erik's wrists and then around the saddle.

"This looks ... looks fun," Erik said with a smile.

"You'll be fine," Terradyn said, looking up at him. The man said something to Warrior.

"Telling secrets, are we now?" Erik said with a foolish chuckle. "Secrets don't ... secrets don't ..."

He felt Warrior moving underneath him as he looked up. The canopy was dark again, only the intermittent rays of light escaping small spaces between branches and leaves. Erik closed his eyes, letting the darkness envelop him like a warm blanket.

Erik opened his eyes, breathing deeply as if he had stayed underwater too long. He was moving but wondered how. He looked down and saw his hands were tied to Warrior's saddle horn. Terradyn was in front of him, a subtle glow about the tattoos on his scalp. He led Erik's warhorse by his reins. Thala plodded along next to them, stopping for a moment to eye another large, tufted squirrel as it scurried up a tree, and then continuing.

"How long was I out?" Erik asked.

"A while," Terradyn said without turning around.

*No dreams. Just darkness.*

"Can I stop leading you now, like some child?" Terradyn asked. His voice sounded irritated at best.

"I'm sorry I don't have magical runes tattooed on my head," Erik spat back. "They look awful, by the way. I think I'd rather be bewitched by some elvish spell than carry those around for the rest of my life."

That was something Bryon would say. Erik cracked a small smile while Terradyn glared at him over his shoulder, dropping the reins.

"Anything happen?" Erik asked.

"Other than enduring your incessant snoring, no. Same things. Voices. Trees and bushes rattling. Flowers glowing and then complete darkness."

"No elves?" Erik asked.

Terradyn shook his head.

"No elves," he replied, "but they're watching us. Waiting."

"For what?" Erik asked.

"Need you ask?" Terradyn replied. "Damn this forest."

As Terradyn hissed his curse through gritted teeth, something echoed in the dark woods. It sounded like a stone bouncing down a cliff, striking craggy rock on its way to the bottom.

"I thought we agreed. No more curses in this place," Erik said.

Terradyn waved him off.

"I could swear," Terradyn said, "these trees are moving. And there is a little more light up ahead."

As Terradyn spoke, the tree line broke, and in moments, they both stared out at open space. Whether it was Hargoleth or Háth-golthane, Erik didn't know, but they were right back at the edge of the forest.

"Shit!" Terradyn said with great feeling. "How did we get here?"

"Is this where we entered the forest?" Erik asked.

Terradyn looked to the sky, watching the faint glow of stars as dusk began to fall. He shook his head.

"No."

"We should camp here and rest properly," Erik said. "In the morning, we will enter the forest again."

As Erik sat watching the fire, Terradyn paced back and forth at the edge of the light. Terradyn's horse, named Shadow Erik had learned, and Warrior stood close, nibbling at cold tufts of grass. Thala purred softly as she curled up into a ball, gently resting against Erik.

Erik closed his eyes and breathed evenly and slowly. He reveled in the warmth against his face and the chill at his back. He tried to meld the two feelings in his mind. The sounds of night, the mysterious echoes and noises from Ul'Erel, the grinding of teeth as horses ate and the soft purring of a great, white, snow cat all became one in his mind. He had never tried to enter the Dream World while he was awake but knew it could be done. Clearly Dewin and Jamalel did it. And he couldn't be so sure the Dream World would come to him while he slept. It seemed so intermittent as of late. He decided he would sit, close his eyes, and consciously search for the place of dreams.

As he breathed slowly, eyes closed, he felt a soft numbness on his face, the space between wake and sleep. He called out in his mind.

*Dewin. Dewin, are you there?*

All around him was darkness and silence, but then a man appeared in front of him, hooded and wearing a black robe. Erik's heart jumped—Patûk again—but as the man turned and pulled back the cowl, he saw it was Andragos.

"Erik, you are alive," Andragos said, a hint of excitement in his voice. "How?"

"A gift," Erik replied. "A life for a life."

Erik stepped closer to Andragos, each footstep creating an echo in the dark space they currently shared.

"My family is safe, because of you," Erik said. "Why? Why do you care?"

The small smile on Andragos face faded.

"Was it out of goodness?" Erik asked. "A sense of righteousness?"

Now, it was Erik's turn to smile.

"Do not fool yourself," Andragos snapped, his face stern and flat.

Erik's smile quickly faded.

"Syzbalo wanted to kill Terradyn and Raktas. I couldn't let that happen, not after all the time and effort and training I had put into them. And the Lord of the East has become a liability. He seeks to control dragons. He seeks world domination. He seeks to ally himself with Chaos. But every time someone attempts such a thing, they bring ruin. And this time, the conqueror's hubris could bring even more destruction upon the world, if his foolishness truly releases Yebritoch and his chaos beasts. You can stop him. You can stop them. For whatever reason, the gods have deemed you worthy of stopping the most powerful man in Háthgolthane. The gods have deemed you worthy of stopping a demon. Do not mistake my motives for kindness."

Erik nodded.

"Very well," he said. "The Dragon Sword has been stolen, as has the Dragon Stone."

"I know," Andragos replied.

"How do I find them?" Erik asked. "This forest of Ul'Erel is a maze, so if I am so important, you'll tell me."

Andragos began to fade, becoming translucent.

"I don't know," he replied, "but Dewin would know. Search for Dewin."

The Black Mage's voice became distant, an echoing whisper.

"Erik," Andragos' voice said before completely disappearing. "I am glad you are alive."

He was gone, and Erik was once again alone in this abyss. He pictured the young Dewin in his mind, a tall and lean wizard with long, brown, wavy hair. He concentrated on his face, his voice, and every little intricacy he could, but nothing was returned. No voice. No image. Then Erik thought of an old man with a hole-ridden robe, liver spots all over his wrinkly skin, and milky, blind eyes. His vision fogged for a moment, and then the image of a hunched figure, sitting cross-legged on the floor, appeared in front of Erik.

"So, the Dream Walker lives," Dewin said with a quick cackle, "and through rebirth has learned to walk the Dream World while awake. Interesting."

"Is it so interesting?" Erik asked.

"Yes," Dewin replied. "Very. You have received a very special gift from Jamalel, and you wonder why. It is because, Dream Walker, you are special."

Erik took in a deep breath, calming himself as he felt the same remorse he felt every time he thought of Jamalel.

"Andragos just told me the same thing, but he did not know how I find Dragon Tooth and the Dragon Stone in a place like Ul'Erel." Erik asked, "He said you would know."

"Did he?" Dewin replied with another cackle. "The Black Mage has much confidence in me. Yes, I can help you find that which you seek. But first, you must know the elvish forest is more dangerous than you think. Believe nothing your eyes see and nothing your ears hear. Listen only to your dreams. They will lead you to El'Beth El'Kesh."

"I have experienced its trickery already, and all we did was end up back outside the forest again. How do I find her?" Erik asked again.

"Again, I do not know," Dewin replied. "Your dreams are your guide, not me or mine. I know not how and where they will lead you."

"More riddles," Erik said.

"Yes," Dewin replied, "the secrets of Ul'Erel are the greatest riddles. But this much I can tell you, you must reenter the forest now. Do not wait until morning. And as the forest shifts, as it speaks to you, you must travel away from the voices you will hear."

"The ones we heard seemed all around us," Erik said.

"They sound that way," Dewin said, "but you will need to concentrate. Find the source. And go in the opposite direction."

Dewin began to fade.

"Thank you," Erik said.

The old man cackled once more.

"It is good that the Dream Walker is alive," Dewin said as he disappeared. "Very good."

hy?" Terradyn asked.

"Because," Erik replied.

"You could have died in your sleep in there," Terradyn said, "and now you wish to reenter that realm of witchcraft *and* during the witching hour!"

Erik ignored his ranting and looked up. The sky was dark, stars twinkling brightly and the moon blazing down on them, illuminating the world in a stark white light. But as he looked at the tree line that signified the Forests of Ul'Erel, there was only darkness.

*I wish I had Dragon Tooth.*

"This is crazy," Terradyn said. "I'm not going in."

Erik turned on the man hard, pointing a finger at him.

"I don't care who your master is, how old you are, or that you have magic tattooed on the side of your head," Erik seethed. "You serve me, at this moment, and you will do as you are commanded ... or are you willing to deny your master's instructions?"

Terradyn was bigger and stronger than Erik. He was a wizard in his own right. And he was an adept warrior, certainly far more trained than Erik. Erik might have had a chance in a fight with

Terradyn if he had Dragon Tooth, but without his enchanted sword, he doubted himself.

Terradyn looked at him, unblinking for a few moments, and then spun on his heel. He mounted his horse and looked down at Erik.

"Well," Terradyn said, more than a hint of sarcasm in his voice, "lead on, leader."

Without response, Erik pulled himself up into his horse's saddle, and the destrier responded with a quick snort. He heeled Warrior, Thala plodding along next to them and Terradyn following, and they passed the first wall of trees. It was as it was before, the trees growing so close to one another they had to ride in single file. Terradyn quickly lit torches, and as before, intermittent gusts of wind tried to extinguish them. Erik heard a whooshing sound overhead and then a whirling sound all around them.

"Where are we going?" Terradyn asked.

"Away from the voices," Erik replied.

"What voices?" Terradyn asked, and as if on cue, they heard a distant voice.

"*Gimel va ha na tet ra'ish,*" the voice said, over and over, and as it moved nearer, like before, it sounded as if it was all around them.

"Damn, this was a mistake," Terradyn hissed, but Erik held up a hand.

"Hush," he said, closing his eyes and concentrating.

Erik listened, and even as other things tried to clutter his ears—the rustling of bushes, the clattering of branches, and the chirping and chittering of animals—he heard it, a single voice. He now felt as if he had moved into the Dream World, and the extra clutter and noise were gone, and he could focus on the voice to his left. A woman's.

When he opened his eyes, the din of the magic forest was back, all around him, but he knew they needed to go right. He pulled on Warrior's reins and faced a wall of trees.

"This way," Erik said.

"How?" Terradyn asked, the irritation in his voice now tempered with curiosity; Erik didn't reply.

He heeled Warrior, and the horse trusted him, slowing walking forward into the wall of trees that appeared more impenetrable than the castle walls of Fen-Stévock. At the edge of the tree line, large roots jutted out from the ground, themselves the girth of a large man, and the horses had to step carefully over them. Thala leaped over as if they weren't there, and looked back as if to ask why the others were so slow. As the noise around them grew thunderous, and Erik wished they could move at the cat's speed, their vision was hampered with thick smoke.

Behind him, Terradyn was yelling, screaming about something, but his voice was drowned out by the sound, but then, just when Erik wondered how they could cope with traveling in such circumstances, he realized that the smoke came from trees and roots that disappeared in the wind. The density of the forest was an illusion, and as the sound dissipated, they were able to move forward more comfortably but still in single file.

"I hope that be the end of it," Erik said, looking at Terradyn over his shoulder.

"Doubtful," Terradyn muttered, for a moment looking like a child who had been denied his favorite treat.

"Are you ready to listen to me now," Erik asked, "completely?"

Terradyn scowled but gave Erik a quick nod.

As they moved deeper into Ul'Erel, the trees would close in like a normal forest and then open to a large glade or meadow. Different flowers and bushes would glow and brighten the otherwise dark forest and then dim, but there was no way to tell the time of day. Erik decided the only indicator of how long they had traveled were their stomachs and if they were hungry or not, but that was not a great help either. Fear had a significant impact on appetite.

They were at a point where they were able to ride side by side when Erik reined Warrior to a halt. A glance down told him Thala had sensed it too because her back was arched after she also stopped.

"What is it, girl?" Erik said softly, but she simply hissed.

He leaned forward in his saddle, turning an ear to the trees in front of them, listening. He could hear voices again, but it wasn't the distant, feminine one they had heard before. There were several this time, and they were conversing, arguing perhaps, in some guttural language he had never heard before.

Erik looked at Terradyn, who nodded before they both dismounted.

"Stay," Erik said into Warrior's ear, speaking Shengu.

Erik retrieved his hunting bow, nocking an arrow and drawing the string halfway. Terradyn didn't have any sort of ranged weapon, so he followed Erik, as did Thala, her soft paws silent as she crept forward, or leaped easily over large roots the men had to either skirt or climb over.

After a short while, the forest opened into a wide meadow, one far bigger than any they had seen thus far. Erik found a root that was completely exposed, its trunk covered in thick, gnarly bark, and he lay on his stomach and stared into the meadow through the gap under the root. Weak sunlight rather than luminescent flowers and toad-stools lit the scene, and he saw three figures, maybe four, all speaking hurriedly, at times speaking over each other.

Erik looked back at Terradyn, holding up four fingers. Thala had stopped, just in front of Terradyn, her whiskers twitching, but otherwise as still as a stone statue. Erik scooted to his left, trying to get a little closer, and as he peered around a tree, he could clearly see two of the group, both elves that were tall and muscular, their pointed ears unmistakable.

One had bright yellow hair, pulled back into a tail, and his skin was almost brown. He wore tight-fitting leggings that were dyed green and tall, brown boots that extended to his knees, and his shirt was loose, billowing at the wrists. He had a longbow strapped across his back, a quiver of arrows hanging from the right side of his belt and a sheathed longsword hanging from the left.

The other elf had pale skin, almost bone white, and had long, brown hair streaked with white, allowed to flow freely. He wore a long, high collared, white robe that covered his feet. He held a simple staff of a red-colored wood topped by an uneven rock that was a deeper auburn in color like no stone Erik had ever seen. As he looked closer, there seemed to be a small, yellow light emanating from the middle of the stone.

Erik leaned further out, trying to get a look at the two when he stopped as the hair on his arm stood on end. He felt a sickening feeling in his stomach, and the air around him grew thick and suffocating. He looked back at Terradyn, the tattoos on his scalp glowing, his eyes the same blue.

"No! They'll feel your magic!" Erik said in a whispered hiss.

As if on cue, the root in front of him exploded into tiny shards of wood, and the concussion of the explosion sent Erik flying backward, his nocked arrow shooting off into the forest as his bow was knocked out of his hands. Thala growled loudly, and Terradyn said something in a language that wasn't Shengu.

"You dare speak the language of black magic in this place," one of the elves said in Westernese, Erik didn't know which one, but his accent rolling and fluid, like water flowing gently over smooth river stone.

Erik rolled to his stomach and looked at Terradyn.

"You used the Shadow Tongue?" Erik asked.

"No," Terradyn replied. "Mages' Tongue."

Erik didn't have time to ask for or get further clarification. He crawled to his bow, coming into a crouch with another arrow nocked. Thala growled, but as she readied herself to jump and attack, someone swung a large branch from above them and caught the snow cat in the ribs, throwing her against the trunk of another tree. She yelped as she fell to the floor, lying still.

"Thala!" Erik yelled and turned towards the opening in the wall of trees created by the elves' magical explosion.

The first elf, with brown skin and yellow hair, stood there, longbow lifted. Another elf stood next to him. This one with pale, milky skin as well, purple eyes, and black hair. He was dressed in the same fashion and also had a longbow lifted and ready to use.

Erik fired, drawing another arrow, nocking it, and letting it loose a moment later. The first would have flown true, right into the first elf's eye, but it exploded, much like the root had. The other arrow thudded into a wooden shield, hoisted by a fourth elf just before it struck the black-haired elf.

The fourth elf wore a mail shirt, but Erik could still see the shape of the she-elf's breasts. Her steel greaves and bracers were embossed with etchings of leaves, and her conical helm held back much of her blonde hair. She squinted harshly at Erik, her purple eyes bright and angry under bushy, yellow eyebrows. Her shield was a simple wooden one, unadorned and unpainted, and she held a sword in her right hand, its long, thin blade glimmering in the sun that spilled into the wide glade.

"*Moggador!*" Terradyn shouted, pushing out with his left hand in a fist, just as the first, yellow-haired elf fired an arrow at Erik.

Erik felt the air move, and a sudden gust of wind knocked the arrow aside and struck the archer in the chest with such force it sent him tumbling backward. The robed elf stepped hurriedly out of the way and then held his staff up, the reddish stone atop it glowing.

"*Gal!*" he shouted.

The earth under Erik's feet shifted and rumbled, and the ground undulated. Then there was a sound of wood snapping and thick, black vines erupted upwards, lined with long thorns. The vines slapped at Erik and Terradyn and the animals like whips, Thala was still too groggy to jump out of the way. One of the vines wrapped around one of Warrior's front legs, the thorns digging deep into the horse's flesh, and he neighed loudly, trying to stomp his hooves but only making his entrapment worse. Shadow was equally struggling, and Erik could see panic in the horse's eye.

"*Warrior! Be still!*" Erik shouted in Shengu as one of the vines wrapped around his right calf.

The thorns were useless against his greaves, but he felt the pressure of the twisted branches tightening around his leg, seeking to immobilize him and cut off the blood supply. Another vine wrapped itself around Erik's left thigh, its thorns digging deep into his muscle; he wanted to scream but stopped himself with gritted teeth.

He saw another vine wrapped around Terradyn's free arm, tearing at the flesh on his forearm and bicep. He swung his massive sword, cutting it in two, a black ichor spilling where it had been severed. But before he could celebrate, another vine wrapped around his sword arm, pulling him down towards the earth.

Erik drew Mardirru's falchion, cutting away at the vine around his thigh and the one around his calf, but as he tried to move to help Terradyn, another vine wrapped itself around his ankle as all four elves moved towards him until they stood before the trapped men and horses.

"Men in our realm," the she-elf warrior seethed. Despite her accent, she spoke perfect Westernese. "You should know better."

The elvish wizard lifted his staff again, the red stone glowing once more, a small ball of fire growing in his other hand.

"*Nar Gurth!*" the wizard shouted, his face and voice full of hatred.

Both archers lifted their bows, one aiming at Erik and the other at Terradyn. The elvish warrior pointed her longsword at Warrior, and the wizard laughed, the ball of fire now casting a demonic glow across his face.

White fur flashed by Erik. Thala's outstretched claws thudded into the wizard's chest as the elf cried out. The vines retreated and, ignoring the arrow that had thudded into her shoulder, the snow cat clamped down on the wizard's throat, tearing flesh, the deep red blood marring her perfect white fur.

When the vines retreated from Warrior's legs, the destrier reared up and kicked out with his forelimbs. One of his massive, feathered hooves struck the she-elf's shield, knocking her back and shattering the wood. Thala leaped to another elf, the yellow-haired archer, but the elf rolled out of the way, coming up to a crouching position and firing an arrow at Terradyn. The missile struck the large man in the right breast, but he didn't seem to notice. His face was red, and his scalp burned with blue light as the magical runes tattooed there came to life.

"*Azgad!*" he shouted, and the elvish bow caught fire, burning the skin on the elf's hands.

The elf screamed as the palms of his hand blistered. When the pale-skinned elf turned on Terradyn, Erik lowered his shoulder, charging at him. The elf loosed an arrow, but it thudded off Erik's pauldrons. Erik dropped his falchion and rammed the elf in the stomach, sending the elf sprawling and gasping for air. Erik was about to retrieve his sword when something hard hit him in the thigh, and the she-elf tackled him to the ground.

In an instant, she straddled him and rained her fists down on his face, harder than he had ever felt before. Her blows were so quick, he had trouble retaliating, and when he covered up his face, she hammered on his chest and ribs. He had felt broken ribs before, and if she kept going, they were on the brink. Erik was about to fight back when a loud voice stopped her in mid-punch.

"*Rik ave vadokan!*" Terradyn shouted, and the elf quickly pushed herself off Erik.

She crouched, one hand on the ground, the other fingering the handle of a dagger sheathed in her belt.

"*Cin bert con in firn in hi near!*" she shouted and then spoke in Westernese, "How dare you command the dead in this place?"

Wondering if the elf he had wounded was back on his feet, Erik looked to his side and saw that a red aura surrounded the elvish wizard. He sat up, a gaping wound in his throat, the blood staining his white robe. He looked to Terradyn, whose eyes were consumed with a blue light, and he held up his left hand. Erik could smell the dead, he heard them, and the she-elf clearly did too. She looked around as the stench of decay and rot surrounded them, as a chorus of the dead screaming and laughing filled the air.

Erik saw their shadows, at the edge of the tree line, in the darkness of the canopy of leaves and branches. They were there, in this place. He hadn't seen them in so long, but the dead were there. The sun spilling into the meadow faded, replaced by a pallid light that looked almost like it came from the moon even though it was clearly day.

"*What are you doing, Terradyn?*" Erik demanded, but Andragos' guard ignored him. The Black Mage had taught his servant too well.

The elvish wizard stood, his eyes black, and lifted his hands and the staff and began to chant. The trees surrounding the meadow burst into flames, as did the grass. Both archers were on their feet again, the first cradling his burned hands close to his body. The other, his face full of the pain in his stomach, fired an arrow into the body of the wizard, but it did nothing. The undead wizard moved closer to his former companions, mouthing a chant that Erik couldn't hear. He scooted backward, picking up his falchion, as he felt the dead closing in.

Erik turned to see a dead man behind him, his skin black with decay. He swung, removing the man's head as another one shuffled towards him. He sliced him open from shoulder to hip, maggots and roaches spilling from the open cavity where his organs used to be. A dead woman clawed at his feet, unable to walk as her legs were gone from the knee down. He swung downwards, removing her hands at the wrists and then stabbed into her forehead.

"*Terradyn! Stop!*" Erik demanded, but the man didn't hear him or care to take notice. His eyes still blazed a brilliant blue, and his tattoos glowed so brightly, it looked like a halo surrounded his head. Perhaps Andragos had not trained him well enough, and the man was unable to break the spell.

Erik heard a cackle behind him, and he recognized the voice. He turned to see Sorben as he stepped from the shadows of the forest, a smile revealing his black and broken teeth.

"You again!" said Erik.

"I like this place," Sorben said, lifting a rusted sword and pointing it at Erik. "I think I'll stay here."

"The Dream World isn't good enough?" Erik asked.

Sorben growled.

"That is not my realm," he said, and Erik turned his nose at the putrid scent that came from the dead man's mouth. "My realm is dark and cold. It is pain. It is torture. It is terror, a place full of horrible things, wretched creatures, and unbelievable depravities."

"It's what you deserve," Erik said.

"No one deserves that!" Sorben hissed, clenching his fist, long, yellow fingernails digging into paper-thin skin.

Two arrows thudded into Sorben's chest, fired from the pale-skinned elvish archer's bow, and the dead man laughed.

"Foolish elves!"

The air dimmed even more and grew cold, and as Erik breathed, his breath formed mist in front of him. Warrior and Thala and Shadow warded off more dead that emerged from the forest, while Erik squared off with Sorben and Terradyn commanded the dead elvish wizard. As more undead shuffled into the small space in which they had fought, a host of crawling creatures followed them—spiders, scorpions, centipedes, and beetles. The snow cat jumped back, behind the remaining elves, as some of the insects began to crawl up Erik's legs, biting and stinging. Sorben threw his head back and laughed.

Erik heard the elves talking and looked at them over his shoulder. The she-elf scowled when her purple eyes, filled with anger and hatred, met his. But her face betrayed another emotion—defeat.

"Min bar na dregen!" the elf said, and Erik was sure she meant they would meet again.

She, along with the two archers, turned and fled into the glade where Erik first saw them, disappearing into the adjacent forest.

More and more dead came from the dark forest. They began to surround Erik and his companions.

"*Terradyn, you have to stop!*" Erik shouted to no avail.

He looked at the undead wizard. The fire that consumed his staff ignited his robe, and his flesh began to turn black as he crumpled to the ground.

"Are you ready to see my realm, Erik?" Sorben said.

There was no way Erik or Thala or Warrior could fight off the battalion of undead emerging from the forest. He looked to Terradyn, the man still mesmerized in his own spell.

"I'm sorry," Erik said as he stepped forward and thrust his falchion into the man's belly.

Terradyn screamed as the blue light in his eyes faded, the tattoos on his scalp dimming. He fell to his knees, sweating and breathing heavily as the undead faded away as if they were dust blown about by a strong wind.

"Just wait, Erik," came Sorben's laughing voice as he disappeared. "Your time will come."

Terradyn looked at Erik and then looked down at his belly, where one-third of the blade still dug into his flesh.

"Wha—" Terradyn began to say, but then he looked at the burning remains of the elvish wizard.

"You have no idea what you have done," Erik said as he removed the blade.

Terradyn stared at Erik for a few moments longer, and then crumpled to the ground, blood rapidly staining the grass beneath him.

## 63

*A*nkara closed her eyes and tried to steady her breathing. She was lost, and every time she used her magic in this place, she seemingly revealed her position to some elvish patrol and would have to run and hide.

"Damn elves," she muttered as she opened her eyes, unable to meditate with so many worries heavy on her mind.

She should have never entered this place. The tales of Ul'Erel weren't just simple ghost stories, and the elves weren't flighty, finicky creatures more concerned with eating grapes or playing flutes as she had thought. They were ruthless, cunning, and dangerous.

She had entered the forest from the east, but she didn't know where that direction was anymore. She couldn't see the damned sun, the canopy of branches was so thick, and the one time she was able to see the stars and moon when entering a small glade, the stars began to swirl around like they were caught in some whirlpool so she couldn't catch her bearings. More damn elvish magic.

As she walked along yet another forest path that probably led her nowhere, her emerald eyes blazing so she could see in the dark—it used the least amount of magic—she heard skittering and shuffling. She crouched and produced her longbow as she sought to even her breathing, but her pulse raced, and she felt her heart pounding against her chest. As well as being lost in this place, a fear she had never known seemed to have filled her mind. The sounds grew closer, but this was a place of almost constant noise, and she sought to concentrate her hearing. In the moment, the distant echoes signified terrifying screams, the air around became heavy and thick, and the putrid stench of decaying flesh struck her nose.

As if protesting themselves, the moss, toadstools, flowers, and leaves all around her flashed a brilliant light, and she screamed as the intensity seemed to burn her eyes. She covered her eyes and willed her night vision to disappear as the smell of rot thickened. The sound shuffling grew louder, it sounded like feet now, and as suddenly as the luminescence had appeared, it was gone, leaving Ankara in complete darkness. In the moment she could see nothing at all, the air grew hot, the smell of decay stronger than ever, and she found herself gagging.

Feeling as if she had no choice, she reached out to her magic, willed her night vision back as she closed her eyes. When she opened them, Ankara gasped before quickly releasing an arrow from her bow, which exploded a man's head that was mostly skull with bits of flesh and hair still stuck to it. A long hiss made her turn, and she faced another man with stretched, yellow and black skin over his face, ocular sockets void of eyes. He reached out with bone-only fingers, and she fired another arrow. His head exploded like the first.

Ankara had never been a pious woman, but at that moment, she began to pray to every Isutan god she knew. She looked down at her feet and the ground fluttered and moved as scorpions, spiders, centipedes and beetles ran over her boots and up her legs, stinging. She said a quick spell and most of the insects that had crawled up her legs burst into little balls of flame, but more came.

She caused her bow to disappear and willed two short swords into her hands. These men that approached her—attacked her—were dead. She had never seen such a thing. She had heard of it, and she suspected her father could reanimate a corpse if he wanted to—he probably had before—but she had never seen the dead walk. More corpses stepped from the trees, hissing and screaming, their faces and bodies in various degrees of decay. Some were recently dead, coagulated blood still clinging to wounds or the bloat of gasses caught in the gut making them look fat. Ankara slashed the belly of one such woman, and a green gas escaped the wound, spewing into Ankara's face and causing her to cough and vomit. She felt not just insects, but hands around her legs, tearing at her clothing. She slashed and stabbed, removing decaying limbs and dropping undead men and women, but they still came, an endless army of death. They closed in on her, clawing at her, biting at her, grabbing her, and she, for the first time in her life, began to panic.

Then, it was as if sunlight had broken through the thick canopy of leaves and branches, and her eyes hurt again, the light too bright for her vision meant specifically for the darkness. She stumbled backward and expected the undead people closing around her to fall on her. She would fight to the end, sending as many of them as she could back to the abyss, but she knew she would die. She just hoped she didn't turn into one of these walking, stinking abominations.

As Ankara lay in the grass, seeing through her closed eyelids that the light around her had dissipated, nothing happened. She opened one eye at first, and then the other. The grass and the flowers and the moss were illuminated again, and specs of something floated through the air, almost like ash caught in the wind after a forest fire. There were no more dead, save for one who shuffled towards her from behind a tree, but just as Ankara looked at the woman with yellow, stretched skin, she dissolved into nothing more than dust and blew away.

"Thank the gods," Ankara gasped, letting her head fall back.

She wasn't able to rest for long, though. Ankara heard distant shouting in Elvish.

"Damn," she hissed, pushing herself to her feet. She reached out to her magic, touching it with just the tips of her fingers, and her eyes blazed emerald green, and she fled, running away from the voices.

## 64

*E*rik draped Terradyn over Shadow's saddle, tying the horse's reins to Warrior's saddle. Thala limped when she walked, but she did her best to stay in front of Erik as he led his destrier through the forest. Every part of Erik's body wanted to rest, but he knew he had to keep moving, away from the site of the battle. Whatever spell Terradyn had cast—probably in desperation—he had opened a portal between the land of the dead and this place. And for all of the hate that filled the elves, they looked genuinely terrified that the dead had stepped foot in their realm.

Erik was sure Terradyn had never tried such magic before, as it looked like he had lost control. Terradyn was a mage, but he was much more a normal man. Erik had not understood the language Terradyn spoke, and it was very different from the language the elves used, but their anger at what he had said and done in Ul'Erel was unmistakable. A part of Erik had hoped he might engage with the elves peaceably, to have explained who he was looking for, but now more would come looking for them, with only death on their minds. In addition, Erik couldn't be sure the door to the world of the dead had been closed properly.

When Erik had to stop to rest, he checked on Terradyn. The large man's breathing was shallow, but Erik was sure any other man would already be dead. What Erik had done filled him with remorse and shame, but he knew it was the only way to break the spell. The dead would have kept on coming, growing in numbers, until they swarmed the forest—the world perhaps. Erik shuddered at the thought.

It was evident the effects of the spell weren't exclusive to the small glade where they had fought the elves. As Erik led Warrior and Shadow through Ul'Erel, he saw dead things—squirrels chewed on, a small deer without a head, and bloody feathers. In a typical forest, these sorts of things weren't uncommon, and life in the wilds was tough for anyone and anything that chose to live there. The mountain people of the Southern Mountains proved that point to Erik long ago. But here, in this elvish realm, until now, Erik had seen none of the normal carnage one might find. He hadn't even seen a tree uprooted, broken, or fallen over, and as he thought of it, he hadn't even seen a wilted flower or a brown patch of grass.

Erik didn't know if things in this forest were eternal—his dwarvish friends had confessed that elves lived very long lives—or if they were simply diligent at maintaining the forest, but it was pristine like the rose garden tended with love by Simone. But now, Terradyn's spell had corrupted it, and Erik could understand why the she-elf, whom he assumed to be the leader of the small group, was so upset at the Mage's language being uttered in Ul'Erel.

Erik looked around the small clearing where he had stopped, and the giant roots of several of the biggest trees he had seen extended as high as a man, blocking the narrow path along which he had traveled. To one side, hidden by bushes and other trees, was what resembled a cave in the roots, and if he needed to, it was place he could hide even the horses.

"We'll stop here, Thala," Erik said, and the snow cat stopped and waited.

Erik pulled Terradyn off of his horse, thinking he would bandage the man's wound with an undershirt he found in Terradyn's saddle-bags; it was dirty, but it would have to do. The man's breathing was shallow still, but the wound had stopped bleeding and, unbelievably, looked to have already started to heal.

"Are you invincible?" Erik asked the unconscious man as he sat, Thala curling up behind him.

Erik brought his knees to his chest and hugged them, looking about as the horses nibbled at the grass, and Terradyn and Thala slept. Stories spoke of the elves as being innovators, builders, artists, and musicians, revolutionaries of justice, and, yet, everything he had experienced in their realm was contrary. Even the way the elves looked at him and Terradyn could only be described as hatred. And for what?

Fatigue began to set in, and he knew it wasn't the magic of this place causing his weariness this time. He was just tired. As he lay back and looked up, he saw one of the large squirrels of the forest perched upon a branch, watching him. Spying on him? As he sought to shrug off the idea and close his eyes, he heard a woman's voice in his mind.

*Rest, Erik Dream Walker.*

He sat up again and looked around, confused and worried.

*Rest. You are safe.*

"I don't trust you," Erik replied out loud, but his eyelids grew heavy as a mist seeped into the forest, reminiscent of early, cold mornings on the farm. It washed over him, and he laid back once more ... even though he didn't want to.

*You are safe here for now. Rest. And Dream.*

Erik opened his eyes, sure he was about to embrace the Dream World again. Since Jamalel had passed his life essence to Erik, he had started to feel different when he was there, and his connection to this place was even stronger. He breathed in deeply and sat up, only to find he was in the small clearing in Ul'Erel. He shook his head and closed his eyes again, but when he opened them, nothing had changed except he was certain he was still dreaming.

It looked different from where he had laid down. Terradyn, Thala, and the horses weren't there, but he had expected as much. Motes floated about him, those that resembled the moon fairy dust, and the sun poked through the canopy above, its warmth and brightness gently touching the forest floor of soft grass and fallen, green leaves.

Erik felt a tug at his mind, something telling him he should turn around and walk, so he did; he was safe while he was dreaming and would follow whatever path seemed right. He passed through meadows and glades, much like the one in which they had fought, and worked his way between tight gaps in thick copses of trees until he eventually stepped out into a wide-open space, but one that didn't have the same dense vegetation surrounding it.

The trees in this place were spaced maybe fifty paces apart, but they were gigantic and ancient, their trunks twice as wide as any he had seen thus far. Their branches, as thick as the trunk of a normal large tree, spread out in perfect, geometric patterns, creating a web of leaves and wood that extended three hundred paces or more upward, where the sun shone in a cloudless blue sky. Then he noticed something even more unusual, and it made him smile.

Ladders connected the branches on which sat what looked like small homes. As he now peered beyond the trees at the edge, he was aware there were homes on the ground as well, some built directly into the trees and some next to them, using the trunk as a wall. As he wandered across the lush green grass, he noticed homes even built into the earth, their doors signified by a large mound of earth or neatly shaped boulder. This was a town, maybe even a city that carried on as far as he could see. It was built into the forest ... was a part of the forest. Was this actually Ul'Erel?

"Birah Shegah," a voice said as if answering Erik's question.

Erik turned.

"This place is named Birah Shegah," the voice, feminine, said again. "It means Second Capital in your language."

The elf's hair was silver-white, and her eyes sparkled and shimmered, and as she moved her head as she walked towards him, her eyes shifted from a deep blue to a purple and back again. She was tall, even taller than Simone, and despite the wide-sleeved, flowing, white robe she wore, he could see a muscular body. Pointed ears poked through her hair, but they took nothing away from her beauty. Erik could think of her face as captivating, even though he could see the smallest hints of crows-feet at the corner of her enchanting eyes. Even though she offered him a small smile, he sensed sadness in her expression.

"Impressive, isn't it?" she asked.

"Yes," Erik replied. "Is this truly what Ul'Erel looks like?"

The she-elf raised an eyebrow and tilted her head.

"Outside of the Dream World?" Erik added.

Her smile deepened.

"Yes," she replied. "This is what the cities of Ul'Erel look like ... more or less."

"So different," Erik said, looking around.

"Than the cities of men?" she asked.

"Not only those," Erik replied, meeting her eyes with his own. "Different than the dwarves."

"Truly," she said with a short laugh. "Let me show you how different."

The she-elf led him into the trees until she stopped at one that seemed to be at the center of all the other tree dwellings. It was the largest tree in the area, and as she looked at it, she began to speak. Her language was fluid, like water gently flowing down a stream, and as she spoke, a branch from high up in this massive tree seemed to follow her command and bent towards them. Once the branch reached the ground, a giant leaf unfolded from its end. It was thick and green and as wide as a rug that might cover some throne room. The elf stepped up onto the leaf, and she jerked her head in an almost child-like way towards Erik.

"Come, Erik Dream Walker," she said.

Erik waited a moment before stepping onto the leaf, and the moment he did, its edges folded up, as if to create a protective barrier, and the branch began to lift Erik and the elf towards the ceiling of the forest.

"Your language," Erik said as they lifted closer and closer to the top of the forest, past ladders and dwellings connected to the tree the whole way up.

"What about it?" the elf asked, now sitting cross-legged on the leaf.

"It's beautiful. So different from any other language I have ever heard before."

"Even dwarvish?" the elf asked with a smile.

"Very much so," Erik replied. "Their language is beautiful in its own way, but very hard. Sharp and angular."

"Their language resembles them," she said, still smiling. "They are a hard people. A tough people ... warriors."

She must have seen the look on Erik's face. He loved his dwarvish friends, and he sought to quickly hide what must have been a look of disapproval. The elf put up a hand before he could say anything.

"They are also a noble people," she continued, "as is their language. A noble and ancient dialect."

Erik smiled and nodded his appreciation.

"I had never heard Elvish before entering Ul'Erel," he said, "but there is something that sounds familiar."

"The Dragon Scroll," the she-elf said.

"How do you know about that?" Erik asked, but the somewhat annoyed look on the elf's face was all the reply he needed. "We are both Dream Walkers."

The elf nodded.

"And the Dragon Riders were elves, were they not?" Erik asked, and the elf's wide eyes told him he had now surprised her.

She calmed quickly and nodded.

"Yes," she replied, "and the reason you are in Ul'Erel."

Erik nodded.

"I've not heard much, but the language from the scroll was similar, but still not exactly like yours."

"The Shadow Tongue," the elf explained. "Both have the same roots, but evil corrupts. Even a language."

Erik wanted to ask more questions, but after they passed by a home built into and onto the tree that could have rivaled any stone-built mansion, they passed by the last treetop of the forest, and Erik held his breath. He looked in every direction, and as far as he could see, there were the green tops of trees. In the far distant northeast, he could see the grayish-blue silhouettes of mountains—the Gray Mountains—and far to the south, he saw a sloping horizon, just beyond the trees—the South Sea.

"This is what Ul'Erel was meant to be," the elf said proudly.

"It's amazing," Erik said, in awe at the vibrant, clear colors of birds and butterflies and trees and distant mountains and oceans.

"Could you have imagined a country like this?" the elf asked, and when Erik turned to face her, she was smiling, but with mistiness in her eyes that suggested she was about to cry.

"Is it all forests and trees?" Erik asked.

"No," the elf said, slowly shaking her head and smiling. "But it's all pure, clean, and uncorrupted."

"I don't understand," Erik said.

"El'Shema'Eret," the elf said. "This was the world, not mountains and plains. Oceans and grasslands. Marshes and forests and jungles and deserts. All pure. All the way El—the Creator—intended them to be."

"The whole world, then?" Erik asked.

"Yes, Erik Eleodum," the elf said. "It was once so beautiful. We—elves—tried to recreate it here, in Ul'Erel, but we have failed."

Erik tilted his head.

"When we ran from the rest of the world—a corrupted world full of evil and despair and sadness—we sought to recreate that which El had originally designed," the she-elf explained. "We would let the humans and the dwarves and the goblins and anyone else suffer in El'Shritûkt'Eret—the corrupted world. But we were fools—as foolish as all the other peoples of the world we thought so foolish. And what we created here, in these forests, were just as corrupted."

"Why stay here, then?" Erik asked. "After all these years, why stay and scare away anyone who enters?"

"Fear, Erik," the elf said. "In a world where faith was meant to rule our hearts, the true master of most is fear."

"Why show me this?" he asked.

"You have seen it," the elf said. "You have seen the heavens, the creation, and the cosmos. Some of us have, and when we come back to our world, we are disappointed. The elves of old were so disappointed with what the world had become that they tried to change it."

"Shouldn't we try to change the world?" Erik asked.

The elf smiled as if she knew—and wanted—Erik to ask that question.

"We cannot physically change the world," the elf said. "It is corrupt by a force much greater than us. We must be the change in the world. Erik Dream Walker, you must be the change. If we are, even though the earth and the sky and the water and the trees will remain corrupted, perhaps those around us will see the purity El intended."

Erik just stared out at the world, and as he watched it, it all seemed to come into view ... not just the tops of forest trees and distant mountains. He saw vast deserts and deep jungles. He saw tall mountain peaks covered in snow and chains of islands. He saw vast grassy plains that melded into dark swamps and marshes.

"I know why you are here, Erik," the elf said. "You must wake.

You are in danger. Follow the blue jay. She will show you the way. She will bring you to me."

"The blue jay?" Erik asked, but the world around him faded. He found himself in the black abyss, but even that faded, and he opened his eyes to a dark forest. "El'Beth El'Kesh."

## 65

*E*rik kept his left hand on Thala's head. He could feel her urgency for aggression as she shook under his touch, but she kept quiet. When he had heard the distinctive sound of marching boots, he had hidden the horses and Terradyn further back in the forest, away from the source of the noise, tying Warrior and Shadow to a tree.

Now, Mardirru's falchion gripped with white knuckles—his longbow broken in his fight with the elves—he crouched behind a bush as a column of twenty elvish warriors marched by. Most of them were dressed as the she-elf had been—mail shirts, bracers and greaves, conical helms, and round, unpainted, wooden shields. They all carried long swords sheathed at their sides. A knight—that was the only title Erik could think of—led the column, an elf wearing full plate, so polished it glimmered even in the dimness of the forest. From the slight curve to the breastplate, Erik surmised the knight was a she-elf, and she carried a triangular shield that reminded him of a Hámonian knight and rode a large mare, white from nose to tail.

A bulegant followed her, a tall, broad-shouldered creature with the head of a bull or bison and the body of a man. Erik remembered seeing several of them in Finlo, using their superior strength and bulk to work the docks. This one had a bull's head of brown fur with large, looping horns. Other than two strips of iron-studded leather that crossed his sternum, the bulegant was bare-chested, and he carried a long-handled ax that would have been a halberd for any man.

Four other creatures marched by at the rear of the column that Erik had not seen before. They were elves from head to belly button, and then their torso became a large horse's body, where the horse's neck should have been. They wore plate barding on their horse bodies and the mail shirts on their elvish torsos. They all carried longbows, but because of their greater height than full elves, these were almost twice the length of a normal bow. They also carried two-handed longswords on their backs. Erik was sure there was no way this was a normal patrol; they were mobilizing. The dead, word of men in Ul'Erel—the elves were on high alert.

He hurried back to where he'd left Warrior and Shadow and crouched beside Terradyn where he lay. He was still unconscious, but his breathing was more normal, and when he had last re-dressed the wound, it had healed even more. All Erik could hope for was no major internal damage, and Terradyn should recover.

"Terradyn," Erik whispered, gently shaking the man's shoulder. "Terradyn."

While Erik tried to get a response, he heard what was becoming a familiar chirping and clicking sound. He looked up to see a blue jay perched on a little branch, just above his head. The bird sang again, a little louder and faster as if to indicate urgency, and Erik knew he couldn't wait.

After making sure the bird was waiting and hadn't flown off, Erik bent his knees, wrapped his arms under Terradyn, and began to lift him, intent on draping him across Shadow again, when something gripped him hard and pulled on him. He looked at Terradyn, and the man stared back at him, his eyes glowing sapphires.

"What are you doing?" Terradyn asked, the tattoos on his scalp blazing.

"No!" Erik snapped, "don't. They'll sense your magic."

"What happened to me?" Terradyn asked, his eyes and scalp returning to their natural colors.

"You cast a spell," Erik said. "You raised the dead."

Terradyn released Erik, and he stood, wobbling slightly.

"And then what?" Terradyn asked, a hand going to his stomach.

"You were consumed," Erik said, taking a step back. "You wouldn't stop. It was like someone else had taken control of you."

As Erik went to untie the horses, Terradyn rubbed his stomach and lifted his shirt. He could see the wound, the skin knitted together, red and scabbed over. Terradyn should have been dead, but if a normal man had miraculously survived such a wound, it wouldn't have looked that good, as if it had been healing for a month or more.

"I was wounded," said Terradyn.

"That was me," Erik said, turning to look over his shoulder. "It was the only way I could think of to stop you."

A flash of anger crossed Terradyn's face, but then it faded.

"Did you mean to raise the dead?" Erik asked.

Terradyn didn't say anything for a moment. The blue jay above clicked and then chirped angrily.

"Yes," Terradyn finally replied.

"Why?"

"I could think of nothing else. I didn't know anything else. It was the only way to stop the elves," Terradyn said flatly.

The blue jay made another sound and then flew over to another tree.

"Can you ride?" Erik asked, and Terradyn nodded. "We need to go," Erik added.

"Where?" Terradyn asked.

"We follow the blue jay."

Terradyn followed Erik as this man followed some stupid bird from tree to tree. He ignored the distant voices and sounds, although they seemed quieter since they had fought the four elves. He had touched the deepest, darkest part of his limited magical abilities, conjured by rote a spell his master had taught him for the direst of situations. He never thought he would have to use it, and he didn't know what would happen to him if he did. Now he knew. Erik had stabbed him, but if he hadn't ... Terradyn thought he probably would have died. Now he rubbed his wound, itching as it healed with remarkable speed. Another benefit of being the Black Mage's personal guard.

He didn't remember anything from when he first cast the spell to the moment he awoke. Rather, he didn't remember anything from the real world. He remembered his dreams ... vividly. Darkness. A great abyss. The smell and stench of death, of piss and shit, of blood, bile, and guts. If he had to guess, it was the ninth level of the nine hells. He could not imagine anything worse.

Terradyn had seen things that most people would consider strange at best, frightening at worst. He had seen all manner of beastly creatures, abominations created by the worst evil of sick and twisted wizards. But the things he saw, he experienced, in his dreams ... they would haunt him forever when nothing had ever disturbed his sleep before. The worst of the memories, the scariest, was simply a huge shadow. Massive in comparison to all the many demonic creatures that came to visit him, it was formless, shapeless, faceless, but it brought with it a chilling sensation that introduced him to raw terror for the first time. There was something else there, though, another shadow, although it had the shape of a giant man ... a man Terradyn recognized.

*Patûk Al'Banan.*

At least, it was a version of the once great general of Golgolithul. All Terradyn really knew was that both sides were evil ... pure evil. He had seen his country—Golgolithul—do some horrible things. He had seen the Lord of the East commit terrible atrocities. He had experienced the full wrath of the Black Mage, but none of that compared to the simple feeling of dread and evil he felt in this black place. And then he woke up, Erik pulling him to his feet.

"Where are we going?" Terradyn asked, seeking to distract himself from the memories. He'd have enough of those when he slept..

"Following the jay," Erik replied without looking back at him. The white snow cat plodded along in front of Erik, stopping intermittently and sniffing at the ground or air, only to continue before Erik could fully catch up to her.

*Of course, what else would we do in this godforsaken place except follow a bird?*

As stupid as Terradyn thought it was, he couldn't help noticing the blue jay would flutter from one branch to another and then wait. They would catch up, and it would call out before fluttering further ahead. As he got more used the idea, the pleasant sound of the blue jay was a welcomed change to the distant, ghostly noises that had caused the hairs on the back of his neck to rise.

Terradyn then noticed Thala stopping, even though they had yet to reach the blue jay again. He felt it, too. The slightest prick of magic. Not his. Someone else's. Not the elves, though. It was familiar —the smell, the taste, the feel.

*Isutan.*

Ankara picked her way slowly through the dense forest of Ul'Erel. She barely touched her magic, giving her the ability to see in the darkness. A large group of elves had just passed her by, accompanied by Kishma—burly men with the heads of bulls or bison—and Kaylytha—creatures with the torsos and heads of elves but the bodies of powerful stallions and mares. Whatever had happened, whatever had opened a doorway between this world and that of the dead, was not the elves' doing. They were scared. But with so many of the Sylvan—elves and all the creatures related to them—nearby, she couldn't touch more than just a small amount of her magic ... It would be her undoing.

Ever since the calamitous breakthrough, the voice of the cloaked man from her dreams was in the back of her head. The presence of the undead must have allowed him in, given him a firmer foothold back in the world of the living, back into her world. But as much as she wanted his presence gone, he was proving useful, giving her directions when to stop or go left or right. He knew where she would find her—their—goal.

Even though his presence gave her power, she could feel him mocking her. He thought nothing of her, and she knew as much. She was a pawn in whatever plan he had, but he needed her, and that was enough. She continued, this phantom guiding her because when the moment of truth came, she would turn the tables. When the prize was his to take, she would snatch it from him and ... Her thoughts were broken by her sensing a different presence, another source of magic that wasn't Sylvan. It was eastern. Golgolithulian. Ankara hid behind a tree and peered under a low branch. The voice in her mind asked:

*What is it?*

*Terradyn.*

Then she sensed something else, a different presence, and she knew who it was. But how? He was dead. Patûk had told her as much. It was no matter. He was moving ever closer to her, and she would kill him again. She would also kill Terradyn.

*Kill them both and give me their bodies.*

She nodded as is if Patûk was beside her. Now was not the time to hide her magic; she needed it. She produced her bow, her green eyes blazing as she nocked an arrow and pulled the fletching to her cheek.

"Kill," she whispered.

## 66

*E*rik couldn't see the bird, and he stopped, Terradyn close behind him. He turned and saw the blue tattoos on his scalp lighting up the space around him.

"No!" Erik said.

Terradyn looked at him, then back at the forest behind them. Something flashed, and he pushed Warrior out of the way as an arrow passed by them and thudded into a tree. Erik slipped from the saddle and stumbled to the ground, but was soon back to his feet, falchion drawn as he grabbed his shield from Warrior's side. At first, he thought Terradyn was the aggressor, but then he peered into the forest and saw her.

"Isutan," Erik hissed.

She came up in a crouch, bow in hand, arrow drawn, and fired. Then again. The two arrows flew towards Erik, fired quicker than anyone should have been able to move. He dodged one and, turning, his shield blocked the other. She pushed out with a hand, and a ball of air struck him in the chest. He watched the canopy overhead pass by as he flew through the air and gasped for air again when he struck the trunk of a tree, all the oxygen escaping his lungs.

Terradyn drew his massive sword. The Isutan laughed.

"Men and their swords."

She fired another arrow, this one at Terradyn. He tried cutting it out of the air, but it struck him, a glancing blow on the shoulder before thunking into another tree. He grunted but seemed to ignore the pain, balling up the fist of his free hand and punching the air. Vines and roots shot up from the ground, all around the Isutan, but, as the vines and roots grabbed at her, she leaped through the air, did summersaults, and avoided the attack. She landed on her feet, just a few paces from the henchman, and was about to fire another arrow when Thala growled and leaped at her.

Even though the snow cat moved with blinding speed, the assassin still had time to aim and release the arrow, which struck the cat in the chest. Thala yelped and crumpled to the ground, trying to get back up, but the Isutan put her foot on the cat's head, pointing yet another arrow at her head.

"No!" Erik said, dropping both sword and shield before he charged at the Isutan.

He must have taken her by surprise as she turned just a little too late. The arrow grazed his cheek, but he drove his shoulder into her stomach, his arms wrapping around her legs and lifting her in the air, every intention of driving her into the ground. But as he tried to drop her, her strength was way beyond her diminutive size, she rolled and twisted and turned, scissoring her legs around his body. She pulled hard on one of his arms, bending it in a direction it was never meant to bend.

Erik's shoulder would have dislocated again, and his arm would have broken, but he remembered his uncle telling him there was no such thing as a fair fight. Her legs moved up to his chest as she twisted and bent his arm, but that was close enough for him to lean forward and bite her inner thigh. She wore leathers, but he put all his strength into the bite and felt skin and flesh tear as his mouth filled with blood.

The Isutan screamed and let go of Erik, grabbing her leg before hissing through gritted teeth. She rolled backward, coming to a crouched position, two short swords appearing in her hands.

"You can't win," she said.

"You're a fool to try and kill me in this place," Erik said.

"You're the fool," she replied, "to think you can enter this place and then exit with your life. At least I have some experience with elves and the sylvan folk."

Erik shrugged. He looked at her emerald green eyes. She wasn't a liar, but she wasn't telling the whole truth either.

"Perhaps," he said.

She shuffled forward, in her fighting stance. Erik lifted his hands, shuffling backward and toward the falchion as Terradyn was moving forward. This wouldn't be an easy fight for her.

"I thought you were dead," she said.

"I was," Erik replied.

"Just like Patûk."

Erik shook his head.

"You work for Patûk now," he replied. "I thought you worked for the Lord of the East."

"I work for myself."

Terradyn was behind him now, and he handed Erik the falchion.

"What price did you pay for your life?" she asked.

"A slight alteration to my hair color. Not as high as what Patûk paid. He sold his soul."

"If he had one," she said with a short mirthless laugh.

"What treasure has Patûk promised you?" Erik asked. "Is it greater than what Syzbalo has offered? What if I offered you something even greater?"

She tilted her head, one eyebrow raised.

"How do you know his name?" she asked.

"The Lord of the East?" Erik replied.

She nodded.

"The wind told me," Erik said with a smile.

"Riddles," the assassin said, rolling her eyes.

"Many wise men I know speak in riddles."

"Fools speak in riddles," she replied.

Erik shrugged.

"The Lord of the East offered me slaves and money. For that, he wants the Dragon Sword," she explained. "Patûk has offered me the Dragon Sword—for myself—and power. For that, he wants the Dragon Stone. I decided I will go with Patûk ... and maybe kill Syzbalo with the sword for being an arrogant prick."

"It is unfortunate you think that way," Erik said, "for the Dragon Sword is no longer the Dragon Sword."

"More riddles, and I don't care. I've seen it. I've seen what it can do, and I have an idea that what I have seen is only a small portion of the power locked inside that blade."

She smirked again and stepped closer to Erik. If she weren't so evil, she would have been a beautiful woman, with olive-colored skin that looked smooth and without blemish, almond-shaped green eyes shadowed by dark brows and lashes, a little, button nose, and a lithe body that spoke of years of training in many different martial art forms. As she stepped a little closer to Erik, he could feel the air around him tighten with Terradyn's magic.

"So, what could you offer me?" she asked.

Erik looked at her. He watched her body, her face, her shoulders, and her eyes. Despite all her bravado, her magic, and her skills, he sensed she was out of her depth. She was scared, and he saw her fear, deep inside those beautiful eyes. She was afraid of this place—Ul'Erel—of him and Terradyn, of the Lord of the East, of Patûk Al'Banan, but she was too proud to admit it, probably even to herself.

"I can offer you the greatest gift of all," Erik said.

"Oh, and what is that?" she asked.

It was his turn to step closer. She was short, her face perhaps chest level to him, and she looked up at him, still a pretense of strength and fierceness in her eyes. She could have stabbed him, slashed him with her swords, but she didn't.

"Your life," Erik replied. "Leave with your life. Return to Isuta.

Ignore Patûk. Ignore him when he haunts your dreams. Avoid the Lord of the East and Golgolithul altogether. And stay away from my family. Go home and keep your life."

She stepped back, rolling her eyes again. More pretenses. More posturing.

"I'm not afraid of you," she said. "I'm not afraid of the Lord of the East. I'm not afraid of Patûk Al'Banan, whatever he is now. And I'm not afraid of this place."

"You are a bad liar," Erik said. "You are afraid of all those things, but mostly, you are afraid of me."

She laughed loudly, and it was genuine, a hearty, guttural laugh that showed true amusement.

"And why would I be afraid of you?" she asked.

"Because I am your failure," Erik said.

She squinted her emerald eyes.

"Failure?" she hissed.

"Exactly," he replied. "You serve the Lord of the East because he has offered you money and slaves, and you know that you could probably beat him without a special sword. You know Patûk Al'Banan could probably defeat you in combat, but he is something otherworldly. He is made of a powerful, dark magic, and so you are all right with his ability to defeat you and control you... for now. And this place... this is a place made from magic and, so, again, you are at peace with the fear you have of Ul'Erel. But me ... I am nothing. I am a man. I know no magic. I have no power beyond what the Creator has given me and what I have learned from training. And, now, I have a normal sword, made of normal steel. And, yet, you don't know that you could defeat me, one on one, in combat. That is *what* scares you. It frightens you and frustrates you and infuriates you that a normal man might be able to beat you, defeat you ... kill you. I am your failure."

She laughed again, but there was an essence of it being forced.

"You are truly a fool if that is what you think. I could kill you with barely an effort."

"Then do it," Erik said. "Fight me now—not the two of us, just me—in this place, without your magic, with just your training. Kill me and prove that I am not your greatest failure."

"With your friend ready to pounce," she replied. "I think not."

"He will not intervene," Erik said, "and if you kill me, he will let you go."

She stared at Erik, and then at Terradyn. She stepped back, shaking her head.

"Then go home," Erik said.

"We will meet again," she said as she walked backward.

"I truly hope not," Erik said as she backed away and into the trees. "If we do, it will mean your death."

Her laughter echoed through the trees as she fled, but this time it was decidedly false.

## 67

*E*rik knelt next to Thala, her breathing shallow as blood soaked her white fur. He couldn't just remove the arrow, dug deep into her flesh. That alone would have killed her. She looked up at Erik, her eyes wide with fear and pain. As he rubbed her head and neck, she still purred under his touch. It was her only way of communicating.

"Can you heal her?" Erik asked.

Terradyn just stared down at them.

"Can you?" Erik asked.

"I don't know," Terradyn replied. "What the Black Mage taught me was only for myself."

"You can bridge the world of the living with the world of the dead," Erik said, more to himself than to Terradyn, "but you can't heal an injured animal. Can you at least help me get her onto Warrior? We need to find the bird."

Erik snapped off the remaining shaft of the arrow and tried lifting the snow cat, to at least start to get her off the ground, but she was big, muscular, and heavy. Terradyn bent down beside him, and as they moved her, she gave a low growl. Thala was Erik's companion—his friend—but she was still a wild animal, and she was scared and in pain. They stopped, and before they could attempt to move her again, the blue jay reappeared and began calling loudly and frantically. Erik looked at the bird, willing she would understand the need to wait, but when he looked down again, he saw a white mist rising from the earth and swirling about them.

"What by the nine hells!" Terradyn said as the mist swirled about him, and he began to cough as he breathed it in.

When the mist touched Erik's skin, it burned, leaving his arms red and itchy. At first, he wondered if this was the work of Patûk and Yebritoch, or the undead, or even the Isutan assassin, but when he heard voices in the mist—elvish voices—he knew it was more of the magic of Ul'Erel. Thala growled as the mist covered her, and when she coughed, blood appeared on her muzzle.

"Quickly," Erik said, coughing too, "we need to get her onto Warrior."

The horse stamped a hoof as the mist swirled about his legs, but it didn't seem to cause him pain. Terradyn and Erik hefted Thala onto his back, draping her—belly down—over his saddle. She looked uncomfortable, and her breathing was uneasy and shallow, but it at least got her above the rising mist.

"We need to go," Terradyn said, grabbing Shadow's reins.

Erik looked up at the blue jay, and the bird fluttered to the next tree.

They led their horses as fast as they could through the dense forest, but the mist followed them and blotted out any hint of light that found its way through the canopy above. Terradyn stopped to light two torches, but they struggled to catch fire, and when they did, they did little more than give off a hazy glow. In the darkness, Erik found himself having to only listen for the blue jay when it perched on a branch that was even the smallest amount above head-height.

Voices followed them as much as the mist did, and even though they were decidedly Elvish, Erik couldn't help thinking they sounded liked curses, angry and hateful. He stopped suddenly, Terradyn almost running into him.

"What are you ..." Terradyn began, but his voice trailed off.

The mist that swirled upwards in front of Erik was forming a cloud that began to take the shape of something, and a partially translucent, humanoid figure appeared, blocking the narrow path they had been following. At first, it looked harmless, like shapes in the clouds, but what might have been its head turned, exposing black orbs that stared at Erik. Below the eyes, a wide maw opened, and the scream that erupted from the apparition's mouth shook the leaves and branches all around them, and Erik dropped Warrior's reins, clutching his ears.

Erik started to yell, but the phantasm of mist swirled and streamed into his open mouth and down his throat. He choked as he felt the thickened mist enter his lungs, and then it seemed to be seeping into his whole body. His arms and legs became stiff, and he could feel it moving about in his stomach. It burned, and he wanted to scream but couldn't.

His vision became hazy as the mist floated behind his eyes, but then it seemed to be moving through them. He could feel it in his ears, and then he gave a huge cough, and as quickly as the mist had entered his body, it left again, forming the same rough image of a humanoid in front of Erik, and he heard it let out a cackling laugh.

"We have to keep moving," Terradyn said, the blue tattoos on his head glowing.

At first, the mist seemed to shy away from him, but then it began jabbing with finger-like projections. Mist should have been harmless, but every spot on Terradyn's skin where it touched formed a red welt and the magical light in the runes on his head dimmed at each attack. It almost seemed as if it was seeking to extract the defensive magic.

Erik tried moving forward quickly, but the mist that eddied around his ankles became thick, and he felt as if he was walking in mud. Two more apparitions rose from the carpet of vapor flowing along the forest floor, both vaguely human in appearance. They twisted and moved as smoke caught in a breeze, lashing out at Erik and Terradyn, caring nothing for their horses. One strike burnt, while the next felt like claws raking across flesh. One would fill his nostrils and mouth, making him choke, while another would seem to pierce his ears like a deafening screech.

Just as Erik thought things could not get any worse, he felt something crawling up his legs and, when the sickening fog parted enough for him to see through it, thorny vines and roots were wrapping themselves around his boots and legs, digging into his flesh and holding him in place. As Erik's breathing quickened, the earth rumbled, and the ground moved to reveal a skeleton, held upright by the vines and roots of trees. The bone of this lost soul was white and void of any lasting tissue, and all Erik could think of was that this must have been the evil mist's last victim.

A deep red glowed in the skeleton's eye sockets; its mandible fell open, and, along with the apparitions, it screamed Erik and Terradyn's doom. Whirling sounds drowned out the incessant call of the jay as tiny lights darted about all around them, but when they struck flesh, they were like a dart, stinging and drawing blood. The grunts coming from Terradyn said he experienced the same thing, but the lights caused Erik to remember something.

"Warrior! Come here!" Erik called, and the horse, seemingly able to move freely because he posed no threat, arrived at his side.

But as Erik maneuvered the animal so he could reach his haversack, the mist must have recognized that the horse was Erik's ally, for the animal screamed and bucked, throwing Thala off his back as creepers tightened around the destrier's legs and red welts began to pepper his gray fur. Erik thrust a hand into his haversack and pulled out a large pouch. He pulled away the string that held it closed, and a light emanated from the bag, illuminating Erik's face in a bright whiteness. Erik reached in and grabbed a handful of moon fairy dust, more than he had ever used before, and blew it from his palm. He prayed it would work because if it didn't, they would all be dead soon.

Thousands of motes of white dust floated through the air, and as they began to descend, the apparitions began to twist and gyrate, seeking to avoid the tiny specs of light. But their dance of evasion was futile, and as the dust settled, the screeching became even louder, and Erik could feel the vines and creepers slither away. Then, as the mist dissipated, Terradyn's magic strengthened. The blue runes flashed to life, his eyes glowed a brilliant blue, and he swiped at one of the phantoms with his sword.

Whatever magic spell it was he'd cast, it made the dust-weakened specters turn to flesh and blood, and they screamed when the steel passed through it before disappearing. The dirt-covered skeleton burst into countless pieces as the fairy dust settled on it and slowly, as Erik's heart rate slowed to a more normal pace, peace and quiet descended upon the forest.

"Damned elves," Terradyn muttered. "I'm getting tired of these pointy-eared devils."

"Me too," Erik agreed.

As the mist disappeared, so did the wounds that it caused, and the welts and burns faded. Terradyn helped Erik pick up Thala again, the great snow cat now unconscious and barely clinging to life. Erik cursed himself for not thinking of it before, but he retrieved the white cloth the ogres had given him and wrapped some of it around Thala's torso. He prayed he wasn't too late.

## 68

The blue jay led them to a tree line, which opened to a narrow glade bordering a wide ravine, to their left was a bridge crossing a chasm that Erik thought he recognized. A wall of rock rose across from their side of the gorge, a cliff above looking over, a small waterfall falling from an opening in the wall. There was no canopy here, so the sun shed as much light as it could, despite a cliff and trees, and Erik welcomed the full sunlight. Ul'Erel was a temperate place, but the weather in this part was hot and humid.

The bridge reminded him of the one in the Gray Mountains that looked as if it were made of ice. As much as the weather pattern moving into the forest had been, that bridge had been guarded by an ice drake and ice golems, but when they eventually crossed it, the world around them became warm and tropical. It was a bridge that had led them to a mystical place and a broken tower made of alabaster white stone. Erik stuck a hand in the money pouch that hung from his belt. He felt two smooth stones in there—one as red as a ruby, and the other as green as an emerald. The red one was a gift from the gypsy Marcus—he had two once, but one had been used to defeat the dragon—and the other, the green stone, he had found in that broken tower.

The jay came to perch on the stone wall at the side of the bridge, and as Erik turned towards it, in the sunlight, he saw the fairy dust had stayed with them, floating around in a protective cloud.

"I've seen this bridge before," Erik said.

"How?" Terradyn asked.

"In the Gray Mountains. It was a bridge made of ice, but turned to black iron as we walked across it."

"Sounds like elvish magic," Terradyn said. "Elvish illusions."

"Why do you think the weather is so different in here?" Erik retorted. Terradyn seemed to be more grumpy since the incident with the dead. "Anyway, it led through a tunnel, and on the other side was a meadow surrounded by a white wall. What looked to once be a tower stood in the middle of the meadow, but it had crumbled and broken so that only the first floor was still there."

"And inside this broken tower?" Terradyn asked, his voice more level having been rebuked.

"Broken statues. An altar. A book with names, only half the pages had been filled. And this," Erik said as he dug into his belt pouch, retrieving the smooth, white stone he had found in the fallen tower.

"An ioun stone," Terradyn said. "I know what they are, but I've only seen one once."

"What are they?"

"Powerful magic," Terradyn said, "Put it away."

As Erik had held the stone in his hand, Terradyn's tattoos had begun to glow, and as fairy dust settled all around them, the earth in front of the bridge began to rise and shake. Both Erik and Terradyn stepped back as two fully-formed drakes rose from the ground, their scales a brilliant green that shimmered like gold—or dragon scales—in the sunlight. Ridges ran above the animals' eyes and around their nostrils, and moss hung in clumps from their chins, giving them the appearance of having thick, unkempt, green beards. Pink tongues flicked from the drakes' mouths, and they stared at the two men with red eyes.

"I don't know if I ever thought I would say this," Terradyn said, exasperation in his voice, "but I'm getting tired of fighting."

This time, Erik had to agree with his companion's mood.

"So am I," he said.

*Your flute.*

The words came into his mind from a woman's voice, and it sounded like the she-elf from his dream. He removed the small wooden instrument, another gift from his gypsy friend, Marcus, from his haversack and lifted it towards his mouth. What was he supposed to play? His mind so fatigued and worried, he couldn't conjure up the memory of a single tune he'd played before, but then the jay began to sing. This more tuneful than the urging call it had been repeating, and it caught the attention of the two drakes. So that's what Erik played, the jay's song.

The bird would chirrup a few notes, and Erik would mimic the sound on his flute like an echo. In time with the simple song, the fairy dust rose again and began to dance in the air as if caught on a swirling, gentle breeze, and then it floated down around the two drakes. Their tongues flickered in and out, catching some of the dust until they eventually lowered themselves to the ground, slowly closing their eyes before, once again, melding into the forest floor as if they were just gentle mounds of dirt.

"I think it's safe to go now," Erik said.

"Are you sure?" Terradyn asked.

"No," Erik replied but added a brief smile to the quick shake of his head.

Stepping past the earthen mounds that had been the drakes, they led the horses onto the bridge. The design and construction of the bridge were exactly like the one in the Gray Mountains, and as Erik looked over the side of the bridge, he stared at a deep chasm. He could see the bottom, many paces below, where a river cut through the steep-sided canyon. The bridge led to a small tunnel, much like before, and on the other side, they came upon a meadow, and a narrow road, made of smoothed rock, led to a gate set into a tall, white wall. This was yet another repeat of what Erik had experienced in the Gray Mountains, the only difference was the absence of Bryon and the dwarves ... Thoughts of them once more brought Simone to mind, but he sought to focus on the task in hand; now was not the time to worry about guilt or wallow in self-pity.

They walked to the gate, a simple double door with a large, iron loop that hung loosely on either side.

"No guards," Erik said.

Terradyn grabbed one of the iron loop handles, and Erik took the other, and they pulled. After a moment of struggle, the gate finally opened, and they came upon a tall tower, standing in the center of a large glade. It looked the antithesis of the horrific black tower at Fealmynster; this pristine white stricture was so tall it should have been visible on the other side of the wall.

The road of paved rocks continued towards the entrance of the tower, around which animals of all sorts scurried about. The squirrels with tall ears that seemed plentiful in the forest were here too, along with small, spotted deer, young foxes, and rabbits. Erik heard a squawk overhead, and when he looked up, a bird floated above him in the air, its multi-colored tail feathers long and graceful.

"This is so similar to where I was before," Erik said.

"Elvish meadows and a white tower were all over the world at one time," Terradyn replied.

"What happened?"

"A story for another time, perhaps. Look."

Erik's eyes followed Terradyn's pointing finger, and he saw the blue jay flutter around the door of the tower. It gave its instructional call and then flew away.

"Stay here," Erik said to Warrior, the unconscious Thala still draped over his saddle.

Erik grabbed his shield, strapped it across his back, and, with Terradyn a pace behind him, walked to the door, gripped the iron loop of a handle, and pulled. It opened into a room that consumed the whole of the first floor, and they were met with shouting, an argument, and Erik was surprised they had not heard it from outside the tower.

The she-elf from his dream stood next to a large, white altar, and she was yelling at another elf, a male, who stood across the altar from her. He had golden hair that looked as brilliant as the she-elf's and wore a sleeveless tunic that showed pale skin and muscular arms that any farmer would covet. About his head, he wore a circlet of simple twisted gold, made to look like forest vines, and when he turned to see Erik and his companion, his eyes were a light purple that shifted to a dark blue, back to purple. That was when Erik saw it, hanging from the male elf's hip. Dragon Tooth.

## 69

*T*he elf carrying Dragon Tooth pointed at Erik and yelled something in Elvish.

"I believe he's suggesting we shouldn't be here," Terradyn whispered in Erik's ear. The she-elf confirmed his supposition when she retorted in Westernese.

"This place was built for all people once. All of the towers were," she said, glaring at the elf who shouted something back.

"And what makes it a lesser language, and why not here?" she replied. "Who says these men are our enemies?"

The elf just rolled his eyes and looked back at Erik.

"That is your problem, sister," the elf said, finally speaking in Westernese.

Erik looked from one elf to the other and now noted several similarities.

*Sister. That makes sense.*

"These idiots have to know that you ignore the superiority of the Elenderel, you and so many others, and here we are, hidden away in Ul'Erel," the elf said, throwing up his hands as if to present the place in which they stood. "What you speak of is blasphemy."

"You are the blasphemer, brother," she retorted. "Speaking of superiority. That is why we are here and not living amongst our brothers and sisters in the world."

She took a step towards Erik as if to present him.

"Brothers and sisters," the elf spat. "You are truly lost," he added and then said something in Elvish.

The she-elf looked at Erik and smiled. He smiled and nodded back. The elf leaped over the altar, landed next to his sister, pushing her behind him.

"Do not look upon the Lady El'Kesh," the elf said. "You are not worthy."

"Stop it, you fool," she said, struggling to get past her brother.

*So, this is El'Beth El'Kesh, which meant this other is Jart'El El'Kesh.*

Erik knew from Dewin that this elf hated men, hated anything that wasn't sylvan, and ... he had hated Rako.

"You have my sword," Erik said, trying to keep his voice as flat and calm as possible.

Being so close to Dragon Tooth, it was as if it had begun to call him. He felt drawn to it, as if he needed it to survive, and knew it was truly his and was meant to hang from his hip and no other.

*Erik, you are here.*

It was Rako's voice. Erik hadn't heard it in so long. His friend, his sentient dagger, the voice that had helped him through so much and saved his life more times than he could count. He had missed Rako. At least his voice.

*It wasn't easy, Rako, but I got this far.*

*You must retrieve the sword from Jart'El, and prevent him from using the Dragon Stone. He has it, and you must take it from him.*

"This pathetic man is the fool," Jart'El said, looking at Erik over his nose.

Erik had heard that accusation before, from the dragon as she looked down on him and his companions in the Southern Mountains. It was a statement of disgust and assumed superiority. He was not the fool because he never considered himself above another, except when they were a threat to those he loved or what he believed to be right.

"Do you not know that this sword is an elvish sword," Jart'El asked, "meant to be wielded by elvish hands?"

"Crafted by dwarves," Erik said.

"Bah!" Jert'El said, throwing a hand up in the air.

"Your hate has blinded you, Jart'El," Erik said, keeping his voice even and, clearly looking for a fight, this enraged the arrogant elf even more.

"How dare you refer to me as if you know me?" Jart'El replied.

"You have been in this world for so many years, yet you still act like a petulant child?"

The elf's face went from pale to red, and he stepped forward, his left hand going to Dragon Tooth's and closing around the handle. He drew the sword, and the sight of the dwarvish steel with a raven and the name *Dragon Fire* carved into it made Erik's heart race. The steel had a green tint to it, but there was no flame as there had been before when he wielded it. It wasn't Jart'El's sword.

"You are indeed a brainless fool," Erik taunted.

The elf fumed and took another step forward. Terradyn moved to step in front of Erik, a show of protection, performing his master's bidding, but the elf held up a hand, and the man flew backward, landing in a heap with a loud and pain-filled groan.

Erik looked at Terradyn and then back to Jart'El. He shrugged as if unimpressed with the elf's magic.

"Don't you see," Erik said. "That blade is no longer the same blade as the Dragon Sword. It is dwarvish steel. Forged by Ilken Copper Head. His mark is on the blade. Surely you can read Dwarvish, even though it is an inferior language."

Jart'El didn't want to, but he couldn't resist a quick look at the blade.

"And even though it retains some elvish magic," Erik continued, "it is now more imbued with dragon magic."

"Dragon magic?" El'Beth asked, catching a steely glare from her brother.

"Oh yes," Erik said. "I placed the dagger that was forged from the Dragon Sword's shards on the altar at Fealmynster—a place I now suspect was once an elvish meadow and tower like this one. Next to that, I placed my sword, the dwarvish-forged Ilken's Blade, and a piece of dragon tooth I acquired when I used *that* sword to fight the dragon Black Wing outside Fen-Stévock. The reason I did all that was so that Rako could combine them all."

"Rako," El'Beth gasped.

"That traitor" spat her brother.

"He reforged the Dragon Sword," Erik said, finally drawing Mardirru's falchion, "and it is now Dragon Tooth, marked with the raven of Copper Head and marked with my dwarvish clan name—Dragon Fire. You see, it is now my sword, and you will no longer be able to use it control dragons."

Jart'El laughed.

"You men are so stupid," he said, "First, I will strike down Black Wing and her mate, Shadow Tooth. Next, I will strike down that fool of a leader, the Lord of Golgolithul. And then I will bring the world to heel so that they understand the might of the Elenderel and experience the peace that only we can bring the world. I have the Dragon Sword. I have the Dragon Stone. All I need is the Dragon Crown, and I will rise as the first of a new line of Dragon Riders."

*He is no better than Syzbalo. He is no better than Fréden Fréwin. He is no better than any other fool in this world who thinks their people are better than all other living people.*

"And what of the Lord of Chaos? What about Yebritoch?"

"What are you talking about?" Jart'El asked, but then he shrugged his shoulders. "It doesn't matter who tries to stop us, from demons to the Shadow. We will prevail."

"Brother! Have you truly gone mad? What are you," began El'Beth, but Erik held up a hand to silence her.

"What of the Dragon Scroll and the spell?" Erik asked.

"Ha," Jart'El chortled. "I know the spell. I don't need some scroll in order to recite the words. I was there when Rako wrote them, when he created the ability to control dragons."

*Rako?*

*Yes, Erik. It was I who created the Dragon Scroll. In my moment of worst weakness, I was no longer satisfied with just riding dragons, creating an unbreakable bond with some of the most majestic creatures in the world. I wanted to control them.*

Jart'El laughed. He must have seen the look on Erik's face.

"Yes," he said. "Your precious Rako is the one who started all this. He is the wicked one."

Erik shook his head.

"Everyone makes mistakes. He learned from them—has been punished for them—and you want to head down the very same path. Even now, when you know Yebritoch is after the same thing, as well as the Lord of the East and others, you wish to make the same mistakes Rako made."

"The Lord of the East is nothing," Jart'El, "as is Yebritoch, compared to the might of the Elenderel. The Lord of Chaos is nothing, even with his beasts."

Erik charged, falchion held in both hands, but Jart'El leaped out of the way. He jumped onto the altar before flipping over Erik and landing behind him. He was agile and no doubt strong, but Erik turned in time to block a strike from Dragon Tooth. He kicked out, but missed, the elf rolling to the side.

Now back on his feet, Terradyn came to Erik's side again, his massive sword drawn, his blue tattoos on the side of his head glowing. As he swung his sword, the elf rolled forward and came back to his feet. He said a single word, and a bolt of light spread from his left hand and struck Terradyn in the chest. He flew backward again. The fairy dust that had followed them into the tower floated around Jart'El, almost surrounding him, but he waved a hand with a grunt, and the dust fell to the ground as if it were sand thrown into the air.

"Moon fairies," Jart'El said with a disgusted grunt. "Backward and bucolic. What sort of man has earned favor with moon fairies?"

Jart'El looked to be casting another spell, but seemingly in mid incantation, he spun, backhanding Erik and knocking him to a knee. Terradyn was on his feet again, stumbling a bit and weak, but he came at the elf one more time. The elf blocked several attacks, easily knocking the great war sword aside and slashing Dragon Tooth across Terradyn's belly. He stumbled to the side, giving the elf time to cast another spell. A fist made of air and wind punched Terradyn in the chest, sending the man flying across the room again.

"So, will you use your magic on me?" Erik asked. "Or will you fight like a soldier?"

"Oh, I don't need anything special to defeat you," the elf replied.

Jart'El turned hard, bringing Dragon Tooth down towards Erik, but he had retrieved his shield from his back and held it up. The sword glanced off the dwarvish shield, but the elf struck again and again. Pain shot through Erik's body with each strike, and he felt as if he might drop the shield when he saw Terradyn on his feet again. The man's tattoos flashed, and he held out a hand.

"De'sine!" Terradyn yelled, and the elf's sword hand stopped in midair.

As Jart'El struggled against whatever magic held his hand and arm, it gave Erik enough time to stand. It was only a moment, but it was all Jart'El e needed to gather himself again.

"Pathetic magic," he said, turning to face Terradyn, throwing his own hand forward.

The man lifted off the ground and still suspended, the elf made a fist, and Terradyn began to choke. Throwing his hand forward, the man flew through the air, striking the wall near the ceiling, twenty paces high, and then dropped to the floor with a loud crunch. El'Beth cried out her brother's name, and Jart'El turned.

Erik rushed him again, ramming into the elf with his shield. Jart'El looked surprised as Erik pushed him back onto his heels. He swung at the elf, barely missing his face and swung again at his legs.

The elf jumped, only to have to bring Dragon Tooth up to block Erik's third strike.

The elf kicked out, catching Erik on the inner thigh and bringing him to one knee again, and then punched Erik on the nose. Erik's eyes watered, and he felt blood rush from his nostrils. He could taste it in the back of his throat. Erik swung up, but Jart'El caught his wrist. He stared at Erik, looking at him, eye to eye. He was searching for something. He was searching Erik's mind, his thoughts, his memories. Erik could feel it. The elf's eyes went wide.

"Jamalel gave his life essence to you," Jart'El hissed, a snarl on his face. "You think you are special. Others think you are special. You are nothing. You are dust. What a waste."

The elf swung with Dragon Tooth, but this time, it was Erik who caught his wrist, dropping his shield and reaching up. As he caught Jart'El's wrist, his fingers touched the hilt of Dragon Tooth. The blade glowed a brilliant green. A flame sparked and spread along the steel. Jart'El's eyes widened, and Erik smiled. He felt the resistance in the elf's arm give by the smallest amount, but it was enough for Erik to push Jart'El's arm towards his face.

The blade touched the elf's cheek, and he screamed as his flesh seared, leaving an angry, red wound. He dropped the sword and kicked out at Erik, sending the man back. Erik dove at the sword, but Jart'El, ignoring the wound on his face, was reaching for it too, but something stopped his arms from moving. Erik's hand wrapped around Dragon Tooth's handle, and he slid along the stone floor on his stomach. He came to his feet quickly and saw El'Beth chanting quietly, both hands lifted to the ceiling, and her eyes glowing a brilliant purple. She was helping him against her own brother.

Jart'El finally broke free and faced his sister. He said a single word, and El'Beth's flowing, white gown fluttered, tightened around her body, pinning her arms to her sides, and a piece of a sash that she wore around her waist slithered up her body like a snake and wrapped itself around her mouth. She struggled to speak against the cloth, but it was no use. Erik gripped Dragon Tooth with both hands.

Jart'El's eyes went wide as green flame burned along the blade of Dragon Tooth, and a calm came over Erik as he held the sword that was especially made for him. He smiled as the elf pushed his hand forward, lightning coming from his fingertips, but Erik easily blocked the attack with his sword. The green blade seemed to consume the magical attack, each bolt causing the flames to glow brighter and fiercer. The elf struck again and again, each time, with the same result.

Erik looked beyond the elf, watching as El'Beth's face turned red as she screamed against the cloth covering her mouth. She closed her eyes, breathed in deeply, and wailed. The gag tore to pieces, bits of fabric floating gently to the floor, and her gown loosened, and she lifted her hands again.

"*Brother! Stop!*" she yelled. "*He'll kill you!*"

Jart'El ignored her and stepped towards Erik, who readied Dragon Tooth. Jart'El was beyond reason, and Erik remembered a position his friend Wrothgard had taught him, one to use when faced with a such a man who was as strong as he was angry. Erik would crouch and jab … the Striking Viper.

"*Brother!*" El'Beth screamed one more time, but still, he ignored her.

He lifted his hands in front of him and sparks appeared between his palms as they faced each other. They turned into a small ball of flame, which grew bigger as the elf chanted, its red light glowing against the elf's face and lighting up the wound on his cheek. Erik remained in his crouch and then, as Jart'El moved to throw the ball of flame at him, Erik punched his blade forward and closed his eyes.

Erik expected to be washed over by deadly fire, but he heard a gasp and pain didn't come. He had felt his sword strike something and after a deep breath, he pushed harder. When he opened his eyes, Jart'El looked down at him, his hand still ready to throw a magical ball of flame that was no longer there. Hate, surprise, regret, and despair all seemed to fill his eyes before he looked down to see Dragon Tooth driven into his belly, hilt deep.

Erik looked at El'Beth. Her hands were extended, towards Jart'El. She had stopped him again, frozen him to save Erik. Tears filled her eyes as Jart'El crumpled to the floor, and Erik retrieved his blade. El'Beth dropped her hands, and they both took a few short breaths as they stared at each other. Between them on the floor, his hate and anger still with him, Jart'El drew his last gulp of air.

## 70

*E*l'Beth El'Kesh knelt on the floor, Jart'El's head resting in her lap, and wept freely, her tears falling over his face. He didn't look angry anymore, and the wound on his cheek where Dragon Tooth had burned him looked to be an even greater contrast to the dead elf's placid features.

"He was almost two thousand years old," El'Beth said, rocking back and forth with her brother's head in her hands.

"I'm sorry," Erik said as she began to sob, grief-stricken for the loss of one so close to her for so long. Erik waited until she'd cried out all of her tears, and eventually, she wiped her eyes and nose with a sleeve.

"He wasn't always this way," she muttered and then sniffed. "He was good, once. Righteous. It wasn't until the Great Schism ... and Rako ..."

"Why did you help me?" Erik asked.

"Why? Because he was wrong, and you are right. It was not about elf against man, but good against evil. That was what he had become. Hatred and anger have been consuming him for the last thousand years," El'Beth said and then looked up at Erik with red eyes. "Do you know what is imprisoned in the Dragon Stone?"

"Rako," Erik replied.

She shook her head gently as she stroked her brother's face and tidied his hair.

"He is, but that is not all. How can I describe this? Jart'El had gone astray, diving deeper and deeper into a sickness that turned all of his good intentions into evil ones. You know who Yebritoch is?"

Erik nodded.

"Have you ever heard of his Beasts of Chaos?" El'Beth asked.

"I have," Erik replied. "A dwarvish friend told me a story about them. But it sounded like just that, a story."

"It's no fable," El'Beth said. "Eons ago—a long, long time before Jart'El or I were born—Yebritoch was served by four beasts, one in each of the four corners of the world, but all were imprisoned—in a battle supposed to end all battles—in stones by four elves, all dragon riders. What you refer to as the Dragon Stone is one of those stones. Its green color means it is known as the Emerald of the East and is the resting place of Orentus, the Beast of the East."

"But Rako was imprisoned in there as well?" Erik asked.

"That was my brother's solution, his punishment for Rako," she replied. "Rako would be tormented for all eternity in the same prison as one of the most devastating forces the world had ever known."

"So why is it called the Dragon Stone?" Erik asked.

"Because it held the last, true Dragon Rider; Rako was the sole descendent of the Dragon Rider who commanded the battle that captured the beasts," El'Beth said. "When the stone was taken from Jart'El by those who knew he would use it for evil, it was given to the people of Hargoleth. It was easier to tell them it was an ancient, petrified dragon egg."

"So you lied to them?" Erik asked.

"My people did, yes," El'Beth replied.

El'Beth rested her brother's head gently on the ground and stood.

She walked to Terradyn, lying unconscious on the floor. She touched him on his forehead, just with the tip of her index finger, and he breathed deeply. As if time had been speeded up, a deep gash on his forehead began knitting together, and bruises on his face disappeared. Erik presumed that any injuries beneath his clothing would also be healed. She left him in a deep sleep, also resting his head gently on the floor.

"Now bring in your cat," El'Beth said, standing up. "I saw she was badly hurt."

Erik opened the large double doors, clicked his tongue, and Warrior trotted into the room. The she-elf removed the white, ogre cloth from the snow cat and touched her gently between her eyes. In only a few moments, the animal stirred, looked around, and leaped frantically from Warrior's back. The wound on her chest gone, her bloodied fur was pure white once again. El'Beth reached down, open palm to Thala, and the snow cat licked her hand. She scratched the cat behind the ear and then shooed her and Warrior back out of the room. They left as if they had been following her orders for years.

"She loves you," El'Beth said as she closed the door behind the animals. "Thala would give her life for you. As would Eroan. Although, you still call him Warrior. Terradyn would as well. He came to you as a task from his master, but now he wishes to protect you for himself."

Erik glanced at the sleeping Terradyn and then looked down at his feet.

"That is a special gift, Erik, to have friends willing to lay down their lives for you," El'Beth said.

"Or a curse, Lady El'Beth," Erik said, now looking her in the eyes.

"Please, just Beth," she said, and he nodded.

Erik smiled.

"My sister's name is Beth."

"I know," she replied.

She walked to the large, alabaster altar in the middle of the tower floor and lifted her hands. She spoke a few words in Elvish, and a green stone appeared in the middle of the altar.

"This stone," Erik said, "why did your brother want it so badly? Did he just want to prevent Rako from being released?"

Beth shook her head.

"For all of his power, he had no idea it was hidden in the lands of Hargoleth," Beth said with a sad smile. "And a part of me thinks he had forgotten about it over the last several hundred years, even if he wouldn't admit to it. I am sure a part of him wanted the stone so he could simply gloat as Rako's spirit languished in his prison, but ultimately, my brother wanted to release the beast Orentus."

"Release a Beast of Chaos?" Erik asked, eyes wide.

"Yes," Beth replied, shaking her head. "He thought he could control the beast, use it for *good*, at least, the good of the Sylvan folk who agreed with him. The stone, rather Rako, also holds the secret to the Dragon Crown."

"The last piece of the scroll," Erik muttered.

"Yes," Beth replied. "Before his imprisonment, Rako had already given the crown, the dagger, and the scroll back to the dwarves, and they scattered them. Only King Fire Beard and his descendants, King Stone Axe and his descendants, and Rako knew of their locations. You know what happened to Fire Beard. The current King Stone Axe of Thrak Baldüukr admitted to me not too many years ago that they have since lost any indication of where these relics were, and so that leaves Rako."

"So, not only did Jart'El want to control a Chaos Beast, he wanted to control dragons as well?" Erik asked not expecting an answer to the rhetorical question.

"The relics of the Dragon Riders are not just meant to control dragons," Beth said, and she looked to the ceiling, seeing something that wasn't there, something distant and in the past. "The true Dragon Riders and their dragons needed no such artifacts. They had a bond that was unbreakable, a friendship beyond anything, a love beyond any other love."

"Rako's dragon?" Erik whispered with revelation.

Beth looked at him, tears in her eyes.

"His life didn't end when my brother imprisoned him in the stone," she explained. "Rako's life ended the day his pride killed Marduka, the Queen of the Dragons, and his mount. It didn't matter how much I loved him or how much he loved me. His will to live was gone."

"So, why the Crown and Sword?"

"If discovered today, Erik," Beth explained, "they would be symbols of leadership to my people. The elf bearing the sword and wearing the crown would be recognized as the true ruler of the elvish people. And Jart'El would have led our people out of Ul'Erel and to war again. Finding the crown would have led him to the Dragon King as well."

"Dragon King?" Erik asked.

"Yes," Beth replied. "The son of Marduka. He is over a thousand years old, but to dragons, he is only an adolescent, and he is hidden and safe. But now that Black Wing has revealed herself, and has most certainly awakened her mate, Shadow Tooth, they will be searching for Marduka's son. I am sure Jart'El thought he could take the Dragon King as his mount, but it would have never worked. He wasn't a Dragon Rider. He never would be, and any dragon would have killed him if he tried. But, nonetheless, he is in danger and must be found. Only Rako can reveal the way to the crown, and the crown will reveal the way to the Dragon King."

"But why didn't Rako reveal the way before?" Erik asked. "To you, or anyone else?"

"Because of the magic Jart'El used to imprison him in the stone. I couldn't stop my brother from casting the spell to trap Rako's spirit, but I added an element that kept Rako from showing Jart'El—or anyone else—the way before he was trapped. It also kept him from revealing himself to me as he had you—to anyone in Ul'Erel. This was a secret I have kept until now."

"Why?" Erik asked.

"I am a Lady of Ul'Erel, a member of the elvish noble court. So was Jart'El. Whether we believe in reunifying with the rest of the world, staying here in Ul'Erel, or dominating all others, to openly oppose another noble in our court, let alone one as high ranking as my brother, would have made me an outcast."

"So social status was more important than love," Erik said, a twinge of anger in his voice.

Beth must have sensed his frustration. She must have felt it herself, for she turned away slightly, her cheeks coloring with embarrassment.

"It would have meant I couldn't continue my underground resistance against those in our courts that wish to remain secluded here," Beth explained, "or worse, desire to subjugate everyone else in this world. That was the sacrifice I made, my position rather than my love, and believe me, it has eaten away at me for a thousand years. But it was the only way."

"I'm sorry," Erik said, now feeling guilty for his accusation.

"Don't be. I've had a long time to practice burying my memories. My brother did too."

Beth looked longingly at the stone.

"Once we find the crown, the stone must be hidden away again," Beth said. "Orentus must once again be forgotten lest Yebritoch find him and release him. He was the second most powerful of the Chaos Beasts."

She looked at Dragon Tooth.

"The sword will release Rako," Beth said. "He will then show us the way to the Dragon Crown."

"But won't this also release the Beast of Chaos?" Erik asked.

"No," Beth replied, but her voice didn't sound so sure. "It is held in there by a deeper magic. I am sure we will be safe from releasing Orentus."

"You don't sound so sure," Erik said.

She looked at Erik with a small smile.

"I am sure, Erik," Beth said.

"In that case, it will also reunite you with Rako," Erik said, returning the smile.

"No, I'm afraid not, it is simply his spirit. His body has long passed from this world, and he belongs with El. He will show us the way, and then he will be finally able to go to where he truly belongs."

Erik considered this for a moment, and a look of sadness came into his eyes.

"So, if Rako can't be by your side, I can't go home, can I?" Erik asked.

Beth looked at him, tears now in her eyes as they deepened until they were almost black. She shook her head.

"No, Erik, you can't. We need you still. Rako needs you."

With a shrug of acceptance, Erik drew Dragon Tooth, the green flames dancing along the blade, blazing brighter than he had ever seen them before.

"I now understand why Jart'El couldn't use the sword to release Rako. It wasn't his. It didn't belong to him. Only the true wielder can release its former master."

Erik nodded.

"What do we do now, then?" he asked.

"Place the sword on the altar," she commanded. "In that way, you are putting the reforged Dragon Sword next to the one who once wielded it."

Erik nodded, knowing he had to trust her, and he placed his sword on the altar and stepped away. Beth began to chant in Elvish, and as she lifted her hands and closed her eyes, Dragon Tooth's green flame intensified. As it did so, the green Dragon Stone, began to glow, and Beth clapped her hands twice before she opened her eyes and said, "Be free."

The air above the altar shifted and shimmered, and there stood Rako, just as he had in Fealmynster. Beth put her hands to her mouth as she began to cry. Erik smiled.

"It is good to see you, my friend," Erik said.

"And you too," Rako said.

The elf stepped off the altar, and Beth ran to him, tried to throw her arms around him, but she passed right through him as if he wasn't there.

"I am not truly here, my love," Rako said. "You know that. I am no longer bound to the stone, but I am still not truly free."

"How do we truly free you?" Erik asked.

But Rako ignored him. He looked at Beth, and she at him.

"Just one more kiss," she said. "I just want to feel your arms around me one more time."

Rako looked at Erik.

"Erik Eleodum," Rako said. "Erik Dragon Fire. Are you truly my friend?"

"Yes, of course," Erik replied without hesitation.

Rako closed his eyes, and Erik saw a bright flash. He blinked wildly, and when he opened his eyes, Simone stood in front of him.

"My love!" he cried out and ran to her, cupping her cheeks in his hands.

Erik kissed his wife deeply, breathing her in, feeling the warmth of her lips against his, the smell of mint and lavender, the softness of her skin. He wrapped his arms around her waist and pulled her to him, feeling the swell of her belly against his stomach. He would never let go of her, and she held him even tighter.

"I'm sorry," Erik cried.

"Oh, by the Creator, how I have missed you," Simone said.

"My love," Erik said. "I have missed you more than the rose misses the sun at night. No one has missed anyone as much as I have missed you."

They held and kissed each other for a while longer, and when Erik finally pulled away from his wife, still cupping her face, he blinked, and El'Beth stood in front of him. His stomach knotted, and his breath caught in his lungs.

"Oh, I'm sorry. I thought ..." he began to say, but she stopped him by putting a finger to his lips.

"Be still," she said, tears streaming down her cheeks, but a wide smile on her face.

"I don't know what happened," Erik said, dropping his hands to his side.

"Rako," she replied. "You saw your wife, and I saw Rako. He entered your body, only for a moment, and possessed you for lack of a better word. And I got my wish, the one thing I wanted more than anything else in this world, to hold and kiss my one true love one more time."

"It was so real," Erik said, wanting to cry also. "You were Simone."

"And I was, to you," Beth replied. "And I am sure she felt your presence, back on your farmstead."

Beth closed her eyes, still smiling wide, and sighed.

"Thank you for that, Erik," she said, opening her eyes. "Thank you for your friendship."

Rako was there again, standing and watching.

"Thank you, Erik," he said, a smile stretching across his face as well.

Erik nodded and turned to Rako.

"What now?" he asked, but Rako had already begun to fade.

"I can't yet leave this world," Rako said, "but I will show you the way to the Dragon Crown. Once you find it and piece it back together, I will truly be free."

"But how?" Erik whispered, but he received no answer.

As the visage of the elf became more translucent, he was mere smoke, ready to be blown away by an errant wind. Erik had not really known the elf as he had Turk or the other dwarves, but he couldn't hold back tears as one of his greatest friends passed away from the world. As he put an arm around the shoulders of a sobbing Beth, the last essence of Rako disappeared.

"In another life," Erik said, "we would have fought together, side by side. I would have given my life for you, and you me."

*We did.*

Erik couldn't help smiling at hearing that voice once more.

*Will I hear you in my mind again? Is that how you will guide us?*

*You have Beth by your side now, Erik. You must trust her. You will never hear me in your mind again, but I will see you in your dreams.*

$\mathcal{E}$rik looked out through the open door to the wide, green meadow that surrounded the White Tower. As Thala basked in the sun and Warrior and Shadow nibbled at the grass, it looked such a peaceful scene. There were squirrels and deer, even foxes, none of which seemed to take notice of each other as they went about their daily business. All the while, Terradyn snored behind him.

With a sigh, he turned back to Jart'El's body lying beside the white altar. He didn't know what the tradition was with elves in how they treated the dead, so he waited for Beth, who seemed to be in some sort of trance. Or maybe she was just mourning the loss of two loved ones. Eventually, she turned to Erik and nodded, her eyes still red-rimmed, but looking more decisive. She turned back to face the altar, arms outstretched, and as she chanted, an image began to appear above the huge white stone that formed the altar top.

Erik thought at first it must be some kind of special cloth in which to wrap her brother's body, but then he realized that not only was the image translucent, but there were markings on it. He stepped closer and recognized the indication of landmarks and cities, and Beth began tracing her finger south along a wide river to where Erik could only assume was Wüsten Sahil. The map ended at a structure that looked like a single mountain peak.

"Is this the way to the Dragon Crown?" Erik asked.

Beth nodded.

"Where can I find some parchment?" Erik asked. "Do you want me to copy it?"

Beth shook her head.

"No. I will remember."

As the image of the map disappeared, Beth smiled.

"Now you understand what Rako meant," Beth said, "and he is now at peace. Thank El for that. Now help me please."

Erik helped her lift her brother's body and place it on the altar. As he stepped back, he heard chirruping above him and looked up to see three birds, with their wide wings and long, multi-colored tail feathers, hovering in the air as if there was an unseen wind. Beth looked up at them, nodded once, and they flew away as one, out through a stone framed window.

"I pray my brother's heart is right when the golden carriage comes."

"Will you bury him?" Erik asked, looking at the body.

"In due time," Beth said. "Now, let us go and sit outside; there is one more mystery hidden within the Dragon Stone that I need to discuss with you."

They settled on the grass next to Thala, and Erik stroked her head as Beth held the stone in her lap. She closed her eyes and mumbled something as the Dragon Stone glowed green, and she closed her hands around it. When she opened them again, she held a smooth, green stone in her hand, one much smaller than the Dragon Stone, and it resembled the two stones Erik already possessed. Ioun stones.

"You possess two more of these," Beth said. It was not a question.

Erik reached into his belt pouch and removed both the white and red ioun stones.

"Where did you get them?" she asked.

"The white one I found in the broken white tower," Erik replied, "in the Gray Mountains. It was protected by ice golems and an ice drake."

"One of the lost towers," Beth said, her voice low and contemplative. "The Tower of the White Rose."

"This red one was given to me by a gypsy friend after his father was murdered."

"The dead gypsy was called Marcus?" Beth asked.

Erik nodded his head.

"He is the same one who gave you the dagger that was a shard of the Dragon Sword," Beth said, "and the flute you carry with you."

Erik nodded.

"Your falchion," El'Beth said, "is the sword of this man's son. It was the father's."

"What about it?" Erik asked.

"It is the sword of an elvish guardsman."

"Truly?" Erik asked, more to himself than to Beth.

"Curious, that a man would have these things," she added, "although, I suppose if any man might have them, it would be a gypsy."

"Marcus was a good man; his son is also," Erik said.

"I am not suggesting he wasn't," Beth said. "Only that gypsies are well-traveled. I am familiar with these Ion Gypsies. That is what their clan is called, yes?"

Erik nodded.

"They are astute followers of El, yes?"

Erik nodded again.

"I will ensure that his sword will be returned to him, this gypsy friend of yours if you wish?" Beth asked.

Erik nodded.

"There were two of the red stones," Erik said.

"Red ioun stones are the most common. What happened to the other one?" Beth asked.

"The best I could say is that it sacrificed itself, to save us—me—against Black Wing."

"That makes sense. Each different color of ioun stone has a different quality and gives the owner varied attributes, or enhancements. Strength, speed, vision, magical ability. If you were to say the correct spell, the stones would float about your head, and you would feel their power, but no two similar ioun stones can work together, with the same person."

"So the stone knew it could sacrifice itself because there was another?" Erik asked.

"More like Rako—through the dagger made from the Dragon Sword shard—helped even though he was trapped here in the Dragon Stone. He caused the stone to do what it did. He was a powerful wizard as well as a mighty warrior."

"But what is so significant about these stones?" Erik asked.

"The Dragon Crown had five points," El'Beth explained, "and each point contained an ioun stone. A red, blue, green, white, and black ioun stone. We must have all the stones in order to reforge the crown as you have reforged the Dragon Sword."

"Couldn't someone just find another ioun stone?" Erik asked after a moment of silence. "Why hide this one away in the Dragon Stone?"

"Blue and green ioun stones were common as well," Beth said, "until Jart'El and those he followed destroyed them all, save for the green one hidden in the Emerald of the East and, as Rako has just revealed to me, the blue one hidden in the Sapphire of the South."

"Is that a Chaos Stone also?" Erik asked.

"It is," Beth replied. "It seems the dwarves hid this prison with the key to reforging the crown."

"Why?"

"I do not know," Beth replied. "But as Yebritoch begins to regain a foothold in this world, it is vitally important we find it."

"What does his return have to do with the Beasts of Chaos?" Erik asked. "Other than they are devastating."

"That, I also do not know," Beth replied. "They were imprisoned so long ago. I just know that releasing them is a part of the key to releasing Yebritoch from his abyssal prison physically."

"And both the crown, the blue ioun stone, and another Beast of Chaos is in Wüsten Sahil," Erik added.

"Correct," Beth said.

"And we have three of the five ioun stones," Erik said, holding his hand open and presenting the white and red one he possessed and nodding to the green one in Beth's hand. His eyes widened with an epiphany. "My cousin found a black stone in Fealmynster."

"Yes, he did," Beth replied with a smile.

"How do we get the black ioun stone from Bryon?" Erik asked.

"We need your cousin to come here."

"No, he can't do that. He is protecting my wife and unborn child," Erik replied.

Beth pushed wisps of hair out of her eyes as she looked at the ground, pondering.

"Surely, the dwarves are also helping to protect your family?" she asked.

"I would hope so," Erik said, "but I don't know how many, and for how long."

"What if I were to help?" Beth asked.

"How do you mean?" Erik replied.

"What if I sent elvish warriors to your farmstead, to aid in the protection of your family and your people."

Erik looked at Beth with wide eyes. Western Háthgolthane hadn't seen elves in a thousand years. How would they be received?

"Do you think they would get along with the dwarves?" Erik asked.

"They would have to, wouldn't they?" Beth replied and even managed a wry smile.

"And how would Bryon know he needed to come here?" Erik asked. "He is a stubborn man, and I wouldn't chance to hope he would listen elves telling him he had to leave."

"You are a Dream Walker, are you not?" Beth asked.

Erik nodded.

"Then walk in his dreams," she added.

Erik shrugged.

"The way to the Dragon Crown and the Sapphire of the South is through the deserts of Wüsten Sahil," Beth said. "Your cousin can meet us on our way."

"Maybe be in Finlo?" Erik suggested, knowing he had to trust Beth.

Beth shrugged.

"If you like. We could use his sword."

"He carries an elvish blade," Erik said.

"Really?" Beth asked. "Now that I didn't know."

"Aye," Erik said. "Ilken Copper Head, the dwarf that first forged my sword, said it was a powerful, elemental magic. Bryon took it off the body of a mercenary."

"Interesting," Beth said, tapping her chin with her fingers.

"If you are sending elves to protect my family, we could use Turk's ax as well," Erik said. "And Nafer's mace."

"Tell Bryon to bring them," Beth said, "when you meet him in his dreams."

"I miss my wife, Beth," Erik said. "I fear I won't be there when my child is born."

"I can imagine," Beth replied.

"Of course you can," Erik said. She had waited a thousand years for Rako.

"What do you think you are having, a boy or girl?" Beth asked with a smile.

"I don't know," Erik said with a shrug. "I don't care. I just want a healthy baby who knows he or she is loved and cared for."

"That is the right answer," Beth said. "That is all any of us could ask for. I am sure El will grant you such a prayer, be it a boy or girl. And he or she will truly know they are loved. That, I know from meeting you in your dreams and talking now."

Erik nodded, his thoughts back with Simone as he ran his fingers through the grass. It's touch brought him back to the here and now.

"What are these places? These meadows with their towers?"

"We used to have them all over the world," Beth explained. "They were training centers, schools, academies, and so much more. Before we retreated to the forests, the elves concerned themselves with helping others in the world. These were places where we would teach young men and women about magic, teach them to read and write and teach them about El. But our pride got the best of us, and men became suspicious of us. And over time, they simply became unused, the elements wearing away at them like they do anything else."

"Fealmynster was once a tower, like this one?" Erik asked, remembering what Dewin had told him.

"Yes, it was," Beth replied. "A very special tower, much like the Tower of the White Rose—Lahvan Shoshanah—a tower only for human girls. We called Fealmynster the Tower of the Black Thorn—a school only for human boys. They were unique compared to all the others."

"I saw that in a book I found. It had only girls' names in it. But special? Unique? How so?"

"It is a long story. Perhaps one for another time," Beth replied with a smile. "Just know that it was the men and women trained in the Tower of the White Rose and the Tower of the Black Thorn that helped defeat Yebritoch the first time. You see, it wasn't Elvish Dragon Riders, or Dwarvish Bear Cavalry, or Kishma Juggernauts, or Kaylytha Archers that saved the world, Erik. It was men and women like you. So ordinary and, yet, so special."

Erik couldn't help but smile. As his world expanded, from an ignorant farm boy to a mercenary to a hero, humans seemed rather unordinary compared to all the other different peoples that inhabited the world.

"For now, let us rest. You may stay here, in this White Tower, where you and Terradyn will be safe. Jart'El had many allies and followers among the sylvan people, but they would not dare seek to harm you in this place. Outside these walls and in the realms of Ul'Erel, I cannot be so certain, even if you are traveling with me. People will know I had a hand in my brother's death. I have much praying and meditating to do before we leave."

"I am glad you are coming with me," Erik said with a smile, but Beth didn't smile back.

"This is a dangerous journey," she replied. "More dangerous than the one you took to find me here. You must understand that."

Erik felt his stomach knot, but he nodded.

"Rest now," she said. "Walk your cousin's dreams tonight and summon him and your dwarvish friends. If we are to meet in Finlo, we will leave in seven days."

Beth stood and, as she looked down at Erik, she smiled. At that moment, she looked like Simone again, and he wanted to hold her and kiss her. Instead, he scratched Thala's head.

## 72

S yzbalo stood in the darkness. Only a select few were privy to the space behind the large curtain that hung behind the royal dais, and most who did find themselves in the area never left. The only light in the room came from a magical portal, a raised piece of stone, filtering a hint of illumination upwards. The Lords of the East had used it for traveling about their city and kingdom for hundreds of years, not only to spy on their people, but to enter places that had no doors, like the dungeons and the magical laboratories.

Syzbalo looked over his shoulder as Melanius shuffled behind him.

"I don't understand why Kimber and Krista couldn't join us," Syzbalo said.

"We must do as we are commanded, my lord," the goblin Akzûl said with a bow, and a look of disgust crossed Syzbalo's face.

*Who is he to command me?*

"Careful, my lord," a familiar voice said, breaking through the otherwise quiet of the darkness.

"What do *you* want, Patûk?" retorted Syzbalo.

He saw Akzûl bow as the former general of Golgolithul—and

traitor to the Lord of the East—came into view, emerging from the darkness.

"You, of all people, should know that powerful beings can hear the thoughts of others ... especially in this place."

"Indeed," Syzbalo replied, and then looked down at the goblin. "Stop groveling, especially to this worm. I was beginning to like you."

The Lord of the East looked back at Patûk, and the smirk across the dead man's face was gone, replaced by a rictus snarl.

"You are lucky I cannot unleash my power on you," Patûk hissed, pointing a bony finger at Syzbalo.

"Come now, traitor," Syzbalo replied, "you know you are not as powerful as me, no matter how much you grovel at the feet of ..."

"Careful, my lord." It was Akzûl's turn to offer the same warning.

Syzbalo grunted and then looked at Melanius, who looked scared, his eyes wide and staring into the darkness. The Lord of the East looked to the goblin again, who stood firm by his side but had a look of caution on his flat face. The goblin gave him an affirming nod, but when Syzbalo turned back to Patûk, the old general's lip curled in distain. Al'Banan, the general who had turned against him, was a shadow of the man he was when he was alive. The skin on his face looked stretched, his cheeks sunken and gaunt. As his cracked lips pulled back into a rictus, snarling smile, they revealed brown and broken teeth.

"You are somewhat of a sad shadow of your former self, Patûk," Syzbalo said, seeking to drip sarcasm.

"We are all shadows," Patûk Al'Banan replied evenly. "Shadows serving shadows. It comes down to which shadow you choose to serve."

*Myself.*

The thought passed through Syzbalo's mind the moment Patûk asked the question, but again the former general could read his thoughts.

"Quite typical" Patûk said, his voice low.

Syzbalo heard movement from the darkness surrounding them, a slithering like a giant snake, and the hair on the back of his neck stood on end. Patûk cackled under his breath.

Terror had always dwelt in the darkness of this room. It was the greatest mystery of the Keep of Fen-Stévock, but to step into the blackness was to step into a nightmare. A low rumble shook the room, causing the low light emanating from the portal to shimmer and sputter. A growl rolled from the darkness, and a chorus of hissing followed. Patûk dropped to one knee.

"The Lord of the East wishes to be as powerful as me," a voice said from the darkness, a low, grumbling deeper than anything Syzbalo had ever heard.

"No," Syzbalo said to the darkness, dropping his chin to his chest. He hated doing so, but could not help it.

"You lie," the voice said.

"My lord ..." Melanius began, but the voice cut him off.

"*Silence!*" the voice said. It wasn't really any louder than before, but the room shook as the word was spoken. "You are but an insect. Speak again, and I will crush you."

The voice wasn't angry, or hateful, it was, quite simply, pure evil.

"Your latest chosen one has failed her mission, minion," the voice said.

Syzbalo presumed the voice was addressing him, but he saw Patûk bow lower, to almost cower rather than be subservient.

"She will pay for her failure, Your Malevolence," Patûk replied. "I will destroy the Isutan bitch."

*Ankara. She served him as well?*

"Yes Syzbalo," the voice growled. "But then she knew better and changed her allegiances. What good it did, though, minion."

Syzbalo couldn't get used to his thoughts being so easily read. He was sure he could block out even Andragos when at his best.

Patûk bowed quickly.

"I will not fail you again, Master," Patûk said.

"See that you do not," the voice said, "else I send you back to oblivion."

The voice was silent for a moment.

"It is good for you Syzbalo—for your continued existence—that you have obeyed and allowed my followers into your army," the voice said, and Syzbalo saw Akzûl standing a bit taller. "Of course, not all the goblin-folk serve me, but many do. For your obedience, Syzbalo, I will grant you more power."

Syzbalo smiled and gave a slight bow. Almost immediately, a tingle crawled along his skin, and he felt the hair on the back of his neck rise. As air filled his lungs, his vision was clearer, and his hearing became crisper. The power his new master had just given him was intoxicating.

"The elves now have Orentus' prison," the voice said. "And soon they will begin searching for the others, working with the man your assassin failed to kill. They must be stopped. If my return is to happen, we need all four Chaos Stones."

"I will stop them, Master," Patûk said.

"No," the voice said, "I need you elsewhere. Whom do you serve, Syzbalo Stévock?"

*Myself.*

The thought came unbidden, and Syzbalo's stomach clenched as he realized his error.

"*No!*" the voice said, and a shadow like a black fog swirled about the Lord of the East. "Your power comes at a price."

As if whipped by a sudden wind, the darkness around Syzbalo began to tighten around him like a tangled sheet during a nightmare. He began to choke as he heard a scream, and another whirlwind of darkness surrounded Melanius, lifting the old magician into the air and stretching his body like pastry.

"*Whom do you serve?*" came the voice louder still, filling the swirling darkness all around the Lord of the East.

Syzbalo clutched his throat as he felt his face flush, and his eyes bulged as he gasped for air. He felt his lungs fill with fire, his bowels twisted, and the most acid bile burnt his throat and filled his mouth. The power he had just touched was gone, and he felt naked.

*You, my Lord Yebritoch.*

The swirling darkness stopped, leaving Syzbalo standing on legs that would barely hold him as he gasped for breaths. Akzûl stood still, unmoving and unchanging, but Melanius crumpled to the ground, motionless for a moment, and then groaned loudly.

"Now you understand," Yebritoch said, his voice still deep but more even.

Such power. Even as Syzbalo rubbed his neck and took in gulps of air, the thought of that kind of power was intoxicating, arousing even.

"You will forget all ideas of expanding your pathetic empire, Syzbalo."

Syzbalo was about to curse the Lord of Chaos in his head but managed to stop himself. He heard sarcastic laughing.

"Do not worry, servant," Yebritoch said, "soon, you will help me rule the world, and your little conquests will seem a drop of water in the ocean. For now, you will stop the elves and this Erik Eleodum from retrieving the prison of Archanaraug. You will procure the stone for me, as well as Orentus' stone, so I might release both he and Archanaraug."

"Erik Eleodum is dead, master," Patûk said with a low bow.

"He lives, minion," Yebritoch said.

"I killed him with my own sword," Patûk added.

"*Silence!*" Yebritoch's voice shook the very foundations of the keep. "He lives, thus, proving your failure. I wonder why I saved you from destruction."

Patûk prostrated himself.

"It will not happen again," Patûk said.

"No, it will not," Yebritoch said.

"How do I best go about this task?" Syzbalo asked, and when he saw the sidelong glance Akzûl had given him, he added, "master?"

"You are a powerful wizard Lord of the East," Yebritoch said. "You will find a way. Know that you will eventually need to attack Ul'Erel."

"Attack—" Syzbalo began but stopped. His protests would do no good. He composed himself. "Andragos has started to oppose me. He is proving a nuisance."

"Do not worry about the Black Mage," the voice said. "I will take care of him."

"And me, Master?" Patûk asked. "Can I slay the Isutan woman who failed us?"

"No, my goblin followers Syzbalo has allowed into his borders will take care of this Black Tigress. For now, General, you will go north and find the prison holding Anradag. I cannot fully rule the world with only two of my beasts, but with three, we can wreak chaos this cursed world hasn't seen since the beginning of time."

"Yes, master," said Patûk, bowing again. Syzbalo could see the look of disapproval on Patûk's face; he wanted the death of Ankara by his own hand.

"Good. I will not be delayed any longer, and you should all remember this."

*Erik Eleodum.*

Syzbalo squeezed his fists, digging his long nails into the flesh of his palms until he drew blood. He wanted nothing more than to make Erik Eleodum pay. Pay for failure. Pay for disobedience. Pay for being a simple farmer whom idiot people now revered.

"I can feel your hate," the voice said. "That is good. Let it grow and receive again my gift of power."

Another black mist flowed from the darkness again, filling Syzbalo's nostrils as he breathed in. As it reached out to his magic, suddenly he felt even more powerful than before. As new incantations and bewildering spells filled his mind, his fingertips tingled with the power and strength flowing through him. He was invincible.

Although Syzbalo knew what hid in the darkness of this place, he never went there. The darkness was death. But, suddenly, the darkness disappeared, the floor illuminating in a pallid, moon-like light, revealing the horrors that hid in shadow.

Thousands of tunnel crawlers hissed as the light hit their gray skin. Winged and horned demons, with wolf snouts and hawk beaks, talons and claws, scales and knotted fur, spiked tails and wide-spread wings roared and snarled and snapped. Dead soldiers, the remnants of men with pale, stretched skin and sharpened, brown teeth and black armor drew their swords and axes and spears and shook them. Bones and skulls littered the floor where bodies hung from chains and hooks, dangling from the ceiling. Blood filled pools and offal burned on altars. Melanius screamed, covering his face with his hands, Patûk stood and laughed, and Akzûl smiled and bowed.

In the middle of it all, a black smoke swirled about, and Yebritoch, the Lord of Chaos, spoke again.

"Remember what you have seen and do not fail me," Yebritoch said, the smoke swirling and diving as if moved by each word he spoke. "The price for failure is greater than you could ever conceive."

The darkness returned, and while Syzbalo sensed the presence of Yebritoch had left, he still bowed before he turned, grabbing hold of Melanius and dragging him along. He parted the curtain behind the royal dais, stepping out of the darkness that consumed the room behind him. He took a breath and then gathered his thoughts, certain he was blocking them from anyone.

*I won't fail, and when I have killed Erik Eleodum, retrieved the Stones of Chaos, and the Dragon Sword and the Dragon Crown is mine, I take my rightful place as Emperor of the World. All men and creatures will bow before me and exalt my new name. It is I who will be The Lord of Chaos.*

# BEFORE YOU GO!

**Before you go!**

Thank you for reading *Stone of Chaos*! I love writing because of readers like you. You may not know this, but reviews are super important, especially to unknown authors such as myself. They give other great readers an idea of what to expect from my story. If you have time, please leave me one. It can be a short one if you're busy; even just one sentence will do!

Leave a review for Stone of Chaos

For news, updates, new books, and free stories
Join My Reader Group

Ready for the next chapter in the Demon's Fire Journey?

# DEMON RISING: CHAPTER 1

All Bryon Eleodum could see was waist-high grass that fluttered back and forth as if there was some breeze, but he felt nothing. He thought he was asleep, but his dreams were never like this. On the rare nights he didn't have nightmares about his cousin Befel burning, or tunnel crawlers tearing his flesh from his bones, or freezing to death alone, he dreamt of women or ale...or both.

He looked around saw the hill. He was sure it wasn't there before. A single willow tree stood in the center and while it was far away, but he could see the silhouette of someone sitting under the falling branches. He felt the ground rumble beneath his feet and when he turned, he saw a mountain range behind him. That definitely wasn't there before. It was black and, even though the sun sat high in the sky, it was dark over the mountain range, with black clouds that emitted purple lightning.

*Damn this is mad. I think I'd rather dream of mountain trolls or dragons. I must be drunk.*

He turned back to the hill with the tree. It seemed closer.

"Bryon," a voice said and he turned.

Erik stood there. He was in his mail shirt, his sword hanging from his belt, his shield strapped to his back. He looked a little leaner, especially in the face, than he had remembered him, his shoulders perhaps a little broader. He almost couldn't see it, but a bit of white touched the edges of his hair, just above his ears, as well as his beard, right over his chin. He smiled.

"Erik," Bryon said.

"Cousin," Erik replied.

"You look terrible," Bryon said with a short laugh. "I hope this isn't how you look ten winters from now. I don't think Simone would still love you."

Erik chuckled.

"This is how I look now," he said.

Bryon cocked an eyebrow.

"This is just a dream," Bryon said.

"It is," Erik replied, "but this is really me, in your dream...walking your dream."

"To the nine hells with this," Bryon said. "I think I want to wake up."

"You can't," Erik said. "I need you to do something for me."

"Is that really you?" Bryon asked.

Erik nodded.

"What, by the Creator's beard, happened to you?" Bryon asked.

"I died," Erik replied.

Bryon rolled his eyes. Erik was always melodramatic.

"I was dead, Bryon, and a powerful magic brought me back," Erik said. He reached up and touched his beard, where it had turned white. "This is what happened when I came back."

"Seriously?" Bryon asked.

Erik nodded again.

Bryon stepped closer to his cousin. He felt his stomach knot and a lump in his throat.

"Simone has missed you, cousin," he said.

"I've missed her," Erik replied, "more than you could imagine. Thank you for keeping her safe."

"We've all missed you," Bryon said. His voice turned to a whisper. "You damned fool. None of this would have happened if you hadn't left without us."

Erik laughed. Apparently he heard Bryon.

"Then who would have protected Simone?" Erik asked. "When the assassin came, who would have been there to keep her safe?"

Bryon shrugged.

"Is this what your dreams look like?" Bryon asked.

"Mostly," Erik replied. "Sometimes it changes, but this is normally the place that greets me when I sleep."

"Not bad," Bryon said with a shrug.

Erik laughed again.

"I've missed you too," Erik said.

"What do you need me to do?" Bryon asked.

"I need you to meet me in Finlo," Erik said.

Bryon sighed.

"You just told me you needed me to stay here and protect your family," Bryon said. "Your wife is closer to giving birth than not. You better come home for that or she might truly leave you."

Erik's face turned down and he looked at the ground.

"I don't think I will be there for the birth of my child, Bryon," Erik said. "My journey isn't finished."

"To the nine hells with your journey," Bryon said.

"I couldn't agree with you more," Erik replied, "but there is so much at stake right now."

His voice was serious.

"Meet you in Finlo," Bryon repeated. "Leave your pregnant wife and soon to be infant child and meet you in Finlo. All right. Simple enough."

"Bring the dwarves," Erik said. "Turk and Nafer. Tell Bofim to stay behind."

"Seriously, Erik, you are a confusing person," Bryon said. "What about Raktas? His friend, or companion—or whatever you want to call him—Terradyn left two weeks ago or more."

"He's with me," Erik said.

"Oh really," Bryon replied, throwing his hands up in the air.

"Bring him as well," Erik said.

"Right, well," Bryon said. He felt his irritation rising and put his hands on his hips. Suddenly, his cousin didn't seem like a seasoned warrior and he was a little, annoying teenager again, nagging and aggravating to be around. "Should I leave tomorrow then, right when I wake up?"

"No," Erik said and Bryon cocked an eyebrow. "Wait until the elves arrive."

"Oh, sure," Bryon said, nodding his head facetiously, "the elves. Will they have any unicorns with them?"

"I doubt it," Erik said, his voice and face flat. "I haven't seen any in Ul'Erel."

"Ul'Erel?" Bryon asked, leaning forward and lifting his hands.

"That's where I am right now," Erik said. "Does any of this truly surprise you? We have fought mountain trolls, evil wolves, a dragon, giants, and a wizard. We've befriended dwarves and wield magic swords."

"I guess you have a good point," Bryon said, chuckling to himself.

He looked around this dream world one more time, nodding.

"Why do you need us?" Bryon asked.

"I can't tell you right now," Erik replied. "I don't have a lot of time. But rest assured, I need you now more than ever."

"Alright, cousin," Bryon said. "I will wait until the elves come—I can't believe I am saying that—and I will bring Turk and Nafer...and Raktas with me, and I will ask Bofim to stay behind, with your wife. When should I expect the elves to arrive?"

"A fortnight," Erik replied.

"So we will meet you in Finlo in three weeks then?" Bryon asked. Erik nodded his head.

"And when we get to Finlo...where do we meet you there?"

"Go to Rory's," Erik said with the slightest hint of a smile. "Go to the *Lady's Inn*."

"And from there?" Bryon asked.

"South," Erik said. "We go south."

"How far south?" Bryon asked.

"As far south as need be," Erik replied.

The image of Erik began to fade.

"Do you want me tell Simone anything?" Bryon asked. "Do you have a message for her?"

Erik seemed to think about that for a moment, even while he faded. He shook his head.

"No," he said. "I am sure she hates me. A message from me would only cause her more pain."

"If you think Simone hates you," Bryon replied, "than you are truly more foolish than I ever thought. And as for pain, each day she goes without you seems like more pain than a thousand deaths. If I tell her I have to leave because you told me so in a dream, and assuming she believes me, and you have no message for her, she might then begin to hate you."

"Tell her I love her," Erik said. "Tell her I love her more than life...and that is why I am not there."

Bryon opened his eyes. He sat up. It was still dark outside. He kicked off his blanket. He was sweating even though it was near freezing outside. He rubbed his face hard. Was that really Erik? It was like no dream he had ever had. He looked at an empty, clay jar next to his bed.

"Too much ale," he whispered.

Bryon stood, walked as quietly as he could to the front door of Erik's house—he didn't want to wake up Simone—opened it, and stepped outside. The cold bit at his shirtless chest, but it felt good in an odd way. The moon hung low and large in the night sky. The Gray Mountains loomed as shadows to the north. And Raktas leaned against the fence that surrounded the house, smoking a pipe. He rarely slept. Magic.

Andragos' bodyguard saw Bryon and gave him a short nod. Bryon returned the gesture. He looked to the barn, where the dwarves stayed most the time. They could have stayed in the house—Simone insisted on it several times—but they always said they didn't want to be a bother, as if they could be. Firelight glowed from underneath the barn door. They were still awake. Something caused his stomach to flutter.

He remembered campfires, adventure, the open sky and camaraderie. A foolish, boyish excitement overcame him and he couldn't help but smile. He lifted his elvish sword—sheathed of course—with his left hand. He took it with him wherever he went. Paranoia. Suspicion. Whatever it was, it made him feel safe. He unsheathed the sword and watched the blade glow purple against the dark, nighttime horizon.

"If elves truly are coming," Bryon said to himself with a laugh and a shake of his head, "they can't come soon enough."

# DEMON RISING: CHAPTER 2

Syzbalo stood on the dais of his keep, hands clasped behind his back. Melanius stood to his right, the esteemed place of honor given to the advisor to the Lord of the East. The Isutan magician stood there, shoulders pulled as far back as his arthritic bones would allow, haughty and proud. In any other time, in any other life, he would have never held that position. He was a trickster and his magic paled in comparison to that of Andragos', even with the extra power both the Lord of the East and Yebritoch had given the man, and he was a snake. But he was a loyal snake, which is more than Syzbalo could say about the deposed Black Mage.

The witches—Kimber and Krista—stood behind him, one on either side. Their power was growing as well and, unlike Melanius, Syzbalo trusted them fully. Akzûl, the goblin and now commander of his personal guard, stood to his left. His one hundred and twenty-one Black Wolves stood in the keep as well, along with the rest of Syzbalo's personal guard. The goblin had done surpassingly well in leading the most elite military force in Fen-Stévock—now that the Soldiers of the Eye were gone. He was ruthless and demanding and not at all fair, but that was exactly what Syzbalo wanted.

Syzbalo tilted his head when he heard a low, grumble come from Akzûl. Over the last few weeks, the goblin had served him well and without question, even giving him a different perspective on military advice and movements. The groan was directed towards Syzbalo's guest, a large warrior walking through the colonnade of the keep and towards the raised dais.

"You disapprove," Syzbalo said, looking down at Akzûl.

The goblin looked up at the Lord of the East and his eyes said he did, but he shook his head.

"This is the will of my lord and our master," Akzûl replied. "It is not my place to disapprove."

Syzbalo looked up as the large Moorian warrior stopped just several paces from the dais. His appearance was alarming.

The people of Boruck-Moore typically kept to themselves and their island and were far less social as their cousins who populated the island of Boruck-Kilith. People of Antolika and Háthgolthane typically referred to the Kilithians as cat people, with humanoid bodies and the heads of any number of large cats one might find around the world. Syzbalo had yet to uncover what manner of dark magic created the race, but one could find a dozen or more of them in any large city in Háthgolthane, and they were avid adventurers. The Moorians were much more reclusive.

With his pallid green skin, his pointed, elf-like ears, long, jet black hair, lower canines that grew up from his lower jaw and along his cheeks, and his eyes that were simply white with the slightest tinge of red, the Moorian standing before Syzbalo looked other-worldly. He was taller than most men, perhaps just a head shorter than most antegants, and his arms, shoulders, chest, and legs bulged with muscle any soldier would envy. He wore a mail shirt that extended just past his waist and knee high boots capped with iron. His left hand rested on the dragonhead pommel of a massive long sword—one that resembled the swords used by the northern barbarians of Hargoleth—and he held a rolled up piece of parchment in his right.

"Welcome, Ankathurg of the Second Clan," Syzbalo said with a small bow.

His retinue standing with him on the dais followed suit, although he noticed Akzûl hesitated at first.

The Moorians divided themselves into twelve clans and, where the dwarves and goblins and even humans gave their clans names of strength or fear—like Skull Crusher or Death Dogs—the Moorians simply numbered their clans one through twelve, the First Clan being the most powerful.

"Why has the Lord of the East summoned my Chieftain?" Ankathurg asked, his voice deep and reverberating, matching his size.

Ankathurg was the Champion of Second Clan, and second in command next to the clan's Chieftain, Tugrim. When Syzbalo sent for Tugrim, he knew, even if the invitation hinted that it was Yebritoch who truly wanted them to meet, he would not come himself.

"You know why," Akzûl replied, surprising both the Moorian and Syzbalo.

"If I wished to speak with dogs, I would have visited the alleys of this wretched city," Ankathurg said, his face flat and emotionless.

Akzûl groaned, his sloping brow furrowing and his beady eyes squinting. His lip curled around his little fangs.

"You will be quiet," Syzbalo said to Akzûl, his voice cold iron.

The goblin bowed. Syzbalo turned back to the Moorian.

"My Captain of the Guard is right, however," Syzbalo said. "You know why I have summoned your Chieftain."

"You expect us to ally ourselves with a *man* who appoints a dog as his Captain of the Guard?" Ankathurg said, the first hint of emotion crossing his face as one corner of his lips barely tipped upward in a smirk.

"I expect you to show respect in the midst of the Lord of the East," Syzbalo said, containing himself as best he could. This was the will of Yebritoch, after all, and disobedience was dealt with harshly. "And for the summons of *our* master."

Not all the Moorians followed Yebritoch. In fact, Syzbalo only knew that Second Clan did. They all did, as a people, once, but over the eons, most of the Moorians had turned from the Lord of Chaos, blaming him for their isolation. But Second Clan blamed their peoples unbelief for their isolation and, clearly, the return of Yebritoch meant a return to glory for their people.

"The Lord of Chaos is the only reason I am here," Ankathurg said. He threw the rolled up parchment—the summons—to the ground. "We have no respect for men. You have no honor."

Syzbalo ground his teeth. Ankathurg was trying his patience and he could see all one hundred and twenty one of the Black Wolves, twitching, ready to strike and kill given the opportunity. The Lord of the East didn't quite know the history between goblins and Moorians. He just knew it was bad. They hated each other. Much of it probably had to do with the way Moorian culture and society operated. It was based on strength and resilience, rigid laws and strict rules and guidelines, ultimate loyalty to the clan and, most of all, honor. It seemed the goblins codes were the exact opposite.

Syzbalo, hands still clasped behind his back, walked forward and stepped down the stairs of his dais. Standing in front of the Moorian, he had to look up, even if he was a tall man.

"Your people do not deserve to live, secluded, on a small island in the South Sea," Syzbalo said, "just as the Second Clan does not deserve to its subservience to First Clan."

"Your honeyed words will not work with me," Ankathurg said. He smirked and gave a quick, mirthless laugh. "I am dealing with a dog and a snake."

"How dare you?" Melanius said.

Syzbalo could feel the magic the Isutan was conjuring and, even though he wanted to stop him, he didn't. He was curious as to what this Moorian Warrior would do. His response came as a surprise. He laughed.

"Isutans," the Moorian said. "A snake, a dog, and a rat."

The magic of Melanius increased, a current of power, and Ankathurg seemed unfazed.

"That's enough," Syzbalo said, putting up a hand, and as soon as he said something, he felt the magic dissipate. He looked at Ankathurg. "Yebritoch has commanded we form an alliance, but I do believe our alliance can go beyond what our master desires. The Warriors of Boruck-Moore are a proud and powerful race."

"And..." Ankathurg said, knowing there was more to what Syzbalo had to say.

"And an alliance with the most powerful nation in four continents could only help solidify not only your clan as First Clan, but also open up trading routes and commerce you have not engaged in for many years."

"And what does this alliance do for you?" Ankathurg asked.

"No one compares to the Warriors of Boruck-Moore in battle," Syzbalo said matter-of-factly. "And no one compares to the Navies of Boruck-Moore. Having both Moorian warriors in my army and Moorian ships in my navy would only serve to increase the power and might of Golgolithul."

"And in return for our swords and our ships?" Ankathurg asked.

"Gold. Slaves. Lands."

Ankathurg seemed to think for a while. If Tugrim and Second Clan weren't interested in an alliance with the Lord of the East, Ankathurg would not have come in the first place. But now that he was there, in Golgolithul, an alliance seemed unsure.

"I will send a message back to Tugrim with your offer," Ankathurg said. "You will draw up terms for an alliance. I will review them. If I find them favorable, I will send for Tugrim."

"What of Yebritoch?" Syzbalo asked.

"We will serve Yebritoch, with or without you," Ankathurg said. "We do not need some alliance with men and...goblins to serve our master."

"Even if it is what he demands?" Syzbalo asked.

"He demands this of *you*," Ankathurg replied.

"I see," Syzbalo said.

"Second Clan holds alliance with Third Clan and Sixth Clan,"

Ankathurg explained. "They will follow where we go. I am sure both clans will want something in return for their loyalty as well."

Syzbalo nodded. Ankathurg did not return the gesture.

"I will let you know what Tugrim's response is," Ankathurg said, his reddish white eyes squinting.

"Very well," Syzbalo replied.

Ankathurg turned and left the keep.

"If it were not for the master, I would not treat with the Moorians," Akzûl said.

"If it were not for Yebritoch, I would not treat with you," Syzbalo said. "Remember that."

The goblin bowed. Syzbalo turned to Melanius.

"Put spies to watch the Moorians," he said. "Not that we need much worry about them, make sure my citizens do not harass them."

"Your Excellency," Melanius said with a bow.

Syzbalo looked back at Akzûl.

"Any word from your Death Dogs?"

"The Death Dogs are in Crom, waiting my lord," Akzûl said. "However, the Stone Claws are in Bard'Sturn, waiting for the Isutan bitch Ankara, just in case she crosses there instead of Crom. Out informants say she might."

"Stone Claws?" Syzbalo asked.

"Loyal to the master and looking to advance their position, like the Death Dogs, Blood Hawks, and Black Wolves," Akzûl replied.

"Good. Keep me informed," Syzbalo said. He looked to his witches. "Come. I am apprehensive and could use some rest."

They smiled, each taking an arm, and followed him into the darkness behind the keep's giant curtain.

# ABOUT THE AUTHOR

Christopher Patterson lives in Tucson, Arizona with his wife and three children. Christopher has a Masters in Education and is a teacher of many subjects, including English, History, Government, Economics, and Health. He is also a football and wrestling coach. Christopher fostered a love of the arts at a very young age, picking up the guitar at 7, the bass at 10, and dabbling in drawing and writing around the same time. His first major at the University of Arizona was, in fact, a BFA in Classical Guitar Performance, although he would eventually earn a BA in Literature and a BFA in Creative Writing.

Christopher Patterson grew up watching Star Wars, Dragon Slayer, and a cartoon version of The Hobbit. He started reading fantasy novels from a young age, took an early interest in early, Medieval Europe, and played Dungeons and Dragons. He has read The Hobbit, The Lord of the Rings, and the Wizard of Earthsea many times and heralds Tolkien, Jordan, and Martin, among others, as major influences in his own writing.

Christopher is also very involved in church, especially music and youth ministries, and is very active, having been a competitive power lifter since high school.

He thanks his grandmother for letting him waste paper on her typewriter while trying to write the "Next Great American Novel" and his parents for always supporting his dreams.

.

# ALSO BY CHRISTOPHER PATTERSON

Books in the Dream Walker Chronicles

The Shadow's Fire Series

*A Chance Beginning*

*Dark Winds*

*Breaking the Flame*

The Demon's Fire Series

*Dragon Sword*

*Stone of Chaos*

*Demon Rising*

Other Books by Christopher Patterson

Holy Warriors

*To Kill A Witch*

Made in the USA
Middletown, DE
18 April 2022

64418505R00314